Praise for *Wink Murder*:

'Tightly-plotted, high-pitched psychological thriller . . . what bright new talent Ali Knight does so successfully, and with a welcome fresh eye, is broach the great divide between public and private space.'
**** *Daily Mirror*

'A really enjoyable read'
Martina Cole

'A fast-paced whodunit.'
Woman and Home

'Knight's promising debut . . . crackles from first page to last . . . She could be very good indeed.'
Daily Mail

'A psychological drama that grips from first to last'
Choice

'A tightly constructed, suspenseful thriller that will have you turning pages and keep you guessing all the way to the dramatic conclusion.'
Shotsmag.co.uk

About the author

Ali Knight has worked as a journalist and sub-editor at the BBC, *Guardian* and *Observer* and helped to launch some of the *Daily Mail* and *Evening Standard*'s most successful websites. She lives with her family in London. *Wink Murder* is her first novel.

Learn more at www.aliknight.co.uk.

ALI KNIGHT

Wink Murder

HODDER

First published in Great Britain in 2011 by Hodder & Stoughton
An Hachette UK company

First published in paperback in 2011

2

A CIP catalogue record for this title is available from the British Library

B format paperback ISBN 978 1 444 71535 4
A format paperback ISBN 978 1 444 71536 1

Typeset in Plantin Light by Palimpsest Book Production Limited,
Falkirk, Stirlingshire

Printed and bound by CPI Group (UK) Ltd, Croydon, CR0 4YY

Hodder & Stoughton policy is to use papers that are natural, renewable and
recyclable products and made from wood grown in sustainable forests. The logging
and manufacturing processes are expected to conform to the environmental regulations
of the country of origin.

Hodder & Stoughton Ltd
338 Euston Road
London NW1 3BH

www.hodder.co.uk

To Stephen, with love

I

I snap my eyes open in the dark, sensing something is not right. The room is instantly familiar, coming into focus with the help of the city light that sneaks past the roman blinds. Tasteful prints hang on the wall, armchairs guard the fireplace opposite, one has Paul's clothes piled on it in a disordered mountain, the other cradles my dressing gown, neatly folded. I'm in our bedroom, a place of safety, a haven from life. The other side of the king-size is empty, the pillow fluffed. Paul is not home. I hold my breath because there is the noise again, a shuffly scraping that's coming from everywhere and nowhere. My heart pounds in my ears. The clock clicks to 3.32 a.m. as I hear a crash downstairs. It might wake the children and this thought alone forces me out from under the comforting warmth of the duvet. I am a mother; point one on the job description is to protect them, at all costs. My movements are slow and deliberate as I try to steel myself for what I'm about to do. I pick up my mobile and turn the handle on the bedroom door hard to ensure it opens without a sound. Someone is groaning in the hallway and it doesn't sound like Paul.

I have mentally rehearsed what happens next quite often because Paul is away for work a lot at the moment and I think it's important to know how I would fight for the only thing that really matters to me – my family. I like to be prepared. So, as if I'm a fire warden at work, I'm putting it all into action. I take a deep breath, punch 999 into the keypad but don't press the green button, turn on the light and run for the stairs, shouting as loudly as I can into the night silence 'Get out of my house!', phone aloft like a burning spear.

I thump loudly down the stairs and use my gathering momentum to swing round the swirly circle at the bottom of the banister as a shape heaves itself across the kitchen at the end of the hall. 'Get out, get out! The police are outside!' I flood my world with light at the flick of a switch as the dark bundle clatters to the floor with a chair. I pull a cricket bat from the coat stand and feel its comforting weight in my palm and am in the kitchen in a second, the weapon close to my chest. 'Get out of my house!' He has his face on my kitchen tiles but as I raise the bat the shape turns to me and I see my husband, staring up at me from the floor.

It is my husband, but not as I have ever seen him before. He is crying, taking great gulps of air, snot running down to his mouth. I toss the phone on the table and drop the bat to the floor. 'Paul, what on earth's the matter?'

He doesn't answer, because he can't. He looks up at me and my former fear for myself is replaced by a more acute worry for him. I try to pull him upright but he is like a dead weight in my arms; he's folded over and crushed, his demeanour transformed. That was why I didn't recognise him from behind, he is not the man he used to be. 'What's happened?'

Paul smashes his fist into the side of his head and groans again. 'Kate, Kate—'

'Oh my God, what's going on?'

He gets to his knees, shaking, leaving the car key on the floor. Paul is a big man; he's tall, with wide palms, and shoulders you can fall asleep on, it was one of the many things about him that I fell in love with all those years ago. He made me feel protected. 'Kate, oh help me—'

His hands are caked with blood.

'You're bleeding!'

He looks down at them in disgust. He staggers to his feet and I pull limply at his coat, he must be cut somewhere under the thick wool. 'Are you hurt?'

I . . . I, oh God, it's come to this.'

'What?' He closes his eyes and sniffs, swaying. 'What has happened?' He shakes his head and drags himself into the downstairs toilet and starts washing his hands, flakes of blood and brown water swirling away down the plughole. 'Paul!'

He wipes his face on his shoulder and nods his head. 'I killed her . . .'

He shakes the water off his hands and I slap him, hard. 'Tell me what is going on!'

My husband looks at me, his arresting brown eyes blood-shot from his tears. 'What a mess, what a stupid load of . . .' He sighs from deep within. 'Oh fuck, Kate, I love you so much.' And with that he falls right past me on to the hallway floor in a faint no manner of prods, shoves and screams will wake him from.

Something at least becomes clear to me: Paul is pissed. He must be completely rat-arsed. There are probably many things I should do at this moment but first I must pee. I sit on the toilet and stare at the long body of my husband passed out on the floor, his feet turned inwards, his palms up as if he's indulging in a spot of yoga. I am shivering with anger that he could get in a car and drive home in such a state. I shake his shoulders but he doesn't move. I am not a spontaneous person, I need to plan things, to think; I have never imag-ined a situation like this before and I am at a loss, paralysed in the face of so much that needs to be discovered. After a lot of pushing and heaving I manage to turn Paul over on to his back and pull his coat apart checking everywhere for a wound. When I find nothing I am pathetically thankful – blood makes me faint. I sit back on my heels and stare. The hard planes of his handsome face have dissolved into a puffy mess, his strong jaw has receded into his neck. Paul is snoring, his chest rising and falling. The house is silent, my children slumber on unaware. The kitchen clock accompanies him with its staccato beat. The fridge hums and a window rattles. The house settles back into its night-time rhythm. At 3.50 a.m. I get to my feet, tiredness moving over me in waves. I can think of nothing better to do than go to bed. He'll wake up in the end.

2

What seems like a second later a small hand pokes me in the stomach. 'Ava! Stop that!' My daughter is squirming over me in bed.

'Mummy, let me get in,' she pleads, letting blasts of cold air into the warm fug under the covers. Normally my four-year-old wriggling in for an early-morning cuddle is one of my greatest pleasures, her soft, flawless skin so close, cold little feet pressing into my back, but it's 7.10 a.m., my head is pounding, my eyes scratchy. Paul is not here and the flashing memory of last night pulls me sharply upright, my heart banging in my chest. 'Mummy, I'm cold, Mummy . . .' I cannot believe I slept, that I could leave my husband in such a state on the floor. Horrible images of his dead body being casually stepped over by Josh on his way to turn on the cartoons hurry me out of bed. '. . . Daddy's on the sofa hiding under a blanky.'

I stumble from bed, pulling on my dressing gown. Ava scratches her blonde head. 'Mummy, can Phoebe come and play?' I ignore her as I busy towards the bedroom door. It's time to get the truth about last night.

Paul isn't in the front room. I find him in the kitchen leaning against the counter, a cup of tea in one hand and a slice of toast in the other. He is dressed and shaved and talking at Josh, who's bent over a cereal bowl. My husband looks completely normal. 'Here, I made you one.' He holds up a steaming cup and smiles. I don't smile back but cross my arms in a "try me" gesture. He puts the tea down, packs his grin away.

'What happened last—?'

'Nothing.'

'That was *nothing*?'

'I got drunk and maudlin, that's all.' He shrugs as if trying to make light of it.

My eyes narrow in sceptical disbelief. 'But you were saying you . . .' We both look at Josh's head to see if it's moved. I don't need to use the word. I'm not even sure I can say 'killed', it seems so bizarre and melodramatic with the sun shining in the window and talk of congestion on the M25 coming over the radio.

'Don't be daft.'

'So what happened?'

'Nothing!'

'Who were you talking about?' Josh begins to sense something different from the normal morning pattern and like a tortoise emerging from a long hibernation lifts his head from his bowl, blinking at his parents.

Paul glares at me. 'No one.' I hold up my hands and wave them at him sarcastically. He knows I'm referring to the blood.

'I ran over a dog.'

'What's "ran over"?' Ava skips into the kitchen in a policeman's hat.

'I can't believe you drove in that state!'

'Kate, please! I'm contrite enough, I've got an awful hangover.' We lock eyes.

'Shreddies or toast, Ava?' I ask crisply, moving to the cupboard.

'Krispies. I want Krispies.' I reach for a bowl and spoon.

'A dog?'

'Yeah. I felt I had to move it and I got covered in . . . you know.'

Blood. Your hands had blood on them, Paul, is what I want to say, but I hold back. 'What kind of dog?'

'What?'

'What kind of dog was it?'

'Labrador cross, I think.' He looks at his feet. 'I had to drag it, I got upset.'

I stare at my husband as he stands in the kitchen, the beating heart of our home, his progeny around him. I know him better than he knows himself. He often tells me that. And I know that when he looks at his feet he's lying.

'You know what breed, but you don't know what sex.' Paul looks blank. 'Last night this dog was a "she". This morning it's an "it".'

He shrugs, his face revealing nothing. 'It all seemed more real last night, I suppose. Dogs can seem like people when they're hurt.' He drains the last of his tea and brushes crumbs off his suit. 'I've got to go.' He moves towards me and gives me a long, tight hug, rocking me slowly from side to side and planting an affectionate kiss in the middle of my forehead. 'Oh, Eggy, you're always looking out for my welfare.'

I have a high forehead, which I've always hated. Almost as soon as I started hanging out with Paul and his crowd, lovesick and in awe of him, to my severe mortification he made his friends laugh by calling me Egghead. But as the months went on and I started to dream that he was falling for me, I became Eggy, and of all his endearments it's the one I love the most. He smiles weakly at me as we walk arm in arm to the front door. I help him into his coat as he hunts around for his scarf and work bag.

'Mum, Ava's spilled milk on my comic!' There are screams and shouts from the kitchen.

'You'd better go,' Paul says, opening the door.

'Are you OK?' I cling on to him for a bit longer, trying

to massage away the dissatisfaction from my unresolved questioning. He nods, pulling my arms away. 'Are you sure?'

'Never better,' he says, but he looks sad as he walks down the path.

'Mum!' I wander into the living room, Ava's scream rising through the octaves. I see a screwed-up blanket under which he spent the night, the indentations of his body are still visible in the cushions. He must have been up early to wash away the effects of last night. When we talked there was something I couldn't bear to ask him, the lid on a box of emotions I was too scared to lift. What could have made him weep on our kitchen floor like that? Five years ago Paul's father died of a sudden stroke. I never thought any man could show such grief as he had then – until last night.

3

My name is Kate Forman and I am very lucky. I have been told this often enough by friends and family and I truly believe it. My successes are many: I have been married for eight years to the most wonderful man on the planet, we have two beautiful, healthy children and a house far bigger and grander than I ever imagined I would live in. I'm thirty-seven years old, I don't have to dye my hair and I can still wear the clothes I bought before Ava was born (though not Josh; motherhood takes it's toll on us all, however much we pretend otherwise). Accident, design, hard work or chance, I don't really care; I am happy and so is Paul, and that is all that counts.

I know that Paul is happy, because he admitted to me recently that he thought he loved me more than our children. He asked me if I thought that was wrong, and I laughed and shook my head. I sometimes think I don't deserve Paul. His family is much grander than mine, he went to a top public school, his mum lives in a manor house in a nice bit of countryside, he grew up with a tennis court, lots of brothers and sisters, first editions on the shelves and paintings that may or may not be valuable, nobody seems to know or care. It's all much more impressive and romantic than my mum and stepdad's sterile box on a suburban estate, photos of mine and my sister Lynda's graduation hung proudly on the lounge wall.

I met Paul on my first day at university. I was Katy Brown

then. In fact, he was the very first person I met after I'd left home. I arrived at the station with my bike; Mum was bringing my stuff up in the car and was meeting me on campus. Paul was the third-year student driving the van ferrying strays and cyclists to our accommodation. I was the only one he picked up on that run and I fell in love with him instantly. He was deeply tanned and ridiculously fit after a long summer break somewhere in Europe. He drove one-handed with his elbow jutting out of the rolled-down window, the late-summer heat bringing a pleasing other-worldliness to our journey. As we careered round huge roundabouts and sped down the dual carriageways of a big and unknown city, I felt an unadulter-ated joy at what life held, sensed excitements that have been hard to recapture since. He was two years older than me and teased me not unkindly for being a fresher. He was flirting and I lapped it up. He had big brown eyes and dark hair that sat up in tufts, which he would rub distractedly. He still has all his hair today. As he lifted my bike out of the back of the van I couldn't believe that university would be so full of such gorgeous, exciting men. Needless to say, it wasn't. In the next few weeks I scanned the campus but caught only brief glimpses of him. He waved at me a couple of times through the crowd that surrounded him, and that's as far as it went. I made new friends, threw myself into first-year university life, got distracted by other relationships. I came to London after graduation giving him barely a thought. Five years later my friend Jessie started dating Pug, and besides having a ridiculous name Pug hung out with Paul.

Paul was married to Eloide then. At first I thought Paul must have said Eloise, but no, even her name had to be different – and difficult. She was a natural blonde. I'm not proud of what happened a year later, but they had no children, thank God, which made things cleaner. We just had a connection that couldn't be denied. The first night we spent together was one of the most supreme moments of my life. It goes without saying that the sex we had was . . . I have no words to properly describe the intensity, the honesty of it. I got pregnant two months after his divorce came through.

Our story doesn't end there, it just gets better and better. Paul proposed on a weekend in Paris when I was seven months gone, we were married when Josh was one. Our baby looked so cute on our wedding, wriggling in his little white sailor suit with blue trim. My mum jiggled him all through the service in the pretty rural church. Afterwards she cried and told me I'd done very well.

We've moved house three times since we've been together; from the flat to a pretty Victorian terrace to our imposing three-storey near the park. Paul runs a TV production company and has been very successful. We've traded up. If things stay as they are, who knows what we might acquire or how soon Paul can retire. I don't work full-time any more. Before I met Paul I worked in market research analysing consumer behaviour – 'poking our noses in and getting paid for it' we used to say over the water cooler – but after I had Josh my interests dovetailed with Paul's and I got my break as a TV researcher, which I've been doing ever since. I now work on *Crime Time*, a tabloid-style weekly show that relies heavily on CCTV footage and viewers' mobile phone videos to catch criminals, from petty thieves to murderers. Even though I work three days a week, Paul still says that I'm 'dabbling'. While sometimes that annoys me, it's also fair to say that my sphere is the home, Paul's is work, and we unite in the middle, like a neat Venn diagram.

This morning should be like any other, fiddling with packed lunches before hustling Josh and Ava off to school. Normally I can take almost anything in my stride but today the children's bickering shoots right to my irritation vein. There is milk all over the kitchen table and chair, Josh is flicking a sodden magazine so splatters hit the paintwork. My children are spoiled, and guilt steals over me at how I overindulge them, overcompensate for what was lacking in my own childhood. Paul doesn't mind though, he's very forgiving.

I step through the kitchen chaos and pick up Paul's cricket bat, untouched and ignored by his unsporty son, and return it to its place in the hall. I'm suddenly struck by how close I came to really battering him with it, and he doesn't even know. Roll on 12.30 and lunch with Jessie. Today I'm drinking wine.

4

Jessie's not my longest-serving friend but she's the most entertaining. We've arranged to meet in Trafalgar Square, I assume because she wants to have a scoot round the National Gallery, but when I start walking up the steps she turns the other way, showing no interest in seeing Impressionist masters or elbowing tourists to get to the postcards in the shop. 'Let's have lunch outside, it'll be fun.'

'Outside?'

'Yeah, let's get a picnic and eat it by the lions.'

'Are you mad? It's hardly a nice day.'

'Where's your sense of adventure? Come on, it's on me after all.' She grins cheekily, I'm seeing her for lunch today because she recently had an exhibition and sold a painting and is buying me a meal to celebrate.

We queue at a noisy sandwich shop and take the death run across lanes of revving traffic, then sit on the edge of one of the fountains. Greaseproof paper flaps in the gusts of wind as we tuck into sandwiches and pour wine into plastic beakers.

'So, how are you?' I ask, picking tomato out of my bacon triangle. 'Work going well?'

She bobs her head from side to side, munching. 'I've been meeting some new potential clients. Maybe something will come of it. I feel I'm on the brink of something exciting.'

'That's great.'

'Or I'm just listening to bullshit.'

'Well, that's the lot of the artist, isn't it?'

'My lot, anyway.' Jessie has only ever had one love: her art. She worked in bars and nightclubs to put herself through art school, lived in squats so she could buy canvas, still has to work today to afford studio rent and materials. Every spare moment she has she uses to paint. 'What time is it?'

I peel back my coat sleeve to find my watch. 'Nearly one. Why?'

She doesn't reply, her eyes roaming around. 'Oh, there's someone I know.' Jessie waves at two young men sitting further round on the fountain. 'Don't look now but the one on the left behind you is someone I'm sort of seeing.' I peer over, taking in a guy who looks about twenty with a goatee. 'He's nineteen.'

'You should be arrested!' I say, faux scandalised. Jessie has dated, left and been dumped by a million men over the years I have known her. I doubt there'd be room for them all in the National Gallery, while my former lovers would struggle to get intimate in my bathroom. Her life has been lived with many different passions, mine with only one.

The young men wave back. 'Aren't they coming over?'

'Maybe in a bit.'

I shrug, nonplussed. Pigeons swoop and waddle, people huddle. It all looks normal, but something's not right. 'Are you OK Jessie?' She's looking at her phone messages.

She smiles. 'Never better. How's Paul?'

Talking about him today doesn't bring the usual warm glow to my heart. 'He's OK. A bit stressed, maybe. His programmes are going well, I guess. *Crime Time*'s moving up the ratings.'

'Oh yeah?'

'The audience-participation element has really caught on. Viewers are picking up their mobiles and texting in in their droves.'

'Interesting,' Jessie says, chewing a mouthful of mozzarella and rocket. 'Maybe I need to talk to him about how to get my message across. He really knows how to stand out from the crowd. What time is it now?'

'It's one. Why does it matter?' She wipes a spot of mayonnaise off the corner of her mouth. The rumble of traffic is suddenly overlain with the strains of loud music. I can't tell where it's coming from. 'What's that?'

Jessie stands and brushes crumbs off her jeans. 'Do you have your iPhone?' I nod. 'You may want to get it out.'

A bass beat booms out across the square and a couple start to dance not far away. It's impossible not to start moving my shoulders to the catchy tune and now there are four people line-dancing near by. 'See you in a minute,' Jessie says and skips off to where sixteen people are now dancing in two lines. Jessie's boyfriend and his friend have joined in, adding to the expanding quadrant of dancers.

The pigeons scatter with the moving crowd. I'm disorientated, a swirling group of people make weird yet beautiful shapes in front of me. Passers-by stand uncomprehending, a couple hurry away, a down-and-out stands mesmerised. The dancers come in all shapes and sizes, some must be as young as thirteen, others retired. There are housewives, women in stilettos, a man with a moustache.

They've obviously rehearsed their moves as there are now more than a hundred and fifty people dancing in a similar fashion. Jessie's brought me to a flashmob, and just like every other viewer I get out my phone and start videoing. A joyful spontaneity fills me; I rock from side to side, the rhythm in the song impossible to resist, the absurdity of this performance under Nelson's Column impossible to ignore. What the admiral would have made of it all I can't guess.

The music's changed now to a modern, upbeat tempo, the dancers are gyrating more free-form and with more energy.

I know someone must be videoing to upload to YouTube minutes after this spectacle has finished. I stand on the low fountain wall and see a man high up on one of the huge lions with a powerful video camera.

The steps of the gallery, where so much art that once was innovative now hangs behind glass screens, are crowded with onlookers.

Jessie's waving her arms, singing loudly. The music is building to a crescendo, the spectators grin at each other, someone cheers. With a final flourish the dancers perform their most difficult move and half of them jump into the arms of a neighbour, arms aloft.

Just as quickly as it started, the music stops and the dancers melt away as if nothing had ever happened. Two policemen, their faces teetering between bemusement and caution, stand marooned in the middle of the now-empty concourse. The crowd on the steps of the gallery clap and cheer.

Jessie collapses into my arms in a peal of giggles. 'I couldn't tell you, the look on your face was just priceless!'

'That was great! How on earth did you get involved in that?'

'We organised it through Facebook, had one rehearsal in a warehouse in Clapton and then we just did it. God, I'm so pumped!'

'Look.' The policemen are trying to talk the man with the video off the lion. 'You'll probably be on the news this evening.'

'The closest I'll ever come to fame.'

'Oh, I have high hopes for you, Jessie.'

'Let's go and get another drink.' She links her arm through mine.

'Can I meet the new man?' I cast around, looking for him.

'Oh, he doesn't really matter.' She pulls me away. 'Thing is, I really like this married man I'm seeing. I think it's all spiralling a bit out of control.' She looks at me carefully. 'If you disapproved you'd tell me, wouldn't you?'

'How can I? Remember Paul was married when—'

Jessie makes a dismissive gesture with her hand. 'He was far too young, it doesn't count.'

'Yes it does, he took those vows with someone else, remember.'

'Till death us do part,' she says as we begin to walk up Charing Cross Road. 'It's a good title for a painting.' Her eyes take her somewhere else for a second or two. 'Crowds of people are so powerful, aren't they?'

'Very true. Organise them and they'll do the most amazing things.'

'When you're part of it you'll say or believe anything.'

'That's the first lesson of history, isn't it? Groups of people are easy to manipulate.'

'My heart's still racing!' Jessie's hand is on her chest, her eyes shining.

'Who is this married man?'

'Sshh.' She puts her fingers to her lips. 'I don't want to hex it. After all, the sex is amazing, I think I'd die for it!'

'Don't say that!' I am surprised. Jessie doesn't usually talk like this, talk seriously about her love life. 'Wow. Lucky you.' Our conversation shrivels. She says nothing and I unexpectedly feel a shard of jealousy pierce me.

'What would you die for?'

'Oh.' I shrug. 'Paul and my kids, I suppose.'

'What would you kill for?'

'Jessie!'

'Come on!' She leans into my arm.

'My family. Only my family.'

She wrinkles her nose. 'How predictable and sentimental.' She's still on a high from her public dancing and spreads her arms wide and spins on the pavement. 'I'd kill for an exhibition in New York, the cover of *Art Monthly*, some new boots . . . are you OK?'

Jessie is staring at me as I've stopped dead in the street. As she was prattling on a thought struck me: what would Paul kill for? I had assumed his answer would mirror mine: his family. We used to pride ourselves on having no secrets – until last night. I simply don't believe he could get that upset about a dog. But if the blood wasn't an animal's then whose was it? For a second I think of telling Jessie what happened, but I dismiss it a moment later. I doubt I will ever tell anyone what happened last night. It will remain mine and Paul's secret, till death us do part, and beyond.

5

Paul phones later that afternoon to say I don't need to cook as he's ordering a curry for everyone and he'll pick it up on the way home. I suspect his hangover taste buds are doing the talking and now the rest of us have to fall into line. Curry is not my favourite meal. I lay out plates and half-heartedly try to get Josh to help but his only contribution is to scratch his armpit and yawn.

Ava jumps into her daddy's arms when he comes through the door, causing him to nearly upend the curry bag on the floor. 'Whoa, monkey!' he shouts, scooping her up with one arm and play-acting the desperation of trying to stop falling. Ava squeals as he weaves and bounces off the walls into the kitchen, curry in one hand, child in the other. 'And into the chair she goes . . . and food is on the table! Phew!' He wheels round and gathers me up in a tight and loving embrace. 'It's good to be home.' I squirm away, images from yesterday still too fresh in my mind for me to play happy families. Paul spoons out chicken and spinach and chick peas on to a plate for me. 'Rice, babes?' he asks me over Ava's screams as she spills apple juice.

'Mum! She's soaked me!' Josh throws his poppadom to the table and shoves his sister as I make placatory noises. Ava takes the gulp of air needed for a big howl, but Paul whizzes round the table and picks her up, transplanting her back on his knee, and tries to eat with a child's head blocking his way. 'It's all soggy!' Josh's fork clatters to the floor.

Paul raises his glass of water to mine. 'Welcome to dinner at the Formans',' he says, smiling at me.

'Mummy, are you twenty-seven?' Ava asks, crunching on a breadstick.

'No, darling, I'm much older than that.'

'Are you twenty-one?'

I look at her indulgently. 'No, I'm thirty-seven.'

'That is *soo* old, Mum,' Josh says, head resting in one hand as he shovels rice into his mouth with his fingers. I try to catch Paul's eye but he's staring at the table.

'I saw Jessie today. She took me to a flashmob in Trafalgar Square.'

Now he's interested. 'Really?'

'Yeah, she was in it. It was amazing. I've got some of it on my phone.'

'TV is chasing mobile and the internet now.' He shakes his head. 'If I'm not careful I'm going to become obsolete.'

'She's having another you-know.' I look at him meaningfully. He can decipher child-proof English.

'So who's this one?'

'He's married.'

He groans. 'Poor bastard.'

'Paul! That's uncalled for. Anyway, it's his wife you should feel for. She has to suffer her husband's midlife crisis.' His answer is to drop his nose to Ava's head and breathe deeply. I stand with the curry bag over the opening of the bin and watch him. 'Are you OK?'

He comes back to us from far away. 'Yes, yes . . .'

'What happened last night, Paul?'

He avoids my gaze. 'Nothing happened.'

'Why were you back so late?' I'm all reasonable inquiry, sweeping leftover rice into my palm.

'I was just out with some people from work.'

'Which people?'

He looks at me. 'You're quizzing me.'

'I want to help. I'm here to help you, Paul.' My voice is soft. I want him to know that we are a team, his problem is my problem and we can work through it together. He picks Ava up and pops her on a neighbouring chair so that he can stand and put cutlery in the dishwasher.

'I don't need your help, everything is OK.' He is pacing round the kitchen distractedly, picking up things and looking under them, he's moved his work bag twice. Our conversation is abandoned as I hear him opening the cupboard under the stairs and rummaging.

'What are you looking for?'

'Nothing.' He comes back into the kitchen.

'So who were you out with till the early hours?'

'Lex and I ended up in a bar in town.'

I nod carefully. No surprises there. Lex is Paul's business partner, who loves nothing more than to drink, party and behave like a teenager. Our most common interactions go along the lines of:

Me: Just grow up.

Lex: Come on! Where's the harm?

Paul: (*Silent eye roll.*)

Lex and I are not the best of friends. If this has ever caused Paul trouble over the years they've been in business then he's hidden it very well.

'What time did you leave?'

'I don't remember.'

'I didn't know Lex could make you so upset.' This is clearly the wrong thing to say as he shoots me a look that drains the brightness from my face. 'Where did you knock over the dog?'

'Run over, you mean.' He shudders and shakes his head. 'Near that car park by the bridge.' He takes a long glance at his shoes. 'I don't want to talk about this any more, Kate. The whole thing's unsettled me.'

'Unsettled *you*!'

'Stop grilling me!'

Sadness wraps around me as he retreats into the front room and turns on the telly. He has cut me out. Josh burps and Ava starts giggling, opening her mouth so that half-chewed chocolate raisins plop on to the table. I tell her off far more sharply than she was expecting and she starts to cry, which makes me feel guilty, which makes me feel angry with myself, which makes me livid with Paul for putting me in a bad mood and making me shout. Motherhood: a never-ending turntable of frustration and guilt.

A few hours later I'm lying very still in bed feeling Paul's body settle into the mattress. I cannot get what happened yesterday out of my mind. His desolation and panic churns in me like a bad restaurant meal in my stomach. None of my explanations are palatable. Could Paul get that upset about a dog? I don't believe it, but I may have to – the alternatives are far more horrifying. The spectre of another woman, another passion throwing him off-kilter, sits leadenly with me in the dark. We have been married eight years. Have I missed something? I always thought that if Paul was ever unfaithful I would know, I would spot the signs. I am a watcher. My dad left Mum when I was ten. Lynda and I heard the screaming and shouting from downstairs, the banging door. He never said goodbye. I have seen my dad about four times since that night; I didn't invite him to my wedding and he has never met my children. Josh will be ten next year. The thought of Paul abandoning him at the age I was abandoned is unthinkable, just unimaginable. Mum used to say that it was a bolt from the blue, that she had no idea Dad was carrying on with his secretary. I have made sure in my relationships to never be my mother, outflanked and unaware. Mum's with Dale now, a dull drinker who's 'company'. Lynda has never married or had children, but unlike Jessie I don't think she's happy about it. She was fifteen when Dad left and she has trouble trusting men.

I hate my dad. You see, even someone as lucky as me has their crosses to bear.

I spoon Paul as he slumbers on, curl my foot around his hairy shin and place my cheek in the groove between his shoulder blades. We fit together, we are man and wife.

Everyone likes Paul. He is handsome and kind, but – and I think this is the cherry on the cake – he's not bland. He can remember a funny joke, win the fathers' sprint at Josh's sports day, offer good advice for Jessie's broken heart. But sometimes people tell me 'Ooh, he's a one, that Paul' and I think: good. He never ceases to surprise me; he's never boring, and boredom is the death of all marriages. He's also successful. Two years ago Forwood TV – the name is a combination of Paul's and Lex's surnames (Lex being a Wood) – was bought by CPTV, the household name, FTSE 100 quoted media company. We joked that we'd get to go to soirées at Downing Street and probably meet Elton John, but that hasn't happened. My children will still have to fight for attention and favours and opportunities, just not quite to the extent that Lynda and I had to. The aura of 'special' is still a long way off.

It was hard to remain calm when Paul and Lex were selling the company. It really was an astonishing achievement, causing them excitement and a lot of stress. How are you supposed to feel once your dreams are achieved and you're not yet forty?

The world Paul moves in is cosmopolitan, fast-paced, glamorous and reckless. He employs fifty-five people at the last count, a large proportion of which are women younger, smarter and prettier than I am. Don't make the mistake of thinking that I am bitter about what the beauty lottery has doled out or paranoid about the competition; life has always been this way for me, my looks are not notable and my personality is quiet – I grow on you. I have mid-length brown hair neither curly nor straight, hazel eyes with, apparently, an arresting fleck in them, and a kind smile. Men are normally drawn to girls like Jessie with her stand-out tits and bottle-blonde hair, women to her loud personality and store of amusing anecdotes; however, it was me who walked away with the greatest prize of all my contemporaries: a marriage to and a life with Paul. I pulled it off because I am single-minded. When I believe something is right, and Paul and I were right, nothing can really stand in my way. I worked very hard at putting his needs in front of my own, of living my life in his shadow. I made it impossible for him to live without me. I never tell anyone this of course, it would make me seem surrendered, and I am certainly not that. But after ten years and two kids I'm sensing a shift. It's time I stepped out from that shadow. My man sobbing on the floor, jabbering of killing whatever it was, is not something I will surrender to. I will find out sooner or later what happened that night, and then I will work tirelessly to put it right.

6

The glamour that clings to TV is in direct contrast to the scuzziness of the offices where *Crime Time* is produced. To get to work I cower from juggernauts spraying grit as they hurtle towards central London, and when I get there I never linger under the 1960s porch that has chunks of cement missing, as if some feral animal has adapted completely to its urban environment and started eating it. Inside is no better, the carpet tiles under my desk curl up at the edges like stale sandwiches, stains resembling blood splatter the floor.

I turn on my computer and wave at Shaheena, a fellow researcher who sits opposite. We joke to each other that our grotty surroundings match the subjects that we deal with day to day. A bin bag leans against my desk. Before I can ask what it is Shaheena leans forward and whispers, 'Black Cloud blowing in.'

I sit down and turn to see Livvy, the producer, 'uh-uhing' someone on her mobile as she weaves past office chairs towards us. I haven't worked on *Crime Time* long enough to have met everyone yet, but Livvy has certainly made an impression. She finishes the call and throws the phone on my desk, huffing with irritation.

'Not a good day, I take it?'

Livvy snorts. 'Cretins and morons all.'

I see Shaheena holding back a smile. We call Livvy Black Cloud because she's relentlessly pessimistic, sees disaster lurking at every turn. 'I thought we got viewing figures that were up?'

Livvy doesn't smile. She sits on my desk and swishes a long ponytail back and forth. 'We did.' This great news is not enough for Livvy, it simply gives her further to fall later. The frown deepens. 'But no one is to get complacent.' She points at the black bin bag. 'There are more and more videos coming in from viewers. This is just a sample. You need to go through them and find the hard-hitting stories, footage that really shows the nasty little toe-rags we all live among.' She jabs a finger for emphasis across my computer.

'No problem,' I reply.

Livvy does her best to spread her bad mood. 'Don't get overexcited. It's grunt work.' Nothing I say can persuade Livvy that I really like my job. What she thinks of as tedious, repetitive sorting and collating I see as fascinating insights into the dramas, lives and troubles of the public. That we can then play these videos to millions on TV, help catch individuals who are terrorising estates and make people's lives better makes me love my job. 'And there's more out the back. I'll show you where and you can lug it all back here.'

'What else did the feedback reveal about the show?' asks Shaheena.

'Marika is a real hit, at least something's going right.'

'Ah, the great Marika Cochran,' I can't help but gush.

'Isn't she just the best?' Despite Livvy's mood tending to be dark, even she can't resist the lure of Marika.

'It's a world away from the dancing show she first presented, but she's got such a young and fresh attitude it really fits,' I add.

'God, what a coup it was to get her! It was Paul's idea of course!'

I smile my sweetest smile, which can be pretty saccharine at times. Marika was *my* idea.

Livvy has made herself too happy for too long. The frown returns with renewed vigour. 'Yes, the show's going well as it stands, but I still get "bring it in under, bring it in under budget". God, I miss the free-spending Noughties. Look at this rathole of an office!' The three of us stare forlornly around us and I hazard a guess that I was hired for the main because I was cheap.

'Why *are* we in this office?' Shaheena asks.

'That's a polite description! Some jerk-off at Forwood forgot to do something with leases.' She stands and immediately looks panicked. 'Where's my phone?' I pick it up for her. 'Kate, the tapes.'

Shaheena gives me a pitying look as I trail after Livvy down a poky corridor. She yanks at a heavy door and we are transported into the *Crime Time* studio. Livvy marches past a large living-room set with a leather armchair and sofa behind a glass coffee table. This is where Marika holds court when *Crime Time* is broadcasting, but today the studio is abandoned and quiet. The show asks for the public's help in solving all types of crime, from murder to rapes and criminal damage, and exploits phone and text voting to raise money for community campaigns – a CCTV camera on a dark corner of an estate, new locks on pensioners' doors.

To the side of the set sits a bank of desks where the researchers take the calls, texts and emails from the public, and from where we organise the public vote each week. The show is populist and unashamed to be so.

Livvy bangs through a side door and from there into a delivery bay and starts riffling through a black bin bag next to a pile of cardboard boxes.

'I feel like the people who end up on our show,' I say.

Livvy grunts. 'What fool put them out here I can't imagine.'

I open a bag and see hundreds of envelopes and packages, each one containing a heartfelt letter describing the terrors their authors are living with and, more often than not, a video to accompany it. 'It's crime from the bottom up.'

'The world is full of liars and cheats,' Livvy adds with gusto. 'Come on, you take one side and I'll take the other.'

'You know, when I did my course in interrogation techniques—'

'You did what?' Livvy turns to me in surprise and I realise with a touch of shame that she never read my CV when I applied for the job. Not for the first time I suspect that being Paul's wife made things easier than it should have been.

'A course in how to question suspects, whether suspects are lying, that sort of thing. It was me and a load of policemen (they were all men then) and private investigators with a weight problem.'

'Why on earth—?'

'When I worked in market research . . .' Livvy is looking blank. 'Before I was a TV researcher I worked in market research. I used to design questionnaires and interview people to test their reactions to consumer products – chocolate bars, washing powder or whatever. Problem was, I often thought the results weren't very helpful, because I often thought the subjects were lying. The classic case is when you ask a housewife how many hours of daytime TV she watches, she'll tend to claim she watches none, but then if you ask her what she thinks of Jeremy Kyle, she's tutting at his subjects every morning. So I persuaded my boss to send me on an interrogation course – you know, the "is this person lying?" course, to find out if there might be a commercial application to police techniques. So they paid for me to study part-time.'

We pick up a side each and head back through the studio.

'And is there?'

'Mmm, I think so. I'm still not sure, or maybe I just wasn't very good at reading people.' Livvy nods. 'But I did learn some interesting things. Did you know that seventy per cent of prime suspects end up confessing? If the people in those letters and emails' – I nod at the pile of envelopes in my arms

– 'think their partner or their neighbour is up to no good, it's because he or she probably is.'

Livvy nods. 'Like my fuck-up of an ex,' she adds bitterly. We dump the bag down next to its twin by my desk. She stares into space for a moment and takes the time to be reflective. 'So I guess market research tells you that my love for that Twix' – she points at the treat I've brought in for my lunch – 'is because my boyfriend didn't love me enough?'

'No. It's because you just really like chocolate.' Livvy actually neighs. It's such a startling sound that a second later we are both roaring. Shaheena comes back from the toilet and stands open-mouthed. 'Seriously though, one thing I did learn at all those night classes was that criminals are actually pretty stupid. The clever ones are very rare.'

'Or they just get away with it.'

'Perhaps. Maybe one reason is that groups can be led surprisingly easily. People are easy to manipulate, but we all think we're immune, or aware enough to see it.'

Livvy's eyes glaze over with longing. 'The master criminal. I'd love to catch one of those.'

'So would I.' She has no idea how seriously I mean that.

A trilling cuts into Livvy's fleeting good mood. 'Where's my phone?' She pats pockets in alarm until I hand it to her from my desk. She listens for a second and then the frown is back. 'Tell whatever bonehead did that to get it back from accounts.' She flicks her hair as she marches away.

'Do I detect a silver lining to that cloud?' Shaheena asks.

7

Wednesday night is a celebratory work dinner, another stop on the socialising round that is Forwood Television. One of the company's series (dreamed up and got on air by Paul, obviously) has just been showing and has caused a huge stir. *Inside-Out* is a reality-TV-style documentary about Gerry Bonacorsi, who thirty years ago strangled his wife, apparently because 'she was doing his head in'. Bonacorsi wouldn't be remembered by anyone were it not for the fact that, as he has never expressed any remorse for his crime, and has therefore never been released, he has the distinction of being one of Britain's longest-serving lifers. He is now seventy and *Inside-Out* managed to get the Parole Board to agree to have cameras at their hearings and in the jail where Bonacorsi was, to show how decisions are made about whether or not to release prisoners like him. At the beginning of the series we didn't know if he would get out or not. A month ago, he did. In my opinion he should have rotted in jail till the day he died, but hey, I'm just a wife and part of Joe Public so who am I to say? According to Paul I have a very tabloid take on life, to which I say everyone's a liberal until they've been a victim of violent crime.

So, tonight it's murderers and mojitos; I don't know if they mix that well. Paul's PA, Sergei, has hired the new hot place in town and has organised dinner for about a hundred and fifty people. It's a great way for employees to back-scratch, navel-gaze and get rat-arsed at somebody else's expense. The evening is important because CPTV's founder, Raiph Spencer, is coming with other top brass and Paul is keen to impress. I've bought a new dress and had my hair blow-dried so that it shines and shifts in a lovely wave when I turn my head.

'So, what do you think?' I swish the full skirt in a slow sashay for Ava and Luciana, the babysitter. Ava is sitting on Luciana's knee as Luciana combs her hair. They giggle and coo together. Luciana is the Brazilian au pair of some friends of ours and she does babysitting when she's free. She is obsessed with Ava and plays dollies and 'school' with her for hours, while Josh is left free to watch TV uninterrupted.

'Ah, Mummy looks beautiful, doesn't she?' Luciana says, looking at Ava.

'You look funny,' Ava says.

'That's rich coming from a girl wearing yellow, scarlet and purple,' I reply. Ava picks her nose in an Alice in Wonderland costume, her wide eyes staring at me as her head bobs back and forth in a tango with the comb. Josh doesn't even look up from the TV.

'It's a wonderful colour on you,' says Luciana. 'Paul can be proud that he is with you tonight.'

'Wow,' I giggle, a little embarrassed.

Luciana shrugs her skinny arms. 'Paul is a sexy man. You must stay beautiful, otherwise . . .' She tails off and sighs dramatically. She wags her finger at me. 'Otherwise, men are all the same.' Luciana is twenty going on seventy. How anyone that young and beautiful has learned to be so cynical about men I can't begin to imagine.

'You say all the right things, Luciana . . . I think.' I smile. 'Have whatever's in the fridge, don't let them go to bed too late.' Luciana nods. It's the same time-honoured routine to get me out the house. My mobile rings, the taxi is outside. 'Well, I'm going now, see you all later.'

Josh doesn't reply, the TV blares on. I double-check the contents of my bag and examine my teeth in the hall mirror. They are still there.

Because I'm wearing high heels I indulge in the luxury of taking a taxing into town. We slide past shops and houses and I watch an old woman battling up the road, her body rocking with the effort of carrying her heavy shopping bag. I feel guilty at how cosseted I am, at the good fortune that has come my way. Have I started to take it for granted? I'm trying to decide whether this is a problem when I feel my mobile vibrating with an incoming message from Jessie. 'Just had the best sex of my life! Call me x.' I put my phone back in my bag and let my head loll on the back seat. I must have had a hundred texts from Jessie saying just that. She is nothing if not consistent. "Paul can be proud of you." That's a nice thing to hear. And I am proud of him, aren't I? His sobs from Monday ring in my head. The seat suddenly feels sticky, the air through my window cold. There has been no explanation that has set my mind at rest; uncomfortable thoughts make a fresh journey through my skull. Paul and I need to talk. I crave clarity and a return to my lovely, normal life. The taxi coasts to a stop and I pinch my palm to pull myself together. I am the boss's wife, I have a part to play and I want to play it well.

8

I am seeing Paul inside because he had a meeting that he knew would overrun. Normally this wouldn't matter, but tonight I really need an arm to lean on, or hide behind. I stand forlornly in the queue to get in the door and am asked who I am by a bouncer. The bar is a crush of loud people I don't know and my circuit ends all too soon, leaving me marooned next to the coat check.

'Kate! It's great to see you.' I am rescued by Sergei, a serious-looking Russian in his late twenties wearing a black suit with a black shirt and black tie. Sergei likes black. He is incredibly good at his job and guards Paul like a pitbull guards an East End drug dealer. He kisses me formally on both cheeks and asks after the children by name as Astrid arrives.

'Hiya! Are you Paul's wife?' I nod and smile, having been through this routine with Astrid twice before. Lex has two assistants, one of which is Astrid. Paul and I used to joke that Lex had two secretaries because neither was good enough to do the job on her own. Lex claims there's method in his madness; he hires wannabes who want to be on TV, and maintains that he's often got his best ideas from his "satellite dishes".

'I'm Kate,' I say, smiling.

'Oh bloody hell, that's it, I can never remember anyone's name!' Astrid is Australian. She play-punches Sergei in his rock-solid stomach, her silver top with a cutaway back advertising she's young enough to get away without a bra. 'Let's get slammed!' She hugs me tightly, pressing a plump and fragrant cheek to mine, and grasps my hand as we walk into the main part of the building.

Paul's and Lex's personalities are neatly mirrored in their assistants. Paul hired Sergei because he didn't want the bimbo eruptions Lex has weathered over the years. 'I can't stand being a cliché,' Paul says. 'Who wants to go to work and be distracted by wanting to fuck their secretary?' My dad, that's who, but enough of that.

'Did you know, Kate, that this building used to be a slaughterhouse?' says Sergei.

'So I heard. It's an amazing place.' We both stare up at a beautiful vaulted wooden ceiling.

'I think it's like a cathedral,' a man's voice adds. I turn to find John staring upwards, his Adam's apple casting a sharp shadow across his neck.

'Hello, John,' I say. 'Are things good? You look really well.' His cheek is hollow where I kiss it, his skin grey.

John nods and gives me his sad, faraway smile. He points his glass of fruit juice over my head. 'Look, above the bar they've still got the old meat hooks.' Astrid makes a disgusted sound. Paul has told me over the years how hard it has been for his brother to stay on the wagon, the daily battle with his demons and his addictions. I've heard about his iron will and determination. I respect John but I'm not sure I like him. It's as if there's a film of defeat between me and him, between him and the world. Paul agrees, but nevertheless he's family and that's the end of it. He handles legal matters at Forwood TV, fished from the river of failure by Paul, dried off – and out. Few would have done it, not many would have taken the risk or spent the time, but then Paul is not like most people. He employed his eldest brother after the sale not to mop the floor or paper-push some irrelevance, but to look over vital contracts. 'Give him responsibility and he will respond, he can't stand pity,' Paul said. I'm ashamed to say I completely disagreed with him, told him in no uncertain terms that disaster would ensue, that his company was at risk, but he ignored me. Two years later I have been proved wrong. The whisky and cocaine benders are gone, along with his wife, his fortune, his former career as an advertising lawyer and his sense of humour, and have been replaced by weekly NA and AA meetings, the gym and cigarettes. I look at the meat hooks, their curvy weight illuminated by a hundred down-lighters, dimmers and uplighters, and then I see John studying me. Paul insists he never told John what I thought, but when he looks at me like that, I suspect he did. Blood is thicker than water.

'I believed it to be a fitting venue to showcase Forwood's success,' says Sergei.

'Well, you certainly deserve it after *Inside-Out*. The response you've had to that programme is phenomenal.'

'It's the bollocks!' says Astrid. Her enthusiasm is infectious and we all laugh.

'Do you know where Paul is?' I ask Sergei.

'Has he abandoned you already?' He looks behind him.

'Oh no. We came separately. He had a meeting that went on late so I came on my own.'

I notice a small frown crossing Sergei's smooth forehead. 'Oh.' He pauses. 'Well, let's see if we can track him down for you, I saw him not five minutes ago. He was with some bigwigs from CPTV.'

'There he is!' Astrid shouts. She is tall with legs like a fawn and peers over heads on my behalf. She smiles and waves over my shoulder as Paul arrives and plants a big kiss on my cheek.

'My wife!' He keeps his hand round my waist as if he doesn't want to – or shouldn't – let me go. 'Where's your drink? Come on, champagne for Kate!' He bags a passing waiter and lifts a flute off the tray. Paul is in a dinner suit. He is glowing with health and looks hot and manic, his dark eyes shining. He slaps a guy on the shoulder, is congratulated on something else by another. Paul introduces me to some high-profile industry people and I put all my effort and attention into making them feel at ease. Apparently it's something I do well. I cling to comments like that; I'm not sure my list of accomplishments is very long. As we queue up to find our seats Paul is the centre of attention, the main man around which the evening, this crowd and their careers revolve.

Half an hour later we sit down to dinner. I'm at the table where all the important people are, though at evenings like this I feel as relevant as a third wheel on a motorbike. I'm introduced by Paul to Raiph Spencer. I've heard about him so often over the years and seen his picture in the media often enough that he feels familiar to me even though this is the first time I've met him.

'It's an honour,' I say, gushing more than I should as I pump his hand.

'You'll probably call it a curse by the end of the meal,' he replies, his blue eyes creasing into a smile. His face is sprinkled with large moles from too much Caribbean or Mediterranean sun and he's shorter and thinner than he looks on TV.

'Did you get time to watch *Inside-Out*?' I ask politely.

'Yes, I made time for that,' Raiph replies. 'You know I was at school with Gerry, although he was a bit older than me. I found the programme fascinating.'

'What I think is fascinating is how the lives of two people from the same place can take such different paths.'

Raiph gives a small laugh. 'I think it's fair to say that he and I are the most famous people to come out of that part of Donegal in more than one generation.' Raiph wears his charm with an easy grace, which is at odds with his reputation of being the velociraptor of the business world. He pulls out my chair for me and Paul beams in my direction.

'Notorious rather than famous, surely?' Raiph's career trajectory from son of an Irish butcher to a possible star of *The Apprentice* is a story that's been told many times.

'Do you mean Gerry and me, or just me?'

I smile. 'I'm not sure there's much difference between the two. Although, it would be more fun to be notorious, wouldn't it? Sounds a bit more exciting.'

Raiph ponders this for longer than I would. He's really thinking about his answer. 'I have quite enough excitement in my life as it is, I think any more and my poor ticker would give out.' He clasps the front of his very well-made suit and rolls his eyes. 'I'll let the Forwood boys here have the challenge of becoming notorious.'

Lex joins the end of our conversation. 'Turning a killer into a celebrity was my greatest challenge,' he adds.

'You can't deny that the camera loves him,' Paul adds. 'He made compulsive viewing. He was so different from what people were expecting, and that makes for great TV.'

'To great TV,' Lex says, raising his glass.

'To great TV,' we all toast together.

Sergei's done his seating plan well: I chew my starter listening to an intense man named Jethro tell an amusing story of how to photograph stoats; and the woman next to him repeats a very indiscreet bit of gossip about a rock star she picked up in an editing suite, oh how we roar. I am about to try to warm up a stiff-looking suit two seats away but notice Lex weaving between the tables to the exit. My guess is he's off for a fag. I make my excuses and head for the door. When I get outside he's with Astrid and a group of people I don't recognise. He sees me and nods, beckoning me over.

'Can I cadge a cigarette? I'm trying to give up but am failing miserably.' In fact I haven't smoked for years.

'Course. You and me both.' He holds his lighter for me in a sexually suggestive manner. I find it hard to pinpoint why I don't like Lex. I mean, there are the obvious things: he's arrogant, vain and selfish, but this doesn't stop him being immensely popular, particularly with younger women. I don't get it and I wonder if my unease is fear, the fear that I don't agree with the crowd, or with Paul; that I've missed something.

He smirks and introduces me to everyone and I shoot him a knowing look in return. 'Hear you had a ding-dong of a night on Monday.'

He blows a smoke ring and smiles. 'I cannot possibly divulge, Kate, it's the code of the road.' Of all the expressions that sum up the TV industry, this is the one I hate the most. The collusion between colleagues and freelancers when they're on location, the lying to spouses and long-suffering partners about what really happened in that house in Ibiza, or that hotel complex in Russia, or that caravan in Ireland over the course of a six-week shoot (I mean six-week party). There are jobs that require hard work and then there are jobs on location for TV, if the stories I hear are anything to go by. How many secrets have been sealed in at work that because I am a wife I can never uncover?

Someone sniggers and I look round sharply. Get a grip, Kate, I say to myself. I hold my elbow with my other hand, the cigarette near my ear. 'How boring that tired TV expression is. I've got a better one from the music business.' I lean forward for Lex's benefit. '"Art for art's sake, but hits for fuck's sake."'

Lex laughs and the group relaxes. The nicotine floods my body, making me feel sick.

'Oh, I've got one!' says Astrid, grinding a fag under her

pump. 'A friend of a friend was working on reception in a music company and Sting walked in and came right up to the desk. So she said, "Don't stand so close to me."' Everyone laughs. This would be fun if I wasn't so desperate to know the truth, to clutch at the straws of understanding that Lex won't offer. How can I prise open what really happened on Monday? My head swims uncomfortably.

After five minutes of superficial banter Lex flicks his stub into the gutter. He pats me on the back as he turns to go inside. 'At this rate you'll be filming me for *Crime Time*, now that you've parachuted on to the programme.' He makes an exaggerated gesture of self-defence. My smile is that of an assassin.

Back inside the heat is stifling and the meal drags on. This should be a pleasant dinner, a validation of everything Paul has achieved, but for the first time I'm scanning the room for women who Paul might be attracted to. This is depressing territory and I slam back my wine. At one point Sergei passes and pats me on the shoulder in a gesture that feels like consolation. I think about his small frown earlier, how he attempted to cover his shock when I said Paul was in a meeting. Sour feelings of misgiving swirl inside me.

I'm pulled from my toxic thoughts by a tap on the arm. Portia Wetherall, the CEO of CPTV, is leaning across the seat backs to greet me and I'm so glad to be distracted that I get up and fling my arms around her, gathering her awkwardly in my armpit.

'A penny for your thoughts?' she says.

'Oh, I'm just tired, that's all. I've got a lot on.' I slap my forehead. 'Sorry, I know that must sound ridiculous to you.'

She clasps my hand and repeats 'not at all' several times. 'Don't assume that because I have a high-profile job I'm more stressed than you are. It might well not be the case. I'm very good at delegating.' She smiles. 'Plus,' she holds up a well-manicured finger, 'I don't have children to deal with.' Portia's the youngest woman to ever head a FTSE 100 quoted company. Whenever she moves I fancy I hear the sound of glass ceilings shattering. Portia's older than me, but by how much I can't tell. Her hair is a conservative helmet of blonde in the style called 'older woman', her suit is an expensive and timeless caramel. She's heading one of Britain's biggest companies and I'll bet she's not yet fifty. I can imagine leading Jessie's life if I didn't have my own, but Portia's is as exotic and indecipherable as an Amazonian Indian or Tibetan goat herder, something you marvel at on holiday or gawp at in a documentary.

'I think you're being very generous. Tell me, how often are you at events like this?'

'Oh, once a week I'd say, though this is of course the most interesting one. Forwood events are a real highlight. I think it's because Paul and Lex are such good company, it all flows from there.'

We smile at each other. 'But the longer you have to talk to me the less enticing the whole evening becomes.'

'Oh stop!' She squeezes my hand. 'But between you and me,' she leans right behind the back of the person at the table, 'if you knew what some of the functions I attended were like, you'd realise how scintillating your company is.' I feel a warm glow inside and it's not just the wine. Portia has a rare gift for making me feel special, as though I'm the only person in the room. It's probably just one of the many talents she's used to take her right to the top. 'Talking of interesting people, I met a friend of yours the other day. Jessica Booth.'

'Jessie! How come?'

'Raiph is commissioning a portrait.' She nods towards the founder. 'He mentioned it to me and so I insisted he used my art adviser to draw up a shortlist and she was on it.'

'Well, that's great news! I think she's really talented.'

Portia nods. 'I was in the East End last week and dropped in on her show and met her there. I liked her, and her work.'

'She deserves a bigger platform.'

'It's amazing the genius that so often lies hidden from the world.' She frowns. 'Or is that sad?'

'Common, more than anything, I suspect.'

'That is sad! I wish your friend luck.' And even though I get the feeling she wants to talk to me further, we are interrupted by a suit butting in.

An hour later I see Lex heading for the toilets, the second time in twenty minutes. I surprise myself because for someone who is not spontaneous I make a sudden decision and follow him. I watch a minute crawl by on my watch, fiddling with my shoe outside the Gents before I open the door. There are two men standing in the stalls but, as I suspected, Lex is not one of them. They look at me open-mouthed and hurriedly zip up. I enter the cubicle next to Lex's and stand on the toilet. I still can't see over so I balance on the cistern in my stilettos and peek.

Lex is chopping out a fat line of coke on the porcelain. He nearly drops his twenty-pound note when he sees me. 'Kate! Fuck, what are you doing here, I mean up there?' He recovers momentarily. 'Do you want one? Oh no, sorry, I didn't mean that.' His discomfort is palpable.

'What time did you leave Paul on Monday?' He wipes his nose, squirming. 'Think very carefully about your answer. It's a Forwood showcase tonight, Lex; Paul would not be happy if he knew about this, and if I think you're lying, he's gonna know.'

Lex pauses, rolling the twenty back and forth between his thumb and forefinger until it forms a thin tube. 'I left at nine-thirty. We just had a few drinks.'

'Where did Paul go?'

Lex defiantly bends over and snorts his coke. 'I don't know.

He said he was going home. You're married to him, it's your funeral.' He looks up insolently. 'Sure you don't want a pick-me-up?'

If I had been in the cubicle I would have slapped Lex, I'm bolshy when I'm drunk. I would have leaned in close to his cheeks red from too much partying and adulation and tried to transfer some of my anguish on to his self-assured mug. But I'm not down there among the piss and bleach, I've now been transported to a far more uncomfortable place. 'Oh fuck off,' I say.

I come back into the dining room to find Paul has a microphone and is mid-speech, holding the attention of the hundred or so guests. He turns and smiles. 'I don't want to take up any more of your time, but I do want to talk about the most controversial programme Forwood TV has ever made. *Inside-Out* has been running on your TV screens all winter and ended just last month. It has produced very strong reactions in people and prompted debate from Parliament to the pages of The *Sun*. This is what the best TV programmes do, and I believe that this is one of the very best.' Someone cheers and Paul holds up his hand. 'This documentary shows us real life, with all its contradictions, its messy hues. Gerry Bonacorsi is not a nice man. He is a convicted murderer who strangled his wife, and who spent thirty years in jail for that crime. The decision on whether to free him when he has expressed no remorse is, thankfully, not yours or mine to make. Our job was to show the decisions taken about Gerry, *in real time*' – there is another cheer – 'and so give the viewer the most profound experience of being a lifer – and then a free man – they will ever have.

'*Inside-Out* shows that reality TV, which is the bread and butter of this company yet long derided by some commentators, is a format that can bring about the most thought-provoking programmes. *Inside-Out* breaks new ground in TV documentary making, and I want to take this opportunity to thank the dedicated team who had the vision to see the project through, and Channel 4 for taking the risk to show it, not knowing what the ending would be.' There is a smattering of applause. 'So, thank you all for your hard work.' Cheers ring out in the high-ceilinged room and Paul holds out his long arm and beckons to me. 'But before I finally sit down and let you enjoy the rest of your evening there is someone else that I have to thank, because she's done the hard and never-ending work of putting up with me.' Someone laughs. 'I want you all to stand and raise your glasses to my wonderful wife and partner-in-crime, Kate, without whom none of this would have been possible.' I hear a thousand scraping chair legs, clapping hands like the beating of wings. Cheers ring hollowly in my ears. Paul's arms are wide, waiting to snare me in their embrace.

My husband is a dirty shitting liar.

I am rooted to the spot, my only desire to slap Paul again and again for every missing hour between leaving Lex and coming home to me. But I am conventional and private, hide-bound by status and appearance. You won't find me rocking boats. The slaughterhouse waits, Paul wiggles his fingers at me. I feel faint, the oxygen is draining from the room. 'Honey?' I force out my most dazzling smile and enter that embrace, dropping the catch on the cage of our marriage.

9

The atmosphere in the taxi going home is glacial. Paul is pleading with me to tell him what the problem is. My fear is damming up against my anger and it's all about to overflow.

'Tell me exactly what happened on Monday night.' I am whispering, I don't want the driver to have any chance of hearing.

Paul rolls his eyes. 'I went out, I stayed out too long, I'm sorry—'

'What time did Lex leave?'

He looks at me sharply. 'You've talked to him, haven't you? You're trying to catch me out.'

'You told me he was with you all night!'

'No I didn't!'

'Sshh.'

Paul frowns. 'What do I need to be quiet for?'

'So where were you?'

'I drove around by myself, went to some bars, I wanted to be alone—'

'Alone?' My question hangs forlornly in the air. When it comes to relationships Paul makes sure he has grasped the next vine before he lets go of the first. If I remember rightly he hasn't been single since he was sixteen. Paul doesn't recognise the concept of overinviting or the phrases 'too many' or 'too much'. When he goes away on trips I can hear him on his mobile organising dinner for twelve, a drinking game for some lads; he'll drive two hours from his hotel to meet an old school friend, just to hang out and catch up. If he is ever delayed at an airport he phones repeatedly, filling in the blanks with conversations with me. Paul cannot tolerate being by himself. 'Why?'

He shrugs. 'Sometimes . . . I don't know . . . I just wanted that kind of night.'

'Are you having an affair?'

'Kate! How can you even ask the question?' Right now I have no idea if he's lying or not, I simply cannot tell and this makes me desperate. I had always assumed I would know, that it would be flagged for me in a look or a habit or a comment. But I am in the dark, groping.

'Did you . . . Paul, did you hurt someone?' I still cannot bring myself to utter the word he used himself.

Paul recoils on the back seat. 'What are you talking about?'

'You were saying some terrible things that night—'

'I was off my face—'

'Even so, I'm worried about you.'

'You don't believe me.' He's watching me carefully, his expression impossible to read.

'A dog . . . I don't know, it seems strange. Oh, Paul, please tell me the truth—'

'Wait a minute.' He's whispering intently. 'Are you saying you think I killed someone?'

'Paul, please, I can help you—'

'You're fucking mental!'

'You kept saying "her", I killed "her"!' I am an inch away from his face, my voice low and insistent.

'You think I could do that? *Do you?*'

'*Sshh.*' We both look at the back of the driver's head. 'You had blood on your hands—'

'You're out of your fucking mind!' He's hissing the words at me, his mouth is almost pressed to my ear.

I burst into tears, hours of pent-up anger and stress releasing. 'Oh God, Paul, please let me help you. I'm your wife, you can tell me anything and everything.' I am hanging on his lapels, searching his face for a sign or a clue.

He pushes me away and looks out of the window. 'Nothing happened, Kate.' His voice is flat and cold. There is a tone of menace that I have never heard from my husband before. 'Drop it. It's boring.' When the taxi stops outside our house I swallow my tears and we walk stiff-backed and separately up the path.

10

Paul leaves for work the next morning after implanting a dry kiss on my cheek and I spend the day with weird and obsessive thoughts. I go to school to pick up Ava, leaving Josh there for band practice. I smile wanly at about fifty mothers and one dad, glad that no one actually tries to talk to me; nothing of any note could be drawn out of me today.

'Come on, Kate, chop-chop, Ava can have the maracas today, Phoebe can take the tambourine.' Sarah claps a hand on my back in an ironic hurry-up gesture as we walk our daughters across the playground. It's music-group day, an after-school activity for Nursery and Year One children, which is really an excuse for mothers to gossip and gripe, down hot drinks and pass an hour. Sarah works part-time as a parliamentary researcher, switching from one set of children to another, she always says.

I really, really don't want to go, but I find it hard to say no. I fall over in a storm, if you know what I mean. I fix a smile to my face as we corral our children down the street. Behind my eyes a tension headache starts to throb.

Ten minutes later I am sat cross-legged on a living-room floor as twelve children slam and bash a selection of loud things together, making no attempt to keep up with the energetic Spanish guitarist. Sarah is on one side of me, Cassidy, who in an act of selfless generosity has given her house over to this weekly mayhem, is on the other. I am slowly shifting forwards across the carpet as Becca's dog, a low, sausagy

47

thing with a very long tongue, is trying to lick me. Becca hasn't noticed, or maybe she has but can't be bothered to do anything about it. She's too tired by early motherhood most of the time to do anything much but moan. She's sprawled on the sofa, fighting to get out from under a wriggling two-year-old. Becca is really Rebecca, but she dropped the first two letters. Maybe she was too tired to pick them up. I glumly grind out one rhyme after another until the session ends.

'Thank God for that,' says Sarah in a low voice as she stretches her legs. 'That's my guilt gone for the day.' I make a noise that shows I know what she means. 'You OK? You look a bit peaky.' I see her kind eyes quizzing me, ready to offer consolation and support.

I smile blankly at her. 'What happens if you run over a dog? I mean, is there a procedure you should follow?'

She shrugs. 'Call the RSPCA?'

Our conversation drifts over to Becca and she jolts to vertical with indignation. 'Run over a dog? Pray – that's what I'd do. I mean it, I would grieve for Maxie.'

I catch Sarah's eye as a long tongue coarsened by Pedigree Chum rasps my chin, only just missing my bottom lip. It's time to stand.

'Why do you ask?' Sarah says, pulling plastic from Phoebe's vice-like grip.

'I heard that a dog was found near the car park by the bridge.'

Becca grimaces and deflates back on to cushions. 'That poor mite.'

We pick up triangles and xylophones, congratulations rain down on the guitarist. But the words I'm desperate to hear, the 'it was so-and-so's dog', don't come. No one knows. In this small, gossipy neighborhood no one's heard a thing.

We talk about school and some committees Sarah's on; she mentions something about the council and a pressure group.

'The Belgians should have given you the Congo, you'd have made a better job of it than they did,' I say.

Ava pushes the buttons on the TV and it springs to life. I hear the theme tune to the news as Ava trails out into the corridor. I should turn it off, but I'm too lazy to move. 'Oh leave it,' says Sarah, 'they've had their fun.'

We watch a government scandal, punctuated by screams from upstairs. A report from Iran I only half catch as we say goodbye to the guitarist and I gratefully take an offered cup of tea. 'Mummy!' Ava's shrieks drive me into the corridor. She's trying to grab a scooter being held by another child. When I step back into the living room a photo of a smiling blonde fills the screen, but is blocked a moment later by Maxie's whirring feet as he's scooped up by Becca. I snatch a glimpse of policemen in white crime suits, catch talk of a neighbouring area, that this woman was a filmmaker, she has been stabbed—

Sarah switches channels. Something escapes from my throat as I grab the remote from her and jab furiously, but precious seconds have been lost. By the time I get back to the original channel the report has ended. I am suddenly aware that the room is quiet and five mothers have rustled to attention.

I retreat to the only place of refuge: the toilet. I feel so sick I have to open the window. I do not know when this . . . I cannot say the word, even to myself. I do not know when this *thing* happened. This is a big city and an area just a few miles away must mean hundreds of thousands of people between me and it. Between us and it. But her face. Tears prick my eyes and I have to lean over the sink as I fear I might retch. I know her. Not well, but we have met. She worked on *Inside-Out* and, more importantly, she conceived the format for *Crime Time*. Paul introduced us. Paul bought her idea and fought to get it produced; Paul had many meetings with her. Paul talked about her a lot. Melody this and

Melody that. Paul said she was a rising star, a woman to watch, a name to remember. Melody Graham. Paul knew her very well.

Melody Graham, your star is extinguished.

I never noticed before, but her features, now that I see them disembodied on a screen, bear a striking resemblance to a face that has chased me into an uncomfortable sleep on countless nights as I stewed over the remains of a relationship I could never prise apart. I rest my forehead against the chilly china of the washbasin because Melody looks like Eloide, my husband's first wife.

My fascination with Eloide was instant. Jessie and I had been invited by Pug to a party in a big old house and as we barged through to the kitchen I caught my sleeve on the button of Eloide's designer coat. I made a few lame jokes about being stuck on her, she said she was reeling me in. And she was in a way; she was much more sophisticated and glamorous than me and I thought her achingly cool. She wrote lifestyle articles for a fashion magazine, her mother was French, she bought clothes in Paris, some part of her dad's family were underworld, so the rumours went. Finally meeting her helped me put Paul out of my mind for a while. My fantasies that he felt something for me were just that: fantasies. She had perfect skin with pores no bigger than pinpricks and soft blonde hair that bounced when she moved – I liked secretly gazing at someone so beautiful, it was my way of studying half of the golden couple that seemed at the time to prove to us unfocused and dithering twenty-somethings that young love really could last for ever.

How wrong we all were.

Their end was messy, painful and protracted. I lost far more friends than Paul did – I felt lucky I wasn't stoned by some of my former girlfriends. I'm over all that now, but I didn't emerge unscathed. An open wound still nags at me, never having enough time to scab over. Paul insisted he remain friends with Eloide, and ten years later she's still squarely in his – and therefore my – life. Her job is going to parties and writing about them for a thick and glossy fashion magazine and getting photographed arm in arm with this celebrity or that. She has the perfect job, if you like stuff like that. She has a little black book to die for, if that's your definition of success. Paul and her have lunch in restaurants that ordinary people could never get a table at; they occasionally drink cocktails at bars where Madonna or Robert de Niro or both might be.

She and I meet only at larger social occasions where her tap-tapping stilettos and taut figure are like a knife plunged into the heart of my self-esteem. Eloide lives with a football agent now in a cutting-edge modernist house in south London. Well, I'm not sure one actually does anything so mundane as live in a house like that, they probably reside, inhabit, or dwell. Despite our years together, despite our growing family, despite everything Paul and I share, a gnawing doubt about what their relationship is eats away at me, and the years don't relax jealousy's teeth on my innards.

I tell Paul none of this. My envy bubbles away silently inside my calm exterior, a pressure cooker released only in diatribes to Jessie or my sister. I won, but sometimes I feel like I lost. That might sound harsh, mean even, but I'm as competitive as the next woman, partial victories don't bring satisfaction and there are moments when I'm certain I catch him wondering what he has given up for me. Whether in a French village or packed tightly on a city street, if a girl with long blonde hair and boyish hips walks by Paul turns his head and stares. He doesn't realise he's doing it, if I called him on it he would genuinely raise those dark eyebrows and protest his innocence, saying, 'Kate, are you having a laugh?'

That his love of a particular physical type has been ingrained and shaped by Eloide has never crossed his mind.

Friends! For someone so successful and popular Paul is very naive about the depth of human emotions. There is no way on earth I could stay mates with Paul if he left me for another woman. No. Way. At. All.

I used to find it endearing when politicians or film stars would have affairs with people who looked just like their wives, but ten years younger. It telegraphed to me how much they must have liked the first version. But now I'm left wondering. Is Melody part of a chain of which I, with my darker hair, frecklier skin and sturdy legs, am the aberration?

'You OK?' shouts Cassidy, knocking on the door. 'Thought maybe I was serving up salmonella digestives.'

I make some comment or other, splash water on my face. In five minutes I can go, retreat to the safety and privacy of my own house.

Back in the living room mothers mill about, chomping through carbohydrates. Becca is talking about her child's skin infection. 'So I have to take a pin and try and pop—'

'Oh, save it for *Oprah*.' Cassidy holds her hand up in front of her face, disgust rippling over it. 'So how's Paul? I saw him on telly the other day. He was being very controversial!'

'Oh . . . you know him. He's good, yeah, good.' I nod earnestly as their eyes track me. When Paul sold the company a change took place in my friends and neighbours. Subtle but noticeable, like the day you finally fully recover from a cold. We were invited out more, I wasn't ignored at the school gate, Becca came round in make-up. Success has a mesmerising smell and Paul has intoxicated them.

'Tell us about Lori-Anne's divorce,' Sarah says to Cassidy, and they all eagerly lean in to hear more.

'Oh my God!' Cassidy replies, splaying fingers for emphasis. Lori-Anne is a friend of Cassidy's I've never met. She's doing divorce the big, brash, expensive Californian way and we cannot get enough of it. I used to love hearing of other people's infidelities, the implosion of their domestic fortresses. They were horror stories that didn't affect me starring people I didn't know. How I would laugh when some husband or other announced he was leaving for the twenty-two-year-old who 'really understood him'. These tales were passing entertainments, a way of giving thanks that Paul and I were not like that. Until now. Money and success are a toxic combination. I look around the room and instead of seeing flesh-and-blood allies and mothers with all their glorious and likeable faults and obsessions, I see rivals, competition that's queuing up to undo me and replace me. I'll be the second wife Paul stepped over on his way to the very top, discarded for a younger, blonder, brasher model. 'He won't move out! Lawyer's advice, of course.'

Sarah shakes her head. 'Where's the lover?'

'Living in the pool house! Lori-Anne's started using the phrase in that Michael Douglas film where his wife explains that she wants a divorce and says, "Every morning I wake up and I hate your guts."'

'That's a term of endearment in our house,' says Sarah, smiling.

'I know that film!' says Becca. 'Doesn't she try and run him over?'

'You got it, but Lori-Anne hasn't! She says if she could find where he's parked her off-roader she'd crush him with it! Believe me, if you don't want to run your husband over in an SUV, you've still got a marriage,' says Cassidy.

'Earth calling Kate, earth calling Kate.' Becca is clicking her fingers in my face, just like my mother used to do. I don't like Becca.

'Men leave if they've got enough money that it doesn't matter. That's why successful men often have several wives,' says Sarah. Becca nods and looks at me as if I should pay attention.

'I tell you, if Mike did that to me I'd act out that scene from *Psycho*,' says Cassidy, shaking her head with conviction.

Becca mimes a stabbing motion at me and starts laughing. It takes all of my large reserves of self-control not to punch her in the face.

I I

When I finally get home I put Ava in front of a video and Josh on the computer and read eighteen articles on the internet about Melody's murder. She was twenty-six, she was regarded as very talented and she lived at home. She was strangled and fatally stabbed in the heart in a quiet, wooded area a few miles away. There is a quote from her aunt, her parents are too upset to talk to reporters. I try to phone Paul, but his number's engaged; Sergei's directs me straight to his messaging service. The news will have swamped Forwood TV like a storm surge. I blow up her picture until her features are large pixellated squares. If I could climb into her image I would. She looks less like Eloide now but the blonde hair is the same shade, her mouth a similar shape. The police are appealing for witnesses and anyone who saw her on her bike, which was found abandoned near by. They are looking for a dark-coloured car seen in the area.

The car. I am out the front door in a moment, beeping myself into the car, colour: Prestige Blue, if I remember correctly. I sit in the driver's seat with my hands on the wheel, suddenly feeling self-conscious. All my neighbours can see me. The pedals are too far away for me to touch, Paul's legs are longer than mine. I do not know what I am doing or what I'm looking for. I check the steering wheel, the door handles and the indicators for blood, but find nothing. A search under the seats produces a shrivelled apple core and a page torn from a comic.

I'm almost disappointed. In the police dramas on the telly they seem to miraculously discover a victim's earring at every turn, as if women drop them wherever they go. I want to laugh as I imagine finding a pair of dirty knickers with 'Monday' printed on them.

I walk around to the front of the car and look closely at the bumper. Surprise surprise, there's no imprint of a flailing woman emblazoned across it. The man next door appears and we do the neighbourly wave thing and I pretend that I'm inspecting my plants. The street is quiet and content; *this* should be the reality of my life, but even late-afternoon sunlight cannot cleanse me of my gothic thoughts. Have I confused familiarity with intimacy? Is my husband, in fact, unknown to me?

I'm standing on the pavement looking back at my house when I see it. A cold slap of understanding hits me in the heart. Paul and I bought this wreck and lovingly renovated it; transforming it from a warren of bedsits into a stylish and cherished family home. The large front garden was a Sahara of broken and weedy cement, which we replaced with a granite-tiled parking space and lots of plantings. When our neighbours oohed and aahed, we would admit that we made a mistake: the parking area is too small. The space between our garden walls is very narrow and you need your wits about you to reverse the car in. I home in on the wing mirrors, standing out proudly from the bodywork. You really need to be paying attention to get in there. Paul parked here that night and neither of us has used the car since. His manoeuvring was inch perfect.

Our conversation comes back to me with a clarity that stops my breath. 'How much have you had to drink?' He stumbled but didn't answer, letting my imagination fill in the blanks. I think Paul was sober; cold, calculatingly sober. Did he pretend to pass out in front of me?

I take the stairs two at a time, a new determination upon me. Paul is messy, his personality type brilliant but chaotic. We have had many rows about this over the years, our friends have been both entertained and bored by my tales of his legendary untidiness: coat thrown down in the hallway; shoes left like tripwire by the stairs; I once found the deeds to the house in a pile of paper he'd left to be burned on our fire. But all those years of running around after him are paying off now – I know where everything is. I sort through the washing basket, nothing. I check every pair of his trousers, examine the soles of his shoes, get excited when I find his work bag, but a forensic examination of it reveals nothing but pay slips, a contract, some plasters and an old pack of chewing gum. I pick up his black wool coat; the weather was warm today and he took his mac. I check it for hairs, blood, stains, a life I'm not party to. I smell it. Nothing. I think very hard about that night when he came back. There's something that I can't put my finger on, some detail that's missing. A ray of sun splits the light cloud outside and floods the living room. That night was chilly, it felt like we were still in the grip of winter. Paul feels the cold. I can't find his scarf.

I begin the hunt through my house with the certainty of one who cannot lose. I know this place so intimately, every hiding hole, every dent, which way the floors slope and how toys roll across them, which corners gather dust, where the ants come in. If he's hidden something he doesn't stand a chance. An hour and a half later in the gloom of early evening I have to cross into enemy territory and start on the shed. It is meticulously tidy, a thudding contrast to the chaos he lives in across the garden with me. I pick up carefully rolled balls of garden string, open the lawnmower, cleaned and put away for the winter. He can be quite a different personality if he chooses to be. This thought does not offer me comfort. As I'm yanking at a rake I hear my name being called.

A canal runs along the back of our garden with the towpath on the far side. Paul loved that canal when we first saw the house, it fitted neatly with his fantasies of perfect childhoods – he'd teach Josh to fish there, spot dragonflies, get a boat. I loved the house but I'm scared of water and was suspicious of the mooring rights just beyond our back fence. But Paul got his way and we bought the house. Funny how things turn out, because it's me who loves the canal now – the craft that trawl up and down, transporting plastic barrels and trailing weeds, the bearded men in their narrowboats who stop for a few days before travelling on through the old transport arteries of England, the occasional cyclist who waves from the towpath.

I come out of the shed, dusting grass clippings off my shoulders. 'Hello, Marcus.' Six months after we bought the house, we bought the mooring rights and Paul found an old narrowboat in Worcester. The *Marie Rose* has floated at the end of our garden ever since, serving for a while as overflow offices of Forwood and now rented to Max and Marcus, student friends of friends. Paul and I speculated for several weeks whether they were gay, but Jessie put us straight by sleeping with Max the first time she met him at a barbeque in our garden. She appeared in our kitchen the following morning looking a perfect combination of mischievous and ashamed. Sipping strong black coffee to alleviate her pounding head she christened Max and Marcus the M&Ms, 'because they're good enough to eat'.

Marcus holds up a hand and waves, one foot looking like it's sprouting from a plant pot and the other out of an old bicycle wheel. 'Something in there you can't find?'

'My life?' His boyish grin lights me temporarily before I sink back on to the fence, suddenly exhausted. 'How are things with you?'

Marcus scratches his chest through his T-shirt, which has

the name of a band I don't know on it. 'Yeah, great, really great. We were at a party that lasted two days . . . no wait, maybe three. It was . . . you know.' He shrugs, which makes me smile. Time, such a concern of parents – and of suspicious wives. I make a note that he wasn't here to see Paul drown the scarf – or a weapon.

'Is Max with you?' In answer a head pops up from the cabin and a long body follows. He rubs sleep from his eyes. 'Just got up, I take it?' He yawns and a maternal fondness for my perfect lodgers lifts my sunken mood. Max and Marcus, everything twenty-two-year-olds should be: beautiful, carefree, attracted to the bucolic – and helpful. They'd been in the boat about two weeks when Paul needed help felling a pine and the three of them eventually brought it crashing down across our lawn as the kids and I cowered in the house. Josh fell in love then and there. Max is the only person to get Josh away from the computer; he played catch with him for hours, sitting on his deck in an old chair as Josh rushed back and forth like a terrier picking up the ball he kept dropping.

Cassidy was horrified when I told her about the lovely young men living over the back fence. 'Having to put on make-up to go into your own garden is a real drag,' she said. But Cassidy didn't understand that Max and Marcus served a much more useful function – they made me feel young again.

'Is there anything you need?' asks Marcus. He's referring to my shed-banging.

'Oh. I lost my scarf,' I say.

'I've got one. You can have mine if you like.'

I protest politely. 'It's not like I haven't got about ten back there.' I gesture at my house, groaning with possessions, and feel embarrassed. Were Paul and I ever this carefree, pared down to life's essentials? As I walk up the garden the day's last rays of sunlight are blocked by the shadow of our tall house.

An hour later I am picking bags out of the grey wheelie bin, sorting through a week's supply of chicken bones and tea bags, curry boxes and yoghurt pots, my frustration leaping at every turn. I am empty-handed, the scarf nowhere to be found. I let out an incoherent roar and burst into tears.

I wash my hands, carefully scrubbing away the smell of putrefying waste. A strong headache starts throbbing in my brain. Paul washed blood down this sink only a few days ago. I get out the Cif and scrub the enamel so hard my fingers ache. I pour bleach down the outside drain. My hands are shaking. Get a grip, Kate, get a grip.

12

A suspicious mind has an appalling clarity. Paul comes home from work and hugs me tightly for a long time. The afternoon was draining as the news of Melody's death jumped from desk to desk – a forest fire in dry brush. I tell him I'm sorry and he hugs me tighter. Unexpectedly tears spring to my eyes and he releases me only when Ava interrupts us. He pours two hefty glasses of wine and I watch him pull up a chair and tuck into the dinner I've made.

He chews for some moments in silence. 'This is good. I'm starving, is there any more?' I nod and empty out a dish as he leans forward for some water. I spot the outline of his phone in his trouser pocket. I study it as if I have X-ray vision. 'Tell me something normal, something nice and . . . ordinary. What did you do today, honey?'

I consider replying with 'realised that you might have murdered your lover' but instead I shrug, non-committal. I spent the early evening rehearsing what I was going to say to him, but when he catapulted into the house I was struck dumb, lacking the vocabulary to even know how to confront him. 'Max and Marcus have been on a three-day bender.'

He smiles. 'Must mean summer's on its way. You renewed the travel insurance?' I listen to him scrape his plate clean, watch him wipe his mouth with a napkin, dig something out from under his nail. He's snuggled down in safe, domestic territory. We'll be discussing which hedge trimmer to buy or relating that the light in the fridge has gone next; the banal,

61

unthreatening details that underpin a relationship over the years. I *like* life like this.

Any next step I take will mean drama, and I need to be sure, very, very sure, so I listen and observe. I track him with my ears around the house. He reads Ava a story and I stand below them in the hallway, listening to the floorboards creak. He is sitting on her bed. He talks to Josh about gladiators, says he'll take him to the Colosseum one day. The future. I cannot imagine anything except this moment now as I hunt mercilessly for clues and signs. Were you really feigning being drunk that night? Did you only pretend to pass out, and if so, why? I can tell he's opening the cupboard in Josh's room. You won't find what you're looking for in there, Paul.

I go in to say goodnight to Ava, sit down on the Cinderella duvet, lean over to kiss her, am enveloped in her freshly baked biscuit scent, and something hard is jabbing me in the leg. It is Paul's phone, spilled from his pocket while he read *Angelina Ballerina*. Trust. I guess that's the opposite of suspicion. It takes years to learn to trust, Paul, and it can be destroyed in a moment, that moment when you fell on our kitchen floor, to be exact. My sweat wets the metal as I grip the phone. Do you trust me, Paul? I turn out Ava's light and stand in the corridor, senses alert, not unlike that terrible night when this all first started. The TV is on, you are not upstairs. I scroll through forty-seven texts from work, your family, your friends, every compartment of your life. I find three texts from Melody, all sent on the same evening. 'Please call me,' is all they say.

'Here, I found your phone. You need to be more careful with it.' He looks up from a rerun of *Grand Designs* in surprise.

'Where was it?'

'On Ava's bed.' I throw it on to the sofa dismissively.

He grunts and shoves it back in his pocket. We watch a glass building being erected by a lake. 'You know, we could build our own house now. Have something exactly as we like.' I nod carefully. 'Maybe we should move to the country, get away from all this stuff here.' I watch my husband from the corner of my eye.

'What about your work?'

He almost looks sad. 'Once the full two years is up and the final part of the sale is completed, I won't have to work any more.'

'What about my work?'

He turns to me in wide-eyed surprise, scratching the back of his head. 'You're really into it, aren't you?' I nod. He pauses for a moment and then flashes his brilliant smile. 'Tell you what, we'll found a new husband-and-wife company and dream up TV programmes together as the sheep bleat outside. That way, you can work and I can spend more time with you and the kids.' Maybe there is a window open somewhere, a door that stands ajar, because at that moment a shiver passes right down my spine.

We watch a lot of TV in our house, hours and hours of the stuff. It's fair to say Paul and I love TV. Not for us the daily battle to stop the kids slouching down in front of CBeebies. Paul rightly scoffs at contempories whose livelihood is television but who refuse to let their own children play with the remote. Hypocrisy is so dull. TV is in his blood, it's his passion and it has become mine too. I love that it transports me to other worlds, terrifies and excites me, and that I don't even have to leave my own sofa to live. Today it's doing the job of cheering me up because it's making me feel superior, so when Paul rings around ten and tells me over the jeers on *The Jeremy Kyle Show* to get the news on *now* I just reach out contentedly for the remote control.

'Everything OK?'

'No. Melody was strangled.'

I shift awkwardly in my seat. 'We already know that, Paul.'

'With a white rope with frayed ends.' I can't vocalise my shock and stare dumbly at the pen and sheaf of paper in the newscaster's hands. 'Kate, I've got to go.' Paul is already talking to someone else as our connection is cut. He didn't need to explain what this means. Gerry Bonacorsi killed his wife all those years ago by strangling her with the tools of his trade: his white magician's rope, frayed artfully at either end.

I sit hunched forward on the sofa, transfixed by the scenes unfolding before me. With few facts available speculation is allowed to run riot. A young reporter stands beside some bright green bushes near the spot where Melody was murdered; there's a shot of a featureless building and talk of the Parole Board and the predictable clips from *Inside-Out* and police shots of Gerry. The next time I see Paul he is being interviewed on *Sky News* at lunchtime. Sarah phones just then to give me her support and we both listen to Paul defending *Inside-Out*. He stays cool under the relentless questioning in a dark jacket that he wasn't wearing this morning. He keeps a couple of suits at the office for the times when the media outlets come calling for a quote. Words such as 'guilt', 'responsibility' and 'copycat' ricochet angrily between the news anchor and my husband.

'I'm not sure you're going to see much of Paul in the next few days,' Sarah says.

I groan. Reality TV is a volatile beast. It made Forwood into the success it is enjoys today, but like a wild animal, it can eat its young. The news anchor rams home her point: 'Is this not one of the worst examples of the media highlighting a heinous crime which an unstable attention-seeker has decided to copy—?'

'It is far too early to draw any conclusions, as the police have been saying all day,' Paul counters.

'Oh dear,' Sarah says, 'this story could run in all sorts of directions.'

I shake my head, even though I know she can't see me. 'And none of them are good.'

We listen as the interview continues. 'Do you concede, Mr Forman, that the alternative is even more horrifying: that the blanket coverage of Bonacorsi by your programme may have influenced the Parole Board into taking a wrong decision that has had catastrophic consequences—?'

'No. I refute that—'

'You'd think Bonacorsi had already been convicted, the way they're carrying on,' Sarah says.

We don't hear Paul's full answer as the broadcast cuts clumsily to a police van speeding past a crowd of reporters somewhere in central London. Bonacorsi is being taken in for questioning.

'His taste of freedom was brief,' I say.

Back in the studio they bring on the head of the Parole Board, who looks dumbfounded. 'On days like this I'm glad I don't have an important job,' Sarah says, but her tone is wistful. 'We'll probably have to research all this for questions in the House,' she adds. 'Victims' rights are the hot thing at the moment.' I say nothing and stare at the hangdog eyes of the man who makes decisions that have life-and-death consequences. 'So,' asks Sarah, 'do you think Bonacorsi did it? Was that folksy charm we saw on late-night telly all an act?'

And to that question I have no answer. Now they've brought Paul back and he's calmly defending the integrity of *Inside-Out*. He swings slowly from side to side in the studio chair; a face made for television with teeth to match. He's in complete control. The gap between this image and him on the kitchen floor, mired in snot and blood, a colossus could not bridge.

'Pitch-perfect presentation, Kate. He's a pro,' Sarah says in admiration.

Paul went on a media-training course a few years ago because the interest in Forwood TV meant he was increasingly asked to do interviews. In theory the course told you about using the right body language, how to sell your story in a soundbite, dodge tough questions and not get rattled. A producer I knew was on the course with Paul and said to me in awe that he needed none of their advice. He was the best they'd ever seen – there was nothing he didn't seem to know. The camera simply loved him. 'He's the perfect liar,' I reply and Sarah laughs, but I didn't mean it as a joke.

The rest of the day slides by with nothing to anchor it. Later I go to school to pick up Josh and Ava. We are beaten home by the snails, the children bicker, my head throbs. Josh can't believe that I let him play a game on my iPhone without complaint as I slump into a kitchen chair.

'Mummy, will you plait my hair?' Ava twists this way and that, in maximum-plead position. I reach for a bottle of white and a glass, heck it's already five, where's the harm?

'Not today, sweetheart, Mummy doesn't feel well.' It's as if a builder has told me my foundations, which I thought were solid, durable and unshakeable, have been burrowed under by an unknown pest and my cherished home is about to crumble to nothing.

I suggest Ava dresses up and off she skips. I am alone in my kitchen, the queen of an empty kingdom. The wine tastes sour but on I glug. All my life I have wanted to be a mother. I liked my jobs, I fought for and enjoyed promotions and pay rises, dug in on one side or another at the battle lines of office politics; but they were jobs, not a career, something to pass the time before my real work began. But now both my children are at school the itch to define myself some other way is becoming fiercer. I know this is partly driven by fear, the fear that I have become out of date, outmanoeuvred by changing times and attitudes. Paul is constantly butting up against exciting concepts. Maybe I haven't kept up. I slug back more wine, maudlin self-absorption taking over.

I hear Ava clattering down the stairs in a pair of my high heels and I wipe away my self-pitying tears with the sleeve of my sweater. She drags her feet into the kitchen to keep my stilettos on. She is wearing fairy wings over her Snow White costume and has a twinkling crown on her head. Sometimes my love for my daughter catches me unawares.

'Oh, Ava, you look so lovely.'

'I can't do it up,' her dress is dragging on the floor behind her, Velcro fastenings flapping. I reach out to pull her to me, desperate to snuggle into her youth and innocence, to try to get some of that magic to rub off on me. 'This is my belt, can you tie it on for me?'

In her flawless hand with the little dimples on the knuckles she is holding Paul's scarf, reaching up so that a big, blotchy bloodstain is visible through her tiny fingers.

'Where did you find this?' I hear my voice coming from far away.

'My dressing-up box.'

'I tell you what, you can use my belt.' Ava's eyes open wide in excitement as I pull mine out of the loops on my jeans. 'A special treat.' I pull gently on Paul's scarf, watch it spooling through her palm into my clutches. She lets go and takes my belt, skipping off into the living room.

Paul's scarf is cashmere with a bit of something trendy and pointless thrown in, rabbit wool, alpaca or pashmina, I think I once knew. It's furry with fibres that stick up. It has a tasteful stripe and is not very long. I bought it for him last Christmas. What do you buy the man who has everything? The same things every year, because he keeps losing them. Paul makes even present-buying easy. A beautiful gay man carefully wrapped it in tissue paper for me and said, 'May it keep him warm,' as he handed over the heavy card bag with the thick rope handles. I know how you tie that scarf, Paul, tight around your neck and with the ends hanging short over your chest. The rust-coloured stain flowers like a toxic rose near one end, hard and brittle to the touch. It means whatever or whoever was bleeding was leaning against your chest, but you said to me you dragged that dog, that's what you said, Paul, dragged it out of the road. I feel the panic ballooning in my chest.

This is what he's been looking for the past few days, and both he and I were foiled by our own daughter, who'd packed it away in the dressing-up box, her own piece of treasure. There must have been a lot of blood, fresh and free-flowing. I've lived with blood, Paul, as all women have. I started my periods when I was thirteen. I have been having periods for nearly twenty-five years, I have given birth to two children. Blood on cotton, lace, rayon, silk, wadding and paper, I know what blood looks like, how it spreads on my sheets, other people's sheets, across knickers, into pyjamas and nighties and through the thickest part of denim jeans, even on to the checked seat of a London bus. So I know that stain soaked in deep and it soaked in fast. Did that someone have their arms around you? Was their face or were their lips close to yours? What were they saying? Were they pleading, begging, screaming or dying?

I lay the scarf out flat across the kitchen table as if I'm about to perform an autopsy. I get down close to the blood-stain and smell. Funny how the very stuff that courses around our unique and instantly recognisable bodies is indistin-guishable when spilled, but only to the human eye, not in a laboratory, not under a microscope where blood groups are isolated and identified; a police laboratory. The scarf smells faintly of beer and enclosed spaces. I lay my face on the table and look along the line of the cloth, light catching the fibres. We shed in spring, I've read, like animals, our hair and skin falling from us into plugholes, drifting to the floor beneath the bedroom mirror, clinging to clothes and to Paul's fashionably hairy scarf. I pull a blonde hair from the fabric. It could be Ava's. Could be.

I sit and stare at that scarf as if it might suddenly get up and walk away. The wine bottle is empty, my headache gone. The doorbell rings.

I know this is Paul. He has a key obviously, he just never uses it. He wants his front door to be opened by his children or me, preferably both, for us to welcome him across the threshold as if he's just come back from years away at war. I hear Josh running down the stairs, the click of the lock. I fold my arms and stay rooted to the chair, staring at the scarf. Let him come into the kitchen and see this, explain this away. An image of Gerry Bonacorsi being shoved into the back of a police van flashes through my mind. My state of limbo has evaporated, I am ready for the fight.

'Mum! It's a policeman!'

I move faster than I have ever moved before, grabbing the scarf and racing to the washing machine. I feel as though nothing in my life has ever been as important as getting this scarf through that round door. 'Coming.' I try to sound casual as I slam it shut, heap biological powder into the tray, turn the dial to cold. I've left blood on everything, and cleaned blood off everything. That's what women do, Paul, we clean. I clean for you. Here I am, washing away the danger, obliterating your mistake, your most dreadful error. I am your wife, Paul, I am in it with you. Whatever you've done, I stand by you, as I stood shoulder to shoulder with you at the altar all those years ago. 'I will love him, comfort him, honour and protect him, as long as we both shall live.' When I make a promise, Paul, I keep it. I will clean up for you, I will lie for you. As I wait for the machine to start, precious seconds draining away, I acknowledge the full extent of my wifely duty. To protect the innocence of my children, your success and my perfect life, perjury seems a small price to pay.

'Coming, coming.' I pick up my wine glass as I move to the front door. If he thinks I'm a lush, all the better.

13

The policeman is actually two women, one much taller than the other. They are standing side by side in the doorway with their shoulders touching. One of them looks down at a notebook before saying, 'Is Paul Forman here?'

Josh is staring open-mouthed at them; neither smile. Ava hurries out of the living room and stands behind me, wrapping her arms around my leg. I am very calm.

'No, he's at work. Is everything OK?'

'Are you his . . .' she trails off, waiting for me to fill in the blanks.

'I'm his wife. Is there a problem?' I put the wine glass down on the shelf by the door. The shorter woman tracks it with her eyes.

'This is Detective Sergeant Karen White,' the taller, thinner woman says, 'and I'm Detective Inspector Anne-Marie O'Shea.' They hold up their ID badges as I stand aside and insist they come into the house. I see their car parked on the single yellow outside the house, advertising that there's trouble circling. 'We need his help with something. Do you know when he'll be back?'

'I thought that was him then. He always rings the doorbell when he comes home.' I laugh nervously, filling in the silence. 'I'm sure he won't be long, I can phone him if you want?'

'Have you got a gun?' Josh asks.

'Josh!'

'No, we don't carry guns,' O'Shea says. She's still not smiling. Maybe there's not much opportunity for it in police-work, a bit like working in a funeral parlour.

'They're too busy to answer your questions, Josh, why don't you go and play upstairs?' That's the lamest thing Josh has ever heard; he stands transfixed by the police-speak coming through the radio.

'Come in, come in,' I implore, leading them into the living room. I sit in the chair, meaning they must take the sofa and see our selection of perfect family photographs on the bureau. There is one of Paul trying to surf in Cornwall, several action shots of the kids in sun-drenched locations, and the one I am most proud of, a black-and-white picture of Paul and the kids in a stylish mess of sheets, just enough but not too much of his healthy chest on display, his long arms and strong shoulders protecting them. 'Is this to do with Melody?'

DS White has a face that falls naturally into a frown. She looks at me through narrowed eyes. 'Did you know her?'

'Yes . . . I'm so sorry, can I get you a drink, something to eat?' They shake their heads.

'We want to establish where Paul was on Monday night. To eliminate him from the inquiry,' O'Shea says.

'I thought you'd arrested Gerry Bonacorsi. I saw that on the news earlier.'

'We're talking to lots of people at the moment, that was a leak that really shouldn't have happened.'

'But the white rope, that seems pretty damning, no?'

The two women give each other a look I can't decipher. 'If you can just think back to Monday,' O'Shea persists.

'Monday . . .' I make a show of trying to remember the beginning of the week. 'Today's Friday . . .' I shake my head. 'He was probably here with me. What was on telly on Monday?' I ask the room. Silence replies.

'Are you going to take Mum to jail?' Josh asks.

DS White inhales loudly.

'Josh, can you take Ava into the kitchen, I need to have a talk to the police officers.' Ava starts whining. 'Go on, there are some sweets in the cupboard.' I give O'Shea a conspiratorial roll of my eyes and get a wan smile back. I'm winning her over, but it's work. 'Sweets, sweets.' I wave my hand and they trail uncertainly from the room. 'That's better, I can't think straight when they're around.'

'Tell me about it,' says White.

'How do you proceed with an investigation like this? Are you questioning everyone at Forwood?'

O'Shea gives me a disinterested smile. 'We're working through.' She's giving nothing away and I know that if I played her at poker I'd be saying goodbye to fifty quid.

I nod. 'It's so terrible.'

'We're trying to build a picture of her life.'

'She was just twenty-six. Her whole life ahead of her,' I shake my head and rub my tired eyes.

'Don't I know it,' says White.

'So young,' says O'Shea hunching forward, elbows on knees to stretch her long back. We are silent for a moment. The two of them are over forty, beginning to grey and creak. I'd guess White has kids, probably grown; O'Shea wears a ring but has a tight look of disappointment set around her lips. We are united for a moment in contemplation of the chances we never seized, the things we never did, how far away from youth we have travelled.

'How well did you know her?' asks O'Shea.

'Not well. I only met her once for about five minutes at a party. She worked on *Inside-Out,* which I also worked on, though we never met there. I'm now a researcher on *Crime Time,* which was her programme.'

'So you worked with Gerry Bonacorsi?' White asks and the tone in her voice makes O'Shea look at her sharply. Despite everything she's seen and heard, White is impressed; despite knowing what he did thirty years ago and might have repeated this week, Gerry is a celebrity, a name, he's someone and she and O'Shea and I are nobodies. She can't get the inflection of admiration out of her voice, double murderer or not. She's drawn to the warmth of that celebrity glow as surely as a moth to a candle.

I pause. She's waiting for an anecdote about Gerry. She wants me to sing for my supper, give her something she can repeat to friends and family that makes her job seem more colourful. For a minute I think of making one up. It would be so easy, because I have seen hours of footage of Gerry, singing old Irish ballads in his cell, good-naturedly taking the Houdini jokes from fellow inmates in the washrooms (the magician who could escape from anywhere, except here!), eating prison slop while reciting his grandmother's tea-bread recipe, smoothing his snowy grey hair as he waits for psychologists and therapists and the prison library trolley, just like White has, and I feel I know him, really, really know him. 'I never met him, if that's what you mean.'

It's as if a light has been switched off. White can't hide her disappointment.

O'Shea grabs the wheel of this runaway interview. 'Monday night . . .'

'Monday night, Paul was here with me. I'm sure of it.'

'What time did he come home?'

I shrug. 'A normal time I guess. Seven-thirty maybe, maybe later as Monday is often busy. It could have been as late as nine or nine-thirty.'

'Can you be more specific?' asks O'Shea.

I'm unprepared for their drilling down in such detail. Indecision creeps along my spine as I see her writing my words down in her notebook. The door opens and Josh appears, his jaw crushing Chewits. 'I'm sorry, I don't want to state an actual time as I could be wrong.' This way I reckon I've covered him after his drink with Lex and seem vague in a way that shows I'm unconcerned.

'Can I have a go with your radio?' Josh asks.

'Josh! They're working.'

White hands it to him as it crackles to life.

'That is *soo* cool,' he says, turning it over and touching the aerial.

O'Shea stands up. She hands me a business card. 'We need a statement from your husband.'

'Of course, he'll be happy to help.' I stand and head for the hall, looking at her name on the card.

'What car does your husband drive?' asks O'Shea. I give her the make and the licence plate number and the Prestige Blue colour. 'Did he take the car on Monday?'

I pause, caught off guard. This is probably important and I haven't thought it through. 'He doesn't usually drive to work, so I think not. It sits in our drive most of the time.' She reaches out to unlock the door. 'Do you think it's a copycat killer?' I ask quietly.

O'Shea regards me with cold, clear eyes. I very much doubt that in her Friends Reunited entry she's remembered as 'warm, funny . . . GSOH'. 'I don't *think* anything. I let the evidence speak for itself.'

I swallow. From the kitchen I hear a faint hum of the washing machine doing its work.

14

I have woken up on the sofa with an empty bottle of Baileys. It is 11.30 p.m. I can't remember how many times I phoned and texted Paul once the police left. I have forgotten what I felt once I heard their car pull away. I stagger to the toilet, bashing my hip against a doorknob, and heave into the bowl, shaking and cold. I don't even like Baileys. I splash cold water on my face to try to regain some composure. Paul is not here, I can sense it; the rooms feel colder, colours duller without him. The events earlier today have an air of unreality. I have just lied to the police in front of my children. I simply cannot believe I did that. I've taken a step far beyond where I thought I could ever go. A trickle of cold water runs down between my breasts, producing a shiver. And it was easy. Paul must surely be equally capable of the profoundest deceptions, what else can he do? One stab wound to the heart.

Tears begin to course down my cheeks as I struggle to find some aspirin and attempt to pull myself together. I pick up my mobile; Paul has not called or replied to my messages. Being drunk makes me clingy and maudlin and despite the treacheries of the day, in spite of them, I am desperate to see him, to be folded into his musky embrace, rocked on his knee and consoled like a child for my lie. The mobile jumps in my hand and through blurred vision I answer it, ready to howl and blub anew at Paul. But it's Jessie, calling from a bar.

'You're still awake! Fan-fucking-tastic. I've been phoning all night! Listen, listen, I've been given a one-man show in Shoreditch! How great is that?' I nod at the phone, but cannot speak. 'Kate? Can you hear me?' There are roars of drunken voices behind her.

'Yes—'

'You remember that agent I told you about who came to the last show? Well now he wants to "take me to the next level".' She says this last bit in an American accent.

'Wow.'

'The important thing is the gallery is in with some really high-profile buyers, and some guy who owns half of Sainsbury's wants to buy two paintings for starters – "for starters"! How mad is that? Oh I'm so happy! Hello? Is everything OK?' I am crying down the phone, unable to stop. 'Kate, what's wrong?'

'Nothing, nothing. Really, I'm so pleased for you.' I cannot puncture her happiness with the sordid details of the hole I am in.

'Are you sure?' Some music pulsates in the background. 'Are you crying?'

'No, no, I've got a cold.' My lies are tripping over themselves in their haste to get out of my mouth.

'Hang on a sec.' The music fades, she's outside now. 'What's happening?'

'Don't be ridiculous, everything's fine. That's such amazing news.'

'I know. They're one of the biggest galleries in the East End. They're giving me a retainer, can you believe it? No more of that cadging-money-for-canvas rubbish.'

I should be laughing with her, feeling her excitement infecting me, this is what she's dreamed about and worked tirelessly towards for more than twenty years, served up a million vodka cranberries for, wiped stale beer off tables for.

She stands on the brink of ambition realised, and I have wanted this moment for her for more than fifteen years. But I am choking in despair. 'I'm so pleased for you, Jessie, I really am.' I start blubbing again.

'You *are* crying!'

'Yes, I am, it's overwhelming. All those years of struggle are paying off.'

She starts giggling. 'This is the happiest day of my life.' She tails off and her voice begins to break. I guess she's welling up. 'You know, you always believed in me, Kate, you kept me going. I want to thank you for that.'

'You don't have to thank me. I knew you could do it. You've worked so hard, nobody deserves it more.' And then we are both sobbing down the line.

'Guess what else happened today, Mr Married said he loved me! He was here celebrating with us – well, he's just left . . .' She talks on as I digest her news. I am happy for Jessie, really I am, but there is a terror inside me. All her most exciting moments are still to come; I fear that mine are behind me and I cannot see where fresh ones will come from. She has something entirely her own, work and a career sown by her alone, and she reaps all the subsequent glory. My achievements are only reflections of me, brief flashes in my children or when I stand arm in arm with Paul at a work function or wedding. I always thought I'd hitched my wagon to the white and shining steed, comforted in the knowledge that I could do no better. Jessie's right, I do believe in her, through all of the disappointments and false starts I believed she had what it took. But what about me? Is everything I thought good and true a lie? Have I bought into a fiction of the profoundest kind, built my life and happiness on deceit?

Sometimes when I feel low or simply when I am bored I play back in my mind how I got together with Paul. My own story is a great comfort to me. Its twists and turns and the breath-catching drama of our eventual union still has the power to bring me up short.

Our second meeting was not like our first; I simply bumped into him in the pub one night when I was out with Pug and Jessie, but the joyful unexpectedness of it flipped my heart. I remember tracking a long and muscular arm as it reached over the bar for change, watched the shrug of his shoulder as he pocketed the coins. He did a double take when he saw me, took a second or two to remember, and then hit me with me that cheeky, full-beam smile. He'd filled out a bit, which suited him; he was still tanned, his clothes telegraphed success. At that moment I cursed over and over again because I'd come to meet Jessie straight from a softball league that I played in with some people from work (I think it's not bragging to say I was their best hitter, not because I was the strongest but because I could place my hits farthest away from the fielders, or angle them towards women hanging around in the outfield, which meant that I could bring home three runners on the bases and myself with one thwack) and I was wearing jogging bottoms and had no make-up on. I didn't look or feel attractive. 'If it isn't the girl with the bike! You've changed.' He looked me up and down appreciatively nonetheless. He'd become bolder, more self-assured. Success was already working its magic.

'The man with the white van! I see you haven't changed. I thought you'd greet me with the V-sign.' I flicked two fingers at him and he laughed as Pug and Jessie gawped.

'Katy, isn't it?' He touched my arm with the back of his hand. He had remembered my name. After eight years he had remembered. My grin was so wide.

I tutted and shook my head, looking mock-offended. 'No. It's Kate.'

He sat down next to me and we related the story of how we met to our friends, as if we were already a couple.

'When he took my bike out of the van he said, "Stop and give me a backy sometime."'

'Mate! I hope your chat-up lines have improved since then!' Pug shook his head as Jessie sniggered.

Paul fought back. 'Well, she was wearing this straw hat—'

I clamped my hands across my eyes in shame. 'Oh my God—'

'A boater! You went to college in a boater?' asked Jessie.

'No! My mum bought it for me as a leaving present. She thought that's what college types actually wore! I thought it was sweet. It was just a straw—'

'What were you thinking!' added Jessie, scandalised.

'Give me a break, I was eighteen—'

'Oh dear me!' We all laughed and as Paul went to get some drinks Jessie did her eyebrow-raising 'where have you been hiding him?' look. Later Paul and I sat at the bar, flirting and doing the banter thing for half an hour before he casually mentioned that he was married. As if it didn't matter. I felt so crushed I couldn't speak and he drained his pint to cover the awkwardness.

'Where's your wife?' It was such a strange word to use. He was twenty-eight, when I look at photos of him from that time he looks shockingly young; in fact, none of look old enough to deal with the emotions we were about to unleash.

'At a party for work. She doesn't think pubs are that great.' He toyed unhappily with a beer mat. Ten minutes later I was in the toilets and Jessie had followed me in.

'Who the hell's that?' her eyes were blotters, ready to soak up scandal.

I held up my hand to stop her right there. 'He's married.'

She sagged against the sinks, mirroring my disappointment. 'Fucking typical.' She spun around and a moment later was reapplying lipstick. 'Oh well, fish and seas and all that.'

My love for Paul remained my secret from then on. Jessie

had fixed moral boundaries back then, they've blurred as she's aged, and she assumed I would move on, pick someone else. And I thought I could, that I would really be able to pull that off. Paul stopped flirting with me after he told me about Eloide, as if that would kill his feelings and mine. Big mistake. Huge. It made things even worse because it meant we had to *talk*.

Groups are contradictory; they are public and private. Our nights out were always stuffed with people coming and going, the shifting hordes of twenty-somethings downing pints and wine, and sometimes pints of wine, popping pills and blithering about everything and nothing as people pulled up chairs and roamed in packs. It was a great cover for Paul and I, squeezed together on benches too short, shoved arm to chest in a club queue or taxi. Among so many voices and loud jokes the nuances of our conversations were hidden.

My infatuation with Paul might well have remained just that if two things hadn't happened. First, Jessie and Pug started arguing. I began to hear warning signs from Jessie on the phone after a weekend or when we went to the cinema midweek. 'Pug's really rude to waiters,' or 'Pug's always moaning at me for being late, he's so unforgiving.' They would break up soon. One night in the pub they had a stand-up row about tights versus stockings, of all things. I caught Paul looking at me. Time was running out for us. Once they finished there would be no easy excuse for us to meet.

Second, Pug's work colleague Steve fancied me, flirted outrageously and invited me to a tremendously posh black-tie affair that his friend who worked in PR had got us all extra tickets to.

In a way I was almost glad. My fantasies of getting together with Paul had been long exhausted: I'd survived a thousand disastrous earthquakes with him in which his wife had died; I'd hiked up Mont Blanc on every path in a white-out and found him in the refuge near the summit; I'd had sex with him in every location and every position every night for nearly a year. I was growing tired. I needed a distraction and Steve was it. Besides, Paul would be there with Eloide and having to pretend all night that I felt as little for her husband as I did for Pug seemed like too much hard work. But at the last minute Eloide was called to Paris because a relative was sick. The stars were moving into alignment.

That night has an epic feel in my memory, colours are more intense, my friends more scintillating, I am – for once – beautiful. We all got completely bladdered on free champagne, I won twenty-five pounds on the roulette wheel, Jessie lost a fortune at craps, I bought fags from a cigarette girl and was twirled around the dance floor by a famous singer. Steve and I had hysterics about that as we fell drunkenly on each other, champagne splattering in all directions. I was twenty-seven years old, high on youth and fresh experiences.

A moment later, Paul had his hand on my arm and was pulling me away. 'You don't fancy him, do you?' he said, his eyes dark and dangerous.

'Yes I do.' I had been pining for months for something I could never have and this was my moment to punish him.

He grabbed my elbow and fought his way through a packed dance floor and out of a fire door. 'We need to talk.'

'About what?'

'Don't play with me.'

'You're the one playing games, you're fucking married!'

'He's not right for you . . .' he trailed off.

'Well too fucking bad!' I was hitting him, really punching him. The moment of revelation that I'd hoped for, pined over all those months, made me mad. He was trying to catch my hands.

'Listen to me, you idiot! Eggy, please!' He was very drunk. 'So you can tell me how you want to have your cake and eat it?' He had me pinned against the fire-escape wall, the physical contact I'd yearned for all those months a paper-width away.

'It's not working; my marriage isn't working.'

'Then try and fix it.'

He laughed sourly. 'I don't want to fix it.' He shook his head. 'Because I'm in love with you.'

'Stop fucking with my head!' I was shouting and raving and he was pleading and I wheeled out of the club door and straight into the path of a taxi. I actually got run over. I'm not lying, that's how Paul and I got together. Well, it was more that I got knocked to the floor in a crowded backstreet by a taxi going about five miles an hour. I was probably half falling anyway, unsteady as I was in my platforms, but I remember lying on the tarmac with Paul calling my name dramatically. Everyone made far too much fuss about it. I remember someone actually screamed. I started crying for real with the shock until the ambulance came. It was really one of my fantasies come to life. They checked me over in A & E, I had a badly bruised hip and that was it. 'Your girl-friend's going to be fine,' the doctor said, and a shiver passed right through me. I knew Paul was staring at me but I couldn't meet his eye, the moment was too intense.

He took me home in a taxi and I had to lean on him heavily to get up the stairs to my flat. It was 4.00 a.m., we said nothing to each other as I struggled into the bedroom. He sat on the end of the bed, his elbows on his knees. I started blubbing again, maybe from shock or the painkillers they'd given me at the hospital, I'm not sure.

'You look so beautiful when you cry.' He said it matter-of-factly. 'What a fucking mess.' He hung his head in defeat, his conscience winning what seemed like a monumental battle. 'I should go. I'll get you some water.' He went to the kitchen and I heard him opening cupboards and testing the taps. The sound of him in my flat, in my life, was just beautiful and I held my breath to catch every movement. I watched him walk back across the bedroom towards me, the glass in his hand.

The film of my memory flicks off its spool as the front door opens.

15

Paul finds me on the sofa, my feet tucked under my bum. He does a double take at my swollen eyes and livid cheeks. It seems like years since I saw him, not just this morning.

'Where have you been?' I wail.

'Are you OK?' He sits down in the chair and kicks his shoes under the coffee table, rubbing the tension headache across his forehead. He doesn't wait for my answer before launching into, 'You wouldn't believe the day I've had—'

'I called and called—'

'Yeah, I saw. Sorry, honey, I haven't had a moment. Who could have believed it about Gerry! I'm hoarse with all the interviews I've given today. They're trying to shoot the messenger—'

'Where were you!'

'Stop shouting! I was at the office. I had to listen to Raiph bawling me out, he's panicking in case this reflects badly on CPTV, on him personally, he doesn't give a stuff about—'

'Paul, the police were here!' His hand stops moving across his brow and I can't see his face. 'They were looking for you. They wanted to know where you were on Monday night.'

His hand drops to the chair arm and he swivels to look at me. 'So what did you say?'

I'm clutching a cushion tightly over my stomach for protection. 'They were here about murder, Paul! Here in this house, sat on this sofa, asking questions—'

'Oh, Kate, you're being dramatic, calm down.' He throws

his hand down by his side, trying to make light of what I'm saying.

'"Calm down"? A woman you know has been killed!'

'Thanks for the reminder, as if I could forget!'

'Paul, what happened on Monday?' My voice is rising, anger and panic beginning to mix.

'What do you mean by that?'

'You know what I mean!'

'No, actually, I'm really not sure that I do.'

'You won't tell me where you were or what you were doing!'

'I've already told you.' He's irritated now, shifting in his seat and leaning forward. 'If you don't believe me that's your problem. I'm too busy to argue about it any more.'

'It's not that simple, Paul. I'll tell you what I did tonight! I told the police that you were here. That you were home with me – your wife! Since I don't *know* where you were, that's what I did.'

He looks horrified, his eyes widening in surprise. 'What did you do that for?'

'I had to do it! I didn't know what to think, I was trying to help!' Paul is off his chair in an instant, looming over me. 'I know something happened on Monday. Oh, Paul, just tell me—'

He explodes. 'You think I killed her!' There is a violence about him I have not seen before. 'Why? Come on!' He takes a long step towards me, spit raining down. 'A crime of passion? Is that it? I killed her because I was in love with her, eh? I'd been playing away and things got out of hand—'

'I don't know, you tell me!'

'Melody's dead, Kate. A woman I worked with has died in the most horrible way,' his voice catches in his throat, 'and you think *I* did it?'

'She's like Eloide—'

'Eloide?' He takes a step back and laughs. He actually

86

laughs. 'So that's it. It all comes back to your paranoia and jealousy of my ex. It's been *ten years*!' He puts his hand on his head. 'So, I had an affair with Melody because she looked like Eloide and then I killed her. Oh, and then I made it look like Gerry had done it. Jesus, Kate, that's pathetic. They don't look remotely alike! Do you not think I would notice?' He says this slowly, enunciating every word in case I'm too stupid to follow.

I stand and grip our fireplace so hard I break a nail. No, Paul, I don't. But I can't explain this to him in a way he would understand. He doesn't *see* what people are like. He's a doer, not an observer. In fact he's quite stunningly unobservant. He never notices when I cut my hair and it took him two days to notice when I once dyed it blonde; he thinks Natalie Portman is Winona Ryder; he cannot guess someone's age. 'You're not even taking this seriously, are you?'

'Why should I? You're not being rational.'

'I lied for you! I perjured myself for you!'

'Us. You've perjured *us*! What do I do now, eh? Contradict you? Think of the consequences if you change your story!'

I come towards him and reach out to hold his arm. I'm begging now, really begging. 'Paul, I love you, I love you so much. I am with you all the way. You can tell me anything, anything, and I will support and help you. Just please tell me the truth.'

'I *have*!'

Something snaps in my head as my pleas for his confession are rejected. 'I don't believe you,' I spit, marching into the kitchen and returning with the evidence, wet and clinging to my skin. 'I've got your scarf, Paul. You couldn't find it because Ava had squirrelled it away. It's covered in blood, Paul. Whose blood?' I hold the end in my hand, the stain now a faint brown splodge in the wool. Blood is stubborn. It comes out in the end, but it fights to cling on in fibres and hems.

My husband is making strange noises as if too many words are trying to escape at once. He shakes his head. 'What the—?'

'It's her blood, isn't it?'

He's looking at me with an expression I have never seen before. 'I wasn't wearing that scarf.'

'For fuck's sake, Paul!' I hold up the clammy wool, wave it like a placard at a rally.

He tries the phrase again as if he's just getting used to it. He's more emphatic now. 'I wasn't wearing that scarf.'

'I am not an idiot,' I hiss. 'I know you've been looking for something in this house that you couldn't find. It was this, wasn't it? Tell me the truth! You've been looking for it for the past week but Ava had taken it before you could get to it in the morning!'

'Oh, Kate . . .' his voice trails off. I wait, hearing my heart beating thickly. There is a strange pallor on his cheeks, my beautiful husband suddenly looks old, it's as if part of his jaw has collapsed. A revelation is finally coming, the air seems to tingle in anticipation of the truth finally being revealed. 'You wear that scarf more often than me.' It takes a moment for me to register what he's saying, then I'm screaming and throwing the sodden scarf at him as he backs away towards the door. 'Kate, what have you done?'

'Stop twisting things!' I pick up cushions and chuck them at him.

'Oh God . . .' his mouth is opening and shutting but he remains stubbornly silent as I rail.

'I want the truth!'

He stands still in the doorway watching me. 'I think you know the truth already.' I hear the front door opening and closing as he walks away. I scream more loudly and then swallow, aware that neighbours crowd in on both sides, innocent children slumber above. Clammy pashmina hairs stick

88

to my hands. I climb over the coffee table and pick up the scarf, ripping at it, pulling it apart with tremendous force. I start to use my teeth, biting the soft and clean-smelling wool, fibres cover my tongue and tickle the back of my throat. Guilt, rage, fear and a thudding jealousy give me extra strength. Five minutes later a fresh burst of tears leaves me shivering on my living-room carpet. I have ended the evening as I started, alone.

16

'Will I die if I fall in there?' Josh asks, leaning too far over the rail of the boat as we chug west up the Thames.

'Yes,' I say, 'get back from there.' I reach forward and pull at his arm.

'I don't know,' Lex chimes, 'you could swim to the bank. It'd be a laugh.'

I curl my arms tighter around Ava who's crowded on my lap in a silent heap and kiss the top of her head. I don't have the energy for arguing today.

'It's not like a swimming pool, Josh, there are currents that can pull you under. Water is very deceptive,' adds Paul.

Like people, I think as I stare at the brown water, almost the same colour as the tea Paul woke me with this morning. He was detached when he handed over the steaming mug and sat on the edge of the bed. 'You'd better get up. It's our trip to Hampton Court today.'

And so here we are, the Formans with Uncle John and Lex in tow, playing happy families but without the other family – Sarah cried off at the last moment as one of the kids was ill. Paul and I are remarkably civil with each other today – the calm after the storm.

'Remember, Josh, Lex isn't a parent—'

'As far as I know!'

'So he doesn't see the risks that I see.'

'I'm not a worrier like your mum,' he adds, inclining towards Josh conspiratorially.

'You don't need to be,' I reply. 'You don't have the responsibilities that I have.'

'That's not true,' he adds, standing up and shoving his hands deep into his trouser pockets. 'I have a company to run. That's just as hard as bringing up the sprogs.'

'How do you think this is playing out for the company? Can we be really damaged by this?' asks Paul.

'No one is doing any work because no one can talk about anything else, that's for sure,' replies Lex.

A casual observer would think us a strange group as we bow our heads in unison and shake them in disbelief at what has happened so close to us.

'There's speculation in the papers that it might be a copycat killing,' says John.

Paul looks unconvinced. 'We always made sure the details of how he killed his wife were not broadcast. Thank heaven for the two-minute delay.'

'I'm not saying we broadcast the details, but have you done a search on the internet? It's all just a few clicks away, the details of the trial, all the sordid stuff.'

'We're just going to have to let things run their course,' says Paul. 'People are in shock, you've got to give them time. I'm in shock! Astrid sobbed on my shoulder for about twenty minutes yesterday.'

'She probably never even met the woman!' scoffs Lex dismissively.

'The police could well come and interview people at work,' John adds.

Lex moans. 'Yet more distractions.' He looks my way. 'I can't believe they talked to you.'

I nod, spitting hair out of my mouth that the wind off the river was trying to stuff in. 'I couldn't really tell them very much, I'd only met her once.'

'They haven't been to see me yet,' Lex adds.

'You should be glad. It was horrible. They make you feel guilty even if you're the most innocent person in the world.' I hug Ava tighter to me and stare at the deck, wondering if I'm imagining a stretchy silence opening up.

'She had a great future ahead of her,' Paul adds, shivering. 'She was a real ideas person. Sergei sent some flowers to her parents.'

'I think we need to put some thought to the image of Forwood,' John says. 'She met Gerry because she worked on our programme—'

'You're worrying too much. *Inside-Out* is being rebroadcast on cable, that's how much of a flop it is!' Lex is talking over John as if he's not there. 'It's great publicity. It might sound crass—'

'There's no *might* about it, Lex!'

At this he rounds on me. 'Oh I get it. Kate thinks she's above all this. But I've worked bloody hard for a long time and if I make a programme so successful it's on the front page of every newspaper in the land, that's good enough for me.'

'Whatever the cost?'

'Do you know, Kate, that the sale of magic sets has jumped several hundred per cent since *Inside-Out* aired? That's the power of telly. Imitation!'

'I can think of a victim I wish this imitator had chosen—'

'That's enough, both of you!' Paul holds up his hand, seeking a truce.

'Mummy, why are you arguing?' Ava asks, staring at Lex.

'Arguing is when two people disagree on something,' Lex replies. 'But your mum and I are actually very alike, we just express ourselves differently. I'm think I'm a little more honest.' Lex gives me his best smile and I reply with a sarcastic grimace.

Ava shifts on my knees and pops her thumb back into her

mouth. Am I just like Lex? I watch him standing with his back against the captain's cabin as if he wants to command the boat. Paul's used to our bickering, he's been listening to it for years. Paul and Lex are an unlikely couple who have worked phenomenally well together. Their first big success was *Whodunnit?*, a reality-TV variant where the audience gets a say in the outcome of a crime drama by being able to vote for different endings. The revenue from the 09 numbers brought in the money to make reality-TV documentaries and crime shows that cemented the company's reputation as a cash cow with kudos. *Inside-Out* is the latest – and most controversial – of those.

Whodunnit? allowed Lex to proudly proclaim, 'I can make anything happen on TV.' He is driven, maniacal about success, he wants to go all the way. He has me all wrong, I am not at all like him, but I feel no desire to put him right. The soft warmth of my daughter in my lap reminds me that I am already so much luckier in life than my lonely sister, Lynda, or my poor mother, still smarting with her unrequited feelings for my father. But I know Lex has no interest in hearing this; losers' stories from the provinces are tedious to the privileged; I am cagey even with Paul about my broken and utterly ordinary family. Lex is jabbing his thumb and forefinger in the air to make a point, Paul is rapt. To be honest, the kind of wealth and profile Lex craves scares me. I like the status quo; the certainty that Paul is my husband and that he loves his family. Maybe there's such a thing as too much success; it unbalances people, separates them from who they are. I imagine being tipped over the side into the cold and dirty water as Paul cruises away, my screams unheard amid the noise of the pleasure craft.

'Are you shivering, Mummy?' Ava asks.

I hug her in reply and tune back in to Paul, who's reassuring Lex. 'Keep the crowd on side, produce what the viewers want and we can see this crisis through.'

Lex grunts. 'As long as it's not like *Whodunnit?* and some other fucker gets to pick the outcome!'

John has retreated back into his shell as Lex and Paul talk on. He stands alone as we bump against the dock, the third wheel staring back down the river we have travelled. 'You OK?' I ask.

'How's the job, Kate? Going well?' I nod and he ruffles Josh's hair so he doesn't have to look at me. Josh squirms away from his uncle in embarrassment.

We had planned to have a picnic but when Sarah cancelled I gratefully seized the chance to buy overpriced sandwiches and buns. The day is cold and few people are around. After dragging the children through Henry VIII's bedroom and enduring Lex's insinuations about venereal disease (which thankfully Josh is too young to pick up on) we emerge into the gardens and arrive at the maze. We find our way to the centre without much problem and are back out quicker than I expected. Ava is sullen and Josh looks bored. This was supposed to be the highlight of our family day out, but it's less than we hoped.

'Right, now we're going to play a game,' says Paul, picking up on the energy lag. 'Hide and seek in the maze.' The kids look unimpressed. 'You've got to find me.' He is swallowed up by the hedges as John and I offer words of encouragement to the children. Lex pretends he's a ghost as we creep along a walkway. The kids giggle and run ahead, John following. I turn off down a path and find myself alone. I walk for a bit, enjoying the silence. Thick hedges of yew surround me, patches of bright green fuzz signalling the start of the growing season. Far away I hear a scream. I dwindle to a stop and rest against a railing. This is the first moment I have been alone all day and I feel exhausted. Last night has a hue like a lurid melodrama, I am too tired to process what it all means.

On the other side of the hedge I hear Ava's voice. 'Uncle John, where's Mummy?'

I don't move – let them come to me.

'We've got a problem,' John says, quietly but distinctly.

I hear a grunt and something I can't catch. 'She never signed the paperwork.'

'I thought that was all finalised!' It's Paul.

'Well, it's not. I looked through it this morning. She didn't sign. Unless there's something at her house, we don't have it.'

Paul's swearing. 'Where does that leave us?' John says something unintelligible. I peer through the hedge, catching only the briefest glimpses of colour and movement and smelling cigarette smoke. 'We're keeping this between ourselves, don't mention this to anyone.'

'Let's go this way, Daddy!' Ava's voice seems to boom after her dad's private conversation. There's a strange taste in my mouth. What am I not allowed to know? I almost jump out of my skin as I am tapped sharply on the shoulder.

'What are you looking so guilty about?' asks Lex.

'Sure you're not transferring?'

Lex grins, his sharp little teeth glinting. I smooth my hair, trying to regain some composure. 'Come on, let's hunt them down.' I set off fast down a narrow path, but Lex pulls at my arm.

'What's the hurry?' He links his arm through mine and slows to the speed of ambling lovers. 'Tough week, eh?' I say nothing. 'I didn't mean to upset you earlier on the boat, it's just that I want the company to do well, Kate, I really do.'

'Are you saying you're more committed than Paul?'

'No, but at heart Paul isn't a reality-TV guy. He wants to make worthy shows about the Lebanon or children with no eyes in Africa or whatever, but they don't make any money. Like it or not, this company sold because—'

'Of you.'

Lex shrugs. 'If you like.'

'I don't recall *Whodunnit?* ever getting the media profile you've got over the Gerry Bonacorsi programme.'

'Oh, Kate, I love the way you stick up for Paul at every turn, whatever he does! God, I want a wife like you!' Lex brushes the thick bank of yew with his hand, sending ripples across its surface.

A thought strikes me. Paul often does TV work, has done interviews all week, defending *Inside-Out*, promoting the company. Press and TV have clamoured for him, over and over again. They never asked Lex. For a man as vain as him, that must have hurt. Forwood TV is a partnership, Lex and Paul own forty-five per cent each, a variety of investors the rest. I wonder how enduring this partnership is. If Paul left Forwood or was disgraced, he could be forced to sell his share of the company and the other investors would be given the first opportunity to buy those shares. Lex could end up holding a controlling interest, and he'd make a lot more money when the sale is finally completed. A murder conviction would definitely be a reason to force Paul to sell.

'You find out where Paul was on Monday night?' Lex is as predictable as a carnivore chasing antelope: he attacks the jugular. 'Presumably the police asked you?'

I try to give him my withering look, as if to prove his verbal punches don't hit me. 'They weren't concerned about that. They were asking about her generally, how well Paul knew her.' I could kick myself. In trying to sound casual I've walked straight into a worse trap. Lex gives me that grin again, as if he's brimming over with secrets.

'Strange. You seemed pretty keen to find out where he was in those missing hours.' He holds my gaze. 'In the light of what we now know, I'm not surprised.' The grin has gone. He's deadly serious – and still tightly holding my arm.

'He was with me.' Lex can't keep the shock out of his eyes.

At that moment Josh, John, Ava and Paul appear around a corner and rush towards us. 'Mum, I found him first,' says Josh.

Ava is on Paul's shoulders, shouting, 'I can see over everything!'

Lex lets go of my arm as fast as if he's been scalded. He's never married. His relationships last a few months. I stare at him defiantly so there is no mistaking my intention. For better or worse, I have chosen my side and he'd better know how seriously I'll root for it. Am I imagining it, or do I even see, for the very first time, respect reflected back at me?

17

Paul spends most of the rest of the weekend giving interviews and talking to John and Lex on the phone. On Monday morning I hurry Josh and Ava to school with the cold efficiency of the discarded woman. I've been granted my wish to work from home today but end up sitting down at the computer to search for electronic clues. The machine takes ages to hum to life as I tap impatiently on the table top. I want to be put out of my misery. I want to find something concrete, evidence of an affair at least, anything would be better than this unknowing purgatory of smoke and mirrors.

I type in Paul's work email address and password. This is by no means the first time I've logged on to his email, and I've never thought of this as his private territory, that I'm trespassing on the unwritten codes that underpin our marriage. The red writing is irritatingly familiar; they don't match. Several attempts later and I am staring at a horrible new reality: I haven't typed the letters incorrectly, Paul's changed his password. I sit very still, processing the significance of this. I know all the day-to-day details of Paul's life. I haven't consciously sought them out, they have seeped in from our years together. Or I did. His pin number, where his bank account details are kept, which taxi company he has an account with, what's in his will. But now I'm locked out of his email, his personal communication with the world. And right now I have more than a curiosity to get in there and scroll through his inbox and the deleted and sent items, I have an insatiable obsession with being in there. I am his wife, it is my right.

I splay out my hands on the desk and try to grip the wood with the tips of my fingers, my nails scratch the varnished surface. I will break in if it the last thing I do. They work out passwords all the time in films, just type in the dog's name and that's the end of it. But I'm not in a film, this is real life and my husband has locked me out. Three hours later and I'm still here; I cannot do it. I have tried everything, logical and illogical. I know everything about Paul, every fucking detail of his life, and I have failed. I started logically, calmly and methodically. My name. The children's names. Other family members and then nieces, nephews and grandparents. I typed in old schools, his favourite teachers. I tried former addresses – with and without the road and the number. I listed work colleagues old and new, his former girlfriends, his football club, the nickname of his football club, his tortoise's name followed by the house he grew up in (this was a game we played in the pub years ago, Hercules Hamleigh is a mediocre porn-star name), his favourite holiday destination, where we got married, where he married Eloide, and of course I tried Melody, with and without her surname. Nothing. I typed in the names of books on the shelf next to the computer, the *Marie Rose*, his favourite public figure, the names on the designer clothes he wears, the builder we last used. I typed in the programmes he commissioned, the series he won prizes for and then I threw the keyboard across the room, upended a cup of tea and howled. He is playing with me. He is messing with my fucking mind. At that moment I hate my husband. I hate him more than I thought possible.

Paul is arrogant. He's got a reason to be: he runs a big company, wins prizes for his work, employs many people. He's well educated, finds it easy to win arguments about abstract things, can take an alternative view just for the fun of it. He's brighter than me. He beats me at games: chess obviously, Monopoly, he can finish a crossword and he slaughters me at Scrabble. This last hurts. Every time it hurts, but I try to pretend it doesn't. When he lays his last tile down and adds up the final score with the stubby pencil we keep in the box, he gives me his pitying-playful look and says, 'Nearly, if you'd just picked up that J . . . who knows?' Then he gives a little laugh. I want to rub that smile right off his face. Make that 'scrub', it's worth four more points.

I go to the loo and calm down a bit, but I leave the tea dripping on to the carpet. There's a piece of paper with some business notes scrawled on them on the side of the desk. I try them all. Nothing works. I look at his spidery handwriting. He writes in capital letters, which I've always found odd. Maybe it's a bloke thing. He certainly can't spell. He beats me at Scrabble but he can't spell. He's so talented but he often shouts at me from his laptop, 'Does "lose" have one o or two? How do you spell "sheer"?' It's his Achilles heel. From left field comes a thought, since she's been on my mind rather a lot lately. Eloide is a tricky name. I wonder how long it took him to master. Before I have time to think about what I'm doing, I type 'melodie'. I press return, and am rejected. I type 'meledy'. I press return . . . nothing. 'Oh, Eggy, Eggy,' I say to myself, tears starting to drip down my nose. I type in my nickname twice as I need a minimum of six letters and suddenly I am in.

I wipe away my tears with a shaking hand. My achievement at cracking his code doesn't give me any satisfaction, it simply leaves more questions without answers. I force myself to concentrate on the job before me. His inbox is dull. There is nothing from Melody at all, no cheeky jokes full of sexual innuendo, signifying a long-established fuck fest, no passionate missives from a young and love-struck admirer.

His deleted and sent items are similarly uninspiring. I feel cheated after all that effort and the hours I've spent. But am I surprised? Melody is dead. She was murdered. The most obvious evidence purge is an email. I feel I've arrived at a party long after the most interesting guests have left. In that situation I might as well just start tucking into the buffet. I go through everything else, just because I spent so long breaking in here. There are a few email exchanges with Lex; it sounds like he's angling for a bigger share of the company. Typical. Lex is a L'Oréal guy, he always thinks he's worth it. There are cool, almost abrupt emails from Portia detailing CPTV's liabilities and umbrella strategies, whatever they are. She always copies someone else on these and she never signs off with the niceties I'm familiar with. She has a job so busy she long ago dispensed with the superficial. There are emails from Sergei offering to do Paul's overdue expenses; a round-robin dirty joke from Astrid; and an art invite from Jessie that's full of exclamation marks. Then I find an email exchange with John where Paul is asking if Forwood TV needs to protect itself. John has attached a long article about intellectual property rights. I follow this thread, they are trying to get clarification on who owns an idea as opposed to a programme that's been commissioned or made. 'Get her to sign a contract straight away,' Paul has written.

'It's drafted, but she's stalling, she's waiting on legal advice,' John replies a day later. The date is three weeks ago. Paul has not replied. I feel discomforted by this, seeing work disagreements set down in black and white, but then my eyes settle on something far more interesting: an email from Eloide. 'Well, I suppose you're right. Why don't I invite her round for lunch. Would that make you happy?' The familiar tone grates. There should be a pecking order of familiarity with me at the top. Then I notice there are also no emails from me. Not one. I write to Paul a lot, mostly with appointments for his diary, sometimes I tell him I love him. A few clicks later I find them in the deleted folder.

I have a flashback to a private view I once went to with Jessie. We're standing in front of a painting, being barged from right and left by the crowd. She holds her glass of white up to the canvas. 'This is my favourite in the whole room.'

I glance dismissively at some not very well-painted peaches and a pineapple in a kitsch bowl against a dull black background. 'This one? You're kidding.'

'I love it.'

'But it just looks like a bad still life to me.'

'See how dark the background is. The absences, the holes if you like, are what makes the picture.'

I shake my head. 'I just don't get it.' Two Japanese students walk in front of the canvas and then move on and I look again. Suddenly the background of the painting has jumped forward, creating a delicate pattern of swirling and vibrant shapes, like a beautiful piece of black lace over the picture which is in contrast to the solid fruit and bowl. The optical illusion is amazing. 'Actually, that's really clever.'

'It's an old painting trick but the artist's done it in a new way here. Gaps create as many shapes and patterns as objects,' she smiles, triumphant. 'Now, there's a void in this glass that needs to be filled,' and she turned towards the bar.

Paul may have cleaned up his email. But for every pattern he obliterates a new one is left. Unfortunately it seems the new design is writing out his wife.

The phone rings. 'Mrs Forman? Are you coming to get your children?'

'What?'

'It's the school reception here. Josh and Ava are waiting in the welfare room. I presume you're near by?' Her tone is crisp and accusing.

It's 3.45 p.m. I have completely forgotten the time, have

spent the entire day on Paul's email grubbing around in his work life. I have not eaten or moved from the study. I spring into harassed-mother mode. 'Of course, I'm nearly there, I got terribly delayed, the traffic—'

'Make haste, my dear.'

She cuts off my tired excuses. She's heard them every day for years from women juggling too many balls. For a mad moment I consider telling her how it really is. 'I think my husband is a murderer.' She probably wouldn't even bat an eyelid. 'Be that as it may, my dear, make haste,' she'd say, and click the phone down.

18

That evening the police come back for Paul's account. I'm unnerved they're working so quickly and ticking so many boxes. A dull ache starts in my stomach; the slow churn of fear and misgiving. They hover in the hallway, adjusting bags and shedding coats. I'm about to explain that Paul is out on his run and that he won't be long when he clatters in the front door. He stands before them, hands on hips and half bent double, panting heavily. Paul does nothing by halves.

'Mr Forman?' asks O'Shea.

Paul nods, trying to catch his breath. He's wearing a long-sleeved breathable top and shorts, and a dark stain of sweat is spread over his chest. 'Please . . . come in here,' he pushes past us and opens the living-room door, politely gesturing for us all to enter, and we pass inches from his ramped testosterone. He holds on to the door handle for support as the policewomen cast around for somewhere to sit. 'Sorry,' Paul tries to joke, 'I'm not the . . . man I was.' He brushes the sweat from his neck and I see the outline of his stomach muscles through the sports fabric. White starts fidgeting.

'We need to ask you some questions about Melody Graham,' O'Shea begins, hovering on the edge of the sofa, refusing to be enticed into its relaxing depths unless she gets too comfortable and misses something.

'Of course. Umm, do you mind,' he starts, a bit embarrassed, 'if I have a shower first?'

'OK, if you're quick,' O'Shea replies.

Paul disappears. 'Do I need to leave the room?' I offer nervously.

They look surprised. 'No, stay here if you want.' I console myself that they think this lead is cold, that their real suspicions are directed elsewhere. I'd watched earlier on television as Gerry Bonacorsi was released from custody. He'd stood on the steps of the police station, his head sandwiched between the shoulders of men in good suits. I couldn't make out if he was very small or they were very tall, but the effect was to make Gerry look like a prematurely aged child in a tracksuit. The voice-over had sniffily mentioned 'insufficient evidence' as the reason for his release and the viewer was left in no doubt that this was not to be believed.

A man in a suit who was probably Bonacorsi's lawyer was trying to hurry him past the cameras, but Gerry falteringly began to talk, stroking his white hair. 'It felt a bit like home being back in there, to be honest.' Gerry squinted against the white light of the flashes. He looked as though he couldn't understand why people were interested. 'The police have been very friendly, to be sure. I wish I had someone who could back up my story about where I was on the night the young girl was murdered, but I'm afraid I don't. I just had a nice walk about, you see. It's been a long time since I could walk.' He held his hand up to his face as questions flew from every angle. He didn't know which way to turn. 'I'm sad that someone might be copying what I did. It's not right. She seemed a very nice girl. Such a shame.'

We wait in silence as the hissing sound of a shower starts up near by. I catch White's eye and explain that we've got a bathroom downstairs because the pressure's better. It feels surprisingly intimate to hear water splashing over a naked body and I look away embarrassed. White scratches her nose.

A few moments later Paul reappears, his hair tousled and

his skin glowing. 'Sorry about that,' he says, collapsing into a chair and pulling one foot up into his lap to put on a sock.

O'Shea gets down to business. 'What was your relationship with Melody Graham?'

'I worked with her on a documentary we made recently. She did research for the programme.'

'How long have you employed her for?'

'I don't. She worked freelance. Probably for about six months in all.'

'How well did you know her?'

'I'm not sure I understand.'

'Did you socialise together, that sort of thing?'

Paul shrugs. 'A bit. Well, not really. I'm very busy but there was the odd evening drink and she was at the wrap party for the programme. I wouldn't say that I know her, exactly. That would be too strong a word.' White scribbles something in her notebook. Paul's foot goes down to the floor and he crosses the other one over his knee. The second sock goes on.

'How did you meet?'

'She came into the office because she had some programme ideas. I run a TV production company, I meet lots of people; it's important to know who's out there and what they can do. It's a way of trying to stay ahead of the competition.'

'So she wanted to make programmes?'

'Yes.' He stands to tuck in his T-shirt with quick, agile movements and picks up his watch, pushing it over his hand and clipping it closed on his wrist.

'But she ended up working as a researcher for you?'

I sit motionless in my chair, looking at my hands. My cuticles are dry and the ends of my fingers chapped. Too much scrubbing things clean.

Paul tucks a label in and, fully dressed now, shifts his focus to the interview. He puts his feet flat on the floor and his forearms on the chair wings, his fingers hanging over the front. It's the position you take a lie-detector test in. 'That's often how things are. She had done in-depth interviews with lots of different types of people. My business partner Lex Wood recommended her to the producer and he hired her.'

White frowns, there's something she's not getting. 'Did Lex ever interview her?'

'Not that I know of.'

'It was nice of him to give her a job then.'

'She had impeccable credentials, otherwise she wouldn't have got the gig, but she was also good-looking. That's important to Lex. He noticed her when she was meeting me – the office is open plan. He likes having pretty girls in the mix, so to speak. It might not be right but it's how TV works.' Paul doesn't hesitate as he says all this. He's defiant, challenging them to find fault with this reflection of the world. O'Shea's lips thin and my heart sinks. Paul's not choosing the easy route and I wonder as I look at the tramlines of effort that run from her nose to her lips what protracted battles O'Shea has fought over the decades, how many years of overtime she's had to put in to be where she is now. Physical advantage is not a pleasure she's ever experienced, like me. 'And for the record she did a very good job, she was full of ideas.'

'What exactly was that job?'

'She did a lot of background research on Gerry Bonacorsi' – O'Shea grimaces at the mention of his name – 'set up some to-camera interviews with his family, and she was present at some of the filming sessions that we did in jail.' O'Shea sighs as if irritated. 'Maybe I'm speaking out of turn,' Paul continues, 'but am I right in thinking you didn't agree with the Parole Board's decision? In your line of work I imagine you normally don't when they let people out.'

'You can say that again,' White interjects, becoming

animated. 'Life should mean life, otherwise why am I getting up in the morning?'

O'Shea shakes her head. 'At least the public know what we're up against now.'

'I'll take that as a compliment, if I may,' says Paul. His smile is mirrored by the policewomen. He's won them over. 'Melody also devised the concept for *Crime Time*, which is on air at the moment. We had a series of meetings with her to discuss all that.'

Two heads nod on the sofa. 'What were you doing last Monday night?'

'I went for a drink with some work colleagues and then I came home.' He names Lex, Astrid, Sergei and John and the bar they went to. 'Lex left first at about nine-thirty, I guess, and we left a while later.'

'Did you drive your car?'

'Yes.'

'What time were you back?'

Paul pauses and gives me a glance. His face betrays nothing, its angular planes the same as they always are. I see White's tired eyes waiting and watching. His foot twitches. 'I was back by ten.'

A friend of mine works as an addiction counsellor at a hospital. Her job description includes words like 'alcoholism', 'prescription drug dependency', 'obsessive compulsive disorder', 'depression', but she says her job is all about shame. The shame women feel about their failures and shortcomings, which means they hide their drink and drug problems from their partners and children, often for years, and they hide them very well. Their secrets are walled up inside their relationships, the fear of the consequences of admitting the truth stalking their every waking hour. My friend's job is to unpick the fear and shame and secrets. Just like a police officer's. At this moment I am so ashamed at what we are doing my chest is like lead. For the first time I think about Melody, not as my husband's lover, as a threat to my family, but as victim.

My greatest fear is the death of my children. I am fully aware that this is a grinding cliché, the least imaginative thing a mother can think, but it doesn't make it any less true. The dank weight of a body as I pull if from a villa swimming pool, the scratch of the material covering an armchair that I sink into when a policewoman tells me one of them is gone, the backup officer hovering on her shoulder. When I conjure this image my eyes fill with tears and my nose blocks and the panic starts to expand across my chest, and then a moment later I force a happy thought in to break up the unbearable images. All in all it takes about thirty seconds and I get on with my life. How are Melody's parents continuing? One minute, two minutes, five, ten, an hour, a day, a week, a lifetime. The police really walked up their path, brought the horror down on their heads. Has my husband done that to them? I swallow the saliva that has gathered in my mouth.

'So you were back home by ten at the latest,' O'Shea repeats.

'That's correct,' says Paul. There is no hesitation, no sign that he thought he stood on any kind of threshold before he crossed over.

For a mad moment I think of getting to my feet and shouting that he's lying and pointing my finger in accusation. Images of Paul being thrown over the coffee table by White, handcuffs shining as they are brought down upon him, flash through my mind, but I remain mute. I look at my wedding ring, feel the way it digs into the flesh of the fingers that surround it.

White turns her pen over and jabs it into her pad, sending the nib retreating into its cheap plastic cover. 'OK, I think we're done here.'

I'm surprised I can get to my feet, that I can open the lock without my fingers shaking. Paul stands behind me on the doorstep of our home as we watch the policewomen walk away down the path. He puts his hand on my shoulder, a controlling weight. I shut the door and we are facing each other. The first time we came to this house we trailed around after the estate agent, the rain pounding outside, the canal a misty smudge beyond thick trees. He went to wait in the car at the end of the tour through a series of bare and bedraggled rooms to "give us a little minute together" and we stood just here on the pile of junk mail, sniffing the damp. I knew then and there that this was our house, that we could transform it and live out our happy future here. 'You love it, don't you?' he'd said, seeing my eyes dart excitedly round the high ceilings and come to rest on his expectant face. And I did. But not now.

He puts a forefinger to his lips and then he winks, slowly and deliberately. He strides into the kitchen and pops the top on a bottle of beer as if he's celebrating the end of a trying week at work.

Paul and I have a secret language, most couples do. Not just words and expressions, but gestures. In Miami we once saw a woman whose hair was shaped in such a way that it looked like she had a duck sitting on her head. There were sections dyed all sorts of shades of brown that flicked out like tail feathers over one ear, a black clip above the other ear formed the beak. Now, if one of us sees a strange hairdo, we'll turn to the other and flap our elbows by our sides and they'll either nod in agreement or shake their head. We also have his wink.

About two years ago we had a bunch of people round for a bite to eat. I guess other people would call such an evening a dinner party, but I wince at using that phrase, it sounds so formal, too grand for me and my humble background. And

I can't cook, I am more familiar with the freezer aisle of the supermarket than the farmers' market. So I cobbled together a cottage pie and tried to keep it casual so as not to raise expectations.

Lex came, enticed by Paul with the innuendo that my tennis partner Ellen was 'right up his street'. Ben, Paul's actor friend who was back from LA, put in a rare appearance; Sarah and her husband, Phil, walked up from few streets away; John came armed with a New Zealand health drink containing algae; and Jessie turned up two hours late. I'm glad I didn't bother to cook because Ben was on a special diet to be 'screen fit' for a role he'd won in a US sitcom: no carbs after six, no booze, two hours a day with a personal trainer. Jessie refused to eat anything and just drank, Phil had three helpings of everything, proclaiming it all delicious as Sarah rolled her eyes, and I'd forgotten that Ellen was a vegetarian.

We played Wink Murder, but first we downed a bottle of champagne to celebrate us all getting together. I remember John's tongue turning moss-coloured from his health drink. At some point Lex and Ellen started playing Rock Paper Scissors. I thought it was a way for Lex to slap her hand and get touchy-feely but it looked like fun so I played with Phil, and Ben and Jessie's game soon descended to poking each other in the ribs. The empty wine bottles began piling up, Ben moaned about being starving and started drinking, and to celebrate something else I can't recall Paul pulled out more champagne. We all got louder, things got funnier the way they do when you're pissed; Lex showed Ellen some dance move teenagers were doing and Phil began eating my under-done broccoli. John and Ben had an intense conversation about personal trainers and started showing each other their lats, or maybe it was quads. Sarah and I clapped when they lifted their shirts.

'Let's play something else,' Ellen suggested.

'Poker,' said Lex and was drowned out by groans.

'Let's play Wink Murder,' said Paul.

'I can't wink,' said Jessie, pulling her face downwards and blinking at Ben.

'Don't use that face if you want to pull, is my advice,' Lex taunted as Jessie threw a napkin at him.

'This game's all about acting, so, Ben, you don't stand a chance obviously,' ribbed Paul.

'God I'm starving,' moaned Ben, nibbling one of Ava's rice cakes.

'Have you ever seen children play that game?' asked Sarah. 'It's hilarious, they can't lie, they just point and say, "Jonny's killed me," or some such.'

'They can't keep a secret, they have no artifice,' added Phil.

'Unlike us,' said John.

'It's a child's game only adults can finesse,' said Paul.

'Decided!' shouted Ellen.

'Kate has to guess which of us is the murderer,' Paul said. 'You get three goes.'

Sarah laughed. 'Three is loads! There's only how many of us . . .' she glanced round the table, '. . . nine of us!'

'Kate's pissed, she'll never guess,' said Paul.

'Bet you she will,' said Jessie, 'she's very observant.'

'Good idea!' said Paul, getting excited. 'Forty quid she doesn't get it.'

'You're on!' shouted Lex, digging in his back pocket for his wallet. 'You'd better bloody win, Kate.'

'Oh stop,' I remember saying. I don't like it when Paul wants to get money involved, it makes things more serious than they should be. It takes away the lightness.

'You need to leave the room so we can choose the killer,' said Ellen.

'I'll get you assassins dessert.' I weaved into the kitchen, a burst of laughter chasing me down the corridor. I pulled the lemon tart from its box, dug about in the freezer for the ice cream, piled plates and cutlery in my arms and headed back to the dining room.

The atmosphere had changed. The group was quiet, their conspiring looks cutting me out. I sat for a moment looking about. 'Have we started?' I said as Ellen suddenly grabbed her throat and rolled her eyes and slumped forward on to her empty plate, arms flailing.

Phil began clapping. I watched Ellen's back shudder as she giggled. 'One down,' said Paul, smiling.

'Come on, Kate, my money's at stake!' said Lex.

I didn't have a clue who'd done it. Our dining-room table is round, so I could in theory see everyone, but this didn't make it easier. 'It's Ben,' I said.

'He's not that good an actor!' scoffed Lex. Ben smiled his 'Hollywood', turning two-thirds of his face towards me and showing all his perfect chiclet teeth, but he shook his head.

Two long minutes passed, until Jessie suddenly said, 'Oh! Was I supposed to die then?'

'Jessie, for fuck's sake!' Lex barked. He is competitive to the end.

A low strangle started in John's throat before he tipped his chair all the way back, gripping the table edge with white fingers. He lost his hold and the chair toppled backwards, sending him slamming into the ceramic tiles. I actually heard his head hit the floor with a crack. 'Are you OK?' John's body was twitching awkwardly, eyes closed.

'Crikey,' said Phil.

'Check he's OK!' Sarah shouted, standing up.

Sarah is my sensible friend, she's punctual and unflappable. She has also bothered to do a first-aid course and if she was alarmed I thought maybe I had better be too. 'John?'

I leaned over and touched his face. Nothing. I shook his shoulder, hearing chairs scrape as people stood and craned. 'John!' I said much louder.

'Is he really hurt?' asked Ellen, back from the dead now.

I stared at John and heard Jessie scream above me. 'Is that blood?' Behind John's head a dark red smear had appeared.

'John?' I shook his shoulder again. He didn't move. 'Oh my God.' I crouched down next to him, the blood looked shiny and fresh. On an impulse I felt his neck as someone gasped above me. 'Call an ambulance!' I looked up at the circle of heads above me as someone passed me a mobile. I punched in 999 and then stopped, my finger on the green connect button. I had heard a snigger. I looked round at John, flat out on the floor with a huge grin on his face, a big green tongue stuck out at me and a bottle of tomato ketchup in his hand. I punched him on the arm as the room erupted in hysteria. 'You bastard!' I really was angry, I had been genuinely scared for him. John has no limits, he's always taking things that little bit further than I find comfortable.

'She felt his neck! She felt for a pulse!'

'Call an ambulance! Call an ambulance!' mimicked Lex.

'Imagine if she had really dialled!'

'I didn't think that tomato-ketchup gag would work, but it was phenomenal!' added Phil, full of admiration.

John was still on the floor, wiping Heinz off his hair with a napkin. 'So come on, who was it?' he said to me.

'What?'

'Who murdered me?'

I had forgotten about the silly game, awkward feelings of being the butt of all their jokes swirling round inside me. 'Oh I don't know,' I said, keen for it all to be over. 'It's Sarah,' but she shook her head.

'It's interesting how our allegiance is with the murderer and not Kate, the detective,' Phil said, pulling the lemon tart towards him and hunting for a knife. 'By colluding with the killer, we're also setting up someone who's innocent.'

'Oh, Eggy, he had you good and proper!' Paul said, wiping away tears of laughter. 'So you're two down.'

I stared at Paul, but a loud noise on my left made me jump and look away. When I turned back Phil grabbed his throat and said, 'I'm dead, but I assure you I haven't been poisoned by this delicious pudding.'

'Three down,' said Paul.

'So, Kate, who did it?' asked Ben.

'Come on, choose me, you know you want to,' pleaded Paul. He was right, I thought it was him. But he knew I thought it was him and he was expecting me to pick him. So I tried to double bluff him. 'It's . . . Lex.'

'Oh, Eggy!' Paul reached in delight for my face across the table and tried to snog me.

'Kaaate!' Lex threw his two twenties in the air. 'Didn't you see him chuck that fork on the floor to distract you? Are you blind?'

'You did really well, Kate,' said Jessie, stroking my arm.

Paul took a sip of champagne, holding out his hand for Lex's money. 'You only win at this game because other people let you, Eggy.' And then amid the roar and chatter of our friends he winked at me. I doubt anyone else saw such a small gesture between the two of us. It was a celebration of his cleverness, an admission that he could outwit me and that I loved him for it, because which wife doesn't love success in her husband?

Paul was not wrong. When we closed the door on the last person that night we had sex right there against the hallway wall, a hurried, intense and physical fucking. After eight years together he brought me to one of the most intense orgasms I've ever had.

I stand in that same spot now looking at Paul's cricket bat

in the stand. The green cotton winds its way up the thick handle. I imagine it in my capable hands, held like a baseball bat, whistling fast through the air towards the back of his head. Paul knew I would lie to the police, he knew I would cover for him and he never even had to ask me. His fake drunken ramblings led me down a path where I colluded all on my own. My husband has played me, but this time the stake is not forty quid, it is much, much higher than that.

19

In the early hours I break into Paul's office. I leave at 2.00 a.m., closing the front door without a sound. Our bedroom is at the back of the house so he can't hear the car pulling away. I take his set of office keys that he keeps in the study and park down the side alley. I am wearing dark clothes and a torch is shoved in my trouser waistband. I know the alarm code because I have occasionally done research from this office and small details like this are the kinds of things I know about Paul. He may be smarter than me but I have a very good memory for literal things. I don't forget.

Paul's office is an old bath factory in a cobbled mews, with full-height metal windows and a wooden floor that's attractively grooved. You can almost imagine labourers with sinewy arms and strong shoulders dragging the heavy cast iron across the floor to be taken to the city's upmarket addresses on horses lined up outside. The desks Paul and Lex 'sourced' ('bought' lends a pedestrian ordinariness to the task, which Lex in particular feels he's above) are from an abandoned university library. They sit under industrial-looking lights that hang down from the high ceiling. There is a table-football game in the corner by the kitchen, beers in the fridge. The reception area is decorated with flowers and a garish wall-paper of reeds and kingfishers, and someone very pretty usually sits behind the stylish 1940s desk. It's the kind of place where if you're not having fun you're made to feel ashamed.

Once I've punched in the code and unlocked the door, it is pitch black inside. I daren't turn on any lights, so I grope forward pointing the torch at the floor. Paul's desk commands a corner site partially shielded by a large plant with delicate leaves. He has never had a private office, which is no surprise for someone who can't bear to be alone, and TV production is an open-plan kind of business. I sit down in his chair and let my eyes grow accustomed to the dark. I have strolled through this office many times to meet Paul before evening events in town. I have taken the eyes that tracked me, the faces that assessed me as the boss's wife, in my stride. I used to perch on the edge of Paul's desk and drink a beer while I waited for him to finish up, though recently there's been a pair of old cinema seats near by and it seems inappropriate not to use them.

I let the torchlight pass over every object on the desk. I pull the Rolodex towards me (Sergei is so efficient he keeps a paper copy of Paul's contacts) and insert my nail as close as I can to G. I end up in the Fs: Film Council, Florists (Maynard's), Forman Kate, Graham Melody. This last card has been written by Paul. How ironic. He's slipped his lover right in next to me. I pull it sharply from the roll, and tuck it into my bra.

I open the drawers of his desk and try to hunt through the chaos of pens, staplers and contracts on Forwood's distinctive pale blue company paper. Back when Paul and Lex were starting out and there were just the two of them in one small room in town Paul used to seek my opinion on far more than he does now; we had a lengthy discussion about the colour of Forwood's paper, we dithered between Old Vellum, Parchment and Milk Blue. Milk Blue won.

Get on with it, I tell myself sharply; don't get distracted. I want to find this thing Melody never signed. There is a postcard from Jessie on the desk. One of her paintings propped up against the computer screen. I sit in Paul's office chair, my toes just reach the planking below. From this position he can see the whole office, lord of his kingdom, and watch what's happening in the mews outside. Astrid's desk is at right angles to his in the middle of the room. She faces Lex, who she works for, but is in profile from here. She's got an orchid next to her intray; a Bach Flower Remedy for stress and a tube of expensive hand cream standing on its lid. Her drawers are locked. She's the keeper of Lex's secrets. Did she ever field Melody's calls to Paul? Hold the phone to her pert breasts and mouth at Paul 'it's her', putting her through with a knowing glance?

I suddenly think of my dad and Barbara, cooped up in that boxy 1960s office building, Monday mornings more delightful than they should be as their desire for each other began to cut my mum out, their passion growing against the backdrop of the car park and the dual carriageway. We may now have pricier clothes, trendier interiors and better-quality lunches, but the dynamics of office life remain stubbornly unchanged from one generation to the next. Relationships are just as likely to grow over the laptop as they did over the telex machine. Unexpectedly my eyes fill with tears.

I can't find the key to Astrid's drawers so I hunt for something to break them open with. Lex's desk is the other side of the room near the window. It's lighter here so I turn the torch off, dig around again. Among his papers I find his gym membership, some Valium tablets, several photographs of him with celebrities, a biography of Don Simpson subtitled *The Hollywood Culture of Excess*, but nothing else.

I move on to John's desk near the toilets. From here he sees the back of most people's heads. It's obsessively neat and ordered, the notepad blank and the lid back on the pen. There is an unopened bottle of Evian on the desk so John can 'hydrate'. Being thirsty is so last century. No personal effects fill his workspace, give any hint of the larger-than-life character Paul insists he used to be. Years of therapy, of NA and AA meetings to keep order and discipline in a life nearly unhinged by addiction have stripped him of colour. It's as if his personality and experiences are now bleached to grey without the chemical enhancers. A sports bag is zipped up and placed under the desk. A lighter is parallel with the keyboard, smoking is the only vice he still allows himself, and he does a lot of that. John Forman, Paul's older brother, carried along in the wake of his younger one's success.

His drawers are not locked but hold nothing interesting, so I bend down on the chair and undo the sports bag. Alongside the Adidas socks and Calvin Klein T-shirt is a Non-Disclosure Agreement between Forwood and Melody Graham. As far as I can make out, reading between the lines of all the legal caveats it seems she had a series idea she wanted to discuss with Forwood. She's signed it. It's dated six months ago. I'm reading it when a crack explodes in the darkness. Someone is in the room with me.

I drop from the chair to the ground. The back of John's desk reaches all the way to the floor in the mid-century style, creating a cubbyhole between his drawers where his chair fits. I crawl into it, hugging my knees to my chest. I want to make myself as small as possible, I have no stomach for a fight. The floorboards groan with the weight of a body passing over them, the footsteps move very close, their weight and confidence sound like they belong to a man. I see torchlight jerking on the back wall and careering off at an angle. He's turning towards the window, inches from me. Silence.

Fear drips down my back and I'm reminded of the summer when Lynda caught a fieldmouse in our caravan and we watched it cower in the bottom of a Corn Flakes box. When I ran my finger along its spine it flinched, its chest panting triple quick. I feel as trapped and helpless as that fieldmouse now, my fate in someone else's hands as I have no excuse at all as to why I am under a piece of furniture in an office I don't work in in the middle of the night. I wish with a pang of bitter regret that Paul had never woken me that Monday, that he had sobbed and moaned alone, that my peace of mind had never been betrayed.

I carefully poke my head out when I hear the bumping of a chair near the window. The figure crosses to a conference room on my far right so I crawl around the side of John's desk. The front door is visible about ten desks away. After we'd manhandled that fieldmouse and made exclamatory noises for a bit Lynda put the Corn Flakes box in the field by a tree and we waited for the creature to make its instinctive run for life. It never did, the poor thing was paralysed with terror. The conference door swings shut with a squeak and I see a dark silhouette heading away from me towards the toilets. I assume the crouch of a sprinter on her blocks, the glass entrance door hovers before me in the gloom, I know it opens outwards. Lynda eventually grew tired of looking at the clashing red and green colours of the crowing Kellogg's rooster and with a yell and a running kick knocked the box high in the air as I screamed and hightailed it back to the caravan. I didn't look back. I don't want to be that fieldmouse now, passively awaiting its fate.

I'm at the third desk when I hear his grunt of surprise and the sound of him chasing me. He's shouting but I have eyes only for the freedom door that's rapidly enlarging before me. I slam into it with both hands and feel a sharp pain in my wrists as the unyielding door bounces me back almost to the floor. My cheek is slammed to the wood and the breath sucked out of me as the figure lands on top of me. The door wasn't unlocked. My heroic dash for liberty has ended before it really began.

'Are you alone? Are you alone?' He pushes my face into

the floor and yanks my arms behind me. It's very painful and I would protest if I wasn't winded, but I'm incapable of answering his shouted commands and he's not making any sense anyway, there's a crackling radio obscuring his words. I sense cold metal on my wrists and he pulls me round and shines the torch full in my eyes. I still haven't seen his face. 'What's your name!' The room is suddenly frozen for a second in bright light and I see a woman standing over the man on top of me before we are all plunged back into blackness for another second before the lights come fully on. 'Check the back!' he points as the woman runs for the toilets. 'I couldn't find the bloody light switch!' He strains on his knees to check where she's going. 'Poncey architects!' he adds before turning back to me. 'You,' his voice is hard and emphatic, 'are in *so* much trouble.' He pulls me roughly to my feet and I gasp at the pain in my wrists. It's me in handcuffs, not Paul. I almost nod in agreement with him. I really am in so much trouble.

The policeman is called Sergeant Ian Mackenzie and he is pissed off. He seemed pumped and excited in Paul's office, as if this were all he had hoped his career choice would be: physically clearing the streets of burglars and driving the dirt back to the station in his patrol car. But four hours later what he thought was a straightforward breaking-and-entering charge is turning into anything but. He's being manipulated by an astonishingly clever lawyer and I am doing my level best to keep my mouth from dropping open in slack-jawed awe at his verbal and mental prowess. The lawyer is my brother-in-law, John, and, at this moment, my saviour. When Mackenzie gave me my phone call I stared blankly at the ten digits. I could think of only two numbers: my mum's (instantly discounted) and Paul's. Despite my sour anger with him, I am tied to him still. He didn't sound asleep when I called, or particularly surprised when I said I had been arrested.

Maybe there's nothing that'll surprise him now. 'Leave it with me,' he said as if I were a client with a cheque-pending query. Forty minutes later John arrived. Night work obviously suits him as he looks brighter and less grey than he does in the sunshine. For the first time I see the genes that he shares with his brother in his high forehead and strong jaw. Mackenzie and I stare at him in fascination.

'To clarify, Mrs Forman used a key to enter the property, and turned off the alarm using the code that she knows,' says John, glowering at Mackenzie and then me as if we are imbeciles. I nod, eyes on the table. Mackenzie shoves his hands in his pockets in irritation. 'I see no evidence of breaking and entering.'

'We got a call from—'

'From who?'

'The man rang off before we could establish who it was, saying there was a robbery in progress.'

'We may all be thankful for civic-minded members of the public but on the available evidence that is a misinterpretation of events.'

Mackenzie groans. 'She was hiding under a desk in the dark with a torch on her!'

'Not surprisingly, considering someone had just broken down the door in the middle of the night.' Mackenzie tuts. 'What material from this office did she have on her?' John asks.

'That's no defence and you know it!'

'What had she taken from the offices?'

He pauses. 'Nothing.' I feel Melody's card against my bra strap.

'May I say—'

'You are not required to say anything,' John interrupts me sharply. He doesn't want defeat snatched from victory.

Mackenzie stares at me with open hostility and I can't hold

his gaze. The last time anyone looked at me in that way was a teacher at school. I've always been on the right side, moved through life without conflict. I like to please. 'I'm phoning your husband, let's see what he has to say.' He leaves, banging the door.

'There are cameras in here, Kate, just in case you didn't realise.' He looks up at the ceiling. 'They've got microphones.' He smiles, but I know what he's saying. Keep your cool, we'll deal with this when we get outside.

'What happens now?'

'We wait. There's a lot of waiting around in a police station.' He digs in his pocket for some chewing gum. 'It's much harder for everybody now that no one's allowed to smoke,' he adds. I take the next tablet off the little paper-wrapped stack.

A little while later Mackenzie returns, that unflinching gaze upon me again. 'He says you're an insomniac. That you often do things in the middle of the night, that you'd probably mislaid something you needed and wondered if you'd left it in the office the last time you visited.' His voice is sarcastic, he certainly doesn't believe a word of it. 'It's all so conven-ient, Mrs Forman, so watertight, eh?'

'If you have no charge for this woman, you must release her.' John pushes back his chair, a signal that it's all over.

Mackenzie's hands are out of his pockets and are twitching by his sides. I'm not sure if he wants to deck me or John, probably both. A lot of the kids I went to school with were the children of policemen. I remember those dads as strict and sarcastic, just like Mackenzie, with voices that could suddenly turn very loud if we ever dared touch a lounge stereo or leaf through a beloved record collection. He hates me.

John stays close to me while I sign lots of papers at a very high counter and collect my torch, car keys and mobile phone.

We leave the station together through the front door, just as dawn is breaking.

'I didn't know you did criminal work.'

'This is a special case. We want as little publicity about this as possible.'

'We?'

John assesses me with his grey eyes, his face betraying nothing. 'Paul, me, the company.' He pulls out a pack of fags and lights one, looking only momentarily surprised as I take it from his fingers and inhale deeply. He lights another one for himself.

'Don't you mean that you always do what Paul asks?' Now that I'm outside my shame has broken over me with the dawn and my barbs of anger at John are a way of trying to protect myself. 'Why are you always jumping to his tune?'

He curls his fingers towards his right palm and examines his fingernails, the cigarette pointing skywards. A frown takes up space between his eyebrows. 'Is that what you think I do?'

John is someone who answers questions with questions, or doesn't answer at all. Both irritate me. I study my brother-in-law, the gap between what I've seen and what I've heard about him over the years impossible to bridge. He's nine years older than Paul, a different generation. He was the lawyer at an advertising agency until the time he entertained his most important clients in Los Angeles and following a thirty-six-hour bender stripped naked by the pool of the hotel where they were staying and dived in, hitting his head in the shallow end and ending up in the ER. When he came round the first thing he asked was whether they'd won the business. I've never seen this larger-than-life personality. The image of John standing shouting in Venice Beach, the Forman family jewels swinging as hotel guests dived for cover, is quite alien to me. I don't like being the centre of attention, I don't crave all the eyes in the room.

'What did Paul say when he phoned you?'

'Kate's got overexcited.' Or Kate's getting nearer to the truth. I imagine Paul's reassuring chat with Mackenzie. He saved me from a breaking-and-entering charge. Paul covered for me, like I covered for him. Tit for tat. We're united to the outside world but breaking apart within.

'What were you looking for, Kate?' John's thrown his butt in the gutter and is standing squarely in front of me, one of his wide and gym-honed shoulders is twitching but his voice is quiet and calm.

'You and Paul were talking at the maze about something Melody never signed. I want to know what it was.'

John frowns. 'You broke in for that? You have got overexcited.' He sees my stony face and relents. 'She never signed the contract for *Crime Time*.' He holds up his hands to stop my questions. 'I know the show's been running for months. The UK version wasn't at issue, it was the sale to European countries . . .' He tails off. 'It sounds irregular but this does happen. Technically Forwood is free to sell the idea all over the place now. It's embarrassing because it looks like a motive and it doesn't leave a good taste.' John picks a piece of fluff out of his pocket as if he's disgusted with himself. 'Why didn't you just ask Paul all this?'

'Was he having an affair with Melody?'

John's face transforms in an instant. He's come alive. A vein in his temple begins to throb. 'You think he killed Melody?'

I open my mouth to speak, but then the door to the station swings open and Mackenzie barrels out, a cloud of frustrated fury following him. John and I hurry round a corner. 'Questions answered with questions.' I walk away with our conversation hanging.

'Kate!' John calls after me, but I march forward on my trainers. I risk a glimpse over my shoulder after about a hundred yards and he's still standing there, tracking my progress up the street. He doesn't follow.

I don't know where to go. I start weaving down the road, delirious with what I have done. When I first dropped to the floor at the office who did I think was coming to get me? Not assailants with faces I don't recognise but my own husband. I walk for half an hour not noticing where I'm going. *A man called and rang off before* . . . Mackenzie's words shorten my breath. Did Paul call the police? Did he know I would go and hunt for clues? Did he lead them to me? These thoughts make me too tired to move and when a cab coasts past I flag it down.

'Where to, love?' His fingers drum with impatience on the steering wheel when he gets no reply. I give him Jessie's address as the idea of going home is unthinkable. Twenty minutes later I get out next to a boarded-up kebab house and ring her doorbell. I pick grit from my eye as a truck thunders past. Jessie is not a morning person and this is a test of how heavily she sleeps. I hope she fails. After more than five minutes the door finally opens a crack and I see the surprise registering on her unmade face. 'Kate, what are you doing here?' She opens the door wider. Her bed hair is offset with a beautiful and colourful kimono. She looks tired but happy. 'You OK?'

A long stairway leads from the ground floor to her rooms above but instead of walking up them she leans on the door frame, blocking my path. 'Can I come in?'

She pauses for a second too long. 'Of course.'

I follow her up the stairs into the kitchen and see an empty bottle of wine and two glasses on the table. 'Oh, am I disturbing you? Is someone here?' I look around, her reluctance making sense now.

'Kate, are you all right?' She's looking at me strangely as

a hysterical giggle escapes and I find I'm clamping a hand across my mouth. Jessie stares at me, bewildered. Her eyes slide to her bedroom door.

'Someone is here! Is it . . . ?' I turn to the closed door and feel her hand on my arm.

'Please, Kate—'

Something about her warm palm on my elbow with its hints of sympathy, the new nightgear, one of her pictures hanging in the hallway that's the same picture that sits in front of Paul's computer screen . . . I push the door open at the moment when someone in the bed pulls the duvet over their head. I've been mired in subterfuge and riddles for days. I snatch the cloth and yank as if I'm pulling away the layers that separate me from the truth, and come face to face with an astonished and naked bald man. The fact that it is not Paul doesn't lessen my anger. 'You should be with your wife,' I spit.

'Kate—'

He looks as frightened as if his actual wife has caught him. 'Well he fucking well should be.'

'Kate!' Jessie's voice is much louder this time and much more insistent. She shoves me back into the kitchen. 'What are you doing?'

'What the hell are *you* doing?'

Her pale face flushes red. She's angry now, angrier than I've ever seen her. 'Living my life, and if you don't like it too bloody bad!' Her words slap me back to my senses. I burst into tears as she folds her arms.

'I'm so sorry, I didn't mean that.' She just stares at me. 'Can you forgive me?' Her silence says 'no' louder than any words can. 'I thought that was Paul!' She takes a huge intake of breath but before she has a chance to speak I cut her off. 'Paul's having an affair, or has had an affair.' I'm blubbing and weeping, desperate to tell her the rest, unload my real fears and suspicions, but it's not just the man in the bedroom that prevents me. Sobbing on my best friend's landing, I wonder whether friendship can stand a secret like the one I'm holding. I don't know if it's strong enough. Maybe I'll never have the relief of this problem shared.

Jessie sighs. 'I'm sorry.'

'You don't understand—'

'You mean, I can't understand?'

No, I don't mean that.'

'Yes you do.' The antagonism is back, we are going in the wrong direction.

'I broke into his office looking for clues. I was arrested and I've just spent the night in jail.' My manic giggle is back. The mothers that I know would gasp and gawp at this rather amazing news, but the tempo of Jessie's life is such that she thinks it unremarkable.

'Do you love him?' My sobs die away and I stare at her. Do I? Can I love a man who has murdered someone? Should I? Is love unconditional? I open my mouth to speak but don't know what to say. 'You seem unsure.' There is a pause. 'If you love him, fight for him; if not, walk away.'

'Walk away!' I shake my head. 'It's more complicated than that.'

'No it isn't.'

Jessie is interrupted by the bedroom door opening and Mr Married shuffles out, wrapped in Jessie's old towelling dressing gown. 'Adam, this is Kate.' He nods sheepishly. 'Kate's husband is having an affair,' Jessie adds, explaining why I am here at this odd time in such a state.

I love Jessie completely at this moment. Adam looks at the carpet as if he hopes a hole might miraculously appear in which he can crawl away and die. She hasn't realised that me being here is far too like the scene he'll have to have one day with his own wife.

'You know, Kate, maybe this is a good thing.'

'How on earth—'

'It makes Paul human. He's not perfect, he's flawed like the rest of us. Don't take this the wrong way but you've put Paul on this pedestal. He was bound to topple off simply with the effort of trying to stand so straight.'

Adam hands me a tissue, a small act of kindness that I'm very grateful for. 'You don't even seem surprised.' I blow my nose and see Jessie shrug a shoulder, the kimono slipping down to her arm. I stop blowing. 'What?' She looks at me, taken aback. 'You know something I don't.'

Again she hesitates for a second too long. 'I . . .'

'Tell me!'

'There's nothing to tell.'

'Yes there is!'

Jessie looks at Adam and back at me. She makes a frustrated gesture with her head. 'I assumed you knew already.'

'Knew what?'

'Jesus, Kate, think about how you met!'

'I don't understand.'

'He was with Eloide when he met you.' I look at her blankly. 'Pug told me . . . oh this is all so long ago, it doesn't matter—'

'What did Pug tell you?'

Jessie looks awkward, crossing and uncrossing her arms as if she's trying to find a comfortable place for them. 'That you were not the first. He'd cheated on Eloide before. More than once.'

20

Eloide sent me a get well card. After I was knocked down by the taxi, taken home by her husband and given my first instructions in mind-blowing sex. I opened an envelope to find the words 'Well-Behaved Women Rarely Make History' emblazoned across the front of a 1950s-style card. Inside she told me to flirt with the doctors. I limped into my bedroom then and lay down on the crumpled sheets, stained with Paul's semen, sweat and saliva. He'd already left a T-shirt behind, the start of the migration of clothes and toiletries into my flat, the marking out of territory. I buried my face in it, thrilling to his smell. I almost came right then. Eloide had written that she hoped I'd be up and about soon. My mind was a fizzing picture of me pinned to this bed, Paul corkscrewing inside me as I cried out over and over and over. I should have known that it takes practice to get that good. Lots of practice.

The morning after our first adulterous night together I woke to see him buttoning his shirt and fishing his jacket off the floor. He had the air of someone keen to get on with his day, his body spent and his head full.

'Where are you going?'

'To wash away my sins,' he replied as he pushed a foot into a shoe.

My world tilted as if someone had sat down on the side of my sin-drenched bed. He was going to chuck me, I thought, but when I looked up he was smiling at me. 'Not really. But I do have to go and tell my wife that our marriage is over.'

It took him a few months, but he did tell her. When he decides on something he always sees it through, right to its end. He's very determined and focused. He pushed on, not knowing what lay ahead, and he carried me along with him.

Gritty dregs catch on my tongue as I drain my third cup of coffee at Jessie's small kitchen table. Adam's dressed now in a suit and a tie. His cheeks are pink from showering and his glasses slightly steamed. He looks like a million suburban commuters and is a world away from the performance artists, acrobats, G8 protestors and students Jessie normally attracts. He catches me assessing him and I look away, embarrassed. Jessie hovers over me awkwardly as if she might need to suddenly catch me. Her table is wobbly and I knock it back and forth with my elbow in a rhythmic dum-doop, dum-doop motion.

'What are you thinking?'

'That I've been cocooned, living in a bubble. I don't know what's real and what's not.'

'Give yourself time. Don't do anything hasty. Try and find some definite evidence, otherwise you're chasing shadows. Do you want another?' She picks up my cup as my mobile rings for the eighth time. Paul is calling, over and over again.

I can feel my heart fluttering as it runs fast on too much caffeine and shake my head. 'I should go.'

She nods. 'I've got some good news. I won that Raiph Spencer commission.'

'That's fantastic!'

'I was in his *huge* office doing some sketches a few days ago.'

'What do you think of him?'

'I found him a bit scary, very formal.'

'Oh? I met him recently. I thought he seemed a bit of a

pussycat. With a sense of humour that doesn't come across when he's interviewed on TV.'

'Blimey. Maybe he's bought into the artist taking a little part of your soul away with them. He seemed nervous and aloof when I was there.'

'I had dinner with him not long ago. He talked a lot about his childhood, Ireland, his dad's shop. You know he told me that one of his earliest memories in the shop was adding up the pennies in the till at the end of the day.'

Jessie shakes her head. 'I don't know how you get that kind of stuff out of people. But if I know it's there, I'm getting it out of him at our next sitting.'

'Well, good luck with it, Jessie. He's very high profile and great for your career.' I pull on my coat as the doorbell rings.

'Who's that?' she asks.

'I'll get it on my way out.'

She envelops me in a hug and her familiar musky perfume. 'Take care.' She looks closely at my face. 'Remember, it's not like anyone's died or anything.' She gathers me tighter as I cry. 'He's still a good man, you know.'

'Goodbye, Adam. I'm sorry I barged in on you like that.' He gives me a salute as I leave.

I come down the stairs and open the door to find Paul standing outside. He's in a dark suit and a black coat and, contrary to what I might have expected, he seems well rested, clean-shaven and, as my mother would say – dashing. He looks at me kindly as he waves up the stairs to Jessie. She can't resist and waves back, smiling.

'How did you know—?'

'She's your best friend, it was an obvious place to start. You weren't answering your phone after all.' He's calm and if he's being sarcastic I can't detect it. We start to walk to the car. 'I went in early to pick it up before it got towed.' He paused before adding, 'The children were asking where you were.'

At the mention of Josh and Ava a tear starts to brim but I fight it back. A blonde in high heels turns her head as we pass, checking out my husband. He doesn't notice. Or maybe she's checking out what on earth I'm doing with him. Paul's wearing his best suit and looks like a master of the universe and I'm made aware of the drab, black clothes I threw on in the middle of last night. After a night in the cells, the smell of desperation and failure cling to me in the briskness and energy of a commuter's morning. She's probably wondering what routine he's using to dump me.

'Where shall I take you?' His kindness is worse than anger. This must be how the mad are treated. I bet even Mr Rochester did a fair bit of tiptoeing around his raving wife.

'To the Tube. I can get home from there.'

He nods as he indicates and pulls out. 'What did you tell Jessie?'

Here it comes, the casual inquiry to see how far my suspicions have leaked. He's probably pretty sure I haven't told anyone else. 'It was more interesting what she told me.'

'Which was?'

'That you were never faithful to Eloide.' He swears under his breath. 'I think you might be a very different person from the one I—'

'Of course I'm different! I'm thirty-nine! It was more than ten years ago.' His hands are off the wheel as he gesticulates. 'I'm not proud of what I did, OK. If you want me to say sorry then fine, that's what I'll say. But affairs happen for a reason. And I don't have those reasons with you!'

'How can I believe you when you've never told me this before?'

'Because it's not important. It's not about you, it concerns someone else.' The old feeling of being kept out resurfaces in me. His pact with his ex-wife, the connection I can never break. Feelings of betrayal reawaken. 'Stop looking at me like that!' He turns sharply at a corner and accelerates so that I am pressed back against the seat. 'You know your problem? I think you've got an inability to be happy. You look for problems to cling to.'

'What?'

'It's because of your mum—'

'Oh please—'

'She's broken and so you think you must be too.'

'This sounds like cod psychology from I know exactly who!'

'See, there you go again, raking over the past, which you can never change!'

I shake my head. 'It's not my mum and her broken marriage or my unhappy sister that's filling my thoughts, it's the blood you had on your hands that night, your raving—'

'No. It's not that at all. You could believe my explanation but your background won't let you.'

We're about to launch verbal assaults into domestic territory that has been fought over too many times already and I'm in the kind of mood where I'll launch the atomic bomb and start criticising his mother, when an advertising hoarding catches my eye. 'Oh, it's Gerry.' We both stare at a giant photo of a serious-looking Gerry Bonacorsi, glowering at us from across the street. 'Good decision? Watch and make up your own mind. *Inside-Out*. Every night from 9.00, online 24 hours a day.'

'That's the new campaign because the interest is sky-high again. They're repeating the whole series on cable. Our share price has jumped.'

'That's convenient.' He ignores me. 'They've made him look more dangerous this time, haven't they? They used to use those pictures that highlighted his laughter lines.'

'He didn't kill her,' Paul says, shaking his head. 'And this copycat theory is bollocks. She wasn't only strangled, she was stabbed too! It's hardly an exact match.'

'I heard on the radio someone saying that because he's old he can't use the brute force he used the first time. He needed to incapacitate her first.' Paul makes a frustrated sound. 'It's got your series back on air, hasn't it?'

He turns on me, angry now. 'Yes it has. And you know what? I'm glad. This is the best programme I ever made. I'll defend it again and again, like I've been doing since last week.' He leans his elbow out of the window, 'Did you find what you were looking for in my office?' He's staring straight at me now, challenging me to explain why I stepped over the boundary into his workspace.

'Why did you lie for me when Mackenzie called?' He's stopped in neutral in the street. A truck honks impatiently as commuters take the opportunity to weave in front and behind us. A cyclist coasts past us by the kerb, bumping the wing mirror. We are hemmed in on all sides by our lies, our suspicions and our secrets.

'Because you're my wife. You're the mother of my children.' There's sadness in his voice. We've made a pact with each other. It's a Gordian knot and I know that those knots can't be untied, only hacked apart. 'Livvy phoned yesterday. She mentioned that you're doing good things on *Crime Time*.'

A horrid thought occurs to me. 'Have I ruined my chances now that I've been arrested?'

'And discharged. Everyone else on that show has probably been done for something or other. Don't worry.'

He pulls up outside a Tube station that's sucking people in through its doors. 'I'm going to a meeting with a reputational management consultant over how we position Forwood through this mess. The joy never ceases.' He looks away through the windscreen. 'You know, Kate, I've never been happier than the day I married you.' I open the car door and am carried away from him before I can think of a reply.

I pick up a free newspaper from a metal rack by the stairs.

Gerry's face stares out from the front cover, a smear of rage across it as his arms are held by a policeman on either side. His white hair is messed, his crooked teeth caught at an unflattering angle. The photographers were tipped off that he would be taken in for questioning and they sure got their fill of photos. Nice. 'Back inside' says the headline.

Gerry Bonacorsi shows the world the anger that made him Britain's longest-serving lifer yesterday as the former magician who strangled his wife gave police a volley of foul abuse as they took him in for questioning over the murder of TV researcher Melody Graham. Bonacorsi's controversial release into the community may be short-lived, according to a spokesman for the prison service. 'Convicted murderers have strict conditions attached to their freedom and resisting the police in this way may contravene those conditions.' Aspects of Melody's murder bear a striking resemblance to that of Delia Bonacorsi's in 1980, for which Bonacorsi served thirty years in jail. He was finally freed just over a month ago after reality-TV programme *Inside-Out* filmed his life in jail. Police questioned the suspect for four hours yesterday before releasing him without charge.

On page 5 I find a colour picture of Delia, smiling shyly at the camera. Around her neck she wears a cross that was not enough to save her from the man closest to her.

21

I'm two streets away from my house when my mobile rings with a number I don't recognise. It's Eloide asking if I'd like to meet for lunch today. Normally I politely decline (ill children are the gold standard of excuses) and I sense we're both relieved that we can sidestep her attempt at continuing a friendship neither of us want. But today as I reach for my door keys a frisson of victory flows through me. I'm party to new and dangerous information that changes the dynamics of our threesome. It's petty, but whoever said we had to put away childish things as we got older was delusional. I'll break bread with the enemy.

'Yes, I'd like that.'

There's the beat of a pause. 'Great!' She's committed now whether she likes it or not.

When I get up to my bathroom I change my mind and want to cancel. I look older than Gerry Bonacorsi; my guilt and the lies I've told, not to mention my night-time activities and sleepless night, have given me a grey, unattractive pallor. A scalding shower, a smearing of foundation and four aspirin are the best I can do to remake me and I head out at midday. I nearly fall asleep on the train.

Forty-five minutes later Eloide opens her smoked-glass front door and leads me into her pristine cubey kitchen cum dining room cum chill-out zone. Or rather into her boyfriend's. It's his house. The last time I saw Eloide was at a Halloween party here. I attend these functions because I don't want to leave Paul and her together, I need to crane, take notes and file gestures and atmospheres away. Eloide was wearing the very latest dress shape in black silk, chunky bracelets and towering designer shoes with fringing that swayed like a hula dancer as she moved. She had to bend down to kiss my cheek. Paul says it's important we appear at these events because Eloide knows a lot of high-profile TV people and sure enough Paul got stuck into industry gossip while I swapped platitudes with another marooned wife about Eloide's garden doors. Don't make the mistake of thinking this conversation was dull, quite the opposite. If you drill deep enough, you can sometimes uncover the most extraordinary revelations. It's a technique I learned when I worked in market research; you discover how to ask the right questions. Turns out that Hannah preferred blinds to curtains to cover those large expanses of glass because an intruder can't hide behind them. Hannah (she was tall with a long nose that she could probably touch with the tip of her tongue) had a fear of being attacked in her own home after being mugged five years ago. She grabbed my hand. 'It's weird. I never talk about that now. I had no idea it had affected me so much.' There, in a nutshell, was the power of ladder-technique questioning.

A loud peal of laughter interrupted our heart to heart. Paul was telling Eloide a joke on the other side of the room. She lifted her fringy foot high behind her as she laughed. She was the dazzling hostess, in demand and on form, and we were the planets orbiting her sun.

Today she's wearing a miniskirt, ballet flats and sheer tights. She has very good legs. She's got on a blouse with a pussy bow and billowy long sleeves. It's the only item of clothing I've ever seen her in that I haven't coveted. She's not wearing make-up and instantly I feel my red lipstick is too try-hard, my foundation cakey. I'm not sure she's even brushed her hair. Eloide is careless with her looks in a way that only the truly beautiful can be. She has no idea how irritating that is.

She pads across a marble floor and perches on a chair by the kitchen table, crossing her perfect legs at the knee and the ankle.

'So. How are things with you?' She smiles as if I'm one of her B-list celebrities she wants a quote from.

'They could be better, to be honest.'

'I can imagine.'

'So you know about Melody?'

'Yes. Paul told me.' *Paul told me*, the three most annoying words in the English language. 'He said you'd both been interviewed by the police.' I nod, my irritation jamming on maximum.

'It's just so terrible . . . poor Paul.' She begins to smooth her hair with a hand and then stops. 'Oh, I mean, not just terrible for him . . .' She looks at me imploringly, realising she's being crass. 'I meant that he worked with her . . . God, let's rewind and start over, can we?' Nervous laughter accompanies her as she rolls one hand over another. She's illustrating with gestures, just in case I'm too dumb to understand.

'What exactly are we starting?' I cross my arms, wishing I hadn't come.

'Would you like some coffee?' She sways to her immaculate kitchen cupboards and pulls out a gleaming coffee machine. 'I don't want there to be bad feeling between us. We were friends once and I hope that we can be friends again.' She pushes the percolator plug into the socket with a clunk and looks at me brightly.

She's got to be kidding. Is she pitying me? Oh God, don't let her know about my husband and Melody. 'I don't mean to be rude, but life's too short, isn't it? I know Paul's put you up to inviting me for lunch. But you must have lots of friends, you certainly don't have gaps in your social life. I don't see why you're trying to force it.'

She nods as she pulls out a filter. 'I can understand why you see it that way. But – and I don't want you to take this the wrong way – I still care for Paul even though he left me for you. He was a huge part of my life and I still want him in my life. I wanted to know if you had a problem with that' – she draws quotes in the air round 'problem' with her fingers – 'and if you did what I could do about it.' I look at Eloide in her fashion-forward home, the sunlight bouncing off her shiny surfaces, her shinier hair. I feel like a fat ugly toad. I run my foot up the hard edge of her modern table leg, reassured by the sense of certainty is gives me. I like borders, knowing where something starts and another thing ends. Eloide likes mixing it all up: Asian fusion dishes, open relationships, staying friends with old lovers and ex-husbands, calling your parents their real names, not Mum and Dad, yoga retreats in Ibiza. It's all too Swedish for me, her boundaries bleeding into one another like paint colours swirling in a tin. 'So . . . some coffee? It's great with a touch of cinnamon.'

Oh no it is not. 'I'll have a tea. Builder's, please.'

'Of course.' She pulls open a cupboard and I see packets and boxes lined up neatly. How did she cope with Paul's untidiness? Not well, I imagine. His infidelity? Even for someone unfettered by convention that must have hurt – a lot. *I still want him in my life.* I watch her open a new packet of PG Tips, pop the curve of cardboard in her kitchen bin – no, make that the custom-made recycling station. She pulls open a drawer and winces as she catches a finger on some-thing sharp. She swears loudly and I soften towards my former rival. I was her friend another lifetime ago. Paul hurt her and I hurt her. She takes some goat's milk from the fridge and pours it into her cup. 'Don't worry, I've got normal for you.' She flashes me an amused look as I let out a sigh of relief that's probably louder than I intended. The sun slices across the table and a spiky plant sways on the decking outside. It feels like California and I'm suddenly in the mood for confessions, for *talking about my feelings*.

'Maybe I do feel uncomfortable with your ... friendship ... with Paul' – I'm already struggling with my terminology – 'because yours is not the normal reaction. Most people would want to run away from the awkwardness of the situation, start anew, if you like. Because you – and he – don't it makes me ...' I shift my shoulders to fill in for my lack of words. It's a long way from the English suburbs to LA easy-cheesy truth-spilling.

She smiles most brilliantly. 'I think I understand. But life is always moving on. Paul and I are entirely different people from when we were married, but I'd rather work out unresolved issues than run away. It's not about regaining the past, it's more about providing a connection that helps me make sense of my life as it goes forward.' She levers her hand like a flight attendant as I nod. I'm quite enjoying this. 'And it's easier to make sense of it if there's no bad feeling with you.'

'Sometimes I feel you're pushing in a bit too much.'

She looks shocked. 'Then I apologise. I honestly didn't realise that's how my actions might be interpreted. I have no ulterior motives. Most of the time we talk on the phone about work, I tell him who the up and coming people are, feed back gossip I pick up in the toilets at nightclubs. He tells me titbits about TV, some of which are useful for my blog.' We lock eyes. 'Which I know he told you about, so don't pretend otherwise.' I don't reply, because she's right. Eloide doesn't only cosy up to celebrities at book launches and hotel openings, experience her career through the stage-managed, smiling shots of the accredited photographers. She's changing with the times, adapting to the harsher, more cutthroat hunger for celebrity titbits. She runs a no-holds-barred gossip blog where all the really salacious stories go. The blog's anonymous and she's very keen to keep it that way.

I take a big gulp of tea. 'Have you discussed you and me with him?'

'A bit.' I wait for the shard of jealousy to pierce me, but I feel nothing. 'He says he's a relationship pacifist.'

'What on earth does that mean?'

She giggles. 'I *think* it means he just wants everyone to get on.'

'I'm glad he saves those phrases for you, otherwise we wouldn't have lasted as long as we have!'

Eloide laughs. 'Oh, Kate, your scepticism about . . . I need to be careful here I don't want to unintentionally offend you' – she holds her hand in a stop gesture, – 'the value of therapeutic methodologies is unparalleled.'

'Oh stop. A cup of tea and a chat work just as well most of the time.'

We mirror each other's smiles. 'Or, in my line of work, a Bellini and the deck of a yacht.' Eloide picks up my drained cup and her own and removes them to her Corian-topped kitchen island.

For the first time in ten years I don't have a tightness across my belly being in Eloide's company. I sink back into the surprisingly comfortable white plastic moulded kitchen chair as she sweeps some imaginary crumbs off the table with the back of her hand. I look at the cups on the island, more white on white. She's placed them with their rims touching and the handles outwards and balanced the teaspoon across the rims. Some people get paid good money to label someone living like this as having obsessive compulsive disorder. I think she's just bloody tidy. I look at this immaculate kitchen space and think how little time it would take my children to ruin it.

'How is Lex coping at the moment?' she asks. 'If ever there was a man who needed therapy, it's him.'

'Why do you say that?'

'Oh! He's so driven, wound up like a spring.' I nod, distracted. I'm looking at the cups. 'If things don't go his way he gets very angry. I think he has rage issues that need to be . . .' Those cups. Something is tugging at my memory but I can't see what it is. The cups and the balanced spoon are a little white sculpture, they're like a painting and I've seen that pattern before somewhere . . . '. . . that anger usually intensifies as one gets older . . . Kate?'

The white plastic chair tips over behind me as I stand up sharply. 'You've been in my house.'

'What?'

'You've been in my house!' I've grabbed Eloide's arm and I'm squeezing. I've seen those cups before, supporting that teaspoon, on my own draining board. How long ago was it? A month? Two or three? I put a Sainsbury's bag down next to them and the spoon clattered to the floor. She'd been in my kitchen. Where else in my house had she invaded? I've discovered a cuckoo in my nest, trampling over boundaries.

My fury at being taken in so readily by a bit of bleached decking and a nice day explodes. 'This is bullshit!'

'Let go!'

I yank her arm and she's almost pulled across the table. 'You make me sick, spouting pseudo psycho claptrap –'

'It's not what you think—'

'Stay away from my husband and don't you ever dare go near my children or I swear I'll kill you.'

'Kate, I only wanted us to be friends—'

'Friends! Friends confide! They support each other, they don't sneak around each other's houses when they're not there. I'd never tell you anything!'

She's crying now and I think it might be from the pain of my fingers in her arm. 'Stop it!' There's a strange noise and I realise I'm screaming as I yank her arm harder and I see the scared 'O' of her gasp, and then I stop as the pussy-bow blouse sleeve has ridden up her arm and I'm looking at four livid cuts above the wrist. White scars in her perfect flesh surround the fresh gashes.

'What fucked-up crap is that?' She stops writhing as I loosen my grip and she slowly and with quite a lot of dignity pulls her sleeve back down over the mess.

'I'm sure you find that shocking. Not the thing a girl with the best job in the world is supposed to do.' She smoothes her hair. 'If you're wanting secrets, there's one.'

'Why do you do it?' Eloide throws her hands up in a useless gesture as tears begin to run across her high cheekbones. I scowl, unmoved by the crying. 'Secrets again. Well, here's one. I think Paul killed Melody. What does the party girl think about that?' I can't believe I'm telling her. That this suspicion I've lugged around with me for over a week I'm now unwrapping in front of my enemy. I'm spewing my troubles on to her fragile psyche. I want to see if she's strong enough to cope with them.

I think I expected Eloide to grill me for a motive or denounce my suspicions as groundless. What I get is her laughter, the full belly roar of the hysteric. I exit her house to the normality of puffy English clouds and a red Post Office van angrily swerving around the road humps. Her manic laughter chases me past the wheelie bins, hidden behind wooden slatted screens. How ironic that Paul always wanted us to get on.

22

A problem shared is a problem halved, my mum used to say. God, she talked a lot of nonsense. A woman who spends her life repeating and rehashing gossip for a magazine and anonymously online now knows something explosive, something she shouldn't. A few cuts exchanged for a murder isn't a fair deal. I've vomited my troubles on to the person least able to keep her counsel, and with the widest audience. My heart returns to its heavy thud as I try to push the mounting dread of what I've just revealed away. I'm nearing the school gate; this is safe, sane territory. I'm so tired I drag my feet along the tarmac. As I lead my children home down my street I notice a car behind us.

'Mrs Forman?' A man is leaning out of the window between the parked cars. 'Can I have a word, Mrs Forman?' He pulls into the kerb at a bad angle and jumps out. 'I'm Declan Moore from the *Express*.' I grab Josh and Ava's hand and with a yowl from my daughter I half run up the street, my children's legs cartwheeling in air. 'Just a few questions about Melody Graham, Mrs Forman.' He's keeping pace, rasping already, physical exercise is something he left behind at school along with graffiti in the toilets.

'I have nothing to say,' I begin.

'There's no need to be scared, Mrs Forman, just a few words about what your husband thinks—'

'No. You can't expect me to comment on an ongoing investigation.' I pull at my children's hands.

'Chillax, Mum,' Josh says indignantly.

He's recording my voice on his mobile, ignoring my pleas to be let alone. 'What's your reaction to Lex Wood's arrest?' When he sees that I've stopped to recover from the shock he closes in on me with renewed interest. 'You don't know, do you?'

Josh is tugging at my sleeve. 'Know what, Mum?'

'I don't understand.' Despite knowing I shouldn't say anything, I've started to blabber.

Declan holds the phone nearer my face. 'Like I said, he's been taken in for Melody's murder. Any comment?'

I look down helplessly at my bag on my shoulder, into which my phone is buried and probably beeping. I feel the warmth in my children's hands radiating back at me. 'I can't believe it.'

He nods. 'How long have Lex and your husband been business partners?'

'Mummy, I want to go.' Ava's eyes are saucers as she stares up at Declan.

'Ten years.'

'Where'd they meet?'

'They worked at Channel 4 together.'

'Are they close, would you say? Do they have a close relationship?'

I turn my feet towards home, wishing him gone. He doesn't take the hint and we are a huddle of bodies that moves down the pavement, Declan dodging saplings with his recording arm outstretched.

'What was Melody's relationship to Lex? What's your view on the copycat theory? That he's trying to make it look like Gerry did it?'

'I have no view. I really don't know.'

'Can I have your husband's mobile? The bloke who answers his phone won't give anything away. He guards him closely, doesn't he?'

I stand my ground and tighten my grip on Ava's hand. 'No. Give me your card and I'll give it to him. That's the best I can do.'

I can see my house now but there's another Declan standing outside it. He does a double take at us and starts to bear down.

'Mrs Forman, I'm from the *Sun*.'

'Please leave me alone. That's enough.'

'What does this mean for Forwood TV?' asks the first Declan. 'Can they continue to produce crime shows if one of the bosses is in jail?'

The second man is standing in front of me, blocking the way. 'I'm with my kids, have a heart!'

They remind me of beggars in a Third World country, one little outstretched hand appeals to your vanity, you almost love them as you dispense your trifle, then eight others surround you and you'd beat them off with a stick if you had one, your fear trampling on your feelings of being had.

'If you just take a few moments to answer my questions I'll be gone,' Declan adds. I keep my head down to stop being photographed, push past him and ram my key in the lock. 'Mrs Forman, the public want to know what your family think!' Questions are still being shouted at me as I shut the door.

'Mummy, who are those men?' Ava asks. I'm shaking as I explain as calmly as I can that someone Daddy and Lex and Uncle John knew has died and the police and the newspapers are trying to understand what happened to this person to make her family feel better because it's sad when someone dies, and the men outside work for the newspapers and they are asking questions so that they can write about it and let people know the truth. Ava eyes look huge in her small head as she nods. 'Mummy . . .' I hold my breath. '. . . When I grow up I want to be a mermaid.' She skips off into the kitchen; the wall seems the only thing still keeping me upright.

A noise makes me turn. Josh is sobbing on the stairs, great wordless gulps punctuated by his little shoulders heaving.

I love terraced houses. Being jammed in next to others makes me feel protected, safe. The street is only yards away from the living room and on summer evenings you can hear a woman's stilettos as she walks quickly home, the rumble of a pull-along suitcase as it bumps over the uneven paving stones. Someone in this street works for an airline, I'd guess. I didn't grow up in a house like this and I know my mum can't understand why, with Paul's success and the size of our family, we don't live in a bigger, newer place in the suburbs, a garden running all around and a nice fat garage. 'All those stairs!' she exclaims, as if walking up and down them is too much for an invalid such as myself. When I told her Paul likes to live close enough to central London to cycle to work, Mum muttered, 'A man of his status.' She comes from a world where important people drive, because driving insulates you from her other great fear: people who want to do you harm, which in her view is nearly everyone.

I'm in my garden now with the late-afternoon sun full on me, wondering if my mum understands the world better than I. Suspicion, anger and sadness twist round one another in my heart. The garden hides us from the men out front who made my nine-year-old child cry. Paul and I watch Josh throw a tennis ball to Max and Marcus as we study Josh's movement and attitude for signs of distress. The M&Ms are a welcome distraction and still the only thing that will get Josh off the computer and out into the fresh air. They help us play happy families.

'Do you think he's OK?' Paul asks me, keeping his voice low.

'He won't talk to me. He cried for a long time.'

Paul makes a dissatisfied noise. 'Good throw, Josh! D'you think he understands what's happened?'

'Some of it at least.' I pause. 'Which is more than me.'

Paul pulls at a leaf on the nearest bush and it bends towards us, springing back with an accusatory rustle. 'Apparently he went to meet Melody for a drink. They were seen in the pub together near the woods where she died.'

'Christ! Why didn't he tell anyone?'

Paul starts folding the leaf in his fingers. 'I have no idea.'

'Was he shagging her?'

Paul looks at me warily. 'Lex tried it on with everybody. You know that.'

'That's not what I asked. I asked if he was shagging *her*.'

The ball flies over Paul's head and Max strides over to pick it up. He's budding with youth and energy, not unlike the vivid green leaf Paul's just shredded.

Paul's mobile rings and he drops the remains of the leaf on the grass. 'I don't know, Eggy. I just don't know what to believe any more. Oh Christ, it's Astrid.' He answers as he returns to the house.

I walk down the garden and beyond the trees to the canal. I stare at the empty towpath across the sludgy water, wondering how long it'll take the reporters to work out that there's a back view of our house should they wish for one. Marcus jogs past in his Bermudas, a light sweater clinging to his six-pack.

'Marcus, can I ask you a favour?'

'Course.' He tries to flick the ball up with his bare feet into his hands as Max comes back and stands in front of me, hands on hips.

'There are reporters outside the front of the house,' I tell him.

'Cool!' He casually tosses the ball from hand to hand.

'Well, not really. Paul's business partner has been arrested. It's very serious.'

'How serious?' asks Max, scratching the back of his head.

'They think he might have killed a woman he worked with.' Marcus whistles. 'If you see anyone hanging around on the towpath, can you come and tell me?'

'No worries.' He drops the ball and I pick it up. I turn its squidgy roundness over in my hands, trace the curvy grooves with a finger.

'You sure everything's OK, Mrs F?' asks Max.

'No.' I hurl the ball as high and as hard as I can up the garden and shout, 'Picnic table.' It bounces once on the wooden top and ricochets like a pinball against paving stones and the wall of the house.

'Nice throw!' Marcus is impressed.

'Those reporters better watch out or I'll do that to them, but with something a lot heavier.' Marcus gives me an appreciative long-body glance and I tingle like a teenager, revelling in how great it feels to be even momentarily fancied by someone born in 1988. 'As long as they stay away from my children, then it's OK.'

'I'll keep my eyes peeled,' Marcus says.

'Think of us as the guard dogs in the garden,' Max adds, putting a comforting hand on my knotted-up shoulder.

I come in through the back door to find Paul in the kitchen trying to extricate himself from Astrid's southern-sun embrace. She sees me and her big hair envelops me, bringing on a sneeze as some spiky blonde ends tickle my nostrils. 'Oh, Kate, it's just awful, isn't it? To think I used to travel with him in his car!'

'Well, even I've done that with him.'

'Yeah, but to think that someone you know can be so . . . so . . . different from what you think.'

'Indeed.' Paul rolls his eyes behind Astrid's blonde halo. 'Do you want a drink?'

'Fuck yeah! Do you have rosé?'

'Sorry, no. Only white.'

She sits down at the table and takes the gulp of a sheep shearer after a ten-hour shift. 'You know, when I think about it now, he always had that funny look in his eye.'

'"Funny look"?' Paul raises his head from his iPhone.

Astrid is warming to her theme. 'Yeah. Kind of sinister—'

'Oh please,' scoffs Paul. 'He's being questioned, he hasn't been charged!' Astrid looks blankly from me to Paul.

'The police haven't actually said that he did it,' I explain to Astrid.

'Yeah, but he met her that night and he didn't tell us that in the pub, did he! I mean, I'm just in a state of shock—'

'Astrid, it's very important that you speak to no one about this, do you understand?' Paul is using a finger for extra emphasis. 'With Lex indisposed I am now your boss, none of us know for how long. You are not to speak to the press or your friends about this, is that clear?' She nods. His mobile rings again. 'I've got to take this call,' Paul goes into the living room leaving us alone.

'Have you moved anything on Lex's desk?'

She takes another long gulp of wine. 'Oh God no, I haven't had time. There was a load of things he wanted me to do, but you know I'm so busy at Forwood . . .' Now it's my turn to glug. 'He wanted me to go to her *house*—' she leans forward even though there's no one else in the room and actually looks over her shoulder – 'to get stuff she kept there, but I can't do it. It's kind of . . . creepy—'

'What things?'

'Recordings, paperwork, I guess, he never said exactly what—' Something interrupts Astrid's train of thought. She's staring out of the kitchen window. 'Who's *that*?'

Marcus pokes his head in the back door and holds up the cricket bat and some stumps. 'I'll put these in the shed, shall I? The dew might damage them otherwise.'

'Oh, thanks.' Marcus pauses, blinking like a woodland animal at Astrid. I go through the motions of introductions. 'Um, Marcus, this is Astrid, Astrid, Marcus.'

'You a cricketer?' Astrid asks, her smile on full beam.

'I play with Josh sometimes . . . and with my friend Max— well, not just Max of course, you know, other people too . . .'

Astrid's beam has set on lock. I almost feel sorry for Marcus, shifting awkwardly from foot to foot, unable to look away. He's only twenty-two, Astrid, have a heart.

'My brother used to play for Canberra. He said it was important to keep your bat well oiled.'

Marcus's Adam's apple pogoes like it's 1977 as he backs out of the door. Astrid waves with the tips of her fingers and crosses to the window to watch him retreating down the garden. 'God he's hot!' She turns to me with a scandalised look. 'You're a dark horse, aren't you, Kate!'

I start to protest but realise I can't be bothered. I quite like Astrid thinking it might be even a little bit possible. 'Is he your type then?'

'Fuck yeah! You don't see shoulders like that on many English guys, I can tell you.' She fluffs her bouncy hair as Paul's urgent tones filter through from the living room.

'Listen, if it's a help, why don't I go to Melody's house. It's no bother.'

'He really is A1 puurfect.' She turns back to me, her bum resting on my worktop. 'Oh, don't worry, I said I'd do it.'

'But if you feel uncomfortable . . .' I let the silence stretch. 'I'm sure you're needed at the office, tomorrow will be a very important day.'

'No. It's my job.' She's digging in.

I nod. 'I guess Sergei can deal with the press and the TV companies. They tend to all come together so there'll be quite a crowd.'

'Oh.' Astrid's paying attention now, her ambition tuning

into a golden opportunity. 'Yes, of course, I'm needed at the office. Well, if you really don't mind?'

'It's no problem. Paul can give me the address.' I pick up my wine glass, thinking of Melody's card that I hid behind some books.

At the mention of Paul's name a frown crosses Astrid's forehead. 'Then again, I should really go. I know what Lex has done is *terrible*, but it's important to always be professional. Now that Paul's my boss it's imperative I help out in every way . . .'

She's already moving on, planning how to enhance her career, how Lex's demise can help her. She's as hard-headed as Lex had always claimed. She'll go far. I admire her, she's pure TV – but *I'm* going to Melody's house . . .

'Astrid.' I interrupt her sharply and she looks up startled. 'There's something I need to ask you.' I fold my arms and assume a look like thunder.

Her big blue eyes stare into mine as she twists a lock of her long blonde hair nervously round a finger. Her eyebrows rise in terrified anticipation of what I'm about to say. She's thinking double quick what indiscretion I might have discovered, what I have over her. I wait a long, long moment. 'Do you use Aussie 3-Minute Miracle?'

An hour later I wave Astrid goodbye, after we've hugged tightly on my doorstep. We've shared excessive toe hair, the best colourists, chemical peels, her dreams of daytime TV fame. I'm left in awe of the career mountain she has yet to climb.

'What on earth were you two finding to talk about?' Paul asks, emerging from the bedroom.

'Oh, stuff you wouldn't be interested in.'

Paul shakes his head. 'You've got this knack of being able to talk to anyone. It's a very underrated skill.'

'Yup.' I smile. 'Who was that on the phone?'

'John.'

I see my coat hanging on the banister and remember something, rummaging inside the pocket for the journalist's card. 'He wants you to call him.'

Paul shoves it in his nearest pocket. 'Him and all the rest.' Paul stands on the stairs so that his feet are at the level of my head. He suddenly punches the wall and springs back, staring at his knuckles. 'Ow. Fuck, that really hurts.' He waves his hand in the air and sucks his knuckle, looking very sorry for himself.

'I can almost hear Lex laughing at that.'

Paul sinks back down on the stairs above me. 'I never realised how much I might miss that laugh.' We both sit in silence staring at the front door, as if we're expecting someone to come through it and save us from ourselves. My mobile flashes with an incoming text from Eloide. 'Call me,' she's pleading.

23

'Kate, get in here now! Now!' Paul is yelling at me from the living room. Today is a workday and I've been dressed since seven, harried the kids along since 7.30 a.m. I'm making sure nothing can derail my carefully laid plans to be in on time, on the ball and full of ideas. I've tried to put the reporters in the street and the revelations about Lex to one side as I help Ava into her coat for the walk to school. The darkest thoughts about my own husband I try to shove to my mind's furthest corners.

'Coming,' I mumble, double-checking my handbag for the things I'll need for the long hours ahead. The morning news is on and Lex is standing outside what must be the police station. A crowd is jostling for position as he starts to speak.

'I've been questioned about the murder of Melody Graham, but I stand here this morning an innocent man. You know me as the king of reality TV—'

'God he's not modest even now!'

'Sshh—' says Paul.

'I cannot sit idly by when a woman I knew and respected has died in such a tragic and pointless way. So I'm giving you, the viewers, the chance to keep her murder in the public eye. Today I'm placing half a million pounds in an account at BetFair. You, the viewer, can bet on whether I murdered Melody. If I'm convicted of this crime within the next two years, I will pay out double whatever money you put in. I'll even pay out if I die. If I'm not convicted in the next two years, I'll donate your money to the charity Victim Support, which helps people affected by violent crime.'

Lex is warming to his theme and the crowd listens intently. 'Find me and the terms and conditions on my website lexwoodisinnocent.com and on YouTube.'

'God love him, he's a cocky bastard,' Paul says, shaking his head in wonder and pulling out his phone.

'This must have been very hard for him,' I add. 'He looks really angry.'

'Lex just *feels* popular culture, it's in his blood.'

We watch as Lex continues. 'I want to find Melody Graham's killer. I demand that this be done. I will not rest until this is done.'

I stare at the TV as a crowd swarms around Lex, questions being hurled from all sides. 'This investigation is in chaos, isn't it?' I turn to Paul. 'The police don't really have a suspect, do they?'

As if responding to what I've just said, a reporter, head ducking to move her hair out of her face in the strong wind, begins: 'Detectives in this investigation may well be feeling uncomfortable this morning as Lex Wood, the second suspect in the murder of Melody Graham, has been released without charge. Gerry Bonacorsi spoke to police at length yesterday but is today still a free man. It seems the lack of physical and DNA evidence is hampering attempts to bring this high-profile case to a swift and satisfactory conclusion. As yet' – she's given up all attempts to control her hair and is now standing almost side on to the camera – 'police are no closer to understanding why Melody Graham died, or who killed her.'

'Daddy, I want a huggle,' Ava says, swinging on the living-room door. 'Daddy . . .'

The siren call of his daughter finally pulls Paul away from his phone and he looks down indulgently. 'Of course, baby.'

He picks Ava up by her hands and swings her high into the air where her squeal of delight ricochets off the ceiling. He drops her and catches her round the waist, twists her upside down and tickles her so that he's holding a giggling banshee, squirmy as a bag of snakes. He places her head down on the floor and she folds herself upright.

'Again! Again!'

'I have to go, sweetie.'

She's standing on tippy-toes, rapture bathing her face. 'Please, Dad, again!' Ava's adoration of her father is complete. I make a note to try to remember this moment for ever, because I have no memories of my own father doing that with me.

'If Ava is very good, we'll play sharks when I get home.' He kisses the top of her head and rocks her from side to side, looking up at me. He reluctantly pulls away and heads for the door as Ava hops from one foot to the other in anticipation.

'If Lex calls here, tell him to ring me immediately,' Paul says, leaving the house without kissing me. Our recent arguments have resulted in strange vacuums opening up between us; we creep around each other, shrinking from accidental physical contact. His body and its rumbles and smells are suddenly foreign to me and I can't recall them even if I try. He's started wearing a T-shirt to bed, nakedness seeming inappropriate now. At the end of the day we climb into our king-size and cling to our edges like mariners to flotsam after a shipwreck. It's only in my long, sleepless hours that I find him curled around me, his nose in the gap between my shoulder blades. He's up before I wake in the mornings.

I nod as I pick up my mobile, beeping with an incoming text. I'm expecting it to be Eloide as I've already had three this morning, but it's from Lex. 'You will meet me today. Don't tell Paul.'

Sadness steals over me. Their friendship is cracking, their business partnership could soon follow. Josh thumps down the stairs, his bottom lip a jutting, moody line. I reach out to ruffle his hair because I just can't resist.

'Get off me, Mum,' he shoves my hand roughly away.

It's all change on the chessboard of life and we must take up new positions. If Lex has been released someone else will be arrested soon. Lex wants me to meet him, but there's somewhere I've got to go first – work.

A sharp pain jars up my leg. 'Ow! What did you do that for!'

Josh has just punched me, hard. 'You never listen, do you! I want to walk to school on my own. I don't want to go with you.'

I always knew that, one day, he would ask me this. Another tether holding him to childhood cut. But I hadn't realised how much it would hurt. 'OK, that's something we can talk about with Dad tonight.' I pause. 'Josh, has anyone said anything nasty to you at school about—?'

'Just leave me alone!' he screams.

I guess that's a yes.

24

Rude language is called blue, but red would be a better colour. Livvy is so angry she's turned puce and is ranting at whoever has the misfortune to have to speak. It's our weekly editorial meeting and we're discussing how to respond to Melody's death. None of our suggestions can lighten Black Cloud's mood.

'OK, we're going to divvy up the examination of Melody's life. She was a pretty girl so we want lots of visual on her. Shaheena, get on to her old friends, search Facebook, all that stuff, and get some clips of her we can use.'

'Who's covering the police angle?' Matt, a researcher, dares ask.

'Colin of course!' Colin is the former Scotland Yard detective that gets to cosy up to Marika on the leather sofa when we need technical assistance. 'We'll use Colin's contacts and beg them to release any CCTV footage of Melody that they have. 'Now, what's the update on Melody's family?'

Shaheena has the unenviable task of disappointing the boss. She shakes her head. 'It's a no go, I'm afraid.' Livvy lets out a long sigh. 'Her parents don't want to have anything to do with the programme—'

'Their daughter invented it!'

Shaheena shrugs. 'I've got a cousin who's keen to appear, but she's a bit tangential.'

Livvy is tapping a cheap biro on the side of her desk. Her irritation is fanning out in waves across the room. 'Hopeless.'

There's a pause. 'So . . . on to Lex and Gerry. That the owner of the company producing this programme has been questioned about knocking off the creator of this programme is something I need like a hole in the head . . .' Before Livvy can begin casting around the room for someone else to direct her disappointment at, the door scrapes open. 'Marika!'

An intoxicating smell wafts in with Marika. She's dressed in an outsize Gore-tex jacket with bobbles and toggles in odd places and from which her tiny suntanned wrists and hands protrude. 'Hello everyone! Sorry I'm late, but the boat was stuck in high winds.'

'Thank God you're here!' Livvy lifts herself off her seat, beckoning Marika in with two hands.

'I do apologise, being marooned on the Isle of White is no use to anyone.' She places a waterproof holdall in the corner of the room and sits down. 'It was blowing a force eight and we couldn't leave the harbour. In the end I got a helicopter from Ventnor to Portsmouth, and simply got on the train to get here.' She smiles most winningly. 'No stress.'

'Finally something to cheer!' Black Cloud's face splits into a rare grin. 'We want you to interview Gerry Bonacorsi. They're not charging him so he's fair game. We've got to get him on the programme.'

'I like it,' Marika says calmly.

'Despite the many hours of television coverage of him, he has rarely been interviewed – asked the hard questions. Take him out of his comfort zone, you might get something surprising.'

'Got it,' Marika adds.

'There's a problem,' says Matt.

'I don't want to know about problems!' Livvy snaps.

'He's in hiding after he was questioned by police. No one can get to him.'

'*We'll* get to him. We made him bloody famous, he owes us!'

'Just get on to his agent—' Marika adds kindly.

'Um, he doesn't have an agent,' Matt replies. 'He was living in south London but he's done a bunk.'

'That moronic, pea-brained whacko—'

'Why not try the tabloids?' Marika suggests, unfazed by this setback. 'They're bound to know where he is. I'll phone my editor friend, he'll help us out.'

'Great idea, Marika!' Livvy's clouds have dispersed, momentarily. 'We need to get Gerry on this show. No ifs or buts. I want him found before we go live or I'm going to . . . I don't know what I'm going to do but it won't be pretty.'

'Isn't he dangerous?' asks Shaheena. 'I mean, even if we know where he is, he's a convicted murderer and he resisted arrest when the police took him in. I read a theory that he may be killing people who made him famous on *Inside-Out*. It's a something syndrome, I can't remember the name.' No one helps her out, but Shaheena continues. 'Are we sure we want to approach him, even assuming we can find him?'

'Oh for Pete's sake!' Livvy snorts. 'Talk about carts before horses! Let's find him first and then if we need to we can use extra protection when we do our persuading.'

'I'd love to interview him,' enthuses Marika. 'He's such a contradictory character. On one episode of *Inside-Out* I saw him request *The Female Eunuch* from the prison library! It had to come over from Holloway! We'll talk feminism before we go on air. I wonder if he's read any Betty Friedan?'

Livvy looks alarmed. 'Make sure that doesn't bleed over into the interview. They'll be turning off in droves.'

Marika's laugh is honey on toast. 'Remember it takes a lot of education to look this stupid.' Livvy's laugh is more Marmite on Ryvita, but no less heartfelt.

I risk a smile but it's short-lived as Livvy turns to me, menace in her voice. 'Kate, you're sleeping with the enemy.' All eyes bore into me.

'Excuse me?'

I'd made sure that my relationship to the boss wasn't widely known.

Livvy snorts at my gross stupidity. 'You're our eyes and ears into Forwood. Paul knows Lex better than anyone. Find at least something out we can use.' I nod slowly and feel a blush of shame travelling across my cheeks at all the secrets I'm withholding.

As the meeting ends and we gather up notebooks, pens and laptops I'm surprised by Marika asking me a question. 'So you're married to Paul Forman?'

I nod. She lowers her heavy lashes as delicate eyebrows lift towards her blonde hairline. She nods with appreciation. I steel myself for yet another acolyte about to sing my husband's praises. 'Lucky him,' she says and I want to gather up her pint-sized frame in my motherly arms, she'll be as light and fluffy as candyfloss.

I'm standing in a murdered woman's living room, unsure whether I'm supposed to sit down. Mrs Graham was perfectly polite when I called and said I was from Forwood. She invited me over straight away, as if I were a friend popping in for coffee, but now I'm here awkwardness has taken over. It's not a social call and my lunch hour is not really long enough to do the visit justice.

'I'm glad you came today, I should have mentioned on the phone that Friday wouldn't have been convenient. It's the funeral. They've released the body.'

I sit down. 'I'm so sorry.' Mrs Graham has pale skin and neat, ash-grey hair and is wearing mid-height stilettos and a red skirt suit. She doesn't react to my condolences, staring at me in silence with large, dark eyes. She's a bit unnerving. I'll start to blabber if I'm not careful. 'I brought you – or maybe this is more for your husband – something small.' I

163

reach out from the armchair and hand over a small package. 'It's a new variety.'

'Roses.' She smiles a little and shakes the packet so that the seeds knock against the paper binding. 'How did you know?'

'I only met Melody once, at a party at the Forwood offices. It was when she was putting the finishing touches to the format for *Crime Time*. We had a brief chat and I remember she said, "I'm as precious about my programme as my dad is about his roses."'

Mrs Graham's smile widens. 'It's very sweet of you to remember, and to bring them.'

'I chose the red because, well, because that's the colour of the dress she was wearing that night.'

When people ask me, I say I don't know Melody, and technically that's true. But the exposure to her that I've lacked I've made up for in my imagination. I was introduced to her by Sergei. 'You must meet Melody Graham,' he said. Paul had mentioned her often enough and I was intrigued. She smiled and giggled a lot and insisted on refilling my glass. Astrid touched her shoulder as she passed on the way to the kitchen. She seemed celebratory and social, unaware of how good the programme that she created was going to be, blind to how alluring she was. I was mesmerised as others were, by her age, her charm, her talent and the opportunities she was yet to take.

Mrs Graham nods. 'Red was her favourite colour.' She touches her skirt. 'We were very alike, Melody and me.' She pauses. 'It's a shame Don's not here. He's on his walk. He needs a routine.'

'I want to say that her work is very highly regarded. She was full of ideas.'

Mrs Graham folds her hands in her lap and tucks her legs together like the Queen. 'That was Melody. She was focused. All the cycling, the exercise gene, is Don's.'

On the wall beside my armchair is a succession of photos charting the Graham family's formation, evolution and growth; happy times before the catastrophe. There are the black-and-white christening pictures, chaotic family gatherings, some 1980s hairdos and school photos against a blue backdrop with clouds. 'Is that Melody?' I point at an unsmiling girl in school uniform who's about fifteen.

Mrs Graham shifts in her seat. 'Yes. It's only up there because she liked it so much. She made a big fuss about not wanting to smile. "Pandering to the male gaze," I think she said.' She gives me a look. 'She was always very opinionated. Don gave in of course, but truth be told I've never liked that picture. She looks sullen, which she was nothing like.' Mrs Graham stands. Her voice softens for the first time. 'That's my favourite.' She points to a photo of a young girl, probably aged about eleven, in shorts and a baggy T-shirt, running through shallow water. The picture is all about movement and joy, the girl is really sprinting with the energy of uncomplicated youth, a time before she got her own opinions and started to act on them.

'She's a very beautiful girl.'

'You can use the past tense. We're going to have to get used to it.' She wipes her hands down her skirt and I sense a great effort being made to stop it all toppling over. 'I'm not sure if you haven't had a wasted journey coming here, the police took everything related to her work away with them. There's very little left.'

I follow her up to the stairs, wondering if Mrs Graham's shocking matter-of-factness is the corset which stops her, literally, from falling apart. She takes the steps two at a time, as silent as a cat. 'I identified the body. I knew Don couldn't do it, but now they won't let me alone.'

'Who won't?'

'My family. It's as if I've developed dementia overnight and I need round-the-clock care. My sister's behind it all,'

she mimics a hysterical woman, '"She needs *help*, Don, *help*."'
I don't even like my sister, but now I have to endure daily
visits from her or her ghastly children. Her daughter's coming
round soon, though 'company' is stretching the word. I spent
my life trying to get away from my first family and build one
more suited to me . . . perhaps you don't understand that.'

'I understand only too well, I'm afraid.'

'Now they're crowding around and all my years of effort
have come to nothing.'

'That's one of the saddest things I've ever heard.' It's out
of my mouth before I can stop it and I can't judge if it's
inappropriate. Mrs Graham's hit a nerve. I put years of effort
into building my new family and I fear mine is about to crash
and burn.

'Here we are.' She opens the door to one of the bedrooms
without a pause and we are in Melody's most private space.
The walls are apple green and frame shelves filled with clothes,
books, DVDs and files, a large 1970s desk with a black inlay
top looks over the garden, a computer cable lays marooned;
I guess the police took her laptop away. A neon retro British
Rail sign hangs on one wall, and there's a Moroccan looking
pouffe. The bed is a small double. I can't look at it for long.

'She was very tidy—' I start, but Mrs Graham interrupts.

'Melody? Entirely the opposite,' she says, shaking her head.
'She had box files and loads of notebooks piled around all
over the place. The police could hardly get it all in the car.
Once they'd gone I sorted her room out for her, one last
time. It's what a mother does. This is all that they left behind.'
She picks up a Milk Blue file and hands it to me. 'You could
call at the station and maybe they'd give you back what they've
finished with.' I open the file and find some old expenses
receipts. My heart sinks and it's hard to summon up even a
thank-you. 'Don can't come in here. He starts to hyperven-
tilate, poor man, but I like it. It smells of her.'

'Do you have any idea who killed your daughter?' Mrs Graham gives no indication that she'd even heard the question.

'Do you want to see some of Don's beloved roses? The early varieties are just beginning to bloom.'

We head back downstairs and walk through a dining room that looks little used to some French doors that lead to the garden. Piles of neat paperwork and household bills are lain out across the table; the *Guardian* is beginning to form a tower on a sideboard. I notice a bulky, old-fashioned PC has taken up permanent residence at the head of the table. 'Did Melody ever use that computer?'

'Yes, she did. Lately she was using it a lot. She liked to have the cat on her lap when she worked, I think, and he likes it down here.'

'Did the police look at this machine?'

'They copied everything off it.'

A thought strikes me. 'So they copied the information rather than transferred it?'

Mrs Graham shrugs. 'I can't really say. Don would know.'

'Mrs Graham, do you mind if I take a look at some of the files on here? I'm sure it won't take long.' I'm steeling myself for her refusal or suspicion, but she seems only too happy to help.

'Not at all. Would you like a cup of tea while you do it?'

'That would be fantastic. Milk, two sugars, please.'

Melody really was a hoarder, because her folder on the family computer has hundreds of files stored within it, but they're not named, just a series of dry numbers, as if they've been transferred en masse from somewhere else. I slip a memory stick into the hard drive and copy everything. A few moments later, I'm informed that fifteen hundred files have been transferred. I hear Mrs Graham clinking cups in the kitchen and I rest my head on the table edge. This mission is hopeless; I'm never going to have the time to trawl through all of this; the police will have a team of computer experts with cancelled weekend leave racing ahead of me. The sun appears and its beams of happy yellow illuminate the thin layer of dust on the French polish of the table. I watch the dust motes dancing with an energy I don't feel as my eyes come to rest on something under the computer. Instinctively I pull at it with my fingernail and a CD-Rom appears. *Inside-Out* and some dates are crossed out on the label and 'Neat Feet!' is scrawled underneath.

Mrs Graham appears, holding two cups. 'I just found this under the computer, it's Melody's. Looks like it worked its way under and got lost.'

Mrs Graham comes towards me and reads the label. Her mouth turns down at the corners. 'You take it. I didn't much care for that programme.'

I slip the disk into the Forwood file containing the dull expenses and put it in my bag with the memory stick. 'Can I see the roses now?'

We walk out into sunshine and cross the lawn. 'She put up a struggle, you know, even when the rope was round her neck—'

'I'm so sorry—'

'But she fought. She gets that off me, I'm a fighter. She always wanted to get her own way. She wasn't popular.' I make a noise of protest but she cuts me off. 'Parents always talk about their children like they're perfect, but Melody was far from that. But she was never ignored, never.'

'Did she talk much about her job at Forwood?'

'Oh all the time! She talked as if it were one big family, you know.'

I take a sip of tea. 'We all know how strife-ridden families can be. The harmony's often a myth.'

Mrs Graham frowns. 'Well. Maybe. She liked it very much

at the beginning. Towards the end she went quiet on that a bit.'

'Oh?'

'Maybe things were getting on top of her. It's hard to say.'

'What things?'

Mrs Graham looks at her tea. 'Nothing I can put a finger on. Every look and gesture is overinterpreted once something like this happens.'

I pause, but nothing more is forthcoming. 'I'm a researcher on the crime programme she invented. We have very high hopes for it. We're dedicating the next programme to your daughter.' Mrs Graham sighs as if she's disappointed. We pause by a flower bed and I change the subject. 'I didn't know roses bloomed so early in the year.'

'It's someone she didn't know.'

'Pardon?'

'She was killed by someone she didn't know.'

'You seem very sure.'

'It's the only explanation I can accept.' The doorbell chimes faintly and she gives a small groan. 'That's my niece, most likely, doing her guard shift. She watches too much rubbish on daytime TV.'

'Why do you think it's someone she doesn't know?'

She pauses. 'Don does research on cancer cells. Melody wasn't exactly discovering a cure for Alzheimer's. She was very bright, she could have trained as a doctor or a lawyer. Done things to really help people. I didn't like the programmes Melody wanted to make, I didn't share her dreams. She was putting her efforts into a job that was . . . superficial, silly even.' She pauses. 'It's a stranger, someone mad.' Her voice turns hard and betrays the emotions she's trying so hard to control. 'I refuse to believe she died for *Inside-Out* or some reality-TV variant. She didn't, she *couldn't*. It's dark enough already.'

'But what about other parts of her life, boyfriends—'

'She didn't have any. She worked. That's all she did.'

'As far as you know.'

'The police kept banging on about this, as if we were all stuck in some ghastly Fifties play. I grew up in the Fifties, we really did have secrets then. She lived at home because she liked it. She was saving to buy a flat because she didn't want to waste money on rent. She talked openly to us about drugs and sex and what have you. We're all unshockable now. What secrets are left?'

I feel admiration for Mrs Graham, for her certainties, but she's wrong. There are so many secrets. I doubt she'd be happy about her daughter seeing a married man, for instance, but I don't push it. The newly bereaved attain a special position with their peers: respected and feared. The doorbell chimes again, louder this time. I'm out of time. 'Do you want me to get the door on my way out?'

'Would you?'

'Of course.'

On the doorstep I pass a big woman with a tan and tight, high-heeled boots. We shake hands and she says she's Melody's cousin.

'She OK?' she whispers, peering into the house.

'I'm not sure I can say.'

'My mum says she's never cried yet. Not once.' A streak of mascara pulses down her cheek. 'It's not normal, is it?' She wipes a manicured finger carefully along her lower lid and examines it for black traces. 'I mean, how can I cry for Melody if she's not weeping for her own daughter?'

'There's no hierarchy on grief.'

'There bloody is in this family,' she adds, sniffing.

I hand her my pack of tissues and walk away towards the Tube. As I turn the corner I check my phone and see I've missed some calls and have a message from Livvy. 'Where R U?' I break into a run. I need to get back to the office.

25

By the time I get back Livvy has forgotten why she even phoned me. She waves me away with an angry swish of her ponytail as she grabs a phone. The rest of the day passes in a flash and as darkness falls people begin to snap shut laptops and shuffle bags and coats. I prepare to leave and start tidying, wiping the grooves of my keyboard with a tissue. Shaheena passes on her way out. 'The cleaners do that, you know.' I nod, embarrassed. Old habits die hard. I'm the last to leave, my guilt at my long lunch break chaining me to my desk for longer than is necessary. I flick the lights off when I get to the door and plunge the corridor into blackness. I hurry blindly forward in the unfamiliar space, a jittery panic making unreasonable inroads into my skull. This building gives me the creeps. I'm relieved when I get outside into the driving rain, which is being thrown up on to the pavements by the rumbling juggernauts. I bend towards home but after a couple of steps I have to turn round. The street looks empty, but a little further on I do it again. Someone is watching me, I can feel it.

I quicken my pace and turn suddenly in the street, weight on my front foot, bag banging my leg. I'd rather confront my fears than suffer any more creeping unease. I pause, uncertain, the rain intensifying the shadows and grimy corners. A dark figure peels itself off a wall and heads my way . . .

'You're always so ready for a fight, little one.' It's Lex. 'We need to talk.'

'Have you spoken to Paul?' We hurry side by side down the pavement.

Lex laughs. 'Who, my partner?' He says this with a sarcastic flourish as the rain pelts down harder. 'My car's round the corner. Come on, Kate, let's get out of the wet.'

'I need to get home.' What I mean is, I'm desperate to get home, as soon as I'd left the building my heart and head had turned back to my children, my need to reconnect with them after a long shift.

'I'll take you. You must be tired after being in there all day.' He turns into a side street and beeps open the passenger door of his dark-coloured car. I note the colour match to the vehicle the police are looking for. 'Come on.' Something about his manner makes me reluctant. He's not a big man but he's wiry and strong . . . I shake the thoughts away with the splats of rain. I'm being melodramatic and ridiculous. I've known this guy for more than ten years, I'm his best friend's wife. It's no surprise, considering what's happened, that he wants to talk.

He slams the car into gear and screeches away as I reach for the seat belt. 'I thought about coming in to see your new offices.'

'"New" is stretching the term.'

'Who'd have thought it, you working for me, Kate. But then I thought, if I walk in there, a potential murderer, I might scare the cavalry – I might make Livvy bolt. But I don't scare you, do I, Kate?' I gasp as he swings left straight on to the main road without so much as looking right. 'And we both know why, don't we?'

I watch the speedometer move round its dial. 'How's your website campaign?'

'Oh, you shouldn't waste your money, Kate, by taking a bet; after all, you know I didn't do it.'

Lex drives right through a junction and we're chased down

the road by the sound of angry horns. I try to remain calm. 'But how do I know, Lex? Turns out you met her that night, something you forgot to mention before. Why did you do that?'

'She asked to meet me. Said she wanted to talk over a contract. How was I to know she'd be killed later that night?'

'Why didn't you tell the police this right at the beginning? It looks far more suspicious that you held it back.'

Lex snorts. 'Think you're a crime expert now, do you? There's no physical evidence linking me to her—'

'So you're in the clear.' Lex turns the wheel and swerves across two lanes of traffic, heading for a gap in the railing separating the oncoming cars. Or trucks, as I see one slamming on its brakes uselessly in the rain-soaked road. Lex makes the U-bend and we miss each other by inches. I realise the sound coming from my own mouth is a scream. 'You're going to get us killed! Stop it now!'

Lex is speeding away from my house, taking us north-west out of London. 'I'll stop when I'm ready to stop.'

'Why are you doing this?' My legs are rigid against the front of the seat well, bracing myself for the inevitable impact.

'Now we're getting somewhere! Why? What's my motive for being really really, pissed? Let's talk about motives, Kate. Why do people kill? Passion, or money. Someone set me up, Kate. Someone knew I was meeting her that night, they knew it might be pinned on me. They wanted to fuck me.'

'But the police haven't charged you so it didn't work!'

'Yet! We know that innocent people are charged all the time. And the motive here is not jealousy or revenge or namby-pamby love, it's money. Let's follow the money, Kate. I'm a director at a company that's being bought in instalments, the first tranche two years ago, a little bit last year, and the big prize, the last instalment, the date of which is coming up in a matter of weeks. The final instalment is when we get some *real* cash, isn't it, Kate? It's when CPTV opens the chequebook and pays us off. But if I'm charged with killing someone my conduct is deemed to be unfit for the office I hold and I can be cut out. Just like that.' He lifts his hands off the steering wheel and clicks his fingers as the car veers dangerously towards the barrier. 'I'm classed as a bad leaver.'

'A what?'

'I'm defined as a bad leaver and my share of Forwood is no longer mine!' Lex comes up close behind a car with three people sitting on the back seat. He's punching the horn and I see the pale ovals of their faces turning through the rain to peer. 'Twenty fucking years I've worked, twenty years I've gobbed off – and it pans out like this!'

'It's red! Red light, Lex!' The car in front has changed lanes and we're racing towards a busy four-way junction. 'Slow down!'

Lex slams on the brakes and we skid down our lane so sharply I'm flung forward, hard against my seat belt. 'Know what happens to my forty-five-per-cent share of Forwood?' He's leaning in towards me as the smell of burning tyres wafts through the car. 'It's divided among the other stock-holders.' We stare at each other in silence. The lights change and a volley of horns boom out behind us as Lex doesn't move. 'Why don't you tell me who they are?' Someone shouts an obscenity out of their window. 'You not in the mood for a chat? Let me enlighten you. Paul—'

'Oh come on!'

'And you and John.' Lex lets out a low, cruel laugh. 'You think I sound ridiculous? I'll show you ridiculous! You stand to make a stack you never worked for, eh? Unlike me!' His anger ignites again and he screeches away from the junction. 'And then today I get a letter from your brother-in-law reminding me of my bad-leaver clauses, just to rub my nose a little deeper in the shit!'

He's going to kill us both if I don't get this under control. 'You're not being rational, Lex! The police were always going to question you, like they questioned me.'

'Why did you break into my office, Kate? Which bit of the tale spun by your loving partner didn't you believe?' The car goes over a rise and plunges into an underpass. 'Or maybe, maybe, you weren't breaking in to find something, Kate! Maybe you broke in to leave something behind. Maybe you and him – and that bloody brother, for all I know – are all in it together.'

'I don't have the answer, Lex, there are things that don't make sense. But I'm trying to find out the truth, and I'm not doing it by burning up the A40 and nearly killing myself! I have as much to lose as you,' I hear him swear but I press on, 'In fact I have a *lot* more to lose than you.' It's my turn to be angry now. 'You stand to lose some cash, I stand to lose . . . everything!' I tail off, my voice breaking. I turn to look at him defiantly. 'You know something, Lex? I never give up. With the stakes as high as they are, I'm going to find out the answer, whatever that takes. What I do with the information once I find it is another matter, but I *will* find it.'

I'm not helping. Lex pushes harder on the accelerator, a smile playing on his lips. 'Such a grand speech, such noble intentions! You're a little bloodhound, aren't you?' I grow rigid in the ergonomic bucket seat. We fly past a sign indicating that the three lanes are narrowing to two. 'Sniffing the trail, running after the thrown sticks. It's a good name for a TV show, *Bloodhound*. The hit new detective series.'

'Lex, Lex!' Our lane is beginning to narrow, I don't give a fuck about his media imagination now.

He ignores me, carrying on as if in a dream. 'Bloodhound, the woman who can smell deceit . . . who doggedly—'

I'm not listening but staring at traffic cones and impatient Slow Down messages. 'Lex! For God's sake stop!' He's run out of road and a van is stopping him moving over. I hear him swear softly until a terrible metal tearing rips through his side of the car and we spin down the dual carriageway, ricocheting off the barrier of the central reservation and spinning across the hard shoulder on to a bank and back again across the road and with each crunch I feel an overwhelming desire to smell my children for the last time because at the moment of reckoning I don't believe in anything except my love for them, and with each juddering smack my pain at not seeing them again multiplies. Lex is shouting over the squealing of brakes and there are more horns and then as suddenly as it started we career to a stop on a grassy bank, our rear end sticking out into the hard shoulder.

I sit very still, feeling each thankful beat of my heart, taking each breath as if it's my first. I manage to turn and see car headlights at confused angles and dark shadows running towards us. I understand with a surge of relief that at least we haven't hit another vehicle. Something warm drips down my temple.

'Bloodhound. That's what I'm going to call you from now on, Kate. An idea for just the two of us.' He laughs sarcastically. 'It'll be our little secret. I won't tell anyone, I promise. I do hope you live up to the name.'

He's still on TV programmes and my anger explodes. 'You mad fucker!' I spit.

'You've cut yourself.' He digs in his pocket for something, his eyes never leaving my face.

'No *you've* cut me! You've lost your mind!'

'What were you looking for in my office, Kate? Come on, Uncle Lex needs to know!'

'What was I looking for!' I'm screaming now. 'You just don't get it, do you! You, with your one-track mind – fortune this, status that, money this. It's bullshit! There are a thousand motives you can't even imagine. And yes, that's what I was looking for, a reason so powerful it's worth killing a young woman for. Control. There's a motive! Or how about shame? Oh, but you've never felt that, have you! Jesus, for all I know you killed her because you finally stopped fucking and – horror of horrors – started to trust her and fell in love. And then you tried to kill me!' I reach over and slap Lex hard across the face as my door is yanked open by some people I can't focus on and there are screams and intrusive hands on my body.

'She's in shock!' someone shouts.

'No I'm not.'

Lex pulls out a tissue and holds it on my cut. 'You need to come clean, Kate, I'm swinging in the wind here! You're covering for him and I'm going to find out why.'

'Get them away from the car! It might explode!' A voice is carried over on the wind.

I almost fall out of the door and walk unsteadily up the bank as Lex stands and leans on the roof of his banged-up top-of-the-range motor. I want to pulverise something with my bare hands but instead start to run away.

'Help the poor woman!' a man shouts. I'm almost over the rise when I remember I've left my bag – and the information from Melody's house – in the car. I turn to find Lex chasing me up the hill, my bag in his hand.

'Give that to me.'

Lex gives me a triumphant look. 'Maybe I should keep it till you tell me what I want to know.' He's panting with the adrenalin of having survived the smash, just like I am.

I hold out my hand. 'Give. That. To. Me.'

'Come on, Bloodhound, what clue are you going to give me for this?' We're circling each other on the bank, panting and silent. I'm in too much shock to even speak.

A man runs up and puts his hand on Lex's arm. 'You must wait for the ambulance!' Several more people are closing in and our battle of wills is interrupted.

'You need to learn an important lesson in life, Kate.' He holds the bag high, Melody's pale blue Forwood file unseen just inches from his eyeline. 'Never come between a man and the millions he stands to make.' He throws the bag at my feet and turns back to face the music.

26

I once grew germs in a school science class. I scraped them out from beneath my fingernails and watched them multiply in a Petri dish. I was told by whiskery Miss Dobbs that their number doubled every hour. These little buggers were quick off the mark. I peer into my bathroom mirror, gingerly tracing the wound across the ballooning skin of my temple.

Paul's face is reflected in the mirror. 'For the last time Kate, you need to go to hospital. Something could be ruptured inside. I can't believe you walked all that way home and didn't wait for the paramedics—' I try to ignore him, try to make space to think about Lex's rants. I have been stupid, focused as I was on Paul's dick and where he might have put it, when other possibilities now multiply in my mind as vigorously as those microorganisms on my skin. And there is no antiseptic to stop these ideas, no possibility too outlandish that I don't consider it. 'See, I think you've got concussion, you're not listening.' I look at my husband, lit by the halogen spots in our bathroom ceiling. 'You need to phone the police and report this.' I shake my head. 'He as good as kidnapped you and tried to kill you!'

'No he didn't.'

'This behaviour is central to the case—' I close my eyes to block it all out and when I open them Paul pulls me down on to the edge of the bath. 'Oh come here. Thank God you're OK.' He starts to massage my shoulders and even after all the years that have passed, the present suspicions and our recent distance, I thrill to his touch as he kneads away my tensions and trapped adrenalin. He blows on my cut as tears channel down my cheeks.

'I'll frighten the kids.'

'Sshh.' He kisses the top of my head. 'They won't even notice.'

We rock side to side on the hard ceramic and it reminds me of Josh's birth nine years ago. A hideous travesty of what I'd read in magazines and dutifully noted in antenatal classes, the day after I wobbled to a bathroom festooned with safety handles for half-dead women to cling to. Paul had to partly carry me there and under the yellow glare of the strip lights and saturated with unfamiliar post-birth hormones I sat one bum cheek on the bath edge and wept that I couldn't look after a baby, I was a fraud. Paul rocked me then, too. 'I'm so proud of you, Eggy,' he soothed, running his palm up and down my spine, the only part of me that wasn't aching. 'You'll be a brilliant mother.' After a while he stopped rubbing and peered at my bloodied clothing. 'These gowns are weird,' he'd said, pulling at my open-at-the-back institutional robe, 'your arse is on show to the world. Look! It's even got bows.' I scolded him for making me laugh when I was so sore. 'Bloody hell, when can we do it again?' he'd whispered. I spent most of my time in the shower with its bumpy floor trying to bat him off. I took the luxury of fast-forwarding forty years and saw the two of us, stooped and doddery in upscale residential care where Stannah stairlifts and non-slip surfaces are de rigeur, and imagined him washing me then. The world was romantic enough then for me to see it as an odds-on certainty.

'If he comes here don't let him in the house. I want you to call the police.'

'He thinks he's been set up.'

Our slow rocking stops. 'By who?'

'There seem to be lots of candidates. You, mainly.'

Paul swears softly. 'Bloody Lex! He always did have an overactive imagination. He won't talk to me on the phone.' He glances at his watch. 'He's avoiding me and everyone else at the office. I don't know why.'

'Livvy wants to put him and Gerry on the next *Crime Time* show. We still haven't found Gerry, no one has any idea where he's gone, Livvy thinks the programme lacks drama without him.'

Paul makes a dissatisfied noise. 'He's only just got out of jail, there must be a clue in those programmes as to where he's gone. It's hardly like he's got a lot of friends, is it?' Paul stands. 'If Lex isn't careful he'll be as friendless as Gerry.'

I drag a hand across my tired face. 'He's just very angry.'

'So am I!'

'Never judge a man till you've walked a mile in his shoes,' I counter.

'Oh! So you're trying to understand now! And this from the woman who finds it so hard to forgive! Well, I'm not forgiving him.'

Lex's bad-leaver comment rings in my head. Look hard enough and you'll find a thousand motives. We cling to outlandish scenarios because they're so much more comforting than believing those close to us are capable of the greatest atrocities. But I also know from experience that ninety per cent of the time, the most obvious motive is the real one.

Josh cries out in his sleep and I hurry in to comfort and console.

27

Two days after his dad died Paul went back to work. I stood barring the front door, pleading with him to take more time. 'Work is the only way I'll get through it,' he'd said. 'It keeps me sane.' This morning our roles are reversed. Paul's insisting he can take the children to school, that I don't have to go out 'looking like that'. He half points at my head as if something weird has grown out of it in the night, which in a way is what's happened. Josh looked at me over the breakfast table, Rice Krispies clustered at the corner of his mouth like flies on cattle, and said, 'Eugh.'

'I'm well enough to work, I just look a bit weird, that's all.' I crack a smile, keeping silent at the pain it causes me to do even that.

Paul goes to the living-room window and pulls back the curtain. 'The press will think I did it to you, knowing our luck.'

'Are they out there now?'

'No. It seems we're not important enough to stand in the cold all night for.'

I wave Paul and the kids off and make to gather my things for work, but that's not where I'm going. I've got a hunch and I need to pursue it alone. Last night I didn't sleep. I lay awake staring at a crack in the ceiling, processing every detail I could remember about Gerry. An hour after Paul fell asleep I came downstairs and examined our collection of *Inside-Out* DVDs, lined up neatly on the shelves behind the television.

I watched bits of episodes and fast-forwarded through large chunks. Passively watching was a way to stop thinking about Lex and his motives, his fears and his anger. Three hours after I started, a short conversation – one line really – between Gerry and a prison warder on disk seventeen made me pause, and several minutes later I moved from the TV to the internet, the seed of an idea forming. Two hours after that I was stealthily rooting through a cupboard in Josh's bedroom for binoculars. I had the makings of a plan; foolish and irrational maybe, but a plan nonetheless. Lex's confrontation has worked like a call to action – I'll show him how much of a bloodhound I can be.

Now I'm being jostled by thousands of horse-racing fans, having just paid a tout with a missing front tooth an extraordinarily inflated price for an all-areas ticket to the Cheltenham Festival. Gerry liked a flutter on the horses, I heard him say it once on *Inside-Out*. He loved the swell of the crowd, the swearing and the shouting, the joy and pain all rolled up in those few intense moments as the horses are driven to the finish line; and so I wondered last night whether Gerry would be able to resist the Cheltenham Festival after all that time. Because I also saw from those hours of watching that he took quiet pleasure in the small prison kindnesses that were available: a new book in the library; a cooking class. He wasn't an attention seeker, and what better way to protect your anonymity than being part of a throng of thousands.

But as I'm bumped this way and that, I'm realising that even if my hunch was right, proving it is going to be almost impossible. The tannoy provides a ceaseless and incomprehensible backdrop of noise as the runners and riders are announced for each race. I'm using sunglasses to cover my battered face and I push through the swaying multitudes to try to get my bearings, map in hand. For two hours I walk all round the main stand, scanning faces in a random way, and get elbowed in the hospitality tents with increasing frequency. Lakes of booze are being consumed at a gallop by the punters, the noise of their conversations and laughter gets louder and coarser with each passing hour. I struggle to the champagne bar in the main stand as it's high up, and stand by the window, looking down at the huge crowd. At least from here I have some space to search. I remove the sunglasses and take the binoculars from my bag. Faces jump into sharp focus, their eyes narrowed against the gusty wind. From this vantage point I can see almost the whole race-course but there are so many people, so many thousands of faces and postures, and I'm looking for just one. I don't know what Gerry's wearing or whether he's changed his appearance. After ten minutes I sit down, the impossibility of finding just one person, even if they are here, finally confirmed.

I check the Tote queues, the stands, the swarm around the betting posts, the crowd lining the course, the finish line. I know it's time to admit defeat but the truth is, after a second sleepless night this week, I'm too tired to move. Gerry won't have much money, where would he be? A roar goes up behind me as three horses gallop towards the finish post. I scan this bar, just in case. Nothing. I return to searching with my binoculars; there's a melee around the finish line as hands wave and fists are punched skywards. That's where the action is, that's where the crowd is most intense. I see a woman snuggled into a man's shoulder, a guy in a hat craning to see, a jumping woman with a rolled-up piece of paper raised above her head, and a small man in aviator sunglasses, right by the course fence, standing quite still. The stillness gives him away. He stood like that in the dinner line, for cell inspection, sat like that before the Parole Board. The glasses disguise him a bit, but it's Gerry.

I'm down the stairs double quick, pressing through a crowd

of office workers bent on quenching their thirst. 'Keep your hair on,' mutters one as I barge past.

Once out of the main stand my progress slows as I try to dodge red-faced beer drinkers and an army of people who seem hell-bent on crowding around just me. It's taking so long, too long, to get to the finish line. I think of Lex and his comments from yesterday, 'Bloodhound, running after the thrown sticks.' Will Gerry give me anything? There's only one way to find out.

'Watch it!' I've made a woman slosh beer over her friend and I retreat from their scowls. The crowd is so thick I can't see more than a couple of people in front of me and I'm not tall enough to see over heads. I'm five rows back from the fence, the red-and-white disc of the winning post visible a short distance away. It's impossible to move further forward, so I try to edge sideways, craning to see Gerry's car coat. The crowd starts swaying, murmuring and craning left. I'm pushed torwards the front in a surge as the pounding of hooves fills the air. A man bellows the name of a horse over and over in my ear, shrieks of 'Come on!' ring out. As the horses rush past my feet leave the ground as we press forward to see. As the crowd lets out a collective exhale I lose my footing and fall to the muddy grass, my sunglasses crunched under a wellington.

Two men lift me skywards by my elbows and inquire as to my well-being before I retreat into a bit more space. I trample the confetti of discarded betting slips, cursing. Gerry could have left this spot as much as ten minutes ago.

I jostle and contort my way to where the horses join the winners' enclosure, and then, between two men who are cheering and hugging at their impressive winning bet, I spot Gerry's coat.

I put my hand on his shoulder and say his name and he wheels round in a second. He's shorter than me and I see my face reflected in his sunglasses. I've got splashes of mud on my cheek. 'Gerry, it's Kate Forman, we met a few times on—'

'I know who you are.'

I wipe my face with my sleeve. 'Excuse me, I fell over back there. It's quite intense, isn't it?'

'When you've been where I've been, you love a crowd and hate it all at the same time.'

I smile and nod. 'Can I buy you a drink, some food?'

Gerry shrugs. 'I'm not going to turn down the offer of a drink now, am I? You know what they say, a drink can sometimes change your fortunes.'

We walk towards a beer tent. I keep him talking while I buy a round. 'Are you up or down on the day?'

'Down. If I don't win soon I'll be hitching home.' He turns to me, his face unreadable behind the big glasses. 'How'd you find me?'

'I remember you said on *Inside-Out* that you liked horse racing.' His face is impossible to read so I stumble on, handing him a pint of beer. 'I'm working on a show called *Crime Time* and we're doing a special piece on Melody Graham. We'd very much like you to come on and be interviewed by Marika Cochran—'

Gerry swears loudly, making me jump. His change in tone from friendly and charming to cold and angry is achieved in an instant. 'I don't know who that is and I don't much care. I just want to be left alone.'

'It would just be this once, because of this unprecedented situation. You did know Melody, after all, and there is such a lot of interest in you and in recent events. You may have useful insights.'

'I've got nothing of any use to anyone. Most people have already made up their mind that I did it. Ain't nothing I can do about that.' He puts his glass down on a beer mat, taking care not to spill any liquid. He was obsessively tidy in prison, I recall.

'You've left your temporary accommodation.'

'There's no law against that. It doesn't break the terms of my parole.'

'Where will you be staying tonight?'

'I can't rightly say.' He laughs cruelly. 'Your house?'

He can see that I don't like that. 'I know that you don't have to do the interview, like you didn't have to do *Crime Time*. You could have stopped at any time, but you didn't. Something in you responded to the cameras and I know you know it. You were great on TV.'

He scowls. 'I'm a media plaything.' He stretches his arms out ironically, mimicking Christ on the Cross. 'Are you not entertained?' he shouts.

'This isn't entertainment. This is serving the purpose of doing something to try and discover who murdered a young woman. We can do the interview at any place you choose. What's your mobile number?'

'I don't have one. They make no sense to me.'

'I'll buy you one today, show you how it works.' I realise how bewildering the world must seem to Gerry, isolated from it in 1980 and thrust back into it in 2010. 'I'll go in to town now and come back. Where will you be?'

He shrugs. 'I'll be here, and there, most likely.'

'Come on, Gerry, throw me a lifeline, I'm begging you.' Gerry smiles and I feel uneasy. I don't like the look of that smile and I wonder whether that's what his wife used to say to him all those years ago, said to him right at the end of her life. I change the subject. 'Fame can convict you but it can also protect you. It gives you an opportunity to put your side of the story. This is your chance to show you didn't kill her.'

Gerry takes off his sunglasses. Those Irish eyes are

smiling now, his mood switching between charm and anger in an instant. He raises the pint in a toast to me, turns and incorporates the swaying, sweating rabble in his gesture, winners and losers both. 'How much would you bet on that?'

28

The rest of the afternoon was a series of tests of Gerry's predictability. I gave him twenty pounds for some more bets and arranged to meet him right where I left him in an hour. I bought a Pay As You Go mobile in Cheltenham and stacked it with credit, programmed in my work number, Livvy's and *Crime Time*'s, before returning to the beer tent. A cheer of delight greets me as I enter the tent: Gerry is entertaining a section of the crowd with card tricks. He's very, very good, his Irish patter keeping pace perfectly with his sleights of hand. A hat is on the floor in front of him, the coins building into a little pyramid.

'Here's a young lady who looks lucky today, to be sure.' He does something tricksy with a pack of cards near my face. 'Pick a card—' He doesn't finish the sentence but looks over my shoulder and quickly picks up the hat – security are approaching across the tent. 'Time to go.'

We weave away together, his hat a clanking bag in his hand.

'People have got to spend money here, not earn it, I guess.'

'So true,' Gerry replies. He doesn't seem too concerned that his earnings have come to a halt. 'I've got enough for a forty-five-to-one bet on the three-fifteen. Crystal Clear, she's called. She'll bring me luck, to be sure.'

'Please come on the show,' I say, handing him the mobile. He doesn't reply. I leave him twisting a ring round his finger and I find myself imagining how he came by it.

On the train back to London I phone Livvy to tell her my

coup. She brings me back down to earth. 'Let's see if he shows up. You should have done the interview then and there! I should have got Matt to do it,' she muttered. 'I want you down in Woolwich now.'

'Woolwich?'

'Friend of Melody's called in. She's got some old video footage of Melody playing a magician on stage. It could be useful.'

'Can't we send a bike for it?'

'No can do. She'll only hand it over personally, and that person is you.' I suppress a groan. Woolwich is miles away, the wrong side of London from where I'm travelling into, a long way from my house. It sounds like a low-priority piece of background colour. My painful eye throbs in silent protest. 'No one ever said TV work was glamorous, Kate! Off you go, she's in this evening.' I sink back into the train seat, wishing bad thoughts on my boss. As the train pulls into Paddington I check the racing results from Cheltenham on my phone. Crystal Clear was brought down at the third fence in the 3.15.

It takes hours to complete the task. The friend is chatty and frothy as she plays the video feed for me. Melody and her played together in a drama production at school when they were fifteen. It's not good quality or interesting enough to use and I back out of the house without the tape, by now desperate to get home.

Paul phones as I walk the unfamiliar streets of this corner of south-east London. 'How are you feeling?'

'Terrible.' This is an understatement. I've got a throbbing headache and I feel faint. The only thing I've eaten all day is a BLT double-decker sandwich bought on the train. It sits like cement in my stomach and I worry it's going to come back up the way it went down – fast. 'This whole visit is a complete red herring.'

Paul makes sympathetic noises. 'You need to get home and rest. I'm in Woolwich at the ferry terminal.'

'What are you doing all the way out here?'

'I had a job to do. Marcus is babysitting. You should be in bed, you've had a nasty shock.'

I thank him and trudge to the ferry terminal, my bruise banging against my skull with the same rhythm that my bag bangs against my hip. Maybe my decision not to go to hospital was pig-headed and hasty after all. When I arrive Paul is leaning against a railing. He wraps me in a hug, takes my bulky bag. 'You shouldn't have gone to work today. You're not well.' I slump against his shoulder but he holds me by the arms, a smile on his face. 'But what a job you did with Gerry! Why didn't you tell me you were hunting him down?'

I try to shrug nonchalantly, but I'm basking in his approval. 'I didn't know if I'd find him.'

'Livvy is very impressed.'

'Oh? She didn't sound it on the phone.'

'Oh come on! You know Livvy, she can't say it, but she feels it.'

'I guess you're right.'

Paul pauses. 'But, Kate, I think it's important you don't do things like that without telling me first in future, it could be dangerous. After all, I wouldn't want anything bad to happen to you.'

I frown, and my bruise throbs. I'm ready to admit defeat. 'Yeah, you're right. Where's the car?'

Paul tips his head across the river. 'Over there. We can walk.'

'Oh. Can't we take the ferry?' I'm exhausted and want to sit down.

'It stops running at eight. Come on, you can see the other bank.' He takes my arm and threads it through his and we head for the round brick building that houses the entrance to the Woolwich Tunnel. Paul starts for the stairwell.

'Can we go down in the lift?' I say, pressing the button. My legs feel leaden.

'Look, they're out of service,' he says, pointing to a sign taped to the wall. 'Come on, where's your sense of adventure?' I trail after him, as I'm used to Paul making decisions that are good ones and I'm too tired to think anything through, although I take one look at the rusty handrail and walk down unaided. We descend, going round and round the narrow staircase. I start to feel dizzy and have to slow, Paul moves out of sight below me. It seems a long way down. It doesn't smell good, not good at all, here.

'Paul?' He doesn't answer and I can't hear his footsteps clanging on the metal stair treads. 'Paul?' I start hurrying after him and as if in response to my admission that I'm feeling scared the hairs on the back on my neck rise, making me gasp and stumble. I turn round, expecting something horrible, but there's no one there.

'This stairwell has one hundred steps' I read at the top. I've walked maybe sixty, just over halfway. I want to retreat, travel the grinding miles home by train and bus, get out in the freezing air, but the drowsy warmth of the car is only a walk away, I can sleep like a child as Paul transports me back to the comforts of home. I grab the handrail and move my feet as quickly as a boxer with a skipping rope and run down the steps. I'm in danger of falling, and it will be bad if I do, but fear has set up shop inside my head and won't be dislodged. I fly around the last curve and come up short, panting.

Paul is standing by the lift shaft. He looks serious. He's holding my bag in the crook of his elbow and Melody's blue folder is peeking out of the top. I haven't had time to do anything with it, but Paul could easily have glanced at it and understood where it came from. 'Is there anything you want to tell me, Kate?' I'm trying to regain my breath. 'Because

I'd hate to think that we have secrets from each other.' His arm shifts and my bag squishes, the corner of the cardboard poking up from the leather like a sail in stormy seas. I can't reply. His eyes are cold as we stare at each other in silence. 'Let's go then.'

I turn and have to swallow the saliva that's forming too fast in my mouth. A tunnel with dim and intermittent lighting leads away and down for a long distance before rising again so that it's impossible to see the end. Perspective is playing tricks and the path ahead looks smaller and narrower with each step. My latent claustrophobia tightens its grip on my stomach. We are alone. I've lived in London over half my life. My mum can't understand it, she calls it that 'dreadful, dirty place,' but I love it. It's the most private place in the world. Wherever you go there's a crowd, the comfort and the cover of strangers. I've never felt afraid, a remarkable achievement in a city this big, because I've never been alone. But down here, down in this tomb, there's just Paul and me. No one can hear you scream. No one in their right minds (as my mum would say) would be here at 9.30 at night. No one of sound mind.

Paul heads off and we walk stiffly side by side. 'I guess the Thames starts about here.' I swallow again. We're going deeper, the tarmac pathway descending at a shallow angle. 'I wonder what the weight of the water is above us.'

'Can we talk about something else?' He's doing this on purpose, trying to make me freak. Everyone has an Achilles heel and mine is water. I can't swim. It's one of life's accomplishments that I never ticked off, like playing an instrument or learning to cook. Water terrifies me, drowning is the worst death I could imagine. Ever since I was a little girl I've had nightmares about trying to outrun tsunamis, though they were called tidal waves when I was small; stories about whirlpools made me cry. Paul knows all this, but he's still trying to pull at the frayed edges of my peace of mind.

'Imagine, during the bombing raids in the war they must have had to stay down here all night. There must have been hundreds of people in here.'

I change the subject – fast. 'Who were you seeing in this part of town?'

'An executive from the BBC.'

'It's a strange place to meet.'

'He flew in to City Airport. It's just up the road from the other side of this tunnel.'

'Oh.'

'Look, water!' Paul reaches out to touch the grimy white tiles where a small leak has formed, puddling on the tarmac.

'Come on, come on.' I hurry past, desperate to get to the end of this interminable underground prison, trying to block out the vast weight of the Thames flowing above us – God, what if the lights go out?

'It would be fun down here if the lights failed,' Paul says. He's holding my bag, nonchalantly strolling.

'Stop it!'

'What, don't you trust me, Kate?'

And then with an understanding that stops my legs from moving I realise that he's planning to do me harm. Five years ago, maybe six, images of a picnic on Hampstead Heath flood my brain. It was summer, a run of stifling city days that are seared in my memory because they're so rare and precious. It was early evening, Josh was toddling about and Jessie was there with a friend who was talking about her acting course with great enthusiasm. She said they'd been learning that for actors to gel as a group on stage required a large amount of trust; they had to know that they could depend utterly on each other. They'd tried to build that trust by playing a game where they had to catch each other as they fell. She said it was fun so we played on the grass of the Heath in the early-evening sun, our shoulders bare and our necks sticky.

'Come on, Eggy, fall backwards into my arms,' Paul said. I hesitated, standing with my arms folded across my chest and looking anxiously behind me. 'Come on!' He took a step away, increasing the distance between us. 'Don't you trust me?' He wiggled his fingers, beckoning me to put myself entirely at his mercy. His face was tanned and his teeth glowing.

'Of course I trust you, but you're too far back. I'm not that tall.'

'I'll catch you.' And he'd said it again. 'Don't you trust me?'

'Go on, Kate,' urged Jessie, 'you've got to take the risk. What's the worst thing that can happen?' And so I closed my eyes, made myself rigid and toppled backwards and heard his 'Shit!' too late and slammed painfully, shoulders first, into the sun-baked Heath. I lay there stunned, the breath knocked out of me, faces blocking the light as they peered over me.

He hadn't caught me. I heard nervous, scandalised laughter and broken voices all at once but tuned into only one: the pleading voice of my husband trying to say sorry, trying to explain how it had all gone so wrong. 'I thought that the final part of the fall is the most intense, I was trying to give you a thrill—'

'Or a scare!' someone added.

'– and then catch you at the last minute—'

'She's gonna kill you for that! Jessie had said, shaking her head and trying to give me a glass of wine.

Most of our friends thought the whole thing was hilarious, but Paul and I hadn't. He knew how I would be more than physically hurt by his mistake, that I would read into it a greater meaning about our relationship, that I wouldn't forget and however hard I tried would find it hard to forgive.

The tunnel is rising now, we're at the deepest part of the

river. Our footsteps echo in the narrow space. How black is your heart, Paul? I watch the tilt of his head, it juts forward and down, his straight nose, which I've kissed from every conceivable angle, a vertical line, the crow's feet beginning to form around eyes that I've seen crinkle with delight more times than it's possible to count. His coat flaps open as ever. He stops and turns round, looking back the way we have come. Just as he always hoped, there's no one here with us. Did you really set up your business partner and old friend, kill Melody for money, not for love?

Are you about to complete the plan and kill the mother of your children who conveniently gave you an alibi? Right here, right now? There was no one at the ferry terminal when I met you because the ferry had stopped. Not a soul saw me, passers-by in the street barely glanced my way. You would have come through here unnoticed, a stranger in a part of town we never visit, far from home. Lex's words ring like a mantra in my head. 'Someone set me up.'

On my interrogation course I watched a lot of police videos of suspects accused of all sorts of crimes, from shoplifting to murder. The crimes of passion were the worst (a man who bludgeoned his mother to death with an iron bar; a woman who stabbed her twin sister thirteen times with a kitchen knife) but to me they had an honesty that was understand-able; passions unleashed by our beastly sides, the explosive anger that perhaps lies within all of us. Those killers had been overtaken by a momentary madness that condemned them to suicide watch on the anniversaries of those deaths, because what they did in that split second would haunt them for the rest of their lives. But setting someone up requires the darkest of dark hearts because it's planned.

'It's awful down here, isn't it?' Paul says, coming closer to me. I stop and back up against the curved wall, the tiles cold against my bum. 'You could get properly scared, Kate. Don't

196

ever walk here alone.' His hand goes into his coat pocket and I can't breathe.

He takes another step towards me, one of his shoes creaking in the silence as I stare into my husband's face and at that moment the words from part of our wedding service spring from my mind with the clarity of a bell ringing on a clear Sunday morning. 'Loving what I know of you, and trusting what I do not yet know.' But what do I, in fact, know? Paul, I have lain next to you for ten years, I know where the sweat runs when you orgasm, I remember the look on your face when our children were yanked from my torn body, I have seen you shit and puke and shout with pain. I know your muscle spasms when you fall asleep, where the snot runs when grief occasionally overwhelms your sunny disposition, I feel your deepest fears and laugh at your most arrogant assumptions. I know you want to be cremated not buried, and that you hope Josh and Ava, by then polished and accomplished adults, and I will stand on a suitably stunning cliff in Devon and scatter your ashes to the westerlies.

I shared a life with you, created two new lives with you, expected to end my life with you, spent untold, uncountable hours with you, but as I stand here, deep under the river that flows through the city where we lived that life, I realise that I do not know you at all.

I don't understand what you're capable of, I cannot fathom your intent or your motives. You may be about to kill me or hug me, I can no longer tell. We have destroyed trust. I lied for you, perjured myself in an effort to preserve that perfect life, left Lex to his fate and . . . Oh, Melody, I'm sorry. At the time I thought the choice was not mine to make.

'You look like you're about to faint,' Paul says, pulling a hanky from his pocket and handing it to me. I hold it to my face like a white flag of surrender. 'Come on, lean on me and let's get out of here.'

197

We get to the other end eventually and I can't even manage a groan at the sandwich-board sign signalling that the lift north of the river is also out of service. I drag myself up the endless staircase past the urine puddles. My palm smells like blood from the rusty handrail. 'Wait here, let me get the car,' Paul says at the top of the exit. 'I don't want you walking any more.' I collapse on a low wall and Paul hands me my bag.

'Can you get me some water? There's a shop over there.'

He strides down the road and across the street to the late-night Shop 'n' Save and disappears under the neon sign. I pull out my mobile and O'Shea's card and dial. Our conversation is short as I tell her that I want to change my statement and I briefly explain why. I hear a note of triumph in her voice: job done, she's thinking. I'm still sitting in the same place when Paul returns.

I take deep gulps of Volvic when I'm settled in the passenger seat and then I'm asleep before we've even reached the end of the street.

29

They came in the morning as Paul was swishing a tea bag round his cup. Ava ran to open the door and they were down the hall as I came out to meet them. There were a lot of them: O'Shea and White, several other plain-clothes police and some in uniform. They busied into the kitchen and O'Shea was the one who told Paul they were arresting him. When he'd asked why they'd said 'in the light of new information we've received'. He'd turned to me and stared wordlessly, still balancing the dripping tea bag on a spoon.

'Let's get it over with.' He chucked the tea bag and spoon in the sink and walked to get his coat from the hall and then all hell broke loose. Josh started screaming. He ran after O'Shea as she followed Paul into the hall and punched her in the stomach.

'Leave my dad alone!' Paul was knocked into the coat stand and upended on the floor. One of the other policemen tried to grab Josh but he found large reserves of pre-teen energy and kicked out, eliciting a yelp of surprise and pain from the man.

Ava's howls drowned out the clamour of several voices all competing at once.

'Get your child under control,' White snapped as too many adults barged and knocked into walls and each other in the confined space. Josh was lying on top of a shell-shocked Paul, clinging on as I tried to prise him away.

'Don't go, Daddy, don't go,' Josh wailed into Paul's shoulder as my husband stared up at me, white-faced and mute. The platitudes that I would normally have clucked to bring this scene to a swift finale I couldn't summon, I had no false succour for Josh and Ava. I couldn't comfort or reassure my own children. There in the scratchy chaos of our elegant hallway was the proof that Paul loved his children and they loved him and it was me that was tearing them apart. I tried to conjure Melody's face to give me the resolve to continue, but I could hear only my own terrified and heartbroken children. The life-threatening fear I felt deep underground yesterday hasn't travelled with me to my home, but the truth is the only thing that can give me back my peace of mind.

'Get him out of here,' O'Shea commanded, or that's what I think she said, Ava was screaming so loudly in my ear the crowd became artists performing mime.

Paul tried to stand and a policeman lifted Josh away, I didn't have the heart to do it. Paul left the house flanked by two officers, Josh's wails of 'Daddy!' ringing out behind him. Paul hadn't said a word to me. O'Shea held the door shut with her foot as I locked us all in the house because Josh was trying to run down the path after his dad. She adjusted her flying shirt tails and folded back her hair. 'I hate you!' Josh screamed at me and he really meant it.

'Charming,' O'Shea responded sourly.

'He's a fighter!' a jovial man in his forties remarked but was silenced by one look from O'Shea.

'Give Mrs Forman a minute,' O'Shea added, giving me a nod, but it took a lot longer than a minute to calm my distressed children. I took them to school to keep things as normal as possible but it's hard doing simple things like helping them with their bags and lunch boxes when your heart has been ripped from your chest.

Now, four hours later, I'm sat on the sofa drinking whisky with shaking hands. I've sold out my family, repeated to

O'Shea and a middle-aged man called DS Ben Samuels details of the late hour and the blood on Paul's hands and handed them the scarf. O'Shea's eyes were shining when I brought her that. I've saved her floundering murder inquiry, wiped the egg off quite a few police faces today. I've probably helped her get promoted. My house is being turned upside down as they search for 'material relevant to the investigation'. I hear them rooting through cupboards; one officer is methodically pulling books off the shelf in front of me and flicking through them; someone in a white suit is in the toilet no doubt swabbing the grouting and poking Q-tips down the plughole.

'Let's give him a bit of space,' O'Shea says, casting her grey eyes at the bookshelf searcher. 'Can we go to the kitchen?' We move through to the back of the house, Ben following. 'There's the issue of you withholding information from a police inquiry,' she begins as she stares out of the window at the garden. 'We could charge you for that, but I'm not sure it's really in the public interest, what with the kids and all.' She's trying to be friendly and she's not doing a bad job. I look at her directing the team in my house, she's younger than about half of them. I find myself wondering how many balls she had to break to get to be pulling up a chair opposite the main subject of all this industry. 'We'll be dredging the canal.'

I'm stunned. 'Why on earth do you need to do that?'

'The murder weapon hasn't been found. If I'd killed her, that's where I'd hide it.' I don't reply as she runs a hand across a kitchen drawer. 'Are any of your kitchen knives missing?'

'No. And I'm the kind of woman who would notice.'

She flashes me a look of respect for my household management and I'd take a bet that her cutlery holder doesn't harbour crumbs either. 'Is this the only lock on your door?' She pulls at the old-fashioned key. 'That'll invalidate your insurance.'

I shrug. 'It's terraces all along here. You'd have to swim the canal to get in from the back.' I shudder. 'No one in their right minds is going to do that.'

'Exactly my point.' She's scanning my kitchen windows, unimpressed by their rickety locks and, in one case, no lock at all. She works in a world where believing in the logical won't save or protect you from the meanness and violence of people. 'They'd be mad, you don't want one of them in here with your kids—'

'I get it! Nobody in this street has been burgled from the back in at least twenty years. Have you got a cigarette?'

She purses her lips. 'Gave up five years ago.' She takes pity on me. 'Ben, give Mrs Forman a cigarette, would you?'

'Course.' He pulls out the bits and pieces and I find holding the packet comforting. She stares at me. I'm being subjected to the gut test. I wonder how many have failed this examination over the years.

'How did you get that?' She gestures at my black eye.

'Lex crashed his car with me in it,' I say.

'When was this?'

'Two nights ago. He was pretty pissed off.'

O'Shea snaps at Samuels, 'Do we know about this?' He shakes his head, frowning. 'He was angry with you? Why?'

'He thought he was being set up for Melody's murder.'

'Who was setting him up?'

'Paul, John, me, all of us. He was raving and probably drunk.'

'Do you think he was set up?'

I take a deep drag. 'Lex is spoilt. When things don't go his way he blames other people.'

'Why did Paul kill Melody?'

'I don't know that he did kill her. I never said that he killed her! I just don't get the story about a dog . . . I don't know what to believe any more, who I can trust . . .' I bite a hang-nail, worry flooding my body with the cigarette smoke. Again

Lex's words from our mad car trip come back to me: 'Innocent people are charged all the time'. God forbid if I'm wrong.

They are both staring at me. 'Was your husband having an affair?'

'I don't know.'

'Hazard a guess. Other people think they were.'

'I don't know!'

'Has he been unfaithful in the past?'

'Not with me.' One of O'Shea's eyebrows rises at the corners. 'He was married before.' I look at the floor. 'There was a crossover with me.'

O'Shea pauses and I sense Samuels is enjoying my discomfort. 'This is a lovely house, Kate. You have an enviable lifestyle. Are there money problems, financial troubles, that you know of?'

'No.'

'How would you know?'

'I see bank statements, we have a joint account, that sort of thing.'

'What happened to make you change your story, Kate?'

I look out at the thriving garden, bursting into life as spring marches on. I can just see the red roof of Ava's Wendy house. 'Have you ever heard of the "halo effect"?'

'No.'

'It's a term sociologists use. If someone is particularly physically attractive, we wrongly assume that all their other traits are just as attractive. We think they're more principled than normal-looking people, better company, more honest. Their unusually heightened beauty makes us blind to their flaws. I guess famous people, actors or models, produce this reaction in people.' I see a pair of Paul's socks on the worktop, one is still puffed into the shape of his foot. Even my husband's feet are beautiful. 'I could no longer judge for myself. I want someone else to confirm or deny.'

'So you're saying that Paul's done it and most people would think that he hasn't?'

'I'm saying I don't know. I just want to know the truth. That's all I want.'

'But why did you change your mind now?'

I grind the cigarette into a plate littered with crusts. 'Lex and I don't often see eye to eye, but that night I took pity on him. If he didn't do it . . . Because I can't look my children in the face if I have doubts, and because . . . because . . .'

'What, Mrs Forman?'

I was about to say I was scared for my life but I realise how that will play. I've said enough. 'Nothing.' O'Shea holds a folder against her chest the way one holds a small baby and I wonder if her career is her child. 'What happens now?'

'This lot will be here most of the day. You may have to sign for some items to be taken away.' She stands.

'Where are you going?'

'I'm going to interview Mr Paul Forman.' Samuels accompanies her out to the car, leaving me alone in the kitchen. A door bangs and the vibration sends one of Paul's socks noiselessly to the tiles where it's immediately trampled on by a policeman coming in from the garden.

30

I'm hoping that two packets of Wotsits munched on the way home from school, Love Hearts and Wine Gums at the front door, the comics in front of the video, takeaway fish and chips followed by chocolate cake and computer games will be enough to buy my children's peace of mind. The teachers said they'd been fine but I watch them carefully as they sit in the living room, hunched in front of Disney as a trail of crumbs and sugar dusting settles into the carpet fibres.

After they've gone to bed I settle down with whatever's left: some Wine Gums and cold chips, a beer and a new packet of B&H – as my life disintegrates my pre-child self re-emerges; I've become the smoker and drinker of my twenties again. I sit at the computer with the memory stick full of documents from Melody's house. The Find option and Paul's name returns eight hundred and seventy-one results. 'Graham' and 'Melody' return pages of expenses claims, tax issues, several contracts and the NDAs she signed to discuss *Crime Time*. It's all very dull. Lex's name brings up fifty-five files, some are programme outlines and there's a detailed file on how the public voting on *Crime Time* would work in practice. This is the most interesting thing I've found so far, Lex's creative juices are flowing, it's clear he really gets the concept and his ideas about the public's engagement are spot on; he's convinced it'll be a hit and boasts that they can sell it in many territories. I find myself smiling; he may be flawed but there's no denying his brilliance – he really is the king of reality TV. The word 'Forwood' is hopeless, it throws up four hundred documents. I need to narrow my search, and so I try 'Px', a sign-off that Paul sometimes uses. Eighteen documents are returned. I skim through several before I come to an email exchange from Paul to Melody revealing how excited Forwood is about the idea for *Crime Time* and a gushing reply.

In the next email there's a change of tone.

> Dear M,
>
> I'm sorry if you feel the meeting was difficult. L is very passionate about this space and has some trenchant views. I hope we can come to an agreement at the next meeting that keeps all parties happy.
>
> Px

The next file is from Melody's personal email account mg26@hotmail.com to Paul.

> Dear P,
>
> I'm very upset about this. I can't believe he's asking if I'm serious, when he knows full well that I am. Yes, I'm junior, but I have a right to take my time and get legal advice on my position. I don't want to be bullied.
>
> Mx.

This is followed by a threat of sorts. From mg26@hotmail.com.

> L might not like it but I have the right to take the idea elsewhere. I've said many times that I just want a fair price and a fair deal for this programme. His competitive pressures are of no interest to me, as you can imagine.
>
> Mx.

Paul has replied with,

You are of course entitled to try and sell your idea anywhere
you see fit. I still believe that we are the best company to turn
this into saleable, watchable, successful television and I hope we
can convince you of that. If not, I wish you well in the future.

Px

The next email is disturbing.

Dear P,

I phoned you three times tonight but put the phone down.
I thought it was better to put the following into words and let
you digest it, rather than coming at it cold on the phone.
When I went for that toilet break I stood outside the door
and heard what L was saying about me. I was disgusted but
was too angry and upset to bring it up in the meeting. I
thought I might say things I later regretted, so I bit my
tongue – unlike him, of course. Firstly, I don't have to sign
his contract if I don't want to. I know that's my right and
what he was saying effectively amounted to bullying. I don't
care if time is running out, that's not my problem.

'The other things he was saying about *us* . . . well, what
can I say? I was embarrassed and angry, for you and for me.
He's saying right in front of John that I've 'got it bad for you'.
Is this meant to imply he thinks I'm acting like a lovesick
fool? And then to claim at the end that he thinks I'll sue you
or him for sexual harassment if I don't get my own way is
slander. That's why I left the meeting without resolving or
agreeing on anything, however much he riled me. The
bottom line is I can't work with him, which means, to my
great, great regret, I can't work with you.

Mx.

I try to imagine for a moment what it must have been like
to have been in this meeting; a young woman with a smart

idea trying to be noticed by the TV predators but not eaten by them. She did a better job than I would have done. Here is evidence of how derogatory Lex was about her ambition and her talents, of how widely suspected her crush on Paul was. The only thing I don't know is if it was reciprocated.

This email exchange gives more than a hint of the nightmare Lex is to work for, particularly if you're a woman with youth and looks on your side. Lex is flawed but Lex is smart; did he later wonder if he'd gone too far, had met his match this time? 'Never come between a man and the millions he stands to make.' Melody probably had grounds for a sexual-harassment charge if she wanted to go down that route. She may well have had other evidence that shows this even more clearly. Combined with earlier 'bimbo eruptions' that Lex has weathered over the years that's motive enough for investors to label Lex a 'bad leaver'. That's why he wanted to get the stuff from her house, to see how offended she really was, but he couldn't go himself because it might have looked suspicious, and Astrid, his satellite dish, couldn't even tune into her boss's desperation. Melody was the one standing between Lex and his fortune and he knew it. Is that why he met her late on the night she was killed? Was he begging or planning?

I pick up the phone and dial his number. I want to hear him swear and rail as I pin him down but I get the frustrating 'the mobile you are calling is currently unavailable, please try again later'. Oh, I'll try, you're not going to stop me now.

I bite my nails and log on to the laptop, pulling up lexwoodisinnocent.com. There have been a hundred thousand visitors since Wednesday. There are photos of him with various celebrities and on the disabled ramp at the police station. Either Lex or someone he's hired has linked to the press reports on him and there are a lot. He was always the master of self-promotion and viral marketing and the thing he knows best how to market is himself. 'Take a bet against if you think I'm guilty' is emblazoned across the top of the site. OK, Lex, I'm sending you a message. I pledge a hundred pounds that you're up to your neck in it. I get an automatic reply message in my email inbox.

> Thank you for caring about the murder of Melody Graham.
> By contributing to this website, you are helping keep the
> pressure on the police to solve this murder and keeping the
> case in the public eye. I didn't kill her, and it's more
> important than ever that the police keep up the hunt to find
> out who did.

There's a news feed running across the top of my screen and my eye catches on Forwood TV. The news that Paul's been arrested is out and two minutes later the phone calls start. I can't avoid Paul's mum, hysterical and defiant. It takes me fifteen minutes of hard persuasion to put her off coming to stay and 'help'. I think I'd rather be in jail with Paul than have her hovering, digging at my child-rearing. 'Oh, I'm not aware of *this* channel' or 'I suppose the children have no need for wellingtons in town.' She's followed by my mum, finally in a situation that can showcase her dull fatalism. 'You could always move back home near me when it comes to that,' she says hopefully. Gee thanks, the best offer I ever had. I channel-hop distractedly as we talk, and pause when I get to Gerry in a rerun of *Inside-Out,* at this moment doing press-ups in his cell with his shirt off. The TV's on mute, so I count Gerry doing twenty-five press-ups as my mum prattles on. The muscles in his back bulge beneath his skin as he moves. He stands as my mum rings off and smiles at the camera high up on the wall before firing an imaginary arrow from a bow, straight at me.

31

The weekend crawled past as we waited to hear any news about Paul. He wasn't released; his twenty-four hours in custody extended to thirty-six, and then to longer after the flourish of a magistrate's pen. But life must go on: the children have to go to school; and I have to go to work. I peek out of the side of Ava's curtains at the street below. Two cameramen and Declan Moore are leaning against the front wall. I remember Josh's sobs from the other day and resolve never to put him through that again.

'Can we go this way every day, Mummy?' Ava asks, squealing as the boat rocks. We're getting out via the garden, the canal and the alleyway on the other side. I woke Marcus up by banging on the side of the *Marie Rose* and asking for a lift. He kindly offered to row us across the ten metres of water. I grip the sides till my knuckles are white. We pick up book bags and lunch boxes and I hug Marcus, happy that I put one over on the lot waiting in the cold outside the front door.

'Are you around this evening? We might need to come back this way.'

'One of us will probably be here. I'll come across for you, then you don't have to pull the boat along the rope, you've got the kids and everything. We won't be able to do it for long though, we're off on holiday, a late ski trip to Austria.'

I allow myself the pleasing picture of Max and Marcus slicing through powder as I stare down at the black canal.

'Marcus, I'm afraid the police will be out here tomorrow, probably with divers. They're going to search the canal. I'm sorry if they are a nuisance.'

He smiles with teeth that would make Tom Cruise fret about his dental work as he helps us on to the bank. 'Maybe we can chat about equipment, I love diving. I'll keep an eye on them.'

'Thanks for being so understanding.'

He does something surprising – he reaches out and gives me a hug. The spontaneous kindness brings tears to my eyes. I cling on for a long time, feeling a chest harder than my husband's beneath Marcus's fleece. When we part my children's faces are like owls'.

As we pass through the school gate I sense the whispers. I see heads pressed together and hands held in front of mouths. People I don't know look at me and then gaze into the middle distance. I guess this is what notoriety feels like. We are officially a family in trouble. Sarah puts an arm round me as she says hello to the kids. 'I'm taking you after school, aren't I?' Everyone nods. She leans close to my ear, doing the best whispering of the morning. 'Are the press at your house?'

'Yes. Marcus rowed us over the canal.'

'Oh, well done. Just remember, it won't last long, Kate. I once worked for an MP arrested for bribery. For three days there were thirty people outside his office and his home, then puff, they were gone. You wouldn't even remember his name if I told it to you now.'

'I'm not sure that makes me feel any better.'

She hugs me close. 'Sorry, but it was the best I could do.'

'Thanks. I'll come round to get them after work.'

'OK.' By the time I get out of the playground I've switched into work mode and am moving with a new purpose through the obstacle course of buggies, toddlers, scooters and yakking mothers when I feel a hand clasp my arm. It's Eloide. I flick her away as if she's a spider clambering up my coat.

'I knew this would be the only way to catch you and my guess is you won't make a scene here.' She links her arm through mine as she smiles indulgently at a boy who knocks into her knee. She's right, losing one's cool at school just isn't done, particularly if you're a mother who is in trouble, so we march along together, a parody of old mates.

'I'm going to work so just leave me alone.'

'Only when you hear what I have to say.'

I'm half running down the steps of the Tube station but she's following me. 'I wasn't in your house. Why on earth are you so convinced that I was?'

I snort as I pass my ticket over the sensor. 'Let's just say that I'm observant. You left a little calling card.' She looks blank. 'Teacups and a spoon.' As I say this I know how absurd it sounds and have a sudden doubt as to whether I've imagined the whole thing.

'Teacups?'

I move on to the train and find a seat. She sits down next to me.

'The pattern they made; I knew it was you.'

'Rational, scientific Kate threw me across a table because of teacups?'

'What do you know!' I'm being petulant and stubborn to disguise my doubts and realise too late that she can probably see this instantly. She gets celebrity denials every day of her life; my lies are no less visible.

She must take pity on me because she doesn't pursue it. 'I know Paul didn't do that to your face.' We turn towards each other. 'See. I know. He didn't do that to you and he didn't kill Melody.' She holds my gaze with her arresting eyes. She's wearing a petrol-blue scarf which intensifies the colour of her irises – they shine violet. She adjusts the cutting-edge designer bag on her shoulder – a free perk of her job, no doubt – and immediately I want that bag. She makes it look as if life would be glossier and happier with that across my shoulder.

'It's easy for you to play the hero, see the past in black and white and rose. You don't have the messy contradictions and compromises of an eight-year marriage to consider, or children.'

'However convinced you are about his guilt, you're still wrong.'

I shrug with irritation. Her conviction is endearing and I feel something akin to shame. She's a better, more loyal friend to Paul than I am. I steal a sideways look at her; she's clean and gorgeous-smelling. I touch my ruined face and notice that the man opposite is mesmerised by her. He glances up in awe, shifting in his seat, watches her criss-cross her legs, follows her hand as she scratches a shin.

This passer-by's fantasy of the pretty woman on the train doesn't include slices on her arm. 'Why do you self-harm?' I keep my voice low.

She waits a few moments. 'It's a way of keeping control, I guess. I was bulimic when I was a teenager.' She twirls a tiny and delicate ankle.

'Did Paul know?'

She looks shocked. 'Of course! He was my husband.' I swallow. He'd never told me. He kept her secrets, was loyal to her even after the end. My shame intensifies.

A thought strikes me. 'Were you doing that when we were all partying together?'

She folds her arms, clasping her elbows with her hands as if trying to protect herself. 'Particularly then.'

'I didn't know. I'm sorry.'

She tries to make light of it by changing the subject. 'Why do you think Paul killed her?'

I tell her in a quiet voice the events of that night. 'He was so upset, so devastated.' She sits impassively, nodding. She doesn't look at me. In her silence there is something I'm keen to discover. 'What?'

She avoids the question and regards me under long lashes as we bump along shoulder to shoulder. 'You're unusual, you know.'

'I'm sure you're going to tell me why.' I steel myself for Eloide's particular brand of hippy intuition.

'You're prepared to believe that your own husband murdered someone. You're not afraid of examining the motives of those closest to you. Believe me, you're wasted in TV.' The man opposite sways to his feet as the train shunts to a halt at a station. She doesn't notice his lingering looks as he leaves.

'Why are you so sure he's innocent?' I watch the man outside the window give Eloide one last stare before we plunge back into the tunnel. I don't think she even knew he was there.

'I don't know what happened that night.' Her voice drops to almost a whisper. 'I can't explain the blood. But how he was, one minute here' – she holds her hands above her head – 'the next here' – she knocks the side of her knee – 'devastated; I've seen him like that before. Twice I saw him like that.'

'When?'

She is looking full at me now with those startling eyes. 'You didn't think I'd noticed that man looking at me, did you?' She leans back in her seat, almost disappointed that she's right. 'Don't underestimate me, Kate, you of all people. Paul often says how perceptive you are. That you see things others miss. But you've got a blind spot with me because of what happened in the past. Think about how I can help you.'

'When was he like that?'

She pauses. 'When he had an affair.' Eloide doesn't try to

touch me. She doesn't try to soothe me or pretend she can make it better. 'And it didn't make him any less of a person, or make me love him any less. I can't tell you what happened in those woods that night, but I can tell you Paul wasn't there. He didn't kill her, Kate. I'm going to fight with you – or against you – to prove that he's innocent.'

My station blurs into focus and I sway to standing. She's contradictory: fragile but stubborn, flaky yet more determined than I had realised. For years I've hated her, when maybe I should have admired her. I walk up the steps of the Tube in a swirl of dreadful sensations. I've fallen through a trapdoor into a world I don't recognise where old enemies may be allies and my husband may be my undoer.

32

Livvy glances at me across the studio and does a double take, veering off course towards me. 'Christ! You look as bad as I feel.' She invades my personal space as she tips my chin up towards her nostrils and examines my puffy temple. I feel like a girl being examined by the school nurse. She blows disapprovingly. 'You'll frighten the guests, looking like that. Shaheena will have to do the meet and greets.'

'So I'm officially too ugly to work in TV,' I say, lamely trying to make a joke.

'Few of us aren't,' Livvy replies matter-of-factly.

I don't feel like laughing. I sense the pitying glances from Shaheena and Matt, have seen the silent stares from the floor manager and lighting crew. They've heard the news about Paul. He will be mentioned on the programme tonight. I glance at my mobile. There are no messages. The police can hold Paul for up to seventy-two hours before they have to charge him or release him. The longer he's in, the worse it looks.

We're gathered for the run-through before the live show this evening. Usually, the atmosphere is one of excitement and jokey expectation, a 'break a leg' camaraderie unites us, but today a sour air hangs over the studio. Even Marika in a tight black skirt suit and the highest scarlet heels can't lighten the mood. She talks intently to the programme editor in a corner as they strike words from a paper script.

The make-up artists wander to and fro, waiting for their

moment in a few hours' time. Chet, the director, snaps out commands from the gallery. 'Marika, when you sit down on the sofa, get close to Colin, almost touching shoulders – you need to seem like you're really a team.' Colin tries to give Marika a mock bear-hug, but neither of them have the energy to pull it off with their normal gusto. From my position at the side of the action I feel that it's all my fault, that they are all blaming me.

'OK, Marika, let's try the new position!' Chet shouts.

She nods and picks up her coffee cup. As the opening music rolls Marika normally strides across the set, smiling and gesturing, but today she perches on the sofa edge as a camera zooms in for a close-up and the lights darken. 'That's great!' Chet calls.

'Our mission on this programme is to fight crime wherever and whenever we find it. To make this country a safer place for you and your family.' She pauses and gives a slight shake of her head. 'This week, we're dedicating the show to a crime that we're determined to solve, because this murder involves one of our own, the creator of this show, Melody Graham.' Marika rises from the sofa arm, the camera tracking her. 'Our own managing director, Paul Forwood, is at this moment being questioned by police for this murder. But I stand here before you to stress the editorial independence of *Crime Time*; we allow no interference in what we broadcast from our owners or from the network. We bring the truth, and nothing but the truth, to you.' She turns to face Colin, now making his way across the floor towards a map of the woods where Melody's body was found.

'God she's good,' Shaheena says, and we watch her quiz Colin about road junctions near the crime scene and time-lines.

Astrid and a million lookalike wannabes should listen and learn from the queen of popular TV.

Livvy comes up behind me as we watch the run-through. 'No word from Gerry yet?'

'No.' I've been checking my work mobile all morning to see if he's been in touch.

'Told you. You can't rely on a toerag like that.' She smiles, pleased her world-view hasn't been challenged by someone exceeding expectations. 'I think we've got plenty without him.' She nods towards a blown-up picture of Melody being used as a backdrop to a shot. We stand awkwardly side by side, her boss, my husband, the elephant in the studio.

A little while later Marika turns to camera for the sign-off. 'Remember, this is your evidence, on your show.'

Thumping music starts to fade and Chet shouts, 'And we're out!'

'Coffee?' Shaheena asks and I nod, shoving my phone back in my bag. Shaheena looks up into the gallery. 'Uh oh. Big Chief is in with Black Cloud.'

We head up the gallery steps to find George, the executive producer, who I've not met before, and Livvy bent over a keyboard with a technician.

'What about "This programme is dedicated to the memory of Melody Graham, nineteen eighty-four to two thousand and ten"?' Livvy says.

'Get rid of "the memory of",' George commands.

I peer over their backs. 'You could put "creator of *Crime Time*",' I say.

'Let's keep it simple,' he says. 'We'll do "This series is dedicated to Melody Graham" and her dates. We'll add it at the start of the credits.' Livvy and the technician murmur their agreement. 'God she was young,' George adds, a faraway look in his eyes. 'I was getting stoned in Nepal in nineteen eighty-four.'

Livvy moves out of the gloom of the gallery into the

studio. 'We're meeting upstairs in five minutes!' she shouts to no one in particular. 'Don't be late.'

Sky News is on in the corner of the conference room when I get there and I watch the reports roll across the bottom of the screen like the heartbeat of a patient in intensive care. I catch Forwood's name pulsing past. A copy of the *Daily Mail* is open on the table. They've got a picture of Paul that I've never seen before, one of Melody smiling, Lex in front of the offices. I feel the room filling with people behind me, the paper being pulled from my palm as someone points a finger at Melody's face.

'Look, we're in the *Telegraph*, too,' Matt says, wrestling the pages into submission.

'We're on now!' Shaheena adds as the news changes continents.

'Oh, there's Astrid!' I exclaim as the front of Forwood's offices comes into view. They're filming staff at the door. She's wearing a tight, pale grey 1950s-style suit with a plunging neckline and towering heels; she looks like a young Marilyn Monroe.

'That's the moron who forgot to sort out the lease on the central London building we wanted,' Livvy scolds as Astrid blows a kiss to the camera.

'That's Lex's secretary,' I explain.

Matt can't help whistling his appreciation – and his envy.

'OK,' George says, and we fidget to attention. 'Turn that down, someone,' he adds, pinching the bridge of his nose. 'I know you're all speculating as to what's happening at Forwood,' he begins. 'The truth is, it's a situation that's changing daily. Try not to get distracted by it. You're here to do a job, so do it. I believe that in the end this will be great for *Crime Time*.'

Livvy snorts. 'Well that's a PR spin if ever I heard one. It's a disaster, isn't it? The bosses are under suspicion of having knocked off the creator of this programme—'

'Exactly. Every news report is mentioning repeatedly the programmes Forwood have made, and talking about this one as though it's special. It's a golden opportunity for us, it's positioning us as controversial, fresh, even a little dangerous. Now they've arrested Paul Forman—'

'Uh mm,' Livvy interrupts him and turns to me.

'Oh.' George looks surprised. 'It's you.' He frowns and I feel something akin to shame travel across my cheeks. My bruise throbs painfully. I'm not what he expected and that will make it easier for him to sack me, though he's sure to use that dreaded phrase "letting me go". He twists a pencil round and round his fingers. He's nervous. The room holds its breath and I wait for the axe to fall.

'She's good,' Livvy adds, as if she's inspecting cattle at a country fair. 'It could work in our favour.'

'Nepotism accusations . . .' George tails off.

'This is TV,' adds Livvy as if her boss is a simpleton.

George nods. 'I take your point. Still, public image and all that.'

'If Kate has personally done nothing wrong you cannot get rid of her.' Marika's sultry voice cuts through their bickering. I can tell that they've all been talking about me when I wasn't here, deciding whether I should still be on the programme. 'No woman should be condemned simply by the man she's with. You need to think of *that* public image.'

George starts back-covering in the modern way. 'Yes, yes—'

It's time to end my misery. 'I am prepared to leave without any fuss if you think it would be better for the programme.' There, I've said it, but with a heavy heart. I sense lots of eyes on me. I can't bear not knowing, having my fate hanging in the balance.

George twists the pencil again it a way that should be masterful but he drops it and it falls on the table and rolls away towards me. I realise how hard magic tricks really are, how many hours of practice must be needed to achieve a perfect sleight of hand. George hasn't put in the hours. 'No, no, stay. But we need to keep you strictly low profile.'

'Thank you.' What on earth George thinks a researcher is apart from low profile he doesn't articulate.

'Now, on to tonight's programme—'

'Have you guys seen Lex's website?' Matt asks. 'Look.' His hands fly over his laptop keys and he turns it round for the room to see. 'Its traffic has increased four hundred per cent since yesterday. It's turning into a real phenomenon. There's two and a half million pounds pledged so far. Maybe there's some way we can piggyback on this to publicise the programme—'

'Or imitate it when we run campaigns?' Shaheena adds.

George gets animated. 'See, that's the power of TV and the internet. This programme is going to be huge.' He turns to the website editor, his face darkening. 'We need a meeting immediately we've aired.' Her mouth opens and shuts like a fish.

Livvy sits back in her chair, luxuriating in the scandal we are mired in. 'Let's just hope they don't arrest any more of us before we air tonight.' We all murmur our agreement as we disperse to make final preparations for the show.

Half an hour later Sergei calls, desperate to get hold of Lex. 'I can't find him anywhere. The ship is rudderless, I think you say. The employees need a pep talk, wild rumours are taking hold and I fear people will start blabbing to the press unless he comes in.'

'Have you tried him at home?'

Sergei sighs like I really am the imbecile I feel. 'Home, mobile, gym, mother's, favourite restaurants, his website, email. He's nowhere.'

It doesn't feel right. I tell him to check the hospitals, maybe the motorway smash has had a delayed effect. 'He crashed his car with you in it?'

'It's a long story.'

'I can wait.'

'Another time, really. I'm still at work.' He rings off disconsolate and I try John, who to my amazement answers. 'My God, where's Paul?'

'Still at the station. He sent me away, said he didn't need me.'

'Is that wise?'

'No. But he was insistent, and you know what he's like when he's in that mood.'

'Are they going to charge him?'

'They're waiting for the test results on the blood on the scarf. If that doesn't come through in the next hour or so they'll have to let him go.'

'Were they horrible to him?'

John makes a strange noise down the phone. 'This is murder, Kate, not vandalism of a church hall.'

'Sorry.' I change the subject. 'Have you spoken to Lex? No one knows where he is.'

'No. What's he playing at?' John is annoyed now.

'If Paul's not let out I think Lex needs to go into the office tomorrow.'

'I'm on it.' There's background distraction as John fumbles with something. 'Are the press leaving you alone?'

'Not really.'

'How are the kids?'

'Not great.' Guilt floods me as I say this.

'Well, take care of them, Kate.'

I say thanks, but I'm not quite sure why.

33

I finally get a text from Paul that afternoon saying they've had to release him and he's going home. A desperation to see him overwhelms me; I put him in custody and now he's out and I just want my husband back. I catch Livvy wiping wet hands on her hair as she emerges from the toilets. 'I have to go home.'

She plumps the damp strands. 'Has he been released?'

'Yes.' I wait for the diatribe, the lecture that I'm putting my family before the show. It doesn't come.

'Off you go.' Livvy almost looks happy.

'I'll make it up to you, I promise.'

She gives me a quite beautiful smile. 'You know they're all bastards, don't you?' She pats me on the back as I leave.

I catch a cab home and make it stop next to the alleyway near the canal. As I turn the corner by the water I can't believe the scene that confronts me. In all my years living here I've never seen more than three dog walkers and some foxes use this towpath, but this afternoon there are about forty people crowded on to it. Police officers, slack-jawed local residents and reporters bustle around TV cameras, a police boat, a lighting rig not dissimilar to the one at the studio, and a woman in Hunter wellies officiously carrying a tray of teacups. The weeds and wildflowers that grow beside the tarmac have been pounded to a squelchy mess; the harsh staccato of police radios and the low thrumming of a motor boat drown out the sensational quiet of still water. A diver surfaces, pondweed trailing off one arm, and a bunch of kids 'ooohhh' him loudly. They're dredging up secrets long drowned. From across the canal and through the bare trees can clearly be seen our shed, our garden, Ava's Wendy house, the table on our patio, the barbeque grill and our house. I watch the cameras rolling, the zoom lenses homing in on bedrooms and undrawn curtains. The invasion is complete. I see Declan from the *Express* talking to two young men. I decide I'd better use the front door. I duck back into the alleyway, trudge around to the bridge and back to my road where I have to run the gauntlet of several reporters, my head down.

It feels like a hundred years since I was in this house rather than a few hours. As I close the door I let out a long sigh, expecting to be sheltered from the storm outside, but as I pull off my coat and turn to hang it up a strong shove in my back sends me slamming into the wall, my bag skittering away across the floorboards. In the half-turn I manage to make I see Paul's fist slamming into the wall as I duck.

'How could you do that to me? How could you *really* think I killed her?' He's repeating this over and over. 'Anyone else, anyone else, but not you!' His face is a contorted mask of anger. This is the first time I've ever seen him lose control, really lose it. He punches the wall again and I race for the kitchen and the back door before I slow. There is no escape to be found out there. What are we going to do, fight in the garden with the country's TV stations filming us? I turn the key to unlock the door but even as I do I know I'm never going out there. I swing round as Paul rugby tackles me to the kitchen floor. As I slam into the cold tiles Lex's grinning face explodes in my mind. We could be the star turns on one of his reality-TV shows, acting out the 'money shot' as we collapse in on ourselves, our carefully constructed facade of the perfect couple with the enviable life a sham for all to see and discuss over the water cooler at the office the following day.

'Paul, stop!'

'You really think I killed Melody? You! You think I'm no better than Gerry.' I'm half under the kitchen table. 'In fact, you think I *am* Gerry!' I look up at the underside of the table where we gathered for a thousand family meals. Ava has drawn spiky mountains piercing fluffy white clouds and a sun with fat rays warming a stick family walking hand in hand in the valley. A father leads a mother and two children. Here are Paul and I, fighting under a canopy showing the love and innocence of our children.

He pins my arms to the floor. 'Get off me!' I shout, writhing around.

'How could you do that to *us*!'

Anger explodes in me as his fingers tighten on my forearms. The wink he gave me after his first bald lies to the police, the bladder-releasing fear I felt in the tunnel at Woolwich, the revelation from Eloide and the raw shock of him trying to hit me combine into a lethal cocktail and I want him off me *now*. I knee him as hard as I can in the balls and he pitches forward on to my neck with a groan, but I can't get out from under his heavy weight as his knees are pressing down on my thighs.

'You think I'm the copycat? Well. What about you, Kate, what about you!' He slams my body back on to the tiles and my head hits a chair leg. I spit at him and as he releases my arm to wipe away the phlegm I bite him on the finger.

He shrieks with outrage and pain and something closes off in him and he becomes someone else. His hands are clamped around my neck. 'Is this how it's done? The copycat works like this, does he?'

My husband is trying to strangle me. I claw at his large, firm hands but they are so tight, so determined. I can't talk my way out of every bad situation. I've been struck mute, helpless. My foot bangs into Ava's sun under the table top. Paul's hands squeeze tighter. He's not looking at me, just talking rapidly, but there's such a rushing in my ears I can't hear. I never realised that being strangled would be so painful and quick and Paul isn't aware that he's about to kill me. I'll be yet more proof that those closest to us are capable of inflicting the most damage. This was how Gerry's wife died, all those years ago. All the hours of filming, all the column inches and blogs and discussion programmes and message boards and YouTube clips to try to understand him, and Paul and I are closer to that than anybody. Was Melody staring into these eyes at her end? His face swims above me, the pain in my chest is exploding through my body. I am slipping into unconsciousness. Ava's stick people walk through the valley of the shadow of death.

Paul makes a noise so loud even I can hear it. He springs back, disgusted horror passing across his face. I fling my arm out and scratch him on his face, scrape marks that bring blood springing to the surface. We're both panting. Paul starts sobbing next to me on the floor. He teetered on the abyss and backed away. We lie a tangled mess of bruises and blood as I retch and he moans.

'Do you remember that pheasant shoot?' He's on his hands and knees, crying on our kitchen floor. I can't even begin to speak so he carries on. 'That back-scratching freebie from an American network?' He shakes his head in sorrow. 'And we had to put on all those silly green clothes and pretend like lords of the manor and shoot those birds out of the sky?' I do remember. Inverness, five years ago, I was pregnant with Ava, and a group from suburban New Jersey were acting out *Call of the Wild.* 'I thought no one in England could use a gun!' one of them shouted, and the Scottish beaters scratched their noses. 'I tried to wring the neck on that pheasant I shot

. . . and I couldn't do it . . .' He looks up at me, pleading. 'I couldn't wring the neck of a bird small enough to carry in my hand.' He sits back on his heels. 'He was warm. Under his feathers.' Disgust makes his shoulders shudder. 'I wasn't expecting that.' His face crumples again.

It takes me a few moments to realise someone is knocking. Paul jumps when he hears the noise and bangs his head on the table, sinking back down cross-legged on the floor. I struggle to my feet to see Marcus opening the back door.

'Kate, I think you should know . . .' He tails off as something about the two of us makes him lose his train of thought. He stands awkwardly in the kitchen where I know he used to feel so at home. 'They've found a knife in the canal.'

Paul bows his head and groans when we both turn to look at him.

34

Paul goes to spend the night at John's house. I tell him quietly that I think it would be better. He said sorry many times but we were talking from opposite ends of the room, unable to touch or comfort each other. I collect the children from Sarah's, wondering what the blood test on the scarf will eventually reveal. I'm in limbo until then; veering between hoping and fearing that I've got it all wrong. I watch *Crime Time* by myself in the living room with the lights off. Gerry appears on the programme but I can't even find the means to be excited or pleased that my hunch paid off. I should be, because tonight he's calm and articulate and Marika is entranced. Shaheena texts me when the show is finished. 'He appeared at the studio when we were already on air. Livvy is SO made up! Well done you.' I don't have the energy to text her back.

I wake in the night in a clammy sweat from a nightmare where Melody is surfing on a tsunami in her red dress towards me, her thighs taut as a sprinter's and a triumphant grin on her face, to find the bed cold and empty.

I ring Lex at 6.00 a.m., but there's no answer. I can't even have the satisfaction of his reaction to Paul being released. I feel the tight wool of my old polo neck scratching my chin as I lead Josh and Ava into the school playground. Livid bruises have appeared on my neck in the night and this black top, full of moths that I shook awake after long months of dark slumber, is the only thing I can find to cover them. As my face recovers my body suffers; but even after all the drama I could pass for normal. I wonder how many other women have walked through these gates with a glassy smile and the fading imprint of a male hand upon them. Josh scoots away to swap football cards with a group of boys by the bins; Ava holds my hand as I wait outside the nursery. The sun begins to warm my face, a sign of spring strengthening its grip. I'm too hot in this top, but I'm still here. Paul stepped back from the precipice – he let me go. I look around at the milling bodies, children careering wildly in circles across the concrete, and possibilities fracture inside me. Cassidy asks me if I want to help at the cake sale, Sarah waves and gives me a T sign – yes, I'd like a cuppa and a chat after drop-off. Becca starts moaning to me about night feeds, I politely try to ignore her. The bell rings and I see Josh lining up to go in. I am alone, cast adrift from the comfort and the renown of Paul's shadow. I swallow, which is still painful after yesterday. I am rubbed raw all over, but my wounds will heal. I don't have the fears and the defeat my mother did, I'm a different generation. I have a new career, I still have my children. The bruises will fade, my cut will scab, the love of my children will sustain me. We can, we will and we must recover from Paul's most grievous error.

'. . . so I've decided to cut out wheat.' I look blankly at Becca, I think she's been talking to me for a while. 'Oh, Kate, I forgot to say, I found out whose dog it was.' She watches me blink and frown. 'You know! That day you got ill at Cassidy's, you said a dog had been knocked over? Well, I think it's my sister's Pilates teacher's Labrador. He had a beautiful black coat and was such a loving thing, I remember once in the park he came running up to Maxie and was – oh, are they coming in here?'

'There's three cars!' Cassidy shouts.

'They're not in uniform—'

'What do they want?'

'That one's carrying a radio.'

'So many!'

'Are they going to the offices?'

'I hope no one's been hurt—'

'It must be something serious—'

'They're coming over here!'

'Kate . . . ?'

'Kate . . . oh my.'

Cassidy and Becca back away. My adopted family of the last five minutes has proved fickle. O'Shea walks across the hopscotch game and past the climbing frame. Samuels and White and two others I don't recognise flank her. They stride purposefully, intent on bearing down on me, but I see them in slow motion as things are happening too quickly for me to process. The dog. Can it be? Could the scarf have only dog's blood on it? The grain of my certainty, the sand on which my suspicion was built, has started to slip away.

'Mrs Kate Forman,' O'Shea stands in front of me, 'I'm arresting you on suspicion of the murder of Melody Graham.'

I sense a collective intake of breath from about sixty mothers gathered around me. Perhaps for the only time ever in this Victorian school's hundred-and-fifty-year history, the playground falls silent without anyone having to shout. Samuels takes out a pair of handcuffs and snaps me into them. The click echoes around the buildings that house my children. Someone grabs my elbow and O'Shea and Samuels walk side by side with me to the gate.

'Oh, I knew it,' Becca whispers.

In films the innocent walk with their heads held high, defying those that condemn them. They're heroes, but I walk with my eyes on the cracked concrete, the gawps from my contemporaries burning on my cheeks.

'Murderer!' a woman shouts and the crowd ripples. Samuels

clutches me tighter and speeds up. Clusters of hard eyes stare. We pass the headmistress, the caretaker, a reporter on a national newspaper, phone already out of her handbag, the lollipop lady, her stick hanging as if broken by her side, and Sarah, her eyes filled with tears, who calls to me that she'll pick my kids up after school. I manage to nod as Samuels opens the door of the car. A woman running late pulls her kids away in case they make the mistake of touching me. He holds my head quite gently as he guides me into the back seat.

35

O'Shea is sitting opposite me, elbows and forearms aligned with the edge of the desk. She is irritatingly calm. 'Let me repeat, the scarf found in your house has traces of Melody's blood on it. The knife found in the canal at the end of your garden is the same size and the blade the same shape as the one used to stab Melody. Whose scarf is it, Kate?'

'It's Paul's.'

'Is it?'

'I phoned *you* to tell you about the scarf!'

O'Shea picks up another file on the desk and opens it, subduing its attempts to spring shut by holding its edges down against the table with her palms. She pulls out a photo. 'Can you describe for me what this picture shows, please?'

The solicitor sits forward shoulder to shoulder with me. Even he can't resist a gander. I touch the computer printout, hoping my body heat might reassemble the image. It's me, Josh and Ava grinning stupidly at the camera from a clifftop. We're wrapped up in thick coats and wellingtons. My children stand either side of me and we're leaning into a strong wind, my face partly obscured by a messy tumble of hair. Round my neck is Paul's scarf. I hear my solicitor exhale. I thought Paul was being kind when he offered me that cashmere ribbon of warmth. 'I've got a hat,' he'd said as he opened the boot of the car to get out his coat. 'It's colder than we thought, take this scarf.' He'd held out his arms and looped the scarf over my head, pulling me towards him. We'd held hands as we'd swayed like drunks in the strong south-westerly to the viewpoint, determined to get some fresh air before hunkering down in the pub for the afternoon. The photo was taken at February half-term on the Devon cliffs where Paul wants his ashes scattered.

'Since no answer is forthcoming, I will describe the photo,' O'Shea says to the tape machine. 'Kate Forman is photographed wearing the scarf stained with Melody Graham's blood.'

O'Shea turns over a piece of paper on the table. 'Monday evening, the eighth of March, where were you?'

'I've already told you, I was at home.'

'How many cars do you own, Kate?'

'Why does that matter?'

'Paul took one car that night, but you own another, don't you? Don't you, Kate? It doesn't sit in the drive, you park it in the street.'

'Can I have a cigarette?'

'There's no smoking in police stations, I'm afraid, Kate.' Samuels leaves the room and O'Shea turns to the tape machine, saying, 'DS Samuels leaves the room,' before turning back to me. 'Did you take the car that night?'

'And leave my kids alone?'

'It happens all the time.'

'No, I did not take that car and leave my kids alone in the house!'

'Tell me about your work, Kate.'

'What do you want to know?'

'Well, you were part of the production team on *Inside-Out*.'

'I had a minor role and I worked entirely from home.'

'But you must know Gerry Bonacorsi very well.'

'No, I don't. I've hardly ever met him.'

'But you met him at Cheltenham Races just this week. It was you who persuaded him to appear – yet again – on television. On *Crime Time*. Your work number is in his phone. One of only two numbers, I understand.' I run my hand across my cheek. I'm caught. 'Did he impress you, Kate? Did he give you ideas? He seems to have impressed everyone else. He's the new hero of the hour, for reasons I can't fathom. I'm no fan of the justice system but they were right to keep him in for a long stretch. Just because he can spin a good story in a comfy accent, well I'm not so easily taken in . . .' she pulls on her starchy cuff, irritated that she let her feelings be known '. . . by him or by you. You've seen hours of footage, heard him banging on and on' – at this she rolls her eyes to the ceiling in a sarcastic flourish – 'about his life, his passions, his temper. You were in the perfect position to carry out a copycat murder.'

'This is ridiculous. Why on earth would I kill her? And why would I kill her in that way? It's too obvious! Why would I chuck the knife in the canal behind my house when there would have been a hundred London bins to throw it in on my way home? Same for the scarf. Why would I keep such an incriminating thing in my house?'

'DS Samuels re-enters the room,' O'Shea says. Samuels leans against the wall and shoves his hands in his pockets. 'Why don't you tell us?' O'Shea continues. 'I think you kept the scarf and told us about it to frame Paul.'

'This is madness!'

'Because that's the perfect revenge, isn't it, Kate?' O'Shea is sitting forward now, speaking quietly. She's put too much fabric conditioner in her clothes wash and an unpleasant waft of violets hits me. 'You kill your husband's lover but that's not enough, you want to make sure that he really suffers, that he really understands what he's put you through—'

'Everything you're accusing me of equally applies to Paul. Why isn't he in here?'

'Paul has an alibi.'

'Yeah, I gave it to him!'

O'Shea doesn't take her eyes off me. 'Turns out your husband has another woman who'll vouch for him.' She notes my frown. 'Paul Forman claims that he was with Portia Wetherall after he left the pub that evening.'

'Oh for Christ's sake!'

'She's the CEO of one of the biggest companies in the UK—'

'I know that!'

'This news doesn't make you very happy, does it, Kate?'

'He never bloody mentioned it before!'

'Does Paul keep a lot of secrets from you, do you think? Does he keep other women from you? As his wife of more than – what is it, eight years? – does that make you angry, Kate? Does it make you mad?' O'Shea breaks her gaze. 'Did his affair with Melody make you really mad? Jealous enough to kill her?' I make a scoffing noise and jump as Samuels bangs his hand down sharply on the table.

'You're wasting our time here! He wasn't just fucking her, he was going to leave you for her, wasn't he? He found music with Melody, didn't he, Kate? They were going to make more than just telly together!' I sit on my hands and pinch the back of my thighs. 'I've got a question for you, Kate, what *one* person does less work than a wealthy TV executive and enjoys themselves more? Answer: his wife! You stood to lose your money and your status to a younger model and you killed her for that.'

'I didn't kill anybody!'

'Why did you break into your husband's offices?' O'Shea asks.

The solicitor comes alive and does what he's paid to do. 'As far as I am aware that is not what actually happened that night. Mrs Forman used her husband's key to enter the premises.'

235

O'Shea rephrases. 'What were you looking for in the middle of the night? What was so important that it couldn't wait until the morning?'

'I was looking for evidence to back up or destroy my suspicions. Don't you think I was desperate for it all not to be true! And I did find things! I've got evidence that proves misconduct on Lex's part that would potentially bar him from receiving his final payout from the sale; the financial arrangements with Melody for her ideas are not clear-cut at all. In fact it's a mess, and that's suspicious to me.'

O'Shea waves her hand as if drying nail polish. 'We know all about the finances of Forwood and Melody's contribution to it. It sounds thin to me.'

Samuels tries to pace the room, but it's so small that after two steps he has to turn. 'This is a pointless distraction. You need to start talking, Kate. You need to give us something, or you're going down for murder. They'll be making an *Inside-Out* about you in twenty-five years, but your daughter won't be watching! How old is she? Four? She won't remember you. She'll have to look at a photo to know who you are, presuming he lets her keep any. She'll have a new mother, probably new brothers and sisters, because a man like Paul won't be single for long, will he?'

'Stop it.'

'You thought you felt jealous about Melody, but imagine living your life knowing he's with another woman and *your* children!'

'Just stop it!' It's come out as a scream as the depth of the pit that I'm in begins to become clear.

'I think my client needs a break, this is all quite intense,' the solicitor says.

Samuels leans across O'Shea and looms over me, his large hand on the table. 'Remember, Kate, when you go back to that cell, when you look at those four walls, if you *really* didn't kill her, then he's stitched you up good and proper. So think, Kate.' Samuels taps the side of his head with his forefinger as he moves in close to me. 'Think hard,' he whispers.

'It's important that we take a break now,' my solicitor says.

O'Shea stacks her folders in a pile and aligns the edges. I get the feeling she's not entirely convinced of Samuels's interview techniques. 'Don't think that it's a you-or-him fight,' she adds, her chair scraping back across the lino. 'I might find that you're both in it together.' She turns towards the tape machine. 'The time is twelve-twenty-two, this interview is terminated.' She leans forward to push the off button and stands.

'Just tell me one thing,' I'm pleading with her. 'Did you find any of her blood in the sink?'

O'Shea looks back at me as she opens the door. 'No, but we don't need any of her blood to be in the sink. We've got enough to charge you already.'

The tension of not knowing has finally been broken: he did it. He did it. He. Did. It. The blood on that scarf was hers. The evidence, cold, hard evidence, points to Paul. I wave away the institutional slop, chew my fingers to replace my cigarette craving. I play back in my mind every step from finding him in the kitchen on that fateful night. I can see Paul grinning disarmingly in my mind right now. He is so good at creating atmospheres, at getting people to do what he wants, at manipulating the crowd, the police. Portia would agree to providing an alibi, of course. This nightmare has produced more free publicity and notoriety for *Inside-Out* and raised the profile of Forwood TV to an unprecedented level. Who with ambition could resist a bit of I'll scratch your back, you scratch mine? A little lie here, a big fat lie there, can create new alliances more powerful than I can guess. It's all a game if you're on the winning side, just like Wink Murder.

Never mind those that are trampled on along the boulevard to victory. He planned it all so perfectly. Maybe I've found my first master criminal. He's played me, Lex and Portia perfectly. He's left no flank exposed, no end untied.

And yet. And yet . . . I used to make a living asking questions to get unexpected results. Ask a different question and you get a different answer. What about the dog? The dog doesn't fit. And a master criminal makes sure everything fits. What have you overlooked, Paul? What can I exploit to save myself?

My solicitor comes to see me at my request. He's a thin man with glasses and long sideburns which rasp when he scratches them. The police offered him to me and I accepted with the enthusiasm of a wedding guest deciding between chicken or salmon. John came to represent me, but I sent him away. He's contaminated with Paul, aligned with his brother. So it's Theo with the raspy face and me against the world. 'Do they have enough to charge me?'

'Yes, but they'll be keen to make the case stronger. Connecting the evidence to you is not as clear-cut as they would like. Your DNA is not on the knife, and the scarf could have been worn by you or your husband. They're checking your car but if they don't have anything by now I think it's going to come back clean.'

'Surely this sudden alibi of Paul's looks suspicious?'

Theo rocks back on worn black shoes. 'My job here is to represent you, Mrs Forman. I don't think it helps for me to speculate on other issues.'

'My name's Kate. Stop calling me Forman.'

Theo nods and blows air into his ginger cheeks. 'I did over-hear a conversation in the corridor just now.' He pauses while I look up from the floor. 'Seems that there's a split in the ranks. O'Shea's not a hundred per cent convinced they've got the real story—'

'She hasn't!'

'– but she's a lone voice. The pressure will be building to charge you and have done.'

'Where does she see the gaps?'

'I'm afraid I don't know. They've applied to keep you in overnight as O'Shea has been called away. I'll see you in the morning.' I sink down on to the cell bed's plastic covering. I don't want to see Theo first thing, I want to see my children.

'Can you get me a cup of tea and a Snickers bar?' Theo pauses and scratches. 'Come on, I saw the machine in the corridor.' He nods and a few minutes later I get my request.

I don't sleep at all. I stare at the arrow pointing to Mecca on the ceiling. On my interrogation course I learned that the first thing a police interviewer has to do is stop the suspect repeating that he's innocent. The more he says it, the more convinced he is of it and the harder it is to get a confession. I repeat it so often to myself it becomes a mantra. I keep repeating it just in case I start to waver, because the evidence is building against me like snow crystals on a mountain overhang and I'm about to be sunk by an avalanche. Portia gave Paul an alibi. Paul, you set it all up. I remember you said something to me once. 'It takes as much effort to work on something small as it does on something big. So always aim big.'

You've aimed as high as possible. I think of the picture of me in the scarf. You must have planned this a long, long time ago. I touch the breeze-block wall, trace the grainy roughness under my palm. 'Fuck', someone's scrawled on it. I couldn't put it better myself. I don't understand why Paul would set me up. Extra money isn't enough of a motive, I know him well enough to know that, but I can't see what I'm missing. I need to talk to Lex. I've got to ask the right questions to get the right answers. I have to get out of here. I wipe my hands down my nose and drop them off my chin. If I ever get out, it's you or me, Paul; me or you.

36

It must be the morning because O'Shea is standing outside the cell as it's unlocked. 'Come on Kate, round two.' I follow her and Samuels along a corridor, eager to be out.

She offers me a cup of tea, which I gratefully accept. She's wearing a pale pink blouse with a rounded collar. She takes her jacket off and hangs it neatly over the back of her chair. The iron creases down her sleeves could cut you. I approve. Theo arrives looking crumpled. I can see that O'Shea doesn't approve.

'Tell me about your marriage, Kate.'

'We had a very successful marriage.'

'Had? What changed?'

'I found him with blood on his hands, raving . . . that's what changed!'

'So until just over a fortnight ago it was idyllic in the Forman marriage?'

Is it really such a short time? Has all this happened in only sixteen days? It's not possible.

O'Shea turns to Samuels, who hands her a copy of the *Daily Mail*. 'Is this what you call success?' She opens the paper to a double-page spread which contains at its centre a photo of Marcus hugging me tight by the canal as my children look on. It's taken that day he rowed us across. '*Inside-Out* creator's wife accused of Melody murder' screams the headline.

In what reads like a plot from a TV drama that her husband could have made, Kate Forman, wife of *Inside-Out* creator Paul Forman, has been arrested for the murder of TV researcher Melody Graham, 26. Rumours of an affair between one of British television's most successful and high-profile producers and Melody have produced a potent motive for this latest arrest and, as this dramatic picture shows, all is not as it seems in the TV power-broker's marriage. Marcus Dutoit, 22, a tree surgeon, lives on a narrowboat moored in the back garden of the couple's luxury London home. This unconventional arrangement raised eyebrows among the Forwoods' neighbours and at Forwood TV . . .

I can't keep reading in a linear way and jump to a photo of Astrid, bigger even than the one of Melody. I see she's quoted further down the article. 'Kate seemed such a nice lady, a bit like a favourite aunt, but her relationship with Marcus struck me as inappropriate for someone of her standing . . .' She's described herself as 'Paul's executive assistant'.

'This is appalling . . .' I trail off, hopelessness overwhelming me. Poor Marcus, a small act of kindness misconstrued, a private life splattered in newsprint. 'That has an entirely innocent explanation, and I know you know it.'

O'Shea folds the paper away. 'The problem here, Kate, is that so much of this story is supposed to be innocent. But the scarf, the knife in the canal, come on! From where I'm sitting it's very clear. It's you, him, or both of you.'

'Everyone knew about that canal! Forwood used the boat as an office for a while, a lot of people at work knew how to get to it. You didn't figure that, did you!' I take bitter satisfaction from seeing O'Shea and Samuels exchange looks. 'They used to house the accounts department in there, it was before they moved to the new premises and they were desperately short on space. So anyone could have dumped the knife there.'

'You're clutching at straws, Kate.'

'Yes I am! Because the innocent don't have all the answers! I don't have the answers, but I know I didn't kill her! I'm not saying anything else.' And after half an hour of futile attempts to get me to open up, admit, confess or crack, they lead me back to a cell where I spend the next three hours listening to the raving drunk next door shout profanities and chant.

Two hours after that, when the drunk's cried himself out and has keeled over on his floor, Theo comes in. 'I've got some surprising news. They're going to let you go.'

'What the—'

'She's got *cojones*, this DI,' he adds, shaking his head. 'It's not a popular decision. They might be tailing you, see where you go.'

'I thought the evidence was overwhelming?'

'They can't be sure it's not your husband. His alibi still leaves just enough time to have killed her. It's very tight, but still possible.'

'I suppose I should be glad, but knowing that if I'm out he must be in feels like a lose-lose to me.' Theo scratches his sideburns by way of an answer.

37

A uniformed policeman opens the door to the custody suite and I follow him through to the foyer of the station, where an elderly couple are waiting on chairs. I hesitate to walk out the front door but Theo reassures me the press don't know which station I'm being held at. We emerge, blinking into the late afternoon, and no one gives us a backwards glance. Theo hands me his card. He's interested in representing me in court. I know he thinks it'll come to that unless I get a lot smarter at finding something that gets me off the hook.

I need to talk to Lex. He was there that night in the pub, he met Melody before she died. He wanted to talk to me earlier and now he's gone to ground and I'm going to find out why. His phone goes straight to voicemail. I phone Sarah and have a quick talk with Josh and Ava, swallowing down my tears. Sarah comes back on the line and breezily reassures me they're fine. I force them from my mind as I hail a cab and turn my thoughts to Lex. I'm going to damn well wait outside his flat until he comes home, they always do in the end. But after two hours I'm cold and bored. Paul sends me a message saying he's picked the children up from Sarah. He urges me to come home, but I have to get some answers first.

I put my frozen hand on the fashionable grainy wood of his loft door. Three heavy top-of-the-range locks bar my entry. I want to get in there and hunt for motives and secrets, but I can't exactly walk in. Then I have an idea.

It's gone 7.30 p.m. by the time I get to Forwood's offices. Repeated ringing on the doorbell brings a young girl in a cleaning-company uniform peering round the inner door. 'Is Rosa there? Rosa, the cleaner?' She understands the one word that matters and unlocks the door. Just as I suspected, the room is deserted. Rarely is anyone here beyond 7.00 p.m. I step around bulging bin bags towards a stout woman wearing Marigolds and pulling on a Hoover nozzle. 'Rosa!'

She turns and switches the machine off, wiping her hands on autopilot down the checked apron uniform she wears. She takes a moment to register who I am. 'Ah! Mrs Forman, very well?' Her snaggle-toothed grin is mirrored in my own. My God, she doesn't know. Every evening she upturns the wire waste baskets and crumples up the papers strewn over Forwood employees' desks, but she never reads any of them, never watches the news. She takes none of it in. Most of the staff never speak to her, the majority have never registered her face, she's just part of the army of workers who revolve around and sustain those important enough to have reached the centre of things. She has no idea of the maelstrom of scandal swirling through here, that I have become infamous, that she should avoid me. 'Childrens? Good?'

I put my hand on her shoulder and nod. I open my bag and pull out my wallet. 'Look, I have a new picture.' This is one from about two months ago; we look a perfect, serene and loving family unit. Rosa beams. 'Beautiful! You very lucky!'

'Rosa, I need something important.' I talk slowly because her English is bad. She nods carefully. 'You have keys to Lex's house?' She frowns. 'Do you have keys to his house?' I mime turning keys in a lock.

'Yes, Mrs Forman, I clean his house.'

I nod enthusiastically. John once told me that Lex puts every expense he can through the books to cut his tax liabilities, even his personal cleaning. Good old John. 'I know. Can you give me the keys? It's his birthday tomorrow, we are doing a surprise party in his house.' Rosa looks blank. 'A party. I'll make cake, cook lots of food, then lights out and when Lex comes homes and opens the door, out we all jump – surprise!' I mime like bad vaudeville. 'Can I take your keys and bring them back to you later in the week?'

It takes a few moments before her mental translation is done and the smile breaks out. 'Ah, Mrs Forman, good idea!' She walks over to the stand where her bag and coat hang and searches through, pulling out a set of keys. They glint in my dry palm and I feel the first stirrings of the call to action.

Lex's door opens silently, his brushed-steel hinges working much better than the swollen wood of my own front door that always catches after rain. I've never been here before. Lex doesn't entertain at home, or his entertaining never includes me. As I climb the stairs and enter the loft space, I decide on the latter. The place is huge with low leather sofas, industrial lights, large, confusing pieces of modern art, a cowhide rug and an open-plan kitchen-cum-bar. There's a bad smell from the kitchen bin, though; Rosa and her Marigolds need to visit.

I study his mosaic tiles and have a root through his bathroom cabinet. Nothing surprising in there, but in a small cupboard inset behind the toilet I find some denture fixative. Ah bless. Lex knows that a twenty-five-year-old would find that even more embarrassing than pile cream.

I'm beginning to luxuriate in my transgressions. I pop the top on a bottle of beer from the fridge and start rummaging through a desk strewn with jottings about his online campaign. I find the workings of Lex's mind fascinating: his ideas are linked together with scratched lines, comments are written in margins, question marks truncate other thoughts that are not pursued. There's a thick file with contracts inside, the buyout by CPTV, Post-its stuck to pages that mention accelerators, and pages and pages of subclauses and addenda. His pad of paper is full of writing and I am leafing through the pages when I spot something on a table they call consoles in interiors magazines. I pick up the Panasonic video camera, still in its brown delivery box, and turn it over in my hands. It's top of the range, digital and wireless. There's a packet of media cards in their skin of plastic. I discard all the wrapping and put the items in my bag. Lex won't mind if I borrow them.

As I remove the cardboard there's a noise from the bedroom that freezes me to my seat. A mobile is ringing. It rings for a long time as I stand motionless in a flat that is not my own, eyes fixed on the door that's not quite closed. The silence booms when the rings cease. He's here, and guilt steals over me at invading his personal space. But the flat doesn't reverberate with the noise of another person. I cross towards the bedroom and slowly push the door with one finger, watching it swing inwards without a sound.

The bad smell is you, Lex.

He's lying at an awkward angle across the bed, facing the ceiling. One of his trainers has come off and lies sole-upwards on the carpet. I swallow down my dread and force myself to take a step into the room. His head is an oozing mess where he's been hit by something heavy and blunt, his eyes stare dully up to nothing. Wound twice around his neck is a length of white rope, the ends frayed. Black bruises cover nearly all his neck. He struggled at the end.

I nearly jump out of my skin as his mobile beeps with an incoming voicemail. I can hear my breath coming fast and shallow, I'm about to have a panic attack and that stings me into action. I can't see his phone and realise that he's lying on it. I grope underneath his heavy back, staring intently at the wardrobe doors to avoid his eyes. I pull out the phone but it's got a lock on it and I can't prise open his secrets. I wipe it and put it down.

I stand uselessly, unsure what to do next. Lex, Lex, give me a sign, please give me a sign of what unfolded here. I try to take in the crime scene with a forensic eye. The flat's tidy, the bed made, there are no cups or ashtrays or half-finished bottles of wine or lines of coke. I check the dishwasher. The cycle has run with a selection of cups, plates and cutlery; there are no wine glasses. The drying rack is empty. I check for a dust outline from missing objects, but Rosa does her job well. There's nothing.

This wasn't a social call, but you let someone you knew in here, someone you knew so well that they could surprise you in your own bedroom. I look around for anything heavy that looks like it might have been used to hit Lex on the head, but decide it's probobly been taken. I wonder if it's been dumped in the canal. What did they hit you with, Lex? The blow didn't kill you, but it incapacitated you. You would have known what was coming.

Oh, Lex, forgive me my suspicions and my self-right-eousness. Our car crash together takes on an entirely different hue, the innocent, scared man fighting shadows. I stand for a few more minutes, hoping something is offered up, but there is nothing.

I close the door and wipe it with my sleeve. Out here in the corridor I can hear the thum-thum of next door's fashionable music and a woman's laughter. A guy is enjoying living in a loft in Central London. I bet the postcode attracts women back here with little effort. But I have to get out.

Only when I'm half a mile away do I use a payphone to make an anonymous 999 call. Five minutes further on I fall to the wet pavement and howl, partly with the shock of what I have discovered and also with the horror of how stupid I have been at a moment when I needed to be clinical. I left my beer bottle next to his laptop, my saliva glistening on the rim.

38

Jessie unchains the metal gate outside her studio, struggling in the gloom with the padlock. 'I know it's a pain, but the shop down the road was ramraided the other day.'

'I thought that had died out in the nineties.'

'A recession re-emergence, apparently.' I'm not sure whether a thief would think it worth ruining a car for one of Jessie's paintings but I let that slide. She's here, that's the main – the only – thing that matters. I've got a bit of space to think what I'm going to do next. I can't go home however desperate I am to see the kids; the police would pick me up as the prime suspect in Lex's murder. 'How are you? Have you managed to sort things out with Paul?' I stare at her blankly as she taps her finger against her temple as we head up the stairs to her studio. 'Keep up, Kate! You thought he was having an affair.' It's as if time has wrinkled and I've stepped across vast swathes without a blink. An affair. How quaint that sounds and how far we have moved from there. Jessie's been busying about in her creative bubble, as uninformed and unaware as newly arrived immigrant cleaner. We enter the studio and I sling my bag and myself down on a varnish-splattered school bench next to a Calor Gas heater. 'By the way, I've got a business meeting in about half an hour. I know it's a bit late but she couldn't fit me in any other time. So you may want to make yourself scarce for that, then we can go out for a drink after.'

'Lex has been murdered.' Jessie stops moving, a canvas a

useless prop in her arms. 'I just found his body. The police will think I killed him, they already think I killed Melody.' A look I'm most familiar with dawns on Jessie's face: slack-jawed incomprehension. 'The same method was used on both . . .' I tail off, realising I'm going to have to go back to the beginning. I watch her eyes blinking and her eyebrows dancing as she struggles to process what she's hearing.

'Why?' She's getting angry now. 'Why was Lex killed?'

'I don't know. He must have found something.'

'What did he find, Kate? Think!'

'I don't know.' I study Jessie's brittle fingernails as they clasp the canvas, see hangnails sharp as razors poking skywards, dried out by turps and cold studios, chapped by work at the artistic coalface. Hands say a lot about a person. Melody's fingernails were short and electric blue and clashed with her dress; Paul's hands are warm and soft, used to clicking from one PowerPoint presentation to another. 'Something crucial enough it was worth killing him for.'

Jessie puts the canvas against the wall and rubs her palms down paint-stained trousers and grabs her knees, as if trying to protect herself from what she's hearing. 'You really think Paul did it?'

I start to cry with the hopelessness of it all. 'I don't know, but how I can think anything else! Portia has given Paul his alibi—'

'Portia Wetherall?'

'The same.'

'She's my business meeting. We're trying to find a solution to the problem with Raiph's commission. He doesn't like it.'

'Oh.'

'He insisted on seeing it when I'd only really just begun; he wanted to see my work in progress, something I normally never let people do, but Portia twisted my arm and now he wants me to change it even though it's unfinished! They

250

all think they're the bloody Medicis, ordering people around.'

'Oh dear. I put in a good word for you with Portia, I thought it would be a nice bit of work.'

'Well, in the light of the *uplift*, as the Americans say, in my career, it's looking like a savvy investment for Raiph, and he's still not happy!'

'Where is it?' She walks over to the far side of the studio and pulls back a piece of material protecting a canvas. The picture is in Jessie's usual style, vibrant, primary colours bleed into one another, saucer-shaped eyes sit in livid-pink face flesh. Raiph's grey suit is still just an outline but there are the beginnings of huge, distorted shoulders. It's art that demands attention, a long way from a watercolour on the wall of a restaurant chain. 'Why did he have such a strong reaction? He knew what your style was.'

'He didn't like what I'd written.'

Jessie's 'signature' is a word or phrase that floats in the lurid-coloured space next to her subject's head. On this picture emerald lettering dances next to Raiph's face: 'Green green grass'.

Jessie's mobile rings. 'I'll be right down,' she says, turning to me and registering my look of alarm. 'It's Portia—'

'I can't see anybody—'

'You sure? You want to ask her about her alibi for Paul?'

Our eyes lock in understanding. 'Don't tell her about Lex,' I say. 'I doubt it's public knowledge yet.'

'I'll bring her up.' She picks up her keys and disappears out of the door; several moments later they both walk back in the room.

When Portia sees me she exclaims loudly and makes a show of hugging me closely and kissing me on both cheeks as if defying the prevailing public opinion. 'My God, what are they putting you and your family through!' I stay mute as she continues. 'I know it's hard but you mustn't read those pieces, remember it's only entertainment at your expense. However, I do think Paul's been very slow off the mark here. You need a PR, someone who can represent your family and speak on your behalf. At a time like this you need a professional in your corner.' She sits down on the bench and opens her bag, pulling out her phone. 'You're twisting and turning this way and that in the glare of the media but it's time to take control. Now, I know a very good reputational management firm whose boss is an old friend of mine, you really should give him a call. Mention my name, please.' She pulls a leather-bound notebook from her bag, takes out a sheet of paper and writes a number down. 'Is this your bag?' She tucks the paper underneath it. 'By all means send his bill to my office.'

'Do you want a drink, Portia?' Jessie asks, and Portia accepts a glass of water. Her neat shoes and pricey trouser suit look comically out of place in this rat warren of studio spaces, her convertible is likely to be nicked at any moment outside, but she looks like she's enjoying herself.

'If there is anything else I can do to help, just call me. I mean that.'

'Why did you give Paul an alibi?'

Portia doesn't flinch, she turns to me directly. She's used to awkward questions. 'I gave him an alibi because I met him. I take it you want to know as much as possible about what happened with Paul the night Melody was killed?'

'Yes.'

'That's understandable.'

'Why did you meet him?'

Portia takes a sip of water, looks around for somewhere to put her glass and settles on the floor. She pauses, thinking about what she's going to say. 'OK, Kate, I have often wondered what I'd say if you asked me that, but on reflection the best thing is simply the truth. There's no opportunity for being caught out later if you tell the truth.' Dread begins to rock-climb my spine. 'I've tried to be as specific as I can be about the time, but inevitably I'm not a hundred per cent sure when it was that we met.'

'Which was?'

'Ten-thirty, maybe as late as ten-forty-five.'

Jessie glances at me, amazed. She'd be hard-pressed to remember the day something happened, let alone the divisions of an hour.

'We talked in my car, partly because it was pouring with rain. It was quite a short meeting.' Portia gets off the bench and walks slowly behind it.

'And why did you—?'

'I'm CEO of a company that turns over around two billion pounds a year. I'm captain of a ship that many want to steer, if you'll pardon the analogy. Since the first part of the sale of Forwood, Paul has been a shareholder in CPTV. Shareholder votes are important in deciding a company's direction and who leads said company. I was canvassing Paul's opinion, if you like.'

'Why didn't you say all this right at the beginning? Why did Paul keep it secret?'

'I'm afraid you'll have to ask him that. I don't want to second-guess him but I suppose meeting at night in a car, when you retell it like that, it sounds a little . . . grubby. When the police asked me specific questions I could corroborate. I'm also guessing that Lex didn't know about our meeting—'

'Why not?'

'Lex and Paul are equal partners in Forwood, but in the event of that changing—'

'Is that changing?'

'These are hypotheticals. I wanted Paul on my side. I believe he's a rising star. I feel we can work well in the future and I was stating my case. To be blunt, I'd rather have him on board than Lex.' Portia glances from me to Jessie. 'Founders lose control of their companies all the time. Power blocks and alliances change surprisingly quickly. That's just how business is. I wouldn't be doing my job if I didn't pay attention to that.'

'Is this illegal?' asks Jessie.

Portia laughs. 'Don't be ridiculous.' She walks over to the portrait of Raiph. 'I've found over the years that it tends to be those who have the least experience of business dealings who think of them in the most melodramatic terms, be they journalists, Hollywood scriptwriters – or artists.' Portia smiles her winning smile. 'The truth is really just lots of diligent, law-abiding work.' She regards the painting for a long time, really taking it in, and then gives a low laugh. 'So this is what is causing the kerfuffle.' She pauses. 'I like it, Jessie, I really do. But to get on you have to be smart and that involves compromise. It's true of every transaction, from business to making art.' Portia has a lovely voice. It's soft and melodious but full of quiet authority. When she talks you simply want to listen. I can imagine her having a roomful of men in her thrall. 'Even artists have to compromise their vision or their ideals some of the time.'

'I won't do it,' Jessie blurts. 'Sell out and you're dead artistically.'

'Was Paul drunk when you met him that night?'

Portia turns to me, confused that I'm still on the same subject. 'No, he didn't seem so.' She's back in selling mode to Jessie. 'We all work hard. Jessie, you toil away here in this studio that I'll guess is too cold in the winter and stifling in the summer; Kate's spinning too many plates, wondering when they're going to fall; I grind away at the office. We all want payback for that work. Payback comes in many forms—'

'Did you arrange the meeting?' I persist.

'Yes I did.'

'How? How did you do it?'

'I don't recall exactly but I probably talked to him about it.'

'This is why I hate commissions,' moans Jessie. 'Either you buy into the artist's vision or you stay away.'

'He's bought into your vision,' soothes Portia. 'But the bottom line is that what Raiph doesn't want,' she points at the words on the canvas, 'Raiph gets changed.'

'So he's not compromising!' I say.

Portia looks at me ruefully. 'When you get that powerful you don't have to.'

'What does it mean anyway, "Green green grass"?' I ask, coming up and standing close to the canvas.

Jessie comes alive now. 'It's from the Tom Jones song, about a man dreaming of his childhood home and its beauty and innocence when in fact he's on death row and is only going to get home in a coffin.'

I turn to Portia and we give each other a look. 'And the relevance is . . . ?' I ask.

'I'm making a statement about how far he's come, from his seemingly idyllic Irish village, the innocence of his youth has been corrupted by the callousness of the business environment. He's on a mental death row, trapped behind bars of his own making.'

'And you're surprised he doesn't like it?'

Portia interjects. 'I thought I might be able to talk Jessie round to a more . . . accommodating . . . viewpoint to keep Raiph happy.'

Jessie's digging in. 'He's turning my art into some pretty irrelevance that hangs above a fireplace. I might as well have become an interior decorator—'

'A cushion chucker,' I say.

'Yes, a bloody cushion chucker!'

Portia laughs. 'I can see why you two are friends. Person-ally, I love your work, Jessie, you could write anything next to my picture and I'd take in on the chin. I'm annoyed Raiph got in before me for a commission, to be honest. Now I feel I can't ask for one; I don't want to be seen to be slavishly imitating his ideas. You have to be very careful how you posi-tion yourself, in media businesses and in the art market.'

'Of course you can have a picture!' Now it's Jessie whose in selling mode, smelling another sale. I'm getting annoyed, Portia's not even seeing this alibi conversation as important, but it's life or death to me. It's time to shock her out of her safe zone.

'Lex has been murdered.'

Now I get a reaction, now I'm the centre of attention. Portia loses her composure for a moment as she stares at me and I fancy I see fear in her eyes. 'I didn't know that.'

'Not many people do.' There's an awkward silence.

'How did he die?'

'The same way as Melody.'

'A copycat?' She pulls out her phone, her hand shaking. She's about to dial but thinks better of it. 'Do you know anything about "Bloodhound"? Raiph was asking about it.'

I sit down slowly on a paint-splattered chair to try to cover my shock. I want my voice to sound normal. 'Bloodhound?' I shrug. 'I don't know. When did he ask you?'

'A few days ago. Lex had said it was his next big thing.'

I shake my head, the world coming into sharper focus as elation thrills through me. Got you, Raiph.

'Kate? Oh, Kate, I think—' Jessie's staring out of the large studio windows at the street. Something in her voice makes me rush to take a look and instantly I know everything I need to know. Two squad cars have pulled up outside, dark shapes spilling from opening doors. I grab my bag and run for the exit. 'Kate!' Jessie is shouting after me. 'Wait!'

No, I can't wait Jessie. I'm out of time. I won't go back in that cell and impotently wait for others to write my story for me. With this crucial new information I can compose the ending myself, I am still in control. Jessie has grabbed me and is shoving something into my palm. She's handed me her bike key. 'Take the stairs at the end of the corridor. Go out past the toilets.'

Portia takes several quick steps towards us, her face hard. 'Jessie. You may be aiding and abetting a criminal. That is a serious offence.'

My old friend turns to me as the sound of a door being battered with something heavy ricochets up the stairwell. She grabs me by my elbows, squeezing them tightly to my sides, more in hope of my innocence than having evidence to back it up. 'No compromise,' she whispers fiercely, and then I'm running with a final backwards glance at Portia's astonished face, taking the stairs five at a time before I burst out of the fire door and pedal away down a back alley filled with rubbish, Jessie's bike helmet bouncing in the broken plastic basket as I rattle over uneven paving stones.

39

I cycle so hard that after ten minutes I have to pull up under a railway bridge, my heart clamouring to get out of my chest. Sweat is trickling down my back and gathering at my knees. A heavy-goods train begins to rumble down the track above me, and I scream over and over and over at what I have unwittingly uncovered, at what Portia so casually mentioned that was so full of meaning to me. Bloodhound. Lex left his sign. For me. I see him now, pinned to the bed, blood seeping into his freshly laundered sheets as in his desperate final seconds he thinks of how he can lay a trap, strains every creative sinew to conjure a way to not let this stand. Lex saved his most imaginative act for last, used his last breaths to transmit that message, hoping it would be carried to me and I would understand its significance. Oh I do, Lex, I do. I won't let you down. I howl anew with the pain and the loss, for Melody and for Lex and for myself. He gasped that final word for me because he knew I wouldn't let it go. Bloodhound. I know the how, but I don't know the why, and I scream with the energy and the rage needed to act, to find that why, to follow that path Lex uncovered and see where it leads.

I swing my leg back over the bowing metal of Jessie's ancient Raleigh, spin the pedal to eleven o'clock. Why Raiph? Why? O'Shea is no nearer the answer than I, she's got computers and access to databases and forensics and the law on her side. But all the systems, processes and protocols are no help here. There's flamboyance, an arrogance at work. Raiph silenced Lex, but that scarf ended up in my house. The knife ended up in the canal. I'm going home and Paul is going to tell me what he knows if it's the last thing he does.

Thirty-five minutes of fast cycling later and things don't seem so clear-cut. I roll to a stop five streets away by some garages. I can't just walk into my house, the police will be waiting for me there. I've made sure my phone is off, the SIM in my back pocket. I have no email access. From melo-dramatic thoughts of vengeance I've shifted to the strictly practical: I'm a fugitive with nowhere to spend a cold night. It's a risk that's probably stupid, but I can't resist the pull of home; the void in my chest where my children sit needs to be filled. I blow on my freezing hands and pedal to a bridge over the canal about half a mile from my house where I can access the water. I lug Jessie's bike down the steps of a nearby house and out of sight of passers-by, locking it to a sapling, ducking down behind a hedge when I hear a car coming. There's a low-rise apartment complex on this corner and I skid down the bank past an electricity substation to a high steel fence at the back of the flats. I prowl about, looking for something to help me over, and find a broken chair by the communal bins. I may be three feet taller but scaling the shiny metal is harder than it looks. I make a huge effort and get nowhere before anger resurfaces in me and I heave myself over, ripping my top and scratching my abdomen painfully in the process. Once I'm over it's a long and arduous journey clinging to the canal bank and inching forward past the garden strips of my neighbours. I daren't approach from across the canal, I'd be too visible. I freeze for a long time at one point as I trip a jittery householder's security light. I cut my hands on spiky bushes as I push through thick vegetation. After a long time I see the outline of the *Marie Rose* in the gloom. It's dark back here for London and very quiet; a hidden, abandoned spot that's idyllic in the sunshine but takes on menacing overtones at night. The canal is a pool of oil next to me. I crouch motionless until my legs are numb. I surprise a roaming fox, who scuttles off past a neighbour's beehive. Water slaps lazily against the wooden slats of the narrow-boat, its blank portholes showing that no one is aboard. Max and Marcus aren't back until next week, they won't mind me borrowing it, and in my bag is the key that fits that thick padlock on the door facing me: landlady's privilege.

When I'm sure no one's around I inch forward until I see my house. Josh's bedroom curtains are closed, the light off. He'll be asleep now, his duvet a tangle round his legs, his hair matted to his forehead. The window along glows with light, from this angle I can see the pictures on my bedroom wall and a pile of Paul's clothes on a chair. The kitchen is dark. I wonder if the police are watching the garden from there.

I move behind the shed and can now board the boat without being seen from the house. I unlock the door and slip inside, putting my palm over the glass of the torch I've had in my bag since breaking into Paul's office. The portholes are small but I daren't turn on the light. In the gloom I check the tiny kitchen by the door: a two-ring cooker and a small fridge. Beyond is a fold-away table with benches and through an archway there are two interconnecting bedrooms with a curtain serving as a wall. At the back is a shower room, a storage space in the stern with a washing machine, and another door to the back deck. The place bears witness to the organ-isational skills of the M&Ms, the beds are covered in clothes that didn't make the cut in their holdalls, beer bottles are stacked on a crowded kitchen surface, and a brand-new pair of ski gloves has been accidentally forgotten on the table next to a laptop.

I turn on the electric fire and am suddenly aware I'm

starving and a poke about in the fridge turns up a dried piece of Cheddar and half a tub of yoghurt. I find two crackers in a cupboard and console myself that I've eaten worse. With a cup of black tea to warm my hands I sit down at the table and half-heartedly punch a key on the laptop. To my amazement it jumps to life, the blue light from the screen throwing gloomy shadows round the room. Max or Marcus never bothered to turn it off, and there's no security code. Now I have things I can do. I take Melody's 'Neat Feet!' CD-Rom from her file and put it in the computer. When it starts playing it's so absurd I want to laugh. The film is taken on a small camera attached to the front of a foot. There is a sequence with someone walking along a brown rug, spiky carpet fibres claw at the lens before the camera swivels and a pair of platforms crunch past. I see a hairgrip, a pen lid kicked against a table leg. The microphone is working too well, picking up every squeak and groan of the shoe's leather sole, but the voices in the room are muffled and indistinct. Someone laughs and a woman's finger is waved in front of the lens. Suddenly the camera lurches skywards and shifts forty-five degrees. The wearer has sat down and put their foot on their knee and Astrid is sticking her tongue out into the tiny camera, the plants in Forwood's offices visible behind her blonde halo. 'Flipping hell, Lex, you pointing that thing up my skirt?' she laughs to camera. There's a rumble and a scrape and the scene goes blank. Lex has turned the camera off, his foot-level filming one of his many ideas that are tested and discarded.

A moment later another video starts, this time his shoe is under a table. He's out of the office now, the floor is cracked white tile and the acoustics are echoey and institutional. The camera swings wildy as Lex bounces one leg up and down before slamming it back down to the floor. Opposite him are a pair of purple ballet pumps placed squarely on the floor.

The wearer has bare legs and elegant ankles, I can see the bones spanning out across her feet as they run down to her toes. Lex shifts in his chair, it may well be a swivel, and at the end of the table are expensive, calfskin stilettos and nude stockings on a pair of crossed legs, one of which is being twirled meditatively. It's impossible to hear what's being said, but the film is arresting enough; the body language is very revealing.

On the left of the ballet pumps are a pair of man's black lace-ups, one of which is stretched across Lex's camera and instantly I know its Paul's shoe, the way his foot scrapes back across the broken tiling. There's about five more minutes of bum-shifting and leg jiggle as Lex's camera stays trained on the wearer of the stilettos and she coquettishly crosses her legs and leans sideways. I'm beginning to tire of Lex's flirting when he seems to swing his body and his foot round, and there, hidden under the table away from prying eyes, a secret moment no one is supposed to share, is the purple ballet pump entwined around Paul's ankle, as clear a sign of a hidden passion as it is possible to have. And as the ballet pump disappears up the back of my husband's trouser leg, I know where I've seen that pair of shoes before: sat neatly under the retro British Rail sign in Melody's bedroom, tidied up and presented to me by her mother.

Fifty per cent of married men cheat. Or seventy per cent. Or all of them in the end, no one really knows. More images of chair legs and knees scroll past but I'm no longer paying attention. I was arrogant enough to assume I could defy those odds. That I was special, that we were the special ones. I thought I was lucky. But I've just seen the brutal evidence, the hard truth that I'm just like everybody else, the happiness of my life built on a fiction. Eloide was right – we share a bond, you've cheated on both of us, Paul. How could you do that to me? You *knew* what you were doing. And, more

262

importantly, Lex knew. His experimental film unwittingly captured it all. How he would have gloated as he handed it over to Melody, a toxic little present.

A burning rage starts to fill me for the complacency I had sunk into, the career opportunities I never took, the way I put Paul's needs before my own, the lazy assumptions into which I had drifted. I slap myself just for the hell of it, slam the CD ROM back into my bag and pull out Lex's camera. 'We're in a media world, Kate,' I whisper sarcastically to no one. 'Smile! Cos you're on camera . . .' I read the instructions cover to cover, my mind sharper than it's felt in years despite my exhaustion. I could memorise every word. I set the machine on a kitchen shelf to get the right angle and start the night-light function. It's time to start turning tables . . .

I begin nervously, my voice croaky and too low. I stumble and begin again, stronger this time. 'My name is Kate Forman and I am on the run from the police. I am wanted for the murder of Melody Graham and Lex Wood. This may be my last opportunity to set the record straight, to prove to you that I am innocent.' The longer I talk the more confident I become. I begin with how I found Paul in the kitchen, that the scarf with Melody's blood was in my house; that I found Lex's body. I am mid-flow when my voice dies in my throat. A clunking is coming from the back door of the boat as it is pulled open and heavy steps descend the short ladder.

40

I have time only to sink down under the trestle, cursing silently that I was stupid enough to think the police wouldn't come here. Long shadows are cast across the floor as a light goes on in the stern and I hear cupboards opening, a bag being dumped on the floor. It doesn't sound like the police. I inch forward on my knees, peering round the corner into the corridor. My angle is restricted but the cupboard door under the stairs is open and an outstretched male arm is pulling at something. There's an old green metal filing cabinet in there, left over from the days this was a Forwood office. Someone's rooting around, and a cold hatred fills my heart. I reckon it's you, Paul, and you're up to something. It's the middle of the night, a long way from the hour anyone needs to check financial transactions or old personnel records. The arm picks up a file, its Milk Blue colour looks green under the strip lighting. The heavy drawer is slammed back into its holder with a screech. The arm careers out of my field of vision and the cupboard door closes with a thud. Yanking my head back, I crouch next to the table as several long strides bring a tall figure into the room, but it's not my cheating husband, it's John.

My astonishment is not mirrored in his face. 'So this is where you are. Are you OK?'

'No. What are you looking for?' He waves his head vaguely, avoiding the question. 'Are there police in the house?'

'Of course.'

'They must have found Paul very persuasive, given the blood test results on the scarf, for him to be in there with the kids while I'm on the run out here,' I say venomously.

John stays silent for a long moment before adding, 'He's worried about you. The kids were crying for you.' My heart feels like its tearing a little from my body. John senses this and adds, 'But they're asleep now.'

He places several files down on the table. 'I haven't got long.' He sits down opposite me, within the range of my camera, which is still recording. 'You've caused quite a stir—'

'I didn't kill them,' I snap.

John looks at me from under his thick eyebrows. 'Why did you break into Lex's flat?'

News travels fast, I think; maybe my 999 call wasn't so anonymous after all.

He doesn't believe me so I push on to try to convince him. 'I thought there might be something there that could help me. What I found was his dead body' – John looks away – 'and no clues at all. But I found my clue later. What I didn't know was that Lex had given me the answer a long time ago, but neither him nor I realised it – until now.' John has turned back towards me and is staring so intently in the half-light that I involuntarily say, 'What?' like a dumb teenager.

'Lex gave you the answer.' It's not a question but a statement, and a frown creases his forehead. 'Jonah and the Whale . . .' he tails off and starts flicking through one of the files. He is so perfectly suited to the night as he bends close to sheaves of paper, after dark the pallor seems to leave his face, it's as if the dull struggle to stay on the wagon drains him more during the day. But then evening always was when John would come alive, be the life and soul, extreme and flamboyant and always the last one to leave. By the time the addiction had really taken hold there was no leaving to go home, just a transition from danker and grottier hangouts in ever-increasing frequency. Now his eyes are bright, a quick, nervous energy pulsing through his shoulders. From this angle, with his forehead bent towards me, he looks a lot like Paul. They have the same hands. I push from my mind with considerable effort the image of where Paul's hands have been. 'Jonah and the Whale. What's that parable mean to you, Kate?'

'Do we have time for this?' I reply tetchily, craning round to see what he's reading, all the while aware that across the garden wait the forces that could stop my searching for ever.

'Is your phone off?'

'Of course.'

'The little guy gets eaten by the big guy . . .' He's flicking through pages. 'Forwood gets gobbled up by CPTV, all's right with the world . . .'

'Tell me what you're talking about!'

John slams the file down so hard on the table that it shakes. He looks straight at me, challengingly. 'Only when you tell me what you know.'

I stare into his face, knowing I'm going to have to take a risk. 'Lex and I had our differences but we both wanted to find out the truth. Lex had a special name for me – it was a private joke at my expense. I think he told that name to his killer, to Raiph—'

'Jonah's going to swallow the whale.' John places his hands gently on top of his head and breathes slowly in his Eureka moment. 'So Lex did know!' John leans forward in his seat, knees splayed far apart as he's too tall to fit properly under the table. 'Two years ago when CPTV was buying Forwood Lex would joke we were Jonah being consumed by the whale. Last week I got a text from Lex saying, "Jonah's gonna eat the whale." It was the last message I ever got from him. But how can we eat the whale? We're a tiny company and they're big. Then this morning, I got a letter from CPTV's lawyers regarding the final payment that CPTV is giving us. They're trying to delay, they're trying to get the payout date put back. So I began to ask myself why. One of the reasons would be if they *couldn't* pay. And if they can't pay, it would have to be because they're bust; one of the biggest media companies in Europe would be bankrupt.'

I shake my head, confused. 'I'm not really getting this. As you said, they're huge.'

'Yes, but being big doesn't mean that they've got a lot of cash. This is a deep recession, banks aren't lending money. Even big companies are having trouble getting extra funds, particularly old-style TV companies like CPTV. And something else: Forwood was valued the way it was two years ago because we rode the boom in telephone voting and texting, it was very prof-itable for us. But since then there've been TV-voting scandals and the income all programmes and channels make from that has dropped a lot. There aren't the huge amounts of money to be made that way now – another reason banks won't lend.' John's nodding now, warming to his theme. 'A small company like Forwood can bankrupt a big company and no one realises—'

'Except Raiph and Lex.'

John rises to his feet and I mirror him. We've got it now. 'Jonah would have eaten the whale.'

'Raiph loses the company he founded and built for forty years.' I stare at John as he skim-reads paragraphs.

He looks so like Paul at this moment, an almost boyish enthusiasm reflected in his arms and shoulders. He's still fit and healthy, no squidges of fat are starting to droop over his waistband. Raiph is old, more used to conference-table pastries and the comfy leather armchairs of a gentlemen's club. Would he have the strength to catch a twenty-six-year-old in trainers who cycled? Maybe. Or maybe not.

John is running a finger across lawyers' jargon. 'I've got to show this to Paul—'

'No!'

John doesn't have time to reply as a noise from the stern brings us both up short. The door has opened and someone's coming down the steps. John wheels round into the corridor, alarm crossing his face as his rangy frame blocks the door.

'You OK back there, Mr Forman?' It's Samuels.

'I've been looking through paperwork.' John walks slowly down the corridor to meet him and I hear the squeak of the filing cabinet.

'You were gone a while, I thought I'd better check on you.' His voice is hard and I can imagine him standing with his head bowed, worried about the low beams inflicting a painful knock.

'I've got something I'm trying to work through and I think it could be important.' He's delaying, giving me precious seconds that I don't know how to use. Samuels grunts, a noise that conveys scepticism, and I hear his shoes scraping on wood as I survey the room looking, searching for something, anything . . .

'This place is a sight to see.' Samuels steps down into the corridor, unimpressed by the lure of the boho life. I imagine his eyes travelling with distaste over the curtained bedrooms, sniffing the unavoidable damp, his lip curling at the dribbly shower.

'Forwood TV used this as the accounts overflow before we moved into the new offices. We took the bedrooms out and it was all open plan . . .' John's babbling and my panic is taking hold. I drop to the floor, clawing at nothing. It's nearly all over . . . My finger hooks round the handle of the trap-door to the bilge. 'They loved working here, they used to tell me. It was the summer though, winters are harder. The cold just seeps in. There's quite an array of wildlife back here.'

'What's through there?'

'That's the kitchen and living room. I'll get the rest of the files and come back to the house.'

It's not worked. The sound of a herd of elephants bears down on my grave. I'm laid out like a corpse under the floorboards, my bag on my chest, the padlock from the front door digging into my ribs as cold water laps at my shoulder blades.

'Can't see the attraction myself,' Samuels mutters, swivelling near the sink. 'You have to be a midget to live in here.' John doesn't answer, I hear him shuffling papers near the table. 'Places like this give me the creeps, to be honest.'

'I can tell you don't holiday on the Norfolk Broads,' John says as Samuels walks round the room before returning and standing right over me. Through the thin gap in the planking I can see his arm reach out for something and I see the straps of Jessie's bike helmet swinging in my narrow field of vision.

'Where do you think she's gone, Mr Forman?'

I can't breathe as his heavy tread pushes the planking lower on to me. 'I don't know, Ben,' John says quietly. 'But if she's got a reason to run, then it'll be a good reason. If she thinks she's right she's very determined, but if she *knows* she's right, I doubt much can stop her.'

'I'm not sure you're the person to talk about limits, Mr Forman.' John doesn't rise to this, I imagine him standing still and absorbing Samuels's cheap jibes.

'Maybe so. But I doubt she's going to give up until she understands the truth.' Samuels makes a scoffing noise. 'She didn't kill them.' Samuels interrupts him by putting the helmet down with a clatter. 'Why are you so sure she did?'

'That much motive, that much evidence, DNA evidence! Come on! She killed Melody in a fit of jealousy and tried to make it look like Gerry, and she killed Lex because she was mad as hell at his gloating about the affair and because he could have killed her in that car crash . . . And now she's on the run! The innocent don't run. It's a done deal.'

'You may think so, but you haven't convinced me. I happen to know that Raiph Spencer is at the Natural History Museum tomorrow for one of his charity gigs,' John shuffles the papers for effect. 'I've got some questions that'll wipe away the feel-good glow.'

Samuels pauses and he may be yawning. 'There's a sweep-stake running at the office as to what time she'll be caught. I've got a quid on four o'clock this morning.'

Their steps recede and I dare to breathe again but I stop abruptly as I'm plunged back into complete darkness as the light is switched off. I hear the door locking. The only thing that keeps me from screaming is John's message to me. I hold on to it as tightly as if it's a hook around which my hand is grasped for dear life as the icy, filthy water laps at the back of my neck.

I make myself mentally count images of slapping Paul a thousand times before I push up the door and gasp my way out of my mounting claustrophobia. Max's and Marcus's mess meant Samuels couldn't see the teacup I'd used or the camera, still winking quietly away on the shelf. In a little burst of triumph at my near escape I turn full on to camera. 'This is Kate Forman, signing off for now. It's four o'clock in the morning and Samuels has lost his bet.'

I turn off the camera and put the media card and the laptop in my bag. I need to sharpen up, I can't make mistakes like that again. I don't know whether John will tell Paul I'm here, so in a great hurry I peel off my sodden clothes and stuff them in the bilge and ransack Marcus's wardrobe for something to wear. I look like an overgrown schoolboy in a brown T-shirt, jeans, sweatshirt and a battered leather jacket. My best finds are an Oakland A's baseball cap I can tuck my hair into and a Swiss Army Knife. I take Jessie's bike helmet, which so very nearly gave me away, and strap it on.

I nervously peer from the portholes, surprised no one's running across the garden. Fifteen minutes after Samuels and John walked back up the garden, I clamber out on to the rowboat and am across the water in a couple of minutes. I'd rather run through deserted streets back to the bike than try to climb over the fence by the bridge, cut hands now hampering my progress. Before I disappear into the alleyway I look back at my house, territory of my greatest domestic triumphs, my happiest moments, my former life. I am suddenly so angry that I've been cast out here in the cold and dark while he sleeps in comfort near our children that I pull out the penknife and start hacking at the weeds on the bank, my jealousy and feelings of betrayal making me temporarily insane. I sever the rope that attaches the boat to the *Marie Rose* in a final act of pointless destruction before sinking back on my bum in tears. Paul's bedroom curtains are closed now, the light off. Are you sleeping soundly, my love? Enjoy. It might be the last time you do.

41

I cycle through deserted streets to south London and arrive at a small terraced house with a broken street light outside. I drop the media card through Livvy's letter box and scrawl a few words on a scrap of paper from my bag. 'Use this in the way you know best. Kate.' It feels like a small-scale insurrection against the army lining up to defeat me. I cycle away before anyone decides to wake early. My tiredness is now overwhelming and I slump down in an abandoned garage for a couple of hours before the cold and an unsettling dream of a purple pump winding round Paul's leg wakes me with a start. As dawn breaks I open the laptop and read the news headlines. My face competes with Lex's for top billing. It's as if we're in a warped beauty contest; the photo is the police mugshot they took when my eye was still bruised. I look like a jealous, homicidal maniac.

Copycat killer strikes again. I click the link for the full story.

Top TV executive Lex Wood was found murdered at his luxury London flat last night in what police believe is the second in a series of 'copycat' killings . . .

I skip forward through the paragraphs.

Police are keen to re-interview Kate Forman, wife of Wood's business partner, Paul Forman, after an anonymous 999 tip-off regarding Woods' murder is thought to have been made by Kate

Forman. She was released from police custody only yesterday after being questioned about the murder of Melody Graham, whose killing bears remarkable similarities to that of Wood. Graham, aged 26, was a researcher on *Inside-Out*, a controversial Forwood programme about murderer Gerry Bonacorsi, who was recently released from jail after serving a life sentence.

The decision by Detective Inspector Anne-Marie O'Shea to release Kate Forman is now looking highly controversial as information comes to light that Wood and Forman were involved in a car crash in north-west London last Wednesday, in which Wood was driving. Several witnesses recall that Forman slapped Wood and, although injured, ran from the scene, refusing medical attention. A police spokesperson urged the public not to approach Forman, who had not returned home last night and was last seen at an artists' studio in Hackney, east London.

Paul Forman said last night, 'I am desperately worried about my wife and urge her to contact me . . .'

The king of crime TV: 'Lex Wood obituary.'

When life imitates art: 'The public are right to ask hard questions of the Met in the light of this latest gaffe in a high-profile murder inquiry . . .'

Forwood looking: 'The small company that punched above its weight in a new TV world . . .'

When the past won't let you go: 'Gerry Bonacorsi's life in the media storm.'

I turn off the computer, partly because I fear the battery expiring but mainly because I can't look at any of it any more.

By nine my hunger is eating its way through my bones, and I have to get some food. I leave the garage, cycle back towards the river and cut through an industrial estate where I find a catering van and risk buying two bacon butties and a giant tea from a skinny teenager who doesn't even make eye contact with me. I shove two Twixes and a can of Fanta in my pockets for later. A sugar rush will do me no harm. All my years of middle-class assimilation, of trying so hard to be something I'm not, are being stripped away. I stop in a cold, empty Battersea Park and slump on an isolated bench, the spiky branches of bare trees swaying overhead. I munch through the second bacon butty and an image of my mother fuelling Lynda and me for our walk to school wafts up with the smell of fat; mum's angry little jabs with the plastic spatula at the sizzling meat as if she thought even the streaky bacon was out to thwart what little happiness she had.

I open the computer and click on *Crime Time*'s website. I feel a rush of gratitude for Livvy: the entire front page is given over to highlighting my video. 'Fugitive Kate claims: Raiph Spencer is copycat killer. <u>Click here</u> for exclusive and sensational revelations.' I duly click and the tape that I filmed in the narrowboat is broadcast in its entirety, including John's theory about the financial motive and my hiding under the floorboards when Samuels arrived. I try to play the video again but it won't load. Then I notice that there have been twenty-two thousand views of it.

I finish off the butty and drink the tea, and refresh the computer page. Google news shows that two blogs are now covering my allegations, caveating everything heavily with 'claims wanted fugitive Kate Forman'. I refresh again and get the first mainstream media headline from the *Daily Mail*: *Bungling cop misses 'copycat strangler'*. I skim-read the following: 'A sensational video sent to TV's *Crime Time* and posted on the internet this morning shows Kate Forman, wanted by the police in connection with the murders of TV researcher Melody Graham and executive Lex Wood, hiding beneath the floorboards of a narrowboat as a policeman fails to notice she's just beneath his feet. The video, made by Forman, contains lurid claims that the head of one of

Britain's biggest media companies murdered Graham and Wood for financial gain. Libel lawyers gasped at the ramifications of this accusation, now in the public domain . . .'

I click back to *Crime Time*. The viewing figures for the video have jumped to more than thirty thousand.

I turn the computer off, fearing for the batteries again. Elation thrills me. The tide, which for so long has been pulling me out, is finally working with me. Livvy has taken a risk, an incredible risk, in posting my video. Raiph's lawyers could shut the whole site down in hours, but the message is out there. I need the momentum to build in order to save myself. It's time to confront Raiph, and John left me the message as to his whereabouts.

With renewed determination I point my wheels towards South Kensington. I stick to side roads but after a while I relax as I'm sure no one will recognise me in these sex-altering clothes. On Marcus these same garments move with the fluidity of the young and rangy, creating an attractive artsy whole; on my dumpier frame they rumple and pool to conjure up a sweaty, poor man. And however avant-garde and uninterested in fashion Marcus might be, he'd never be seen dead in this helmet – a triumph of safety over style and a badge of middle-aged paranoia that renders me invisible. So I grind my way north unnoticed, my insteps pushing down on the pedals.

My burst of belief in my changing fortunes is short-lived. I pull up outside the Natural History Museum and swear under my breath. Never has a children's charity event attracted such interest: there's a crowd nearly a hundred strong outside the main entrance, press and photographers mainly but also hangers-on and passers-by, craning to see what all the fuss is about. TV cameras and presenters are setting up on the lawn. It's as if Hollywood royalty is inside, rather than a sixty-five-year-old businessman with a nasty secret that I've brought to light. I see the tops of two bouncers' heads, keeping the unwanted out. A police car cruises past and I cycle slowly away. Raiph's still in there, but my way is barred. I cut east through some side streets and spot a church in a garden square. I need help and my help has run out. I'm becoming desperate. I connect up the separated bits in my phone and call Eloide. I get her breathy answerphone message and hang up. I crouch down by a tree and get out the computer, find her office number near Regent Street, and dial. The receptionist trills that Eloide's in a meeting. No, I don't want to leave a message. Ten minutes later I call again – she's still busy. My frustration mounts. This could be my last day of freedom for a very long time. I track down a florist's local to her office and order a bouquet to be delivered to Eloide, with a hefty electronic tip for doing it right away. A young woman with poor English reads back my message: 'I need your help. Holy Trinity Brompton, KF.'

I pull open the heavy door to the church and crouch down behind a large pillar to one side away from the entrance. As I hoped I have the place to myself. I type 'Kate Forman video' into Google and get seventeen thousand entries. What started less than two hours ago as one post on a website has become an internet sensation. The mainstream media have joined the fray and we all have our fifteen minutes of fame.

Raiph Spencer 'appalled' by accusations

Crime Time defends video – Livvy is quoted at length, her mood defiant and ebullient – 'Claims made in this video by our employee Kate Forman are simply too important to ignore. This type of personal, heartfelt video evidence is what *Crime Time* is all about. We say, if these claims aren't true – then sue. And another thing. The police can bleat about this video being material relevant to a murder inquiry but it was made by our employee, for us. So hands off until you get a court order.'

Libel laws tested – again: 'A series of allegations of murder in a home-made video posted on a crime website have challenged England's libel laws . . .'

CPTV shares dive as panic spreads

CPTV: A personal tragedy for Raiph Spencer

'Serial Mom' makes a mockery of the Met

It's so much bigger, nastier and interconnected than I had imagined. I may have started the ball rolling but now neither I nor anyone else can stop it. If Raiph isn't being questioned by police already, he soon will be. John may well face serious charges for not telling Samuels I was just a floorboard away from him. Half an hour drags past, my window of opportunity to challenge Raiph closing. The church door opens and closes on various people, but none of them are who I want to see. Finally I hear the door opening and the harsh clack of stilettos on stone. She's here. I peek round the column. She's alone.

'Hello?' Eloide calls out tentatively and moves uncertainly into the church. She's trying to adjust to the gloom after the sunlight outside. 'Hello?' She's louder this time. No one else appears so I move down a row of pews to the central aisle. She notices and comes towards me and a moment later we are sat side by side in the empty church, staring at the altar. 'You're the talk of the town.' She whispers in deference to the place we are in.

'I'm not enjoying it.' I whisper back.

She smooths her skirt over her bony knees. 'That video is quite something. You took a risk contacting me. How did you know I wouldn't go to the police?'

'I didn't.'

'You took your revenge on Paul, I see.'

'How do you mean?'

'The video. His infidelity. The whole world knows now.' Shame travels across my cheeks. My children will find out.

I should have thought of my children. What I said in the middle of the night in a fit of pique and rage will be forever there in cyberspace for my children to discover as they grow up. It should have stayed private. I should have kept control. I should have tried much harder to keep control. Eloide drops her head to one side, staring ahead. 'Public protestations are powerful things. I got married in church.'

'Me too.'

'Those vows, in front of everyone, the tears, I really meant them.' She pauses and turns to me, her face flinty. 'Give me one good reason why I should help you.' Her voice is loud and hard in the echoey space.

'I need to find out the truth if it's the last thing I do. For my children, for Paul, for myself . . .' I trail off. 'To find out if the past – if all this – was just a lie, or a horrible game at my expense.' We sit silently for a moment, staring ahead at the altar where we both once stood, the same man at our sides, the vows of forever enunciated for all our friends and family to hear. 'Eloide, I'm sorry. I'm sorry I caused you pain years ago and I'm sorry that I reacted that way in your kitchen.'

'Don't, you don't have to.'

'No, I do. I guess I was jealous—'

'Of me? You can't be serious! I'm a fucked-up mental head who puts her sliced-up arms around famous waists for a living.'

'Talking of which, is Raiph still at the museum?'

'Yes. The police haven't arrested him yet. The wheels of justice grind slow. You're the one they want at this point, remember, which leaves anyone who's anybody suddenly desperate to get into CPTV's charity gig – including me.'

'Do you think you can get me to him?'

She turns to look at me as she stands, a brilliant smile on her lovely face. 'I do.' She takes her phone from her bag. 'If I can't get in there, no one can.'

We stand in the porch as Eloide spends the next ten minutes talking to PRs and party planners, getting frustrated at various points. Time ticks by as she hunts for a ticket to what is for the next hour or so the hottest venue in town.

'It's not going to work,' I say.

'Come on.' She heads off towards the museum and I follow, pushing Jessie's bike behind her bouncing hair. 'I've spent my life blagging my way into nightclubs. There's always chaos around a queue. The front door really is the best way in.'

Even she pauses when we reach the museum. The crowd is even bigger than before. 'God, this is impossible.'

'Nothing's impossible. We'll try round the corner.' I keep my eyes on the pavement as we come across a side entrance. 'Come on!' she shouts, and we march up to the large glass door only to find it's locked. She hunts for a bell, peers through the glass to see if anyone's the other side while I cast nervous glances up and down the street. She swears softly. 'To the back.'

'Why are you being so nice to me?'

'All this effort isn't going unrewarded, I grant you. If I get you in there this will be the most salacious online posting I've done yet.'

'I give you permission to use any of this however you see fit,' I tell her as I chain the bike to a railing.

Eloide links her arm through mine. 'I didn't think I needed your permission.'

We walk round a traffic barrier at the back of the museum and cross a small car park to a huddle of activity by a large set of doors. Eloide does up the top button on her shirt and ties her hair back with a clip from her handbag. 'It's kids, daytime, you know . . .' She looks me up and down. 'I'm glad I'm not trying to get you into a nightclub.'

'Sorry.' I turn away from a police car parked near the entrance. 'Can you use your press pass?'

Eloide tosses her hair. 'That's exactly what won't be allowed today after what's been made public.' I pull the baseball cap down harder on my head and follow Eloide towards the cluster of people. She pushes towards a bouncer who looks carved from stone and starts explaining loudly about her daughter being inside without her EpiPen. He pulls out a phone and with glacial speed asks the name of the school party her daughter is with. Eloide starts babbling about nut allergies and my heart sinks. This isn't going to work. I stand aside as a minibus pulls up, the back doors swinging open. The bouncer's eyes flit between Eloide and around thirty six-year-olds streaming from the bus. He takes one long step forward, holding out his huge arms in a stop gesture. Eloide intensifies her allergy monologue, her hand resting on the bouncer's chest. The children's screams of day-trip excitement are overlain by the shouts of a harassed woman in a baseball cap. Two other adults grab small hands and swoosh the children forward as the bouncer examines a large embossed ticket.

'We're late!' the teacher exclaims, cartwheeling her arms at the door. The bouncer nods silently, not giving way. Eloide's voice rises through the octaves as the teacher remonstrates with someone and a phone trills with a loud rap ringtone and I reach out and clasp a small brown hand that's moving past me towards those doors 'Ryan, stop pulling Thomas's glasses!' she shouts as I smile down at a little boy in a multicoloured jester's hat, and together we inch past the bouncer as Eloide lets forth the sob of a loving mother. I have one hand on the glass door, the other behind me holding that small hand.

'Quiet, children, please, this is a museum!' a woman calls as I take one step and another and another and Eloide's panicky voice fades. The light changes and I drop the hand I'm holding. I walk slowly towards a toilet sign, push open the swing door and listen to it thwump shut behind me. I am in.

I wash my filthy face and hands in the sink, slick back my hair with water and try to compose myself before heading off down a corridor surrounded on all sides by stuffed animals and skeletons. It takes only a few minutes to find where CPTV's charity event is: it would be hard for it to be more obvious.

CPTV has taken over the grand central hall and around two hundred children are being corralled to sit down in preparation for a speech. The walls of the hall are lined with stalls highlighting the work of the charity and offering up freebies to the kids and the adults alike. I see a paper mountain of brightly coloured hats and a man happy to hand them out; pretty women carrying trays of badges and stickers mingle with the crowd, waiters pass through with trays of champagne glasses for the adults. Raiph stands elevated above the children and staff on a portable dias. He seems to float, God-like, above a wriggling carpet of hair beads and hats. The children ignore him and giggle and gasp instead at the giant dinosaur skeleton looming over them all. Youth workers in royal-blue T-shirts and tracksuit bottoms bend and kneel, shushing their fingers to their lips. Behind them and in front of me are middle-aged white men in suits and expensively dressed women with big rings who are rapt as Raiph delivers his speech. They're looking for signs, trying to interpret a reaction to the maelstrom that's swirling in cyberspace about him. His speech is on message and to the point, he gives nothing away. When he's finished a PR enthusiastically leads the clapping as Raiph bends down and picks up the dias himself, tucking it under his arm before a woman with blonde dreadlocks wrestles it off him.

The children move off to the dinosaur zone as Raiph shares a joke with the woman with dreadlocks. He is surrounded by too many people, I cannot get near, and as a museum guard moves through the crowd I turn back the way I've come. I hadn't thought that the last twenty feet would be the hardest challenge of all. I stand in the corridor behind a prehistoric shin bone, weighing up whether I'll have to confront him in the Gents, when I'm ambushed.

'Give me one good reason why I don't call the police right now.' It's Raiph, and he's not happy.

'There's another tape,' I say, walking quickly away from the party under an arch.

He follows me, pulling out his phone and dialing 999, a bitter smile on his lips.

'Unless it's Lex from the grave saying I killed him, there's nothing you have.'

'Your share price has sunk twenty per cent in the last two hours. Are you prepared to take that chance?'

Raiph's eyes are blue and he stares at me for what I imagine are several seconds of rare indecision, his anger and curiosity fighting each other. He drops the phone to his side. 'You're brave. Foolhardy and brave. Trial by media. I suppose you'd call it poetic justice.'

'When you live by the sword—'

'Die by the sword.' He stops walking. 'When this day ends, whether you're in police custody or not, I'm taking my revenge, on you personally, on your husband, on what's left of Forwood, on that producer who posted your video.'

'How's it feel to be about to lose your company?'

'The same as it always does. You think this is the only time? This is the *eighth* time. This is just how business is.' We stand next to a stone relief set into the tiling on the wall. A dinosaur's backbone curves into a semicircle, which reminds me of the antenatal scan of a human foetus. 'I don't usually have to fend off accusations of double murder at the same time.' Raiph pats his breast pocket, picks out an inhaler and takes a short, sharp pull. 'Why are you here? What do you want from me?'

'I know what "bloodhound" is.'

It doesn't register. 'Think carefully about how you decide to thrash out your final moments in the public eye. A friend of mine in the Met told me this morning that the autopsy shows Lex was killed just over a week ago.' The significance sinks in: eight days ago Lex crashed the car. 'Which means I don't have clear alibis for either murder nights. That's inconvenient, but if you think that means I'm taking the rap for this, then you don't know me at all. In your desperation to save yourself, you picked the wrong target to slander. I might suffer the greater temporary public embarrassment, but I'm also the one who can crush you most comprehensively.' He lifts a finger and points at me. 'Your children are going to be paying off your legal bills long after this is over.' Raiph's face is red and blotchy from his anger and his voice rasps. He must use that inhaler a lot.

'You never told Portia that Lex mentioned "bloodhound"?'

'Jonah and the Whale. That was quite clever. Did Paul dream that up, get his brother to feed the line to you? It's so catchy, so right for our soundbite age. And the timing! It puts some *real* pressure on me when I'm trying to raise the financing to save the company. He plays dirty, your husband.' Raiph gives a slight nod of his head. 'It almost makes me respect him the more. But I tell you, I'm going to fight to save CPTV from people who can't possibly run it as well as the present team.'

'Portia.' I say her name aloud, as if trying it out for the first time.

'I'm glad you mentioned Portia, she's my safe pair of hands, she never takes risks she doesn't have to.' I watch his movements very, very carefully. His jaw is strained, the anger at what has ambushed him plain to see, but there was no recognition. The inhaler. Raiph's words. *She never takes risks she doesn't have to.*

283

A man in a dark suit waves, trying to get Raiph's attention. The lawyers are circling. He holds a finger up, a sign that I've got only a few moments left. What if Portia had to take a risk? How far would Portia go to protect her interests? Raiph points to a sign on the wall between our heads for the Darwin Centre. 'Adapt or die, that was Darwin's great discovery.' Raiph coughs. 'And mine.'

I hear a rushing in my ears and I wonder for a minute if I'm going to faint. Anger starts building in me. 'No, Raiph, the great discovery is you fight or die.' I pull one of Lex's unused media cards out of my bag. He reaches for it but I pull my hand away. 'What do I get in return?'

'You're not in a position to ask for anything.' We lock eyes and a moment later something travels across his face. 'OK.' Some of the outrage drains from his features. 'I'll give you a sporting chance, I'll play the Darwinian game. You get five minutes before I call the police.' I turn to go but he grabs my arm, a new intensity fills him. 'Not so fast. What's this "bloodhound"?'

I look at him standing next to fossils millions of years old, testament to their inability to adapt to the times. 'It's me.'

I peel away down the corridor, following signs to the exit on a fast walk but not fast enough to warrant attention, acutely aware that Raiph's five minutes might only be two. For someone who believes in statistics and computer modelling I've just made a decision Eloide would be proud of – I've gone with my gut. Portia, did your interests align with Paul's? The alibi, the late-night meeting . . . I break into a run as I turn a corner and see a cloud of multicoloured balloons bobbing down the corridor, Eloide beneath them.

'Turns out allergies were a dud. Spent a fortune buying these off a guy outside the Tube.' She sees my expression. 'What's happened?'

'Portia . . .' My voice fades away.

'Kate?' Claustrophobia clamps itself to me. Raiph must be on the phone to the police right now, and I need to be away from here, far away. 'Kate!' I run for the door, desperate to be outside. I can see the exit, the small crowd beyond. I slow, pull the cap low, put my hands in my pockets and push my way out.

I feel sick as I unchain my bike and turn on my mobile. It's time to turn my attentions to Paul. Where this all started is where it will end.

'You lying bastard!' I shout into his answerphone. 'I've seen Lex's video. I know what you did. Answer your phone!' I don't care that it might be cradled in a policeman's hand, that there might be a trace on it as I speak. My need to vent at the man I chose to marry, procreate with and grow old with overrides every saner emotion. I grip the bike handles so hard my palms go numb. I hear the beep of an incoming text.

'Eggy, please come home. I'm alone.'

Paul Forwood, this is about me, you and our family. Nothing else matters. We're ending this today. I point my wheels up Exhibition Road and cycle past the grand stucco houses of the merchants who pillaged the world and stuffed all that glory into the museums near here. They had ambitions unbounded, just like Paul. Let's see you fall to earth, my glorious conquistador.

42

I cycle to the road that leads to the alleyway by the canal as a light rain begins to fall. I want to get to my house via the rowboat but I shrink back from a fresh police cordon. They've installed a new police line further back from the canal. In my mind I can see Paul in his pyjamas, gesticulating at the police about the invasion of privacy at the back of the house, demanding they take the gawpers and the scribblers back a hundred feet, our neighbours standing shoulder to shoulder with him. I don't know if that's what happened, but I'll have to retrace my steps from the bridge along the back of the gardens. My trip is much riskier in daylight, but I really have no choice. The rain gets heavier as I heave myself over the fence via the rickety chair and stumble through vegetation, intent on closing in on Paul. Eventually I reach the narrowboat and the garden shed and pause. I'm shielded from the alleyway to the canal on the opposite bank. I'm hoping that Raiph has diverted police attention elsewhere and that Paul really is alone. As I start to walk up the garden to the back door I understand that by now I'm beyond caring. There's nowhere else I care to go.

I try the handle and the door swings in. He's opened it for me, he's waiting for me. I'm taken aback by how comfortable and luxurious my house looks. It is an environment to envy. I tell myself to not be fooled. Nobody's jumped me, there are no staccato police radios. I move silently through into the corridor. The softness of the light tells me the curtains are closed.

The gap between expectation and reality is elastic: whether a canyon or a hair's breadth, there's always a gap. But what I find in the next two steps is something so far removed from what I was imagining my brain can't process it. Gerry is lying on the living-room carpet with a bloodstain covering most of his car coat. His face is turned to me, frozen in its final expression of startled surprise, as if the world and the way it turns remained until the end a mystery to him. In his hand he holds a coil of white magician's rope.

I don't have time to question why he is in my house, dead on my carpet, as a thump from upstairs makes the hairs rise on the back of my neck. There it comes once more from the office above. I step into the corridor and pull the cricket bat from the stand by the door. In the low light every familiar doorway is a menace, every comfortable shadow a potential threat. Now I hear a dragging sound as I take the stairs three at a time, curving round to the first-floor landing. The office door stands ajar, papers are strewn across the floor and the chair is overturned. I step silently into the room and feel my knees losing their lock.

Paul is part suspended from something hooked over the top of the wardrobe door, his hands tied behind his back and tape across his mouth, twisting round and round, a thick white rope with frayed ends around his neck. He's kicking with his feet against the floor that he can just touch. When his eyes alight on me he starts groaning loudly, the sound rising into a higher and higher panic pitch, his eyes pleading and bulging.

I grab the office chair and balance precariously on it, clawing at the knot around his neck but it's set tight and doesn't budge. His hair smells of tar and sweat. It's the smell of fear. I scan the room, trying to find lethal edges on everyday objects. I grab a framed picture of the children and smash it to the floor, picking up a shard of glass with my sleeve and sawing the hard fibres of the rope above his head. My mind is entirely empty at this point as I put every bit of energy into freeing my husband. When the rope is finally cut Paul plummets to the carpet, a streak of blood chasing him down the door. I yank off the duct tape, making him cry out in pain as now a thousand questions compete to get out of my mouth first.

'How in God's name—?'

'Untie me, quick—'

His wrists have swollen welts from his straining and pulling. I cut my hand with the glass trying to saw through the knots that bind his hands. 'What happened?'

He's having trouble speaking as he gulps down air and groans. '. . . thumped on the head . . .' He starts hyperventiliating at the memory of what he's just been through. As I try to calm him I can see a livid lump in his hair and without thinking cradle his head in my arms, telling him over and over that it's going to be OK. Two hours ago I loathed my husband with a deadly passion, now that he's hurt and in danger, I would die for him.

'Who did this? Who did this to you?'

He looks up at me, confused. 'I thought it was you . . .' I'm so surprised I can only stare down at him, more questions crowding my mind.

'Gerry is dead downstairs. Why is he here?'

'Gerry?' He looks blank and tries to stand but staggers like a cow with BSE. He looks disorientated and concussed. 'I don't remember . . .'

'Who else was here, Paul? Think! What happened? Was Portia here?'

Paul frowns. 'I think . . . was that today?' He doesn't look well at all.

'You sent me a text about an hour ago, so think back: this morning you took the kids to school—?'

Paul's eyes refocus. 'I was getting the kids ready, Portia came round to talk about Lex and to say she'd seen you, then while she was here someone phoned to tell her about your video. We came straight in here to watch it and she had to firefight for the company. She was very angry. I had to speak to John . . .' He tails off, his mind cranking back into gear. 'I didn't send you a text.'

Something is so deeply wrong about all this that my fear ramps with every passing second. 'You're bait.' And I realise I have swallowed it.

He frowns, fully awake now. 'What's Gerry doing here?' Paul picks up the cricket bat and shakes his head.

Before I can explain that we're now in a fight for our lives, a sound that feels almost physical shoots up the back of my neck and into my ears. I can hear screaming. 'Paul, tell me the kids aren't here . . .' It's Josh, shrieking. 'Paul . . .' My voice dies in my throat. It's a plea for Paul to deliver me from that sound.

The cry works on Paul like an electric charge jolting him fully awake. He's out of the office and taking the stairs to the top floor two at a time. 'Josh!' He's round the curve on the next floor before I'm halfway up. 'Josh?' He's opening doors, bounding up to the second floor. 'Ava! Where's Ava?'

'Dad! Dad! I can't get out!' Josh is hammering somewhere on the floor above.

'Kate! Help me, Kate!' Josh is not in the bedroom but thumping on the square opening to the attic in the bedroom ceiling. The pole that opens the door and pulls the fold-away ladder down is missing. Paul is grunting with the effort of pulling the guest bed into the middle of the room.

'Is Ava in there?' I shout at Josh.

'Mum! No she's not.'

'Where's Ava?' I spit at Paul. My desperation to see my daughter knows no bounds.

'I don't know!' he says, straining to pull the catch on the attic door. Josh's head pokes through and Paul pulls him down in an untidy tumble. 'How did you end up in there?'

Josh is crying and he can't get the words out. 'That woman who came round—'

'Portia—?'

'– said you needed a box from up there and told me to get it and then she shut me in . . . is that blood, Dad?'

'Where was Ava?'

'Here.' Josh starts sobbing. 'You didn't come and get me!' I hold my son tightly, trying to absorb some of his fear. Paul and I stare at each other over Josh's head. Things are moving fast and it is probably only for a second or two, but that look sums up so much. We are back on the same side. We are fighting the same battle, united in our struggle to save what is most precious to us. Paul's lips are a malevolent line. His chest rises and falls in an ever-quickening cycle. His outrage is escalating. He snatches the bat and heads for the stairs. 'Jonah's gonna eat the fucking whale.'

'Paul, wait!' but before anything else can be said Paul gives a cry as he turns to the short flight of stairs that leads down from the top floor. A door has slammed and with a sinking heart I know which door it is. Our house was bedsits when we bought it, its grand proportions chopped and reduced to accommodate the washing and privacy needs of many unrelated adults. Most of the internal doors groaned under the weight of heavy Yale locks, which we removed. But the lock to the door to the top floor, to its one bedroom and bathroom, we kept, thinking our guests would appreciate a bit of extra privacy. That door now keeps us prisoners.

'Portia! Portia, let us out!' Paul is pleading as he ransacks the bedroom for something heavy enough to get that door down. Ava Ava Ava . . . My heart beats time for my daughter. Paul starts jumping down the stairs, trying to use his feet to break the door. 'Why's she doing this? It doesn't make any sense!'

'Yes it does, Paul. Don't you see? Kill Melody and you and Lex are immediately in the frame. Ruin the reputation of Forwood's directors and the final part of the sale won't happen. One or both of you could be classed as bad leavers. After all, you did have a bloody affair with her!' My anger is boiling up. I slap him. 'I've seen Lex's foot video!' The purple pump tangles its way round my guts, pulling me apart with jealousy. Again and again I slap him, incoherent words tumbling out. I am furious and jealous but most of all I'm full of fear. There are different categories of affair: the one-night bunk-up in a faraway place, a passing passion that could be acted upon or not; and the deadly slow build-up that once unleashed cannot be controlled. Melody was his type, she was a woman to admire and to respect and to share a life with. The stakes could not have been higher. 'How could you do that to me! To us!'

Paul is looking more desperate than I've ever seen him. 'I'm sorry, Kate. I'm so sorry. That night I didn't come home, when I knocked over the dog, I was thinking it all through. I'd ended it the week before and I was trying to sort it out in my head. I made a mistake but I couldn't tell you.' He grabs my hand. 'I was ashamed. I'll make it up to you if it's the last thing I do.'

'Mum?' Josh is standing limply watching us and a deep shame that our grubby secrets are being witnessed by our son lies on me like a blanket. This is an argument for another day, but first we have to get through this one.

'Lex is dead, and her intention is that you will be too. If Portia makes it look like Gerry did it her position at CPTV is unchallenged.'

'But the scarf . . . ?'

'Were you wearing it that night you knocked over the dog? You can't remember, can you? I thought you were, but maybe I was wrong. When you met her that night in the car I think she took it without you noticing, because you never notice things like that, and she used it and she planted it back here. She must have crossed over the canal from the towpath and dropped the knife in the water on her way – Max and Marcus were away, remember? So all she had to do was open the back window and throw the scarf in; it was even better for her that Ava found it in the morning and hid it. She planned this all a long, long time ago.'

'But Lex challenged her on the finances—'

'So he had to go, and now she's trying to tie up the loose ends. My video exposed a financial theory, but with Gerry downstairs it could just as easily be the work of a madman – the unhinged celebrity getting rid of those that made him famous.' I stop. Something has drifted into my senses that makes me stand stock-still. Oh no, it can't be. 'What's that smell?'

'What?' Paul is sniffing and getting nothing.

'It's gas.'

'No.'

I sniff again. There it is, unmistakable, as it curls unseen under the door and drifts up the stairs. The house is filling up with a deadly and explosive cocktail. I race to the wardrobe and pick up an old computer screen inside and hurl it with all my force through the paper-thin Victorian-glass window that overlooks the garden. One pane explodes with an almighty crash and plummets to the patio three floors below, bursting into myriad pieces and spreading shrapnel over the plants. I glimpse the *Marie Rose* through the rain-blurred trees and wish with all my heart that Max and Marcus were there now; that the noise of something shattering would turn Max's head from his navel towards that porthole and he would amble up the grass in his bare feet and save us. But the boat sits unmoving. I curse fate, my life and myself. And all the while my heart screams over and over again for my daughter.

'She'll blow the house.' Paul is standing at the top of the flight of stairs, preparing to launch himself off. We've reached the endgame. He's trying to get through that door, he's clinging, clinging with desperation to the thought that he can. The blood from his weeping head wound has stained the top of his grey T-shirt. He's fighting for his family, fighting for our lives over his own. He stands up another step, judging how high he can go before a jump will be guaranteed to break his legs.

He leans back, about to hurl himself off when I shout.

'Paul, don't!'

He looks up at me, his forehead a hideous brown from dried blood. 'I'm so sorry, Kate.' He launches off and lands on the door with a groan and a thump, but it doesn't budge. He lies winded on the floor for a moment. The smell of gas is growing stronger. The meter is in the cupboard under the stairs, the gas pipes lining the walls. She's cut or hacked through a pipe and now the gas is being pumped out under pressure into the belly of my house.

'Mum, I'm scared.' I am hugging a whimpering Josh in the corner, and a cold, hard rage against the woman on the other side of the door fills me. Paul is panting with the effort just expended. He limps back up the steps, his eyes hold no light. He goes over to the broken window and shouts out, his voice competing with the rain drumming on the neighbour's corrugated iron shed roof. Someone might hear us. But it's only a might and we need much more certainty than that. We need to be saved. Paul peers out for a long moment. When he turns, there's a chink of light back in his eyes. 'You're going through there.'

I join him at the window and look down. Pieces of the smashed computer glitter in the rain on the patio far below. 'I'm going to hold you and swing you and you're going in through the bedroom window below.' I stare at him in disbelief. He opens the second sash window as wide as it will go.

I look out of the window again. 'It's too far,' I whisper.

Paul's talking urgently now. 'It's our only way out. You can't hold me but I can hold you. You can do it—'

'No, Paul, I can't!'

'You must do it. Trust me.'

My eyebrows furrow. The doubt switch has been turned on again, bright and harsh. We stand now not three miles from Hampstead Heath and on that hot summer evening in the moments after my fall when Paul didn't catch me what was it he said? 'Trust me.' It was those same words on our walk through the Woolwich Tunnel that made me turn him in to the police and brought our world crashing down.

'Trust me, Kate, it's our only option.'

I look into the eyes of my husband as he pants with adrenalin. Is this the end you planned all along, Paul? You'd never harm your children, of that I have not the slightest doubt, but me? How hard would you fight for me? There was something else you said on the Heath that day: 'the final part of the fall is the most intense'. How hard is your grip on my life, Paul?

In the end love is all about belief, and belief is blind. You opt in or you don't, you choose A or you choose B. At this moment I'm choosing the window, because going out there brings me closer to Ava, brings this whole ghastly saga closer to its end. I grab Paul's large hand, the hand I held at the altar all those years ago. 'I trust you, Paul.'

He grabs me in what feels like the closest embrace I have ever known. 'I love you, Kate. More than you can ever know.'

I look out of the window and feel the rain pelting. Our

hands will be slimier, the window sill more slippery. Puddles widen across the patio far below. I tuck Marcus's jeans into my socks, zip up the leather jacket and fold up the collar, doing my best to protect myself from the broken glass. Sweat slicks my hand. 'Mum, what are you doing?'

I can't look at Josh, knowing that nothing must distract me from the task ahead, nothing must lessen my resolve. 'I want you to stand on the other side of this room and stay there, is that clear?' Josh says nothing.

We drag the bed close to the window and Paul hooks his legs underneath it, his arms hanging out. 'Eggy, this *is* going to work.'

I smile weakly. 'I always was a good climber.'

'Just get to that door, I'll be on the other side.'

I nod and swing one leg out of the window. I don't look down. I lean back into the room and, facing Paul, bring my other leg out. Paul wipes his hands down his trousers and I grip one wrist, making him wince with pain as I grab the rope welts. 'Sorry,' I whisper. He shakes his head, showing me it doesn't matter. I sense a terrifying weightlessness below the soles of my feet. I let go of the window ledge with an involuntary cry and grab hold of his other wrist. 'Don't look away,' I plead. Paul fixes me with his large brown eyes. For years I've bathed in those eyes, whether with pleasure, pain or ecstasy. If I fall or am dropped, they will be the last thing I ever see.

Paul's grip on me is like a vice. 'On the count of three, push away from the wall and I'll swing you in feet first.' I place the soles of my shoes on the wet wall. 'One.' Josh's bed sits under the window below and should cushion me once I'm through. 'Two.' Terror washes over me in a wave but before I can shout stop and climb back in the window he says, 'Three!' and my stomach drops away as Paul prises me off the wall and I'm swinging through air three storeys up with a pane of glass between me and death. I lock my knees and Paul lets go of my hands and if I had any time I would pray but before I can I slam feet first into Josh's window and then I'm through but elation turns to panic as only my knees are in the window and I scream as my body falls backwards and I see the canal the wrong way up as I flail with my legs and catch the backs of my knees on wood and the remaining glass. I curl up, seeing Paul's blurred head through my tears, and grab on to the sill, straining every muscle in my stomach to get upright. My bum is slipping back out of the window and Josh's door is swinging open and Portia is advancing across the room. She's moving fast but I'm quicker, brute fear curling my spine until I'm finally in the room with my bloodied hands up in self-defence. She's holding a heavy Buddha statue in her hand, the size of a big rock. 'Is that what you killed Lex with? Planning to leave it here when you go?'

'Kate.' Her voice is smooth even now. 'You just don't get it, do you?' She's taunting me as she moves slowly forwards. 'Now that all the actors are gathered, we can finish off the show. And I think you'll agree, Kate, it's going to be quite some show.' A hysterical euphoria floods me as the realisation that I've just survived a swing through the window sinks in. I sidestep towards Josh's desk. I know without looking that there's a brick on the corner with a pile of marbles in the groove. I need to keep Portia talking. My T-shirt feels sticky at the back and I push away the thought of a deep glass cut.

'Why? Why did you do it?'

Paul is shouting above, the smell of gas is coming in waves.

'Oh come on. Don't play dumb with me. Don't make out you can't see my reasons. It's tough to be about to lose everything you've worked so hard for, isn't it, Kate? Your video distraction shows that. The pain of a collapsing marriage—'

'The police know you did it.'

Portia smiles. 'You're grasping at straws. When they get here, and they will in the end, they'll find that you killed Gerry in an ultimately futile act of self-defence.'

'How did you get him here?'

'I didn't. You did. You texted him this morning and enticed him over with an offer he couldn't refuse.' She sees my confusion. 'Oh, Paul couldn't stop talking about it. The pride in his voice that you'd found Gerry at Cheltenham, that he came on TV because he liked you, that you and him had a connection, remember? You should have kept more of a watch on your bag at Jessie's, your phone was practically poking out the top.'

I'm stunned, but I try not to show it. I'm dealing with a woman whose deceptions and quick-wittedness are beyond what I ever thought possible. I hadn't even noticed that my work phone was missing. 'Where's Ava?'

'Oh, the agony of a lost child. Must be terrible, knowing you can't swim.'

My eyes glance involuntarily out of the window towards the canal. She wouldn't . . . couldn't . . . too late – I turn as the heavy black object comes hard and fast across the room at my head. I manage to get my arm in front of my face but my elbow takes a glancing blow and I stagger back into the desk in agony. She's on me seconds later and has a knife raised above my head, bearing down on my neck. Beyond her helmet hair I can see the barrier behind which Paul waits to be released. The Yale is high up on the door, the key still in the lock.

We are in a brute struggle for life. Portia is stronger than she looks and I suspect a lot of time on machines in an expensive gym is paying off now. My hand is holding her wrist, pushing her and the knife blade back while I strain my neck away and with the other hand, feel the objects on Josh's desk. I know each of them by touch: the retractable light sabre, the skeleton-hand pen; a rubber from the Tate Gallery. My fingertip touches something rough. The brick. I hear vicious thumps from upstairs, Paul is redoubling his efforts to get through that door.

I'm seconds from death but I'm extremely calm, all my effort concentrated into getting my hand on that brick. Portia's face is red as she strains to murder me and small thread veins are visible this close up on her nose. It's the first time I've seen the chinks in the perfect facade and it gives me extra strength. I pull the brick towards me with my index finger, hearing a marble roll off the pile on to the desk top. Portia's eyes flick up and I smash her in the side of the face with the London stock, a shower of marbles bouncing over us.

She screams as she drops the knife and I seize the moment to push her off and sprint for the door. My late-night run across Paul's office comes to my mind and how I was thrown backwards by a door that opened the wrong way. I was fighting shadows then; now those shadows have become real and I know who the enemy is. I'm not making the same mistake again.

I'm in the corridor, my hand on the key when the brick lands in my side and pain explodes across my ribs, making me stagger into the wall.

'Open the door!' Paul is screaming.

The key is in my fingers, but every breath I take, every move, is agony. 'Step away, Kate.' Portia's holding a lighter in her hand, swaying.

I move towards the door, triumph surging through me. 'There's no guarantee this place will blow, and you know it.' I can feel the wind blowing fresh air in through the broken window. I'll take my chances. I insert the key in the lock.

'Can you take that risk with Ava?'

I stop in my tracks as she holds the lighter upright, taunting me. 'Fire is very disfiguring on a young girl. Move away, Kate.'

'Open the door!' Paul bellows.

I can't do it. I couldn't live with myself. I can't take the chance that she might be telling the truth. I circle backwards towards the bedroom.

'That's better. The sooner you realise who is in control here the more likely your children will be able to live their lives to the full.'

'Where is she?' Portia shakes her head. 'Where's my daughter? Why are you doing this to us?'

'Do you know how it feels to put thirty years into something? No, you don't. People think family is for ever, that children are a lifetime's work. But children live with their parents for, what, twenty years? My working life is fifty years. My work is my family, Kate. That's a choice I made, I made it freely and I've no regrets. And I'm not going to let a badly drawn contract ruin that effort. It's simply not going to happen.'

'You're insane.'

Portia takes a step towards me, the lighter near her face. 'Like I said, Kate, you don't get it. It all depends on where you stand. This is my life. I'll fight as hard for it as you will for yours. That's intelligence and bravery, not insanity.'

'I never did anything to you!'

'The world is full of victims, I'm afraid. 'This is nothing personal, it's just business.'

'"Business"? You can't kill people for that!'

'You know something?' She's inching towards me. 'I can't stand the trite nonsense of those who spout "on my deathbed I won't wish that I worked more"! It's pathetic. Work is my life Kate. I *love* it!' She puts particular emphasis on that word. 'Just like Paul loves it. I live for the status, the money, the respect, the fame and, yes, the fear that power brings. Do you really think I'd let a tiny company like Forwood, run by people like Lex, take that away? Do you think I could tolerate Lex strutting into my boardroom and demanding to call the shots? Giving me my marching orders at a time when my shares are worth hardly more than I bought them for? You bring up children and expect love in return. If you don't get it you feel cheated. Well that's how I feel.'

I'm back against Ava's bedroom door now, staring at that lighter. I feel the cold metal of the key in my fingers. 'You'd be a laughing stock, the first female CEO of a bankrupt company. That doesn't get you a knighthood.' My toe touches something. I daren't look down, I've made that mistake once before and been punished for it.

'When I found out about Melody and Paul it was the perfect way to get the chaos going. Discrediting Forwood's directors would have given reason to delay the sale date until conditions were better.'

I kick out at the object on the floor, lifting it high in the air. A flash of red and orange passes my eyeline and instantly I know it's Ava's robot. 'Enemies attack! Enemies attack!' It explodes into sound when it's moved and takes Portia by surprise. She stumbles a little, which gives me a crucial second to knock the lighter from her hand and watch it bounce away down the stairs. I slam my elbow into her face and knock her out of the way. I get the key in the lock as she jumps on me and tries to yank me backwards, and the key turns as I'm pulled to the floor. My back explodes in a million shards of spiky pain and I know I have no strength to resist her any more.

Portia climbs on my chest in a parody of the play fights my children have with each other, my arms pinned by her knees. The pain sucks my breath away. From somewhere she produces a rope, puts it over my head and tightens it around my neck. My eyes bulge with the pressure, my head is about to explode. 'That's better. Don't struggle. Sometimes business is unpleasant, deeply unpleasant.' Portia wipes strands of hair off my reddening face as if she's fascinated by the physical trauma she's inflicting. 'Those that stand in the way are dispatched; those that can help are cultivated'. Her melodious voice is calm, almost mocking. 'You think Paul's with you? No . . . Paul's with me.'

I have no more struggle left. My eyelids are a red curtain that fall across my vision and I sense a terrible disappointment. Portia has confused me; in my last seconds I'm left wondering if Paul and her . . . I hear the noise of a heavy pebble dropping into a lake at dusk, but then the dreadful pressure on my chest and my neck is released and with great difficulty I raise those falling red curtains with a desperate intake of breath. Portia has tumbled away to my side and above me stands Paul in the doorway, the cricket bat hanging loosely in his fingers. He looks at me with a blank stare before his eyes roll to the back of his head and he collapses to the floor.

My coughing and spluttering is agony on my ribs but I grab the banister and stand. Josh appears and I try to hug him, but the pain brings me up short. The smell of gas is overpowering, clinging to the back of my throat.

'Open every door and window, right now! Don't use the phone in here, it might blow the house. Go out in the street and get someone.' He sprints into my bedroom, glad to have instructions to follow.

I stumble down into the hall and into the cupboard under the stairs, reeling back from the broken pipe. The hiss of the escaping gas is indistinguishable from the hissing in my head. I have to check whether Portia's threat about Ava is true. If she's hidden her somewhere close to the gas this is the most obvious place. I crawl into the back of the dark cupboard, too scared to turn on the light. 'Ava!' On my knees I try to pull at the old door that covers the disused coal cellar, my chest protesting violently at every yank. It opens with difficulty and I have no choice but to crawl in, groping blindly. She's not here. My Ava isn't here.

I check the rest of the ground floor, my back wetter and wetter, my vision beginning to swim again. I open the back door. No, she wouldn't have risked carrying her across the garden, there are too many neighbours who might have seen. The clear air refocuses my fuzzy mind. A four-year-old girl is so tiny, she can be rolled in a carpet, popped in a box. I weave across the lawn, nausea coming in waves. The Wendy house is home to shrivelled leaves, the shed smells of old grass cuttings and Cuprinol and has long been undisturbed, the narrowboat doors are locked. I shout Ava's name again, drag myself round to the far side of the boat and see that floating on the canal is my pale blue plastic suitcase, transplanted from the top of my wardrobe. I bought it for our honeymoon. Ava would fit in there. My heart drops through into a world where whole new levels of dread exist. Ava is in there.

I can't reach it. I can't swim, and the rowboat is moored on the far side by the towpath where I rowed it over last night and in a fit of pointless spite cut the rope that could save my daughter. I can't jump in and save her, I can't leave her to get help. A boat will pass and upend the suitcase. She'll start to struggle and it will tip. I scream for Paul and I scream for Josh as the paralysis of sheer terror possesses me. She is so near and yet so far. My screams end in a whimper and I battle to get a grip. I rush to the shed and get the rake, but leaning over the side I still can't reach the suitcase. Midway through a torrent of swearing I see the rubber inflatable on this side of the boat. Of course! I'm not thinking straight, my brain a scrambled mess that logical thinking cannot penetrate. I take off my jacket. I drop down on to the side of the *Marie Rose* and look at the water. It's a long way down, but there's nothing to do but roll off the side holding the inflatable. I pray that the splash doesn't capsize the suitcase.

The water is freezing. My baby will be cold, so cold in there. I kick out to the suitcase and pull on the handle, my numb hands have difficulty springing the catches. The lid pops up and through the three-inch gap I see Ava's dark almond eyes, her father's eyes, staring out at me. I throw back the lid of this perverted moses basket and it starts to sink. Ava tips towards me in the water, her eyebrows high parentheses on her forehead. Her mouth is taped like Paul's was, and I didn't notice that her hands are tied in front of her. I grab her round the waist with an arm as she struggles, panic etched on her silent face, my elbow hooked inside the rubber ring. Keeping her afloat is much harder than I realised; several times my head drops under the water as we kick and tussle. 'Put your hands on the ring!' I splutter and kick towards the bank. We inch forwards, my movements getting slower and slower. The grotesque pain in my chest lessens. The water is so cold I'm like an engine seizing up without its oil; soon it will stop altogether. Ava is hardly moving, no signs of protest come from her. She's in severe danger of dying out here with the cold and the shock.

I can't get back on the boat, the sides may as well be a mountain. I change direction and attempt to kick to the bank. I have no energy to cry out or shout. Ava's stopped moving, her head slumps forward in the water, her tied hands start to come away from the ring. 'No!' I try to roll her over to get her face upright, the struggle seems endless. I'm not sure I can do this alone, I have come this far, we are this close.

'Give her to me!' Josh is leaning over the side of the *Marie Rose*, his long wiry arms reaching down for his sister. With a final few kicks I come in closer to the hull. I don't have the strength to lift her up. Her face looks waxy, her eyes are closed. Josh shimmies his stomach further out from the side of the boat, further forwards and down, and he manages to grabs the rope that binds her hands and starts to pull her up to safety. Water drains off my lifeless child. Her eyes flutter open as Josh pulls and I see her feet disappear over the side of the boat 'She's going to be OK, Mum, they're here, they're here.' He's waving urgently behind him at someone in the garden. 'She needs to get warm, she's four years old!' he's shouting. Josh looks so tall from down here. My baby's growing up, he's taking control. He stands with his hands on his hips as I feel the boat rock with many heavy feet, hear disembodied and confused voices. He looks like a man. He looks like his dad.

A second later a burly bloke with a camera round his neck and tattoos on his arm bends down and fishes me out of the canal. 'Bit parky in there!' He puts a hand gently behind my neck and I fold backwards. I see other men with cameras standing and taking pictures, a skinny bloke rushes over and puts a throw from the sofa over my shivering body. The press pack from the street outside who were once tormentors have changed into saviours.

'Great job, son,' the burly man says to Josh. 'The paramedics are on their way, love,' to me.

I try to sit up. 'Ava . . .'

'She's breathing, we need to warm her up.' He peers across at something before looking back and smiling. 'She's under every duvet you've got in your house.'

'Paul . . . Paul—'

But he stops me. 'Now Mrs Forman, you need to lie back and think of England.'

I look up at the white sky, feeling a tear or maybe the start of the next rain shower trickle down my cheek. I hear my daughter's tiny cry as the tape is ripped off her mouth. Never has a yelp of pain sounded so good. The paparazzo gives me a gap-toothed smile as his warm hands smooth sodden strands of hair from my face. I dare to have a small flutter of hope that another day will come to us all.

Epilogue

The hairs on my arm sway in the water like seaweed in a tidal swell. My fingernails appear milk-white against my suntanned fingers. I stand and poke my swimming cap behind my ears; the gurgle and woosh of my own body is distracting and I like hearing my children squeal and their feet splatter across the marble of the poolside. Ava's wearing a rubber ring in the shape of a swan; Josh is growling like a lion.

I take a deep breath and put my hands together, leaning forward in the intense blue and feeling the grooves between the mosaic tiles under my feet. The other end of the pool looks a long way away, but I'm very determined. I splash a little water on my face and squint against the relentless Mediterranean sun. A tall, dark figure in bright shorts wobbles in my water-clouded vision. Paul is holding a pool net by his side, just in case. 'You'll never be more ready, Eggy,' he coaxes.

I'm learning to swim. Maybe I'll take a cordon bleu cookery course next. But today I'm getting to the end of this twenty-five metres.

I got to sit on the sofa with Marika. I got my moment in the television sun. Marika sat closer to me than she ever sat to Colin and held my hand several times as she insisted I told *my* story, *my* way. And I did. My bruised neck was invisible under the thick television make-up. The viewers couldn't see the stitches across the gash in my back or the pills in my bag for the pain in my ribs. Paul wasn't there. Marika's eyelashes had lowered even further in sympathy as I explained that he was still in hospital, that recovery from the severe impact to the head was taking longer than doctors had hoped. For a while it was touch and go, but I was confident he'd pull through. He was a fighter, after all.

The water slooshes between my breasts under my one-piece. My years of wearing a bikini are over and I feel little regret at their passing. Jessie walks past into the house in a fashionable sarong and a cowboy hat, holding a barbeque fork aloft. Her newly separated Adam follows a step behind with a large bowl in which shellfish from the local market suffocate slowly. The wheel of life never stops turning. It's lovely to have her here and this house is big enough for a crowd. Paul suggested we needed to get away from London for a while, recover ourselves, escape bad memories. He was right; the media exposure was intense and, after all, we can afford it.

I kick off from the bottom and doggy-paddle away from the edge. It's not stylish but it's effective. A bit like me, some might say. I've had fan letters at *Crime Time* to just that effect. When I showed them to Paul he got worried about a stalker, but I laughed it off. Let's not get above ourselves, I said.

I learned to swim with a former marine called Bobby. I treated myself to private lessons. 'I don't want you to pick up the bad habits you see in pools all over Britain,' he said, lying me back in the water in the shallow end and aligning my body correctly. 'It's all about your head. A human head is very heavy, it weighs the same as a melon.' I jackknifed to vertical in a panic, spitting water. His comment had brought back the image of Portia's head being split open by that cricket bat ... It was too vivid and too soon. I force the picture away and look over at my children. Josh is doing a cartwheel near some lavender bushes as Ava watches him, scratching her shin with her foot. We took the kids to counselling, of course. Eloide provided a host of celebrity recommendations. Their resilience has been a marvel to us all.

I'm out in deeper water now, knowing the bottom is angling away from my feet. I need to concentrate, but most of all I need to keep calm. Bobby said with an air of wonder that I was one of his most difficult pupils, that I was stubborn in my fear. 'It's all in the mind, Kate. Free your mind.' I think Bobby's a bit of a secret hippy. 'It's never going to happen!' Unfortunately this didn't offer me any comfort. I know that it can – and that it did.

Marika asked the hard questions as we communed on the couch. I tried to ignore my nerves and Livvy giving me the thumbs-up behind the cameras. 'So you really thought for a while that your husband, who you've been with for ten years and is the father of your two children, had murdered his lover and his business partner?'

'Yes.'

Marika sighed theatrically. 'But how did that make you *feel*?'

My nerves fell away as I watched Marika's glossy lips twitching in anticipation of some juicy revelations. 'Just very determined to get to the truth. That was the most important thing of all. For my children, for myself – and for Paul.'

'You've been called a bloodhound, as we know, for your tenacity and your spirit!'

'I miss Lex very much. We often didn't see eye to eye, but he was his own person and I respected him immensely. Without his message to me I would never have got to the truth. I think I have quite a dark side, I'm prepared to believe the most terrible things about people, and that includes those closest to me.'

'Are you together with your husband – as a couple, as a family – now?'

'Yes. We're very happy, happier than we've ever been.'

'Tell us, Kate, how is it possible to rebuild the trust, to love again, after having those thoughts, those terrible suspicions – and let's not forget, your husband did have an affair, which was broadcast to the nation, by you?'

Paul is walking along the side of the pool watching me. 'Halfway, Eggy.' His washboard stomach is tanned a deep brown. He's still regaining the weight he lost in hospital. The sun has etched deep laughter lines round those big brown eyes. Jessie's started calling him a playboy and I'm not sure I like it. I might have to tell her to stop. He keeps pace with me in silence, knowing better than to give me instructions. I'm using Bobby's method and no one else's. I'm over the deepest part of the pool now and I can feel cooler water ballooning up from the depths. Swimming is tiring and the end still looks far away.

I didn't pull my punches. I told Marika the story of Paul's affair. Told her we were working it through, that we had a new honesty and appreciation of each other, that having come so close to losing everything I had forgiven him entirely. I didn't tell her how easy it was. I never wanted to leave Paul for a second, and every gesture and look of his suggested he felt the same. We were fighting an external enemy bent on destroying us and this fused us together in a way few things could. When it was all hanging by a thread, we realised the depth of our bond to each other.

'Now, Kate, you more than most have had your most private moments captured by our increasingly filmed world – the narrowboat video obviously, but the press even took pictures of Gerry dead in your living room, of your daughter being rescued from the canal. Is this a step too far?'

I shrugged my shoulders. 'Lex would have loved it. He would probably have said it was reality TV taken to a new level. I'm just so thankful that Portia didn't succeed.'

Josh chases Ava through the large sliding doors, John swings in a hammock under the willow tree. Sarah and her family are arriving in two days, even the M&Ms said they might drop in later in the summer. All's right with the world until I accidently suck water into my mouth. I start coughing and lose my rhythm. Paul stops his poolside amble. I start treading water too quickly and begin a mental fight between panic and sanity metres from the end of the horizon pool. Paul takes a step towards the edge, swinging the long pole to upright, his senses alert for the next development. We lock eyes. 'You've done the hard bit. You know the rest. Come on.'

Looking into those eyes, squinted into slits against the sun, I forget momentarily the terror I'm feeling and start doggy-paddling towards the wall. 'You're nearly there! Come on, Eggy!' I'm panting now as the beloved edge looms closer, Paul guiding me to safety.

'Mummy's done it!' Ava shouts, her little knock knees blocking the sun.

'Go, Kate!' shouts Jessie. 'You make it look easy!' I don't reply, too scared to try talking.

'Three metres . . . two metres . . .' They're counting down, Ava's little hands tighten into excited fists as she joins in. 'One metre . . .' I touch the rough edge. I'm surrounded by cheers as if I've swum the Channel, not one length, but I'm full of joy at my accomplishment. Josh jumps in beside me and starts splashing, and with a huge roar John dive-bombs us all.

Paul reaches out a hand and pulls me with one arm out of the water and gives me a hug. His legs burn hot against my cool skin. 'Let's break out some champagne. Make that vintage!' Forwood TV didn't bankrupt one of the FTSE's biggest companies. Raiph found financing at the eleventh hour. The speed with which personal rumours about him were circulating and the crashing share price brought several offers to the table.

I sent Raiph a long letter apologising for what happened. I heard nothing for weeks and acknowledged with regret that no reconciliation was ever likely to come, but one day a courier arrived with a package. Inside a heavy cardboard box was a beautiful piece of stone with a tiny multilegged creature imprinted on it. There was no message.

Paul runs a hand across my back as my family cavort around me. My name is Kate Forman and I am very lucky. We're taking a break before Paul gets back into the television fray. A long break. I pick up a towel and wipe my face as a small black dog scoots around the barbeque.

John makes shooing noises. 'I bet it's a walker's dog run up from the road and it likes the smell of sausages.' Paul turns and we watch it for a moment.

After my interview with Marika I was badgered by three national newspapers and two supermarket magazines to do interviews, "at home" photo-shoots and a makeover ('We want to make you more glamorous!'). I turned them all down. I mean, it's just not me. After our lazy and loving family holiday I've got work to do. *Crime Time* has been a huge hit, there's talk of creating a cable channel that runs *Crime Time*-type videos on a loop. Livvy is keen to get me back, perhaps in front of the camera. She says viewers responded positively to my "no nonsense honesty" and I am keen to get more involved. There's a lot to think about.

The dog puts its paws on the table near the barbeque. Paul puts his fingers in his mouth and produces a screaming wolf whistle out of nowhere that makes me jump. The dog bounds over and Paul ruffles its floppy ears, making friendly noises. I hear the distant sing-song of the owner's call and a moment later Paul directs the furball away with his whole arm. The dog hovers uncertainly, torn, but for a second time Paul commands him to leave and it obediently retreats the way it had come.

'Oh sweet.' He looks after the dog indulgently before glancing at me. 'You OK? You seem miles away.'

I wrap the towel around my shoulders. Despite the heat of the day, I'm cold. Something about what I've just witnessed jars. The expert way he controlled that dog . . . 'Paul, how did you knock over the dog?'

'What do you mean?'

'How did it happen? Did it run out at you or what?'

He pauses. 'Why do you want to know?'

'Just tell me.'

He's watching me with an expression I can't read. 'It was raining so it was hard to see. I ran right over it. Maybe it was already injured. It didn't jump out at me, if that's what you mean. It was very badly crushed, as you can imagine.'

He starts to fiddle with the ties on his shorts. I think of Portia; of what she said at the end: *You think Paul's with you* . . . I swallow. 'You know something? I was really convinced it was you, that you did those things in the spring.'

'Kate!' He looks shocked and takes a step towards me, brushing his lovely hand lightly across my cheek.

'Come on, lovebirds, lunch is nearly ready,' Jessie says, walking past.

He stares at me for a long moment, light playing across those eyes that pull me in with their intensity. He smiles his lopsided smile and puts his hand on my shoulder. 'Don't you trust me, Kate?' And then he winks. Slow, sexy and sly.

The sun disappears behind a cloud, except I know that the sky is unbroken azure. I step away, my eyes never leaving his face. A moment passes before I take a step forwards, pulled by the ties that bind us. And I wink back at him.

Acknowledgements

I wish to thank my agent, Peter Straus, at Rogers Coleridge & White, and Jenny Hewson; my publisher, Carolyn Mays, and copy-editor, Sarah Coward, and the great team at Hodder for their hard work on this book. I am indebted to the police officers at Kilburn Station who took the time to answer my questions and show me what really happens behind the front desk; and to psychologists Vanessa Pilkington and Julie Read for their insights. For his unstinting support and belief, I cannot thank Stephen enough.

The new novel by Ali Knight will be coming out in April, 2012

LOVE KILLS

Ali Knight

Five years ago, Nicky was on holiday with a group of friends when her best friend Grace was brutally murdered. No one was ever charged with this terrible crime and Nicky in her grief sought solace in the arms of Grace's widower.

They're now married but he is often out of the country for work, and when Nicky meets Adam, who is young, good-looking and obviously interested, she's tempted.

But what starts as an innocent flirtation leads to a terrible ordeal, and a dark secret. A secret that involves her husband, and Adam, and what happened to Grace all those years before.

Nicky finds herself fighting for answers. But, when love is worth killing for, the price paid for the truth can be very high indeed . . .

HODDER &
STOUGHTON